# ELENA RANSOM

### AND THE FIREBIRD UNIT

by

## J.S. WOOD

*Illustrations by BRoseDesignz*

**Small Frye Publishing**

Atlanta, GA

ISBN: 978-0-9978908-3-9 (paperback)

Printed in the U.S.A.

To Tom and Rachel

Prologue

1

_____

2

_____

3

_____

4

_____

5

_____

6

_____

# ¤ Prologue ¤

Screams of terror echoed through the city. A torrent of anxious citizens crowded between the shining skyscrapers, each one moving in the same direction, running to ensure their survival. In their arms, the frightened people carried crying children and wriggling pets. Keepsakes from their lives were crammed into duffels and strapped to their backs. Androids and Humanoids followed behind their masters, heavy-laden with swollen baggage and hurrying to retrieve belongings that fell along the streets as people tripped and pushed. Some whispered prayers, a few cursed, but others shouted words of encouragement to their kids and loved ones.

"Just a little farther, darling."

"Keep moving."

"We can make it out of here alive."

Amid the pandemonium, a monotone voice repeated loudly over the citycom, "Code zero six zero six zero six. Remain calm and follow your evacuation route. Code zero six zero six zero six. Remain calm and follow your evacuation route..."

This warning did nothing to relieve the panic that was pressing on the city; it only made the women scream louder, the men hurry faster, and the children cry harder.

Contemporary towers flanked the streets, cutting a clear path toward the harbor, but there was no rhyme or reason as people pushed in all directions between the buildings. Smashed glass littered the streets as looters broke through store windows and hurried out with futile trinkets.

High above the chaos, in a comfortably furnished apartment, a young man overlooked the city through a window that spanned the length of the room from floor to ceiling. He could see the frantic faces hurrying to Upper Bay where hover-vessels were waiting to take people to safety.

"Charles!" called a voice from down the hall, but the young man at the window didn't even turn.

"What is it?" he replied.

"Where's the tactical pack with the warm clothes?" the voice called again.

"Under my side of the bed," Charles replied, staring at the pointed buildings and pinnacle towers that were stacked neatly together, their windows ablaze with the reflection of the setting sun.

Charles had lived in the city many years, but had never fully appreciated its beauty until that moment. The receding, sapphire waters sparkled hypnotically in the bay. And there, Lady Liberty stood emerald against a scarlet orange sunset; the statue that was once a beacon of freedom to immigrants coming into the country was now the gateway to usher residents away.

"Oh, Charles!" said a horrified voice, and the young man turned to see that his wife had joined him; her petite frame dwarfed in front of the window. She tucked a loose strand of platinum blonde hair behind her ear and stared with mingled fear and pity.

"Maybe you shouldn't watch them, Sarah," Charles said.

Sarah took a moment to search her husband's eyes. "I'm going to miss taking bike rides through the park with the children. And remember the tree in the park where we had our first kiss?" She smiled sadly. "I'll miss the colors and smells of the flower market in bloom."

"I know. And look at it," Charles motioned at the storefronts that were boarded up. "Everyone covered their windows, foolishly believing that they'll return to the city one day. To their lives here."

"We shouldn't fault them for having hope."

"Sarah, one of the Renegades must have told him we were here," Charles said earnestly. "This is all happening because we were betrayed. There is no hope left for the city now."

Sarah shook her head sadly. "All those poor people will suffer, but Imperator is only looking for us."

"Those people were condemned to death long before we were discovered," Charles replied. "We can't help them, and we never could."

"Perhaps we could save just a few of them," Sarah suggested.

"We have an evacuation procedure to follow," he replied sensibly. "Our mission must be successful. If we start taking in refugees we'll never make it."

"Charles, if he finds us..." But her voice failed.

"He'll never get to us in time," Charles reassured her.

Sarah ran her fingers through his neatly combed blonde hair and ruffled it gently. "I'll get the children. Then, we really should go."

Charles stepped away from the window and took a swift inventory of the room. A series of Optivision holographic screens hovered mid-air above his desk. The constant flickering of light indicated that the archive of data from his mainframe was copying to the two-inch wide, translucent square disk that was resting inside the scanner niche. Two hard-shelled suitcases and two wheeled duffle bags sat in the doorway, as if expecting to move quickly.

In the center of the room, a news reporter stood, describing the massive Droidier invasions that were currently taking place in several metropolitan cities. Charles turned briefly to watch the pretty anchorwoman, who spoke in a strained voice, her holographic image crackling with static.

"Terror reigns over all major U.S. cities this evening as a massive army of Droidiers is moving across the country," the anchorwoman said. "We received word that all private satellites have been destroyed. Our broadcast is made possible today by Snorks Sporting Goods, who granted us access to their private Orbitor, which is on schedule to be destroyed shortly.

"The White House has not yet released a statement to the public, but we have learned that the Droidiers are shooting people with a Decimator Magnum. As you know, this weapon was outlawed last year because it over-stimulates the central nervous system in humans, causing deterioration and, eventually, death. Please take extreme caution if you encounter any of these robotic soldiers. In fact, it is best not to approach them, but take cover immediately.

"Another note of warning: all metropolitan transportation has been compromised. Do not, I repeat, do not try to board the metrorail. However, the underground transit routes are currently functional, and water vehicles are still evacuating to safety. If you have a hover-transport of any kind and can offer to motor-pool with other families, you should do so as soon as possible.

"We don't know how much time we have left for this broadcast." Her image faded in and out slightly. "Follow your evacuation routes and try to remain..." But the anchorwoman froze in her speech, a look of terror passing over her face as her eyes were distracted away from her announcement.

Charles could hear shallow screaming from beyond her holographic image and had the feeling that the news station had been breached. He could not tear his eyes away from the woman as she stared back at him and said, "Good luck to you all. And God bless the United States of America."

The woman then faded away, and the spot where she stood became dark. Charles realized that his time was running out. He hurried over to the desk and removed the two-inch wide square disk from the scanner niche. Then, he entered a seven-digit code onto a touchpad and watched the data scramble until the Optivision screen was blank except for an orange line of text that read "File Corruption."

Charles reached over his desk and grabbed a cylinder contraption, which he laid in the palm of his hand. The numbered keys that encircled the entire outside of the contraption spun and spun until finally a flap opened on one end of the tube. As he slid the disk inside the cylinder, a wave of grievous moaning rose up like a storm from outside the building.

Charles hurried to the window again and saw an Oligarki gunship arrive in front of their building. He witnessed several dozen robotic figures emerge from the vehicle, brandishing Decimator Magnums on their metallic arms. The Droidiers moved toward the building in perfect unison, a flawless army that was devoid of any kind of emotion as they shot pedestrians around them.

Charles watched people flailing on the ground with mouths open, screaming sounds that he could not hear.

"He's here!" Sarah squealed from another room.

Charles felt a twinge of panic that slowly intensified as the imposing figure of Imperator stepped from the gunship. He was shrouded in a black cloak and wore a silver-studded mask that made him appear fierce and indestructible. Charles noticed that Imperator was motionless and composed, yet the Droidier soldiers advanced around the building as if he were directing them with his mind.

"Are we going now, Daddy?" asked a babyish voice, though the sentence was spoken clearly as if an adult were speaking.

"Yes, son," Charles replied, looking down at his two-year-old son, whose tiny hands clutched Charles's pantleg. He turned slightly to see that Sarah was now standing across the room holding their daughter.

Their twins looked very similar, with blonde hair that shimmered from the hololights shining all around the room, but their personalities were very different. While his son was happy to hold Charles's hand, his daughter clutched a stuffed toy horse to her chest for comfort.

"Oh, sweetheart," Charles said, coming toward his daughter and taking her horse. "You can't bring Chocolate Charlie along on this trip."

Charles carried the horse down the hall to the twins' nursery with the rest of the family following closely behind him. A mural of a carousel graced one entire wall and on another wall stood twin beds, dressers, and organizer shelving filled with books, games, puzzles, and riding toys. He hurried inside a richly wallpapered closet that was almost as large as the bedroom.

"What's that, Daddy?" asked Charles' son as the little boy stared at the cylinder contraption with numbered keys.

"It's called a Cryptext," Charles said, holding the small device in his palm so the boy could get a better look. "And it's going to keep some very important information safe for us."

"Should you really be telling them this now?" Sarah asked urgently.

Charles looked at her seriously. "Is your Broadcaster active?"

Sarah pulled back the cuff of her sleeve to reveal a round-faced object that was attached to her wrist.

"Good. Now, launch the Touchdot so we can hide the Cryptext."

Sarah slid a finger toward the Broadcaster and a tiny object the size of a drop of water flew out. From this Touchdot, an Optivision screen appeared holographically in midair. Charles made a few selections from the screen, and a secret compartment opened from the wall above the doorway.

Charles' daughter sobbed in Sarah's arms as she watched him conceal the Cryptext inside her favorite toy. Then, he reached over the door and put the horse inside the hidden compartment. He selected a few more buttons from the Optivision screen, and then the door closed, blending seamlessly with the wallpaper so that it couldn't be distinguished from the rest of the wall.

"Don't cry, sweetheart. I promise that you'll come back one day to get Chocolate Charlie."

Charles' warm smile then transformed into a grimace of determination as he looked at his family. A moment later, the lights blinked and faded to absolute darkness. Then, hovercopters began to converge on the building, shining spotlights through the windows. An unmistakable vibration shook the building.

"I do believe they have just blown out the west wall of the building. That means we're officially out of time," Charles said urgently. "Sarah, let's go."

But suddenly, there was a loud pounding on the front door. Sarah gasped, but Charles put a finger to his lips, indicating that he wanted everyone to remain silent.

"Sarah, stay here with the children," Charles said in a barely audible voice as he pulled an assault pistol from under his coat.

He stepped softly into the next room toward the entryway and looked at the surveillance monitor that was inset in the wall and displayed an image from the other side of the door. A man with black hair and a pencil thin beard stood there wearing a neatly pressed waistcoat. He looked side to side down the hallway in an urgent sort of way.

"Truman!" Charles exclaimed, after he unlocked and threw open the door. "What are you doing here?"

"I got word that an attack was being planned on the city," the man named Truman replied. "Imperator knows you're here."

"Obviously," Charles said lightly, his tension subsiding at the sight of his friend.

Truman smiled and said, "Come along. We have a clear path all the way."

Charles lifted his son into his arms as Truman led the way through the apartment and into a back room where a hefty red cabinet stretched across most of the wall. Truman knelt down and pushed a lever that was concealed under the base of the cupboard. The cabinet moved mechanically away from the wall, revealing a secret passageway. When everyone had passed over the threshold, the cupboard swung shut, and Truman locked the door. Lights flickered awake along the corridor as the group hurried along with determination.

"Good thing they're using small bombs," Truman said sarcastically as there was another violent shake to the building.

"I can't believe we were foolish enough to vote Imperator into the Oligarki!" Charles said as they moved down the passageway.

"We thought he'd protect everyone. It's not our fault he's a traitor. But that doesn't matter now. We've got to get everyone to safety," Truman said. "I brought your new identities. Your hovercraft is registered to Orbitor 10151975 so make sure to set the console navigation to that number. No one will be able to track you."

"Thank you, thank you," Sarah said, holding her daughter a little closer.

Truman threw open another door and they climbed onto an elevator that had no mirror, buttons, or windows.

"I know they disabled electricity to the building, but Tiny has already connected a port to the power cable on this elevator," Truman explained as he held his Broadcaster up toward the wall of the elevator. The Touchdot flew out from the wristband and an Optivision screen appeared.

"When did she do that?" Charles asked, as if they were discussing the weather.

"Before you moved in," Truman replied. Then, he turned to the Broadcaster on his wrist and spoke clearly, "Tiny! We're in position."

The holographic image of a woman with short hair appeared from the Broadcaster and said, "Initiating the sequence."

The elevator lurched once and then began its descent into the bowels of the building.

"You will go to the Galilee Province," Truman told Charles. "The dome over the city is still being built, but the Renegades already have a presence there. You must be successful in getting elected to office when the time comes.

"Take an apartment and put the children into school, maintaining the cover that your daughter was adopted after the death of your brother."

The elevator landed softly and the doors slid open. The Touchdot flew forward into a marble stoned garage that had chandeliers hanging from the rafters. The walls were decorated with tiles and embellished with emblems. Even though there was space for several dozen hover-transport vehicles, only one was left.

"Who is left in the building?" Truman asked Charles sharply as they followed the Touchdot through the garage.

"Edmund on the sixth floor. Poor old chap is determined to stick it out," Charles replied as Truman crossed the garage quickly. *"I'm a New Yorker,"* Charles mimicked old man Edmund, *"I'll stay until the end."*

The Touchdot stopped at the far end of the garage, and the Optivision screen came to life again, scanning the wall. They all watched in silence as the floor gave way at their feet and stairs materialized, leading down into the ground.

Truman led Charles and Sarah into a perfectly circular room with no doors or windows. Two caravan shuttles waited in the center of the room. As Sarah hurried over to one of the vehicles, the side door slid open automatically. She belted the twins into their seats and herself in the passenger's seat.

"Your new last name is *Bowen*," Truman said, pulling several bags from the trunk of the Speedster. "Your new family history, background info, replacement personal identities, and details about your new occupations are listed in the manifest below the driver's seat."

As the trunk closed, Charles noticed a two-year-old boy with black hair sitting in the front seat of the Speedster. His eyes were red with tears.

"Who's the child?" Charles asked Truman as they carried the bags to the trunk of the caravan.

Truman looked heartbroken as he replied, "Collateral damage." He clasped Charles's arm tightly. "Kenneth and Anne's daughter was just killed in an explosion at the White House."

Charles gasped and then looked at his own children.

"They've also been assigned to the Galilee Province with a new last name of *Foreman*. I'll need you to make contact with them after you've settled."

Charles nodded. "Good luck to you."

"And you," Truman replied.

After this brief farewell, Charles jumped into his vehicle and activated the dashboard, opening seven Optivision screens for navigation. Immediately, a wall opened into the underground of the city. Hundreds of hovercrafts were speeding in the same direction away from the Droidier army, the Oligarki, and Imperator. Charles and Sarah's caravan eased through the opened wall and joined the throngs that were leaving New York.

Eleven Years Later

□ | □

# The Girl with Freckles

In the twelfth month, on the nineteenth day, Elena Ransom sat stoically at her pupil station listening intently as Instructor Nettles gave the last few instructions before their final history exam. School had always been a struggle for her, not because she wasn't smart, but because it was difficult for her to fake that she cared about the same, mindless issues the other kids in class talked about.

In a classroom full of twelve year olds all dressed in school uniforms, Elena stood out as an oddity. All the other children were grown to perfection, each to a specific height and all flawlessly shaped according to their gender. Each one was engineered with either ebony black hair and coffee brown eyes or platinum blonde hair with sky blue eyes. Perfectly straight, white teeth complemented the milky white complexion on each of their faces.

Unlike every other student, Elena's fiery red hair was wildly curly, and her milky white complexion was dotted with brown freckles. And if being freckled and red haired wasn't enough, she was also vivacious instead of composed like all the other children had been designed. From her hazel, almond shaped eyes, to her unbuttoned top collar, down to the fuzzy Dalmatian spotted slippers on her feet, there was nothing conventional about this girl. Therefore, school was essentially a lonely place where she had only a couple close friends.

She glanced around the room and scowled. Her classmates stared at Instructor Nettles, each one appearing transfixed on him with their eyes glazed over. Elena remembered back to a recent report card hologram (which had arrived at her home in the form of Instructor Nettles) that had informed her parents that she "did not work well with others" during the Socialization module. Elena had argued that it was pointless to discuss the optimum conditions for establishing a diplomatic relationship with a foreign nation when no foreign nations technically existed.

She had often complained to her parents about school, and yet, this classroom was better than the change that would take place at the start of the next school term. In the first month of the new year, Elena would be going off to boarding school, a requirement for every thirteen-year-old child. Grimsby School of the Republic was located several hours away from home, so there was no chance of sneaking back if she didn't like it. She had grumbled a lot about not wanting to go away to school, but her parents hadn't changed their minds.

However, since she couldn't do anything about boarding school in that moment, Elena tried to refocus her attention on class. She used her nail bitten fingers to brush hair away from her face as Instructor Nettles said, "You may begin your test."

Elena reached forward and activated the center of her pupil station. An Optivision screen materialized in midair. She lifted her right wrist to the top of the screen and scanned her Trademark implant that confirmed her identity. The screen morphed into an identity match where she noted the date, her full given name (Elena J. Ransom), her picture ID (an image taken at her last birthday), her address (Number 10 Tower West) and her Trademark barcode number (03111980). Before any test began she always checked these items to make sure they were listed correctly because Elena couldn't stand the thought of another person receiving credit for her perfect marks in history class.

Elena chewed the last bit of the thumbnail on her right hand as she read the first question out loud: *In what year and in what province was Atlanson founded?*

Smirking at the simplicity of the question, Elena selected to answer the question verbally and spoke aloud:

*Atlanson was founded in 2282 A.D. in the old province of Quebec, Canada, between the Atlantic Ocean and the Hudson Bay.*

The second question was just as easy: *What is the name and type of central government that was created in Atlanson when it was founded?*

To which she answered:

*The central government created in Atlanson when it was founded was the United Republic, a democratic government.*

The third question tied the first two questions together: *For what reason was Atlanson formed and the new government created?*

Elena quickly said:

*Atlanson and the United Republic were formed after a disastrous famine called the Great Drought destroyed the inhabitant lands of the earth eleven years ago.*

The test continued on with similar questions, asking Elena to explain the history of how their country was settled and how it had evolved in the years since its inception. She was able to select different methods for answering the questions, whether verbal, touch-type, or terms selected from a list.

Elena was nearly finished with the fifty-question test when the boy sitting next to her leaned over into her space. He was average looking with ebony black hair, straight white teeth, and a standard physique for a twelve-year-old, but this boy had a nervous look in his brown eyes that wasn't common among teens of that day. He held a Whimsical candy wedge in one hand and had chocolate smeared on his upper lip.

"Elena, what's the answer to question thirty-three?" the boy asked her without even a whisper to his voice.

"You shouldn't talk to me, Pigg," Elena replied, scowling. "Instructor Nettles will catch you again."

"Not this time," Pigg said, though a nervous laugh caused his voice to tremble. "I fixed it after, well, you remember the time you told me to reprogram the hatch doors in Sector 7 so we could go in and out as we please, and I used a portal cipher to decrypt the door lock, but then the door shut on Austin's bag. Although I don't know why he would leave his bag sitting there of all places…"

"Get to the point!" said Elena through gritted teeth.

"Oh, right," said Pigg. "I'm talking to you over the hidden portal, like the one I designed for getting in and out of Sector 7. But, I redesigned a frequency specifically for this class."

Elena sighed and said, "You told me that last time, and then we got caught. My parents grounded me for three months."

"But I found the flaw in the last portal and fixed it. They won't find it this time, I'm sure! At least, I'm almost ninety-nine point nine percent sure, give or take a couple percentage points based on the technology that's been developed in the past thirteen hours."

Elena knew it was wrong, but she and Pigg had been cheating off each other for years. He always gave her answers in mathematics, her worst subject, and she always shared her knowledge of history with him.

Elena looked to the front of the room. Instructor Nettles didn't seem to have noticed the disruption, but was sitting at the front of the classroom staring glassy-eyed in an apparent trance. She knew the Instructor was monitoring all the electronic frequencies inside the classroom, but he hadn't looked over at them once. Elena knew she'd feel guilty for it later, but opened her mouth and spilled the answer to her friend.

"Now, leave me alone. I don't want to get caught!" She snapped.

"Thanks, Elena," Pigg said before leaning back into his space.

Elena turned back to her test and concentrated, breezing easily through the next set of questions. Then, tapping fiercely on the screen touchpad, she answered the three essay questions at the end. After one last scan over all her answers, she felt confident and saved the session on the Optivision screen. Elena knew that her test was immediately transferred over a secure network to the application software that Instructor Nettles was scrutinizing.

A moment later, Instructor Nettles stood from his desk and looked at her saying, "Thank you, Miss Ransom. The very best of luck to you at Grimsby. You are dismissed."

After she was excused, the virtual classroom slowly faded away, morphing into a tiny, white-walled room. Elena stood from her pupil station and stretched, groaning loudly. Then, she leaned forward to rub her hands over her fuzzy slippers. Turning, she walked toward one of the walls and a door appeared, opening automatically. She stepped into the warmth of her spacious, modern kitchen.

Elena's house was silent; both her parents were still at work. Normally, she would have used her free time after class to practice one of her new Simulab extra curricular activities, but there was a note on the refrigerator. She leaned close and read the words, "Clean Your Room!" in her mom's handwriting. She rolled her eyes and swiped her finger across the Optivision screen, erasing the message.

She wandered aimlessly into the spacious living room off the kitchen. The walls of the room were made of glass and aligned with marbled columns. Patches of carpet were tastefully laid between the marbled floors and were adorned with contemporary furniture.

Suddenly, a familiar ringing echoed from down the hall. Elena ran, skidding to a halt at her bedroom door. She scanned the Trademark implant on her wrist against a silver mounted plate and the door opened silently. Her whole bedroom was modern, from the electrolux warming floors to the safety brite lights hanging from the eight-foot ceiling. The walls were lined with titanium panels, which hid away all her possessions.

The rather large bed that was positioned in the center of her room was still a jumble of sheets because she'd never made it from that morning. And, on the edge of the bed, sat a typical looking boy with black hair and brown eyes.

"Took you long enough," said the boy.

"I was just finishing our test, Austin," replied Elena impatiently. She opened the closet door and an avalanche of clothes and shoes spilled out.

"I've been looking everywhere for this shirt!" she said, grabbing it from the floor.

"Focus," Austin said sharply. "You're wasting daylight hours."

Austin's appearance was similar enough to other boys his age but, unlike them, he had a deep scar under his chin, the result of a skateboarding accident one afternoon a couple years ago. The cut had bled like a war wound, but he'd refused surgery, allowing it to heal as a ragged scar.

"The scar makes me different from everyone else," Austin had told Elena when she asked why he wouldn't have it fixed.

Elena had grown up across the hall from Austin Haddock and they'd always been great friends, just as their parents had been before them. He had a charismatic personality and was an energetic student. He never met a person he wasn't a friend to, which was the exact opposite of Elena's personality and one of the reasons why they got along so well. She was jealous that he always seemed to bring out the best in everyone. At school, he was on the honor roll and had been class President, not to mention that he was voted "Most Likely to Conquer the World" by their classmates.

Austin's profile suddenly blinked, the light around him fading in and out.

"You're breaking up a bit," Elena said, sifting through a pile of shirts, smelling each one. "I told Dad that my receiver was failing, but he still hasn't had it fixed."

"Just get Pigg to fix it," said the hologram Austin.

"I suggested that to Dad, but he said Pigg's not allowed to fix anything else in the house since he almost burned down the living room the last time he reformatted the Optivision screen."

"Well, I'm off," said Austin. "See you in the hall."

Austin's profile blinked and faded as Elena slipped on her sneakers. She grabbed a rucksack that was buried under a pile of dirty clothes and ran back down the hall toward the front door.

"Elena," called a semi-monotone voice.

Elena paused by the front door and turned to see the house Humanoid, Tiny, standing in the living room. Humanoids were flawless robots that people could purchase to do anything: cook, clean, help with the children. Each robot was assembled by owner's preference, with one exception. Because they looked so identical to actual humans that it would otherwise be impossible to tell them apart, every Humanoid was required to have short hair so the manufacturer's initials (D.E.S.) could be seen on the back of their necks.

"Your mother said to clean your room." Tiny spoke in the same monotone voice.

"Oh, well...you see..." Elena stammered. "I was just going to run out and get something for Mom right now. She won't mind."

Tiny surveyed Elena's face and said blandly, "I detect deceitfulness."

Elena stiffened. "I'm going out with Austin, little miss noisy. You caught me, all right? I'll be back before Mom gets home, and then I'll clean my room."

"I will tell the ma'am that you were impolite, yet again," Tiny droned.

Elena rolled her eyes and scanned her Trademark against the wall scanner to disarm the front door, which slid open silently. She bounded through the door into the hallway, where Austin was leaning against an elevator.

"Did you bring the new wheels?" she asked.

"They're in my bag. Come on, let's go," Austin said, as the elevator doors opened.

Elena loved riding up and down the side of her resident tower because it gave a spectacular view of Atlanson. Four residence towers that stood like points on a compass anchored the thriving metropolis. Polished rotunda roofs adorned several of the lower buildings, and walking bridges connected many structures. Avant-garde style office suites gleamed with elaborately cut glass windows, while white marbled walkways were dotted with trees, playing fountains, duck ponds, and picnicking quarters.

This elevator was one of the main routes to the nerve center below Atlanson. The Underground of the city included four different levels of shopping, entertainment, and transportation. As the elevator doors slid open on first level, Elena and Austin joined the crowds of people hurrying in every direction. They stayed close together trying to avoid the pedestrians walking from the opposite direction.

Underground One was a vast, strategically mapped infrastructure of restaurants, beauty salons, clothing shops, and grocers. It had always reminded Elena of a picture she'd once seen of the Chapelle Royale inside the Palace of Versailles with its ornate marbled columns, arched ceilings, and mosaic tile floors. The ceiling was a sophisticated hologram, sometimes displaying a crystal blue sky and at other times a Renaissance fresco.

Holographic figures patrolled the walkways, beckoning people to come inside the stores. The walls flashed three dimensional advertisements: from a woman using the newest whitening toothpaste, to the latest perfume bottle on the market, to a small child modeling the most absorbent diaper. Android clerks ushered pedestrians through swiveling doors, and a Cyborg helped a woman select groceries from the organic market.

On Peachtree Street, Humanoids followed closely to their owners, holding hands with human children or walking robo-pets. Women sat in the salon being styled with the latest hair designs. There were people choosing the latest linen tunic fashions, and lying in hydration booths. A man wearing knickerbockers and a fedora picked fruit from a nearby vending cart, while another scanned his Trademark implant into a pane of glass that transformed into a holographic map of the city.

"Good afternoon, Mr. Peter," the window-dimentional greeted him. "How may I direct you today?"

On Decatur Road, a row of Simulab gaming hubs stood together; a place where adults and children fulfilled their physical exertion quota for the day. The virtual machines allowed for jogging, kickboxing, playing tennis, hang-gliding, martial arts, and swimming.

Austin took a long look at one of the tennis classes and asked Elena, "When's your mom gonna give us our next karate class?"

"The day after tomorrow," Elena answered. "Mom went on a twenty-minute tirade the other night at dinner about how those Simulab modules make people lazy and hinder the ability to grow stable muscle mass. She just doesn't understand the sheer joy of beating someone senseless in that boxing simulation."

At the end of the street, Elena and Austin stopped at Dante Down the Hatch, a tavern that sold Elena's favorite fizzy beverage infusion. She scanned her Trademark to pay for the bottles, and then they set off again through the streets.

As Decatur Road curved around and the friends cut through a back alley between the Rising Loafer Bakery and the Murphy's Paw Kennel, Elena had a bit of déjà vu.

Several years ago, she and Austin had stumbled across a Humanoid taking piles of metal down to the waste disposal site. The robot had followed this back alley to a metal hatch door where it entered a code. The door opened into a passage, which led to a strange world of machinery, electric modems, and power grids that formed Underground Four. This level was restricted to pedestrians, but it wasn't strictly enforced, so Elena and Austin had explored until they found a remote section called Sector 7 where they immediately decided to create a hideaway.

"Pigg changed the code recently," Elena said, as she and Austin arrived at the metal hatch door that led down to Underground Four. As she punched in the new code, she and Austin discussed their final history exam, and an argument about Pigg began.

"Austin, I really don't think it's a big deal," Elena said curtly, as he held the door open to let her pass through.

"You shouldn't let him cheat off you," Austin told her. "It's not fair to everyone else in class or to Instructor Nettles."

Elena had heard him say this many times before. Even though they were best friends, he'd never tolerated her cheating, and he had a way of making her feel guilty about disobeying the rules.

"I know I shouldn't cheat," she finally conceded. But then, shrugging it off, she added, "Bad habits and all."

"You and Pigg are not going to be able to cheat at our new school."

"Don't remind me," Elena said, the edges of her words terse with misery.

The pair continued walking down into the deep underworld of Atlanson to the far corner of Sector 7 where a crude clubhouse stood between stack pipes and silver ducts. Austin entered the lean-to, dropped to his knees, and pulled up some planks from the floor. He removed two skateboards from below.

Elena's board was covered with marker art; it was messy and she liked it that way. Austin's board was plain except for a picture of a gigantic bird of prey that looked similar to a hawk, but was bright orange with yellow tips on the wings. This skateboard also had a missing wheel.

"Where's Pigg today?" Elena asked, placing her rucksack on a ratted out cushioned chair.

Austin opened his bag and pulled out a pair of wheels for the broken skateboard. "His mom said he's taking Simulab Fishing today."

"Oh, phooey," Elena said, helping Austin hold the wheel straight as he screwed it in place. "He really needs to learn to ride a skateboard or come with us to karate because I swear he's the clumsiest person I know."

"That's the great thing about Grimsby. We'll do all our exercising outside," said Austin eagerly. "I can't wait to go to school."

Elena looked sullen. For months, Austin had been talking nonstop about Grimsby School of the Republic, and she understood why even though she didn't share his excitement. His father had graduated from Grimsby, but had disappeared on an expedition for his job when Austin was only two-years-old. He never spoke much about his father, but she thought that his absence made Austin feel a bit lonely and out of place. He never actually said, but Elena felt that Austin viewed school as a way to be closer to his father.

Elena bit back the argument growing in her chest about how she thought Grimsby would be a disaster and walked out the back of the clubhouse to the quarter mile long track that they'd constructed for skateboarding. They used the track nearly every day, skating up and down the sloped walls of the underground, across the paths of twists and turns, hills and bumps.

"Only a couple more weeks and then we'll be free," said Austin, dropping his board on the ground.

"As free as you can be at a school with strict rules," Elena said skeptically. "At least here we can sneak out of the house whenever we want. At school we'll be under lock and key."

"But it'll be exciting to live in a dorm and go to class with other kids our age. Don't you think?"

"I guess," Elena mumbled. "But I've always been happiest when it is just us. And, sometimes when Pigg is around we have a good laugh."

"You're so stubborn," Austin replied, shaking his head and looking frustrated. "No one particularly *likes* change, but we should welcome it as an opportunity to learn something."

"Quit acting so grown-up," said Elena haughtily, as they climbed to the top of a skate ramp. "Race you to the bottom," she challenged, leaning forward on her board.

"And you'll lose," Austin yelled as he skated down the ramp.

Stale air whipped Elena's curls around her face as she kicked off from the platform. The skateboard glided easily down the ramp and onto the path. On a typical afternoon they could skate for several hours, racing and learning new tricks.

Once in a while, Pigg would join them, but he was generally so clumsy that, instead of skating, he would perch on top of a ramp and tinker with his PocketUnit or some other kind of electronic equipment.

Elena liked having Pigg around from time to time. He was useful for fixing things, he was a great study partner, and he'd built a magnificent timepiece that hung on the outside of the club-house so they would always know the time of day. But she was always most comfortable when it was just her and Austin.

Austin knew her favorite Simulabs and always let her choose first before they started one. He knew that she had to eat candy in secret because her mom believed that it ruined the human body. He also knew that her greatest fantasy was to run away from home and see the world. Elena was glad that she had someone to tell all her secrets to, and she was equally invested in knowing Austin's secrets.

She knew that he had an addition to java frappuccino. Also, that he was obsessed with everything that had to do with the hospital because he wanted to be a Healing Surgeon like her mom when he grew up. His grandparents wanted him to pursue politics, but Elena had once watched Austin stitch up his own chest after he'd sliced it open on the skateboarding ramp, and she knew he'd never do anything else with his life. She also knew that he sat in the same spot in the park each year on his birthday because it was also the anniversary of his mother's death. Elena knew this because she sat with him all day in silent memorial.

"Oh no! Just noticed the time!" Elena screamed suddenly over the sounds of their skate wheels against the track. "I'm going to be late getting home if I don't go now. Mom wants my room cleaned before she gets there. Race you to the clubhouse."

They both started fast, but on the last turn around the track Elena misjudged her speed and the edge of the ramp. She veered too quickly and fell off her skateboard, sliding down the side of the ramp. The skateboard hit her in the eye, and a metal shard that was sticking up from one of the boards sliced her from elbow to wrist. Blood squirted from her arm, staining her shirt.

## 2

## The Gift

Elena winced, trying to keep blood from getting all over her clothes. "Mom's going to kill me."

Austin hurried to Elena's side and placed his hands on either side of the cut. "Come on. I think there's some gauze in the clubhouse."

He helped Elena to her feet and they walked together back to the clubhouse. Once inside, he pulled some white strips of cloth from a can on the shelf and covered Elena's arm, soaking up as much of the blood as he could.

"I don't think you damaged the muscle, but the tissue is torn pretty bad."

"Go on and fix it," she told Austin bossily. "I've got to get home."

"I really shouldn't," Austin said. "Your mom will be angry if she finds out I healed you again."

"Then don't tell her," Elena said impatiently. "It's not as though you ever leave a mark."

Austin looked nervous. "Remember how mad she got last time?"

"Of course I do. I was the one who got grounded, *remember*? But she can't see this cut or she'll know we've been down here. I promised that I would never come down here again. Puh-lease!" Elena begged.

Austin examined her arm again. "It's not a clean cut and will take some time to mend, but it should look normal when I'm finished."

Austin plunged his hand deep into his pocket and withdrew a thin, silver wand no larger than a pencil. The Suturand, as it was called, was familiar to Elena because it was common for her mom to use the instrument at work. Austin pointed the Suturand toward Elena's cut, and it produced a small laser light at the tip.

For years, he'd been healing her every time she'd been hurt. Austin had even set her wrist when she broke it once before, but Elena's mom had been livid when she found out. That put a brief end to Austin using her as his guinea pig. He had developed his skills into a mastery of the craft by working often on Pigg's and Elena's bumps and bruises, not to mention injured animals.

"At least I brought a fresh shirt," Elena said. "If Mom sees this blood she'll know you fixed me."

Austin got to work stitching the cut on Elena's arm, and she watched, amazed at his technique. He was extraordinarily precise with the positioning of the laser and unfailingly meticulous with each stroke that sealed her wound.

"All done," Austin said, pocketing the Suturand.

Elena's cut was completely gone, along with any trace of damage. She should have been happy, but she suddenly realized that there would be no more days like this to look forward to. She would celebrate a birthday in the morning and then be shipped off to boarding school soon after that.

"What's wrong?" Austin asked.

"It's just...it's about tomorrow," Elena said slowly. "My thirteenth birthday is like a death sentence, with Grimsby waiting to collect my soul."

"Elena," Austin said, sounding insincere as he put his arm around her shoulders. "I'm not sure that Grimsby really wants you either. Anyhow, Pigg and I will be there, so what are you going to do here alone?"

"Find a new friend!" Elena pronounced, but Austin only laughed.

Soon enough, Elena jumped off the elevator when it reached her floor, and waved a quick good-bye to Austin. She arrived at her apartment door confident that her mom, Hannah, was home from work. But, since her trousers were torn, her hair was in shambles, and there was a bruise coming in under her eye, she thought it best to sneak back to her room and get cleaned up first.

Elena used her Trademark to activate the front door, and it slid open silently. She peered through the entrance, but didn't hear or see her mom. She tiptoed across the threshold and was halfway to her room when she stopped dead in her tracks.

"How was school today?" asked a voice from behind her.

Elena turned and gave her mom a wayward smile. She had always thought that Hannah was the most perfectly engineered specimen of woman, even though she was often wearing a high, choke collar hospital uniform and her hair was almost always pulled into a tight bun. Her mom was a brilliant Healing Pediatric Surgeon and had helped pioneer advancements in human genetic engineering. And even though her black hair made her look similar to other mothers, Elena thought Hannah had a special twinkle in her eye that no one else had. But, right now, her brow was furrowed as she inspected Elena's face.

"Look at you," Hannah said sternly. "You look like a tattered gypsy child."

"Austin and I were playing and I fell," she said offhandedly.

"Is that a tear in your pants?"

"Technically, yes. But I'm alright," Elena rushed to say. "Just skinned my knee."

Hannah sighed and said, "Come, into the kitchen and I'll clean you up."

"School was fine," Elena said nonchalantly as she followed her mom. "I aced my final history exam."

"Well, it's a comfort that you have brains beneath that rugged exterior," Hannah said, pointing to a kitchen chair; Elena knew immediately that she was expected to sit. Hannah reached into one of the cabinets and pulled down a bottle of violet potion.

"Tisk." She clicked her tongue. "Just look at that eye. What do you expect me to tell Dad when you arrive home looking like you've been in a fight?"

"You can tell him the truth. I wasn't fighting. Austin and I were skateboarding."

"Wait a minute," Hannah said slowly. "You purchased something at Dante Down the Hatch today."

Elena closed her eyes and sighed; sometimes she hated having a Trademark that recorded every purchase.

"You were in that clubhouse under the city again!" Hannah exclaimed. "I thought we told you not to play down there anymore. After the last time, when you broke..."

"I'm fine," Elena interrupted as Hannah washed her face and dabbed her eye with a foul smelling sapphire cream. "We can't skateboard anywhere else, Mom."

"You were willfully disobedient." Hannah washed her hands and dried them and then withdrew a comb from a nearby drawer. "You know we're going to have to punish you now."

"You could lock me in my room, say, for a whole year," Elena suggested.

"So that you can skip Grimsby? Nice try," Hannah said, brushing the comb through Elena's tangled curls and setting them in a messy bun on top. "You *are* going to school. Student interaction and developing suitable social skills is one of the key elements in human development."

Elena thought about all the interactive cheating she'd done with Pigg over the years and smiled. "Most kids are very *abnormal*. I'm not gonna fit in there."

"Elena, it's a waste of your time to complain about school. You are going and that is our final word."

"I know! You've told me that a hundred go-zillion times, like that's supposed to change how I feel." Elena picked at her bitten fingernails. "Grimsby is such a *wretched* name for a school. It sounds so glum and uninspiring."

Hannah smiled thoughtfully and said, "At least Austin and Pigg are going with you."

Elena couldn't disagree with her mom on that point; it was, in fact, her only consolation. But, she preferred arguing to compromise, so she quickly changed the subject.

"How was work today?"

"Really good, actually. Today I surgically reconstructed the spinal cord of a fetus that would have been paraplegic. Her parents wanted a brown eyed daughter so we..." Hannah's voice suddenly caught in her throat and she looked deep in thought. Elena understood why.

Hannah Ransom sometimes found it difficult to justify her job. As a Healing Pediatric Surgeon, she was constantly fixing, reconstructing, and surgically enhancing the natural order of life into a flawless-looking and textbook-functioning human. Like most people, Hannah had been surgically redesigned to have black hair and brown eyes, traits that the parents could decide before their children were born. Hannah had come to despise the redesigning of human nature as she grew up; nevertheless, she had become a Healing Surgeon.

However, when she finally became pregnant, Hannah vowed to not have the Surgeons "fix" her daughter. So, Elena was born with a head full of red hair and dazzlingly green eyes, features that were not common among humans in that day. Later, peanut butter colored freckles appeared on her nose, setting her even more apart from every other child.

Elena had once called her mom a hypocrite for engineering humans, given that she despised the practice so much. Through bitter tears, Hannah explained that sometimes people did jobs in life that weren't perfect in order to bring some decency to the wrong that was being done. Elena did not understand what she meant, but she hated to see her mom cry. She never brought up the subject again.

"Well, anyway," Hannah said, snapping back to reality. "Dad will be late coming home from work, so what should we do for dinner? Oh!" — At that moment, a bell rang, sending a chiming sound through the entire apartment — "That must be your birthday presents from the store."

Elena leapt from her chair and raced toward the entryway. On the front door surveillance monitor she could see a robotic figure standing in the hall with an arm full of packages. She scanned her Trademark and the front door opened.

The Android handed the packages forward and said, "Delivery for the Ransoms."

Elena scanned her Trademark into the mechanical chest to confirm that she'd received the delivery and took the parcels. As the robot turned to leave, the front door closed again.

"I can't believe you're going to be thirteen tomorrow," Hannah said as Elena reentered the kitchen. "It seems like yesterday that you were running around in diapers."

"Ugh, diapers?" Elena said. "Please don't reminisce tomorrow at my party, okay?"

Hannah laughed. "Hey, since Dad is going to be late, how about we run through the park and get some dinner at Rancher's Cantina."

"Sure!" Elena said, jumping to her feet. "I'll get changed."

Elena hurried to her room and rummaged through a pile of clean laundry on her bed to find her favorite running suit. When she got back to the kitchen she found her mom sitting at the kitchen table speaking to her dad's holographic shape.

"Hey, Daddy," Elena said.

"Hello, Sunshine," said the hologram.

Elena loved it when her dad, Truman, called her by this nickname. Truman was black haired, with a pencil thin black beard, and he stood slightly taller than Hannah. He was muscular, had a strong chin, and always wore a regal looking suit to work.

"Mom said you aced your history exam."

"Was there ever any doubt?" asked Elena, beaming with pride.

"Not at all," Truman answered. "So, what are my women up to this evening?"

"We're going running and to Rancher's Cantina for dinner!" Elena said.

"I'm jealous," Truman said. "But, you should check the weather. I heard the Weather Station is going to test some new timer delays for the rain simulation program."

Hannah opened an Optivision screen by pressing a finger on the window-dimensional pane of glass that was inset into the table. A Weather Station logo materialized. Rain usually occurred like clockwork while Elena was in class.

She'd rarely been outside to see it, and the one time that she and Austin had played in the rain she'd gotten in trouble for dripping water from the front door to her bedroom.

Hannah looked over the report and said, "It looks like they'll be testing zones one and five this evening, so we should be fine."

"What time will you be home, Daddy," Elena chimed in.

"By the time you return," Truman replied. "You ladies have fun tonight. See you later."

With that, Truman's holographic image disappeared.

"Are you ready?" Hannah asked, inspecting Elena's clothes. "Alright, let's go."

Elena and Hannah exited their apartment into the hallway and climbed onto the elevator.

"What is Austin doing this evening?" Hannah asked.

"Grandpa and Grandma Haddock are taking him out to celebrate the end of school," Elena said, pressing her nose against the elevator window.

The evening sun was just beginning to set in the simulated sky, casting an orange-red glow on the trees below them. Beyond the sun, Elena could just discern the thick walled layer of the dome that protected Atlanson from the forces of the natural world.

"I love the way Hampton Park looks when the sun sets. But I wish I could go outside the dome to see the real sun in the real world."

Hannah combed her fingers through her daughter's red hair. "The *real* sun causes cancer, Sweetheart."

Her mom had repeated this so many times over the years that it sounded like a recording. Elena and her family had lived inside the protection of a domed city for as long as she could remember, and they hardly ever talked about life outside Atlanson.

But suddenly, it occurred to Elena to ask, "Have you ever seen the sun without the protection of the dome?"

"A long time ago," said Hannah, sounding reminiscent. "Your dad and I had a farmhouse in the country. You were born there."

"You never told me that before." Elena looked straight into her mom's face, but Hannah seemed far away. "Mom, where did we live?"

Hannah caught Elena's eye and suddenly acted as if she'd revealed a secret because her tone changed and she became serious. "The dome was built to protect us from the harmful elements in the atmosphere. Going outside of its protection is illegal."

Elena knew all this, but it had never deterred her desire to see the world as it was and not what had been created for her. She wanted to ask about the farmhouse, but Hannah had acted so strangely that she was reluctant to bring it up again. She was quiet for a few minutes and then said, "Would you tell me about the world beyond the dome?"

"It was a glorious place before the Great Drought," Hannah began and then she talked for a long time about the grand cities that had existed, the global sea trade routes, and the vast lands that grew orchards and nurtured farm animals.

As they entered Hampton Park and began to run, Elena realized for the first time how much she would miss her mom when she went to school. She was a rare breed, a child who actually enjoyed being in her parents' company.

Hannah was intelligent, honest, and unfailingly patient. She always devoted time to answering Elena's many questions, even the ones that were strange. Hannah was gracious and compassionate to all people, but she was sensible with her time and boundaries. And while other parents sent their children off to spend time in simulation programs, Hannah spent time challenging Elena through physical exercise. Elena had always wanted to be like her mom, but she was more like her dad with a quick wit, sharp tongue, and intuitive wisdom.

Eventually, Elena and Hannah wound around to the main square, which was a particularly interesting part of Atlanson. A multi-tiered building anchored the street dividing two lanes of roadway for shoppers, walkers, and runners. Since all vehicle transportation occurred far below the city, the storefronts glittered with three-dimensional advertisements, laser light shows, holographic clerks, and a myriad of electronic busyness. The streets were aligned with shoe stores, decorating fashions, hotels, grocers, pharmacies, doctors' offices, and a theater.

A while later, after running and eating dinner, Elena and Hannah walked back through the park toward their resident tower.

"Do you think Dad will be home yet?" Elena asked as they climbed back onto the elevator.

"He should be there," Hannah replied.

"Do you think he would mind my company?"

"Of course not, Sweetheart. Why?"

Elena hesitated, but then said, "Lately, he's seemed stressed when he comes home from work."

She watched to see if Hannah's expression would change after she mentioned Truman's job, but it did not. Generally, they did not speak about what he did for a living. She knew that he worked as a classified agent directly for the head chancellor of the United Republic and that his job was complicated and secretive.

"Dad does have a lot on his mind, but he is not stressed. And, he definitely has time to speak with his favorite daughter."

"His only daughter," Elena corrected Hannah.

"But you are his favorite, just the same."

When Elena and Hannah arrived home, Tiny the Humanoid greeted them at the door.

"Welcome home, Mrs. Ransom. Master Ransom is in his office. Do you wish to see him now?"

"Not yet," replied Hannah. "Elena wants to have a word with him."

Tiny gave Elena an ominous look before she turned quickly and headed down the hall.

When she reached the office door, Elena noticed that it was already opened, so she peeked around the corner. Truman Ransom's office was simple and modern, with richly patterned furniture and shelves of personal possessions, family film diskettes, and priceless artifacts that lined the walls. His oaken desk included the latest in Optivision technology, and the oaken shelving that stretched along the entire wall behind him was neatly arranged with Optical images of Elena as a baby, family outings, and important people that her dad had business dealings with.

Truman was sitting at his desk talking out loud to a book that was lying open on its surface. Elena had never seen him do this before, so instead of entering she waited with attentive eyes and ears.

"Imperator has learned of the Firebird Disc, though Roman has assured me that he does not know the function of the Disc," Truman said. "Roman continues to create innovative strategies for protecting the Disc. He is confident that Imperator will not find this artifact and that, even if he does locate it, he won't know how to use it."

Elena did not understand anything else he said, even though she was eavesdropping the best she could.

"Elena, you can come over here," Truman called, and she jumped out of her skin because she hadn't realized that he noticed her presence. As she came in the room, he exclaimed, "Look at that eye!"

"Yeah, I know it looks bad, but it doesn't even hurt anymore."

Elena felt her shoulders sag under the weight of Truman's gaze as he stared at her face.

"Mom said you were in Sector 7 again," her dad said. "What do I have to do to keep you away from that place?"

Elena sighed. "Dad, it's the only place I can be myself."

Truman Ransom smiled thoughtfully and said, "Very well. I will speak with your mom about giving you permission to play down there, as long as it does not compromise your health."

Elena smiled and came close to his desk, asking, "What are you working on?"

Truman closed the book and pressed some strange symbols on the cover. There was a small click, like a lock was being turned.

"This is my Dossier," Truman replied, but after seeing Elena's puzzled expression he added, "It's sort of like a diary."

"A diary?" Elena exclaimed. "That's kind of a girly thing to do."

Truman chuckled. "This is actually very important work."

"About what?"

Truman scratched his chin. "This Dossier is a collection of annotations and evidence I have gathered my entire life. The nature of its contents is extremely confidential and mysterious. Therefore, I think you're a little too young to discuss it now. But one day we'll talk over everything in this book. In fact, one day this Dossier will be yours."

"I don't want your girly diary," Elena said sassily.

He laughed jovially. "I know you think that now, Sunshine. But one day, it will be important to you."

"If it's so important, why do you keep it all in one spot? Aren't you afraid that someone might steal it and see everything you've put in there."

"My dear, there are only two people on earth who can get into this diary. I am the primary guardian, and the other is *you*."

"Me!" Elena squealed. "Why me?"

"Because, you are destined to accomplish greatness in this world."

"But I'm just a girl."

"As you know, there have been plenty of extraordinary women throughout history and you will be no different," Truman replied as he pushed away from his desk and turned toward the elaborate shelving that stretched the entire wall behind him.

The structure was embroidered with rounded emblems, and it was, in truth, simply a beautiful camouflage. Truman slid open the third emblem from the left and inserted his finger into a hole. A moment later, a portion of the bookcase disappeared from the wall, revealing a secret room.

"I don't want to be extraordinary," Elena said as she followed Truman into her favorite place in the entire world.

The space was filled from floor to ceiling with books on shelves, stacked in piles on the floor, and lying lazily over cushioned chairs. Elena remembered the first time her dad had showed her this room. She was only five-years-old and, at that age, already knew that it was illegal to own books. Her dad had explained that he had special permission through his job to keep the books secure, but that she wasn't allowed to tell anyone. So, of course, she immediately told Austin because she couldn't keep any secrets from him.

"But, if I must be anything, why can't I *be* in Atlanson?" Elena asked.

"I believe that Grimsby will be able to teach you more than you think," said Truman as he crossed the room to another desk.

"Like what?" Elena asked haughtily as she watched Truman open a concealed panel in the desk and slide the Dossier into a compartment.

"Athletic training is one," he replied as he replaced the panel on the desk, hiding the Dossier from view. "And how to make friends is another."

"I have friends!" Elena said defensively as she sat down on the lavish carpet in the center of the room where she stared at a map of the earth that was painted across one entire wall.

"Austin and that clumsy little Pigg boy are not the kind of friends I am referring to," Truman said patiently. "I mean friends that are girls."

Elena rolled her eyes significantly and said, "Girls are too silly to be friends with."

"Have you considered the true reason you do not wish to go to Grimsby?"

Elena pouted and lay down on her back. She knew the reason, but she didn't want to discuss it with him. The ceiling above her was a complicated fresco, a celestial patterned artwork that ebbed and flowed like an ocean wave.

After a few moments, Truman said, "Time to choose a book."

Elena was grateful for the change in subject and leapt up at once. She moved around the room, fingering the book bindings as she passed each shelf. It was a weekly ritual for Elena and her dad to read a book aloud to one another. And tonight, they would begin a new novel.

At length, Elena pulled a title from a stack of books on the floor and handed it to Truman. Then, she curled up in the chaise lounge chair across from him and listened as he began to read the first page. She closed her eyes and let her dad's voice fill her up completely.

Elena was going to miss these nights when she was stuck at Grimsby. She didn't understand how her parents could even consider sending her away when they had such a nice life together already. Maybe her dad was right. Maybe it was going to be good for her to try to make some new friends and have some new experiences. But right now, in the quiet of Truman's library, she didn't want anything to change.

"Hey, you two." Hannah had arrived in the doorway. "It's after midnight."

"Aw...yes," said Truman closing the book with a snap. "That's what I was hoping for."

He crossed the room and opened a drawer from the desk. "I have a special gift for you that was given to my mother when she was thirteen."

Feeling excited, Elena accepted a pink box with a red bow that was sitting in Truman's outstretched palm. She lifted the cover off the box and pulled out a multidimensional star shaped drop necklace, with angles and points and crevices.

"It's beautiful!"

"This is a Kairos," Truman said, with a playful grin etched on his face. "The ancient Greeks used this word to describe the supreme or opportune moment in history. It is a moment of indeterminate time in which something special happens. But this necklace, in particular, is believed to have *paranormal* powers."

"Does it?" Elena asked.

"Not that I have seen," Truman said. "But your grandmother did swear that it had the power to heal the sick, cast a curse, and even change the course of time."

Truman picked up the necklace and fastened it to Elena's neck. "I hope it will bring you good fortune."

"Okay, time for bed," Hannah said, slipping her arm around Elena's shoulders.

They walked arm in arm down the hallway and gave hugs and kisses to say goodnight. Elena climbed into bed, feeling tired. But before she drifted to sleep, she twisted the Kairos over and over in her fingers wishing that she could change the course of time so that she wouldn't have to be sent to Grimsby. She knew herself well enough to know that she would not make new friends easily.

Austin would make friends quickly, of course, because he was kind, charismatic, and inclusive. Pigg would make friends because he was a good study partner and he was brilliant at anything having to do with code writing and holography. Elena felt inadequate, like she had nothing to offer. She couldn't face a year of school with so much insecurity.

She tossed and turned until she finally had a brainwave; she would run away from home. It would not be easy because she liked the feel of clean clothes and having a bed to sleep in, but she figured she could make a fine home in the Sector 7 clubhouse. Then again, she knew she couldn't live in isolation.

"Austin!" Elena blurted out loud.

She knew what she needed to do. She would convince him to run away with her.

# ¤ 3 ¤

## Every Fear

After dinner the following evening, Hannah set a purple iced birthday cake in front of Elena as her family and friends cheered. Austin sat across the table with Grandpa and Grandma Haddock while Pigg and his parents sat at the opposite end of the table: his dad, Norman, with his normally goofy smile and his mom, Emelie, with her constant serious and reserved demeanor.

When the singing finished, Elena said, "You know, each year I hope that will be less embarrassing but, amazingly, it gets worse."

"It is a parent's prerogative to embarrass their child," Truman replied.

After the cake was cut and served, the adults retreated to the living room with coffee to discuss boring nonsense about the government. Elena and Austin watched Pigg unzip a pocket on the sleeve of his shirt and remove a diamond shaped object that he placed on the table.

"I got a new game on my PocketUnit," he told Elena and Austin as a blue Optivision screen materialized in mid-air above the diamond.

Pigg accessed the game and lost himself in a world of fantasy.

Elena watched the adults sipping coffee and thought about the many birthdays they'd spent together, the hours they'd shared meals or picnics in the park, and the time they'd spent playing backgammon. She felt sad to be leaving this life for the unknown.

Perhaps able to feel Elena's melancholy, Austin leaned toward her and whispered, "Want to sneak out tonight and star gaze? It's probably our last chance before we leave for school."

"Sure," Elena said moodily, realizing again that they wouldn't be free to roam around at night when they wanted.

"I almost forgot," Hannah called suddenly. She crossed the room and withdrew two flat objects. "You received your Smartslates today from the school. Austin, your grandparents were kind enough to bring yours here so that you and Elena could watch them together."

"The Grimsby Initiation Memorandum!" Austin shouted excitedly, reaching for his Smartslate. "This has everything we need to know before we start school, including the field manual for Basic Training."

"I already watched mine at home," Pigg said, not even bothering to look up from his PocketUnit.

Elena looked at Pigg and shook her head slowly. Even though Austin and Pigg looked similar enough with their standard black hair, brown eyes, and slender physique, Pigg couldn't have been more different from Austin in personality.

Hannah held Elena's Smartslate out toward her, and she reached for it slowly, as though it may bite.

"The screen on this must be ten inches long! Why is it so huge?" Elena asked.

"You'll have extensive hand writing modules in each of your classes," called Truman from the living room. "They had to make the screen large enough for you to write on."

"*Hand writing!*" Elena said incredulously. "I don't see the point in that."

Elena turned on the Smartslate. A round seal appeared holographically in midair with an octopus featured at the bottom, it's long tentacles reaching up, creating a half circle. Connecting the other half of the circle were the wing tips of a bird of prey. The head of a lion appeared in the center, and the words Grimsby School of the Republic were etched into the pinnacle of the seal.

Elena made a selection on the Optivision screen and declared, "It's over three hours long! How many policies and rules could they possibly have?"

"One for every occasion and instance, which will come in handy for trouble makers like you, Austin, and Pigg," Truman said.

"That's actually a lot shorter than the recording your parents received when they first went to Grimsby," said Stephen Haddock, Austin's grandpa. "It took us three days to view the entire thing."

As Elena selected the greeting summons, Pigg looked up briefly from his PocketUnit and exclaimed, "Look! We're all in the same Unit."

Elena noticed the bright orange bird of prey, enclosed by a rich red and warm golden circle; it was identical to the bird drawn on Austin's skateboard, complete with yellow tips on the wings. The words "Firebird Unit" were embossed across it.

Elena knew that a Unit was the group of six boys and six girls who would be chosen at random to work and train together for their first three years of school. She would be expected to share a room with the five other girls in her Unit. She detested the thought of sharing a room.

"We were all in the Firebird Unit, including Austin's parents," Truman said.

"Except me," Norman Pigg interjected. "What can I say? I was born to an Animalia family. But, don't hold it against me."

The adults chuckled, but Elena didn't feel that this was a joking matter.

Austin pulled up another Optivision screen from his Smartslate, and a man wearing a tailored uniform appeared in mid-air. Elena recoiled at the sight of him. His rigid, high-neck collar made her feel as if she were choking.

"Welcome to Grimsby School of the Republic. I am Headmaster Worthen Bentley. We are pleased that you will be joining us in just a few short days.

"As a highly academic collegiate institution with a reputation of turning out the most advanced minds, Grimsby concentrates on developing skills that may be underdeveloped."

"Ugh!" Elena said. "I don't even want to know what that means. Could you please turn that off, Austin? I don't want to vomit up the cake I just ate."

Shortly after all the adults had watched some of the initiation modules from the Smartslates that Grimsby had sent, and Elena had started calling it the *Manual of Manipulation*, her thirteenth birthday party was over. Elena retreated to her room, eager to change her clothes for stargazing.

After she was sure her parents were in their room, she hurried across her bedroom to the window. She opened the latch slowly and peered out over Atlanson.

Her balcony was forty-seven floors above the citywalk, but she was not afraid of heights and had snuck out of the house like this many times before. She climbed over the top of her balcony and onto the next veranda where a public leisure garden was lined with manicured hedges and flower bushes. A trickling fountain sat in the center of the garden, surrounded by lounging chairs. Elena walked to the far side of the terrace and opened a door that led into the building's main hallway where Austin was waiting for her.

Elena and Austin hopped on an elevator down to the main level exit. Then, they walked across the street and through Central Park for about a half-mile before finding their favorite spot on the grass near the pond.

"So, I was thinking we should run away from home," Elena stated bluntly as she dropped onto the lawn.

"Lena," Austin started, sounding exasperated.

"Don't talk for a minute and let me finish," Elena said sassily. "I just think that we could do better not going to that school."

"Tell me why you don't want to go," Austin said. "And be honest."

Elena was quiet for a moment, staring up into the simulation of stars and constellations that were projected into the dome ceiling.

"I like my life. I'm happy here, and I don't want anything to change," Elena replied honestly, the edges of her words threatening to reveal her deepest fears.

"Why does change have to be bad?" Austin asked.

"It doesn't *have* to be bad. I just think *this* is a mistake," Elena said. "I'd be much happier if it was just the two of us rummaging around Sector 7. At Grimsby, I'll stand out. They'll think I'm weird. What if they don't like me?"

Austin turned and looked her square in the eyes. "I know why you're like this. Ever since Jinee told that lie about you, you've been *different* about trusting people."

"She lied about you, too. And you just forgave her," Elena said glumly, thinking about their ex-friend.

"That was seven years ago," Austin almost laughed. "Are you ever going to let it go?"

"Austin, I'm not like you. I'm not a nice person, you know? I think I was genetically engineered not to be nice."

Austin sniggered and replied, "You let one incident when we were little kids affect how you trust people. You can't go through your whole life refusing to make friends because you're afraid of being hurt."

Elena stared at the simulated sky in silence.

"You're the most loyal friend, and you fight for people you love," Austin said. "I *will* help you make friends."

"I guess," Elena grumbled. "But what about the classes. It will be so different from here. What if I fail?"

"I know that you won't be able to cheat off Pigg like you normally do, but remember, you're only *partly* dimwitted at mathematics," Austin teased.

"Hey, that was a completely unnecessary remark!"

"Seriously, though," Austin added after laughing at the face Elena had given him. "I know that you'll do fine with your classes. Pigg and I will be there to help you study. I promise I won't let you fail."

Then, Austin began telling her about all the amazing attributes of the Grimsby campus that he'd read about from the Initiation recording in the Smartslate. He rattled on and on about all the classes and how he was particularly looking forward to a class called *Survival Strategy*. Then, he went into great detail about the Simulab modules that they could compete in with other students. He also spoke about the different clubs and societies they could join.

Elena tried to listen without feeling cynical, but she couldn't make herself feel happy. Austin was already excited about their classes, but she didn't even want to get on the train to go there. She knew that it wasn't normal for a teen to enjoy picnicking with her parents in the park, or to like spending hours of physical training with her mom, or to be happy doing her school work in a way that didn't require her to interact with other boys and girls, but she liked her life. The Sector 7 clubhouse was her sanctuary; her mom was just starting to teach her how to cook; even Tiny was fun once in a while, keeping her company with brain teasers or the books from Truman's library when her parents had to work late.

Elena could feel tears threatening to choke her, but she was officially too old for that, so she pushed them away and focused on Austin's voice. They'd been best friends for as long as she could remember. Would he become a different person once they arrived? She didn't want to change, and she certainly didn't want her friend to change.

Later that evening, Elena climbed back through her bedroom window feeling tired and hungry. She crept toward the kitchen hoping to make a quick snack, but stopped dead in her tracks as her parents' voices drifted down the hall from the living room.

"I'm worried about her leaving," said Hannah in a low voice. "She seems so unhappy about it."

"You know she has to go and you know why," said Truman seriously.

Elena crouched down and eased further down the hall toward her parents. She peeked around the corner so she could see their faces.

"But, are you sure it's safe for her to leave?"

"It is the safest place for her to be. Even safer than being with us," Truman replied. "You know how the Imperator hunts us. It's a miracle he hasn't found our location. The older Elena gets, the more susceptible we are to being caught. He won't expect us to send her to Grimsby, so he won't look for her there. But if she stays she'll be the only thirteen-year-old around here, making her easier to notice."

"Couldn't we send her somewhere else?"

Truman rubbed his hands over his face in a frustrated sort of way. "I already told you how hard work was this week. There have been strange disappearances of top officials. Just today, the Linus family in Crowfield

Plantation vanished without a trace, and the memories of everyone in town have been modified. Could you imagine if Imperator finds us?"

Elena noticed the look of fear on her dad's face.

"It terrifies me to think what could happen if he learned the location of the Firebird Disc. There is nowhere else to send her. She has to go."

"But, Imperator thinks we're underground," Hannah said. "How could he possibly know that we live here, out in the open? Especially when we could be anywhere in the world."

"That logic didn't work so well for the Linus family," Truman wrapped his arms around her mom in a comforting way. "Hannibal is there. He won't let anything happen to her."

"Little Elena shouldn't be spying," said a whisper in Elena's ear. Tiny had arrived to catch her eavesdropping.

"You're so nosy," Elena whispered back angrily before she crept back quietly to her room.

Once in bed, she reviewed everything she'd just overheard. She remembered her dad using the name "Imperator" when she'd overheard him talking to his Dossier just yesterday. She thought she remembered him say that Imperator was looking for something called a "Firebird Disc." The name *Firebird* made her remember school. She was in the Firebird Unit. Did the Firebird Disc have something to do with school? If Imperator was hunting for the Firebird Disc, and there was a Firebird Unit at school, was Grimsby really a safe place?

Also, why would Imperator be hunting for her parents? She quickly determined that it must have something to do with her dad's job with the United Republic. She pulled the Kairos from around her neck and examined it closely. Elena was slightly panicked to hear Hannah sound so worried. Her mom was usually the strong, fearless type.

But then she realized, it didn't matter why her parents were being hunted. If Truman thought it was best that she go to Grimsby so they would all be safe that was a good enough reason. Elena decided that she would force herself to be compliant and not say anything negative about Grimsby from that point forward.

# ◻ 4 ◻

## The Grimsby Channel

"Elena!" Hannah called from down the hall. "Hurry, we'll be late."

Elena stood in the door of her room. Her last week at home had gone by too fast for her liking, but she hadn't complained once about Grimsby in front of her parents. She'd saved that for the last precious hours she'd spent with Austin down in Sector 7. She told him about how Imperator was looking for something called a *Firebird Disc* and how he was also searching for her parents.

"I wonder who Imperator is? I don't remember seeing his name when we studied our government officials at school," Austin had said. "And I wonder why your parents are in hiding."

"I don't know," Elena had shrugged. "I guess it has something to do with Dad's job. So, you can't tell anyone."

"Who would I tell?"

"Do you think I should worry about my parents?"

"No! If I know one thing it's that your parents can take care of themselves," Austin had replied firmly. "But, have you ever heard about people having their memories *modified*? Has your mom ever talked about something like that from work?"

Elena shook her head. "That's weird, right?"

"Definitely weird."

Elena puzzled over the memory of their conversation as she fastened the Kairos around her neck. She slung her carrier bag, filled with a few modest possessions, over her shoulder. After one last fleeting look at her room, Elena turned and followed the hallway to the living room.

"I guess this is as good a time as any to tell you that I feel like I'm going to vomit," Elena told her parents, who were waiting by the front door.

"You're just nervous," Truman said, putting his arm around her. "Come on, let's get Austin and be on our way."

Minutes later, Truman and Hannah escorted Elena and Austin onto an elevator. Elena pressed her face against the window, scanning the buildings, parks, and people of Atlanson with a feeling of true loss. But, by the time the elevator stopped, she forced a smile on her face.

Elena and the others stepped out into the terminal located on Underground Two under their resident tower; it was comprised of six metrorail tracks that efficiently transported people to any part of Atlanson. Elena hadn't used the terminal often because her mom had always preferred to walk. However, the northern section of Atlanson where she and Austin would board the train to school wasn't a journey they could take on foot today.

"So, what's going to happen when we first get there?" Austin asked Truman excitedly as Elena eased into one of the lounge chairs with her carrier bag on her lap.

"You'll have to register, go to your new resident tower, and meet your new roommates," Truman replied. "But be careful who you make friends with because Elena is very picky." He teased and Elena rolled her eyes.

Before long, the metrorail pulled into a station and Elena got off the train with her mouth open in awe. She looked down an elaborate marble staircase and into the cavernous room below that was filled with a bustling crowd.

On the opposite end of the room, an identical marble staircase stood, and Elena could see that another metrorail was pulling into a platform, no doubt bringing more students to the train going to Grimsby.

"Wow!" Elena breathed as she stared up into a vaulted ceiling that was painted over with sea green celestial artwork.

She followed her parents down the marbled stairs to the main station area, which was a nucleus of school-based activity. Students were shopping at booths that sold clothing embossed with Grimsby logos. Grimsby insignia flags and banners were available for purchase. The deli bakery, coffee shop, and gourmet market were busy with people getting a quick breakfast. A group of teens were gathered around the candy store choosing Toffee Spores, Swedish Gummies, Toxic Sours, and Peanut Wafers.

A four-faced brass clock stood atop a booth with the word "Information" scrawled along it. Below, several kids stood in front of window-dimensional glass panes where they could be seen scanning their Trademarks to access a searchable Optivision screen or download a program into their Smartslates.

In the center of the station, a silver bullet metrorail flashed the words *GRIMSBY CHANNEL* spectacularly down its side. Holographic clerks walked up and down the platform giving advice and directions as a display board listed out safety procedures. Teens and parents talked and laughed as students climbed onto the train.

"We're going this way to check-in," Hannah called out as she led the way down the platform to a row of turnstiles where dozens of boys and girls were scanning their Trademarks to gain access to the platform.

"This is where we part ways," Hannah said, motioning toward the turnstiles. "Just scan your Trademark over there and you can get right on the train."

"Look, there's Pigg," Austin said pointing down the platform.

Pigg's mother was obsessively combing his hair with her fingers, and then she straightened his shirt, tucking it firmly into his pants.

"You can meet with him later," Hannah said. "You only have minutes before the train leaves. Elena, give me a hug and a kiss."

Elena embraced Hannah, giving her a strong hug as she breathed in her mom's lavender scented hair. She forced herself to remember that it was best for all of them that she go to school.

Truman knelt down so that he was below eye level with Elena. "Be safe, Sunshine, and try to have some fun at school."

Then, he hugged her tightly, and she breathed in his favorite cologne. Elena wanted to tell him to be safe, but she didn't want to sound suspicious so she gave him a quick peck on the cheek and lifted her carrier bag onto her shoulder. As she scanned her Trademark into a turnstile, Elena turned back; her parents stood arm in arm, smiling and waving at her. She was going to miss them.

She swallowed the growing lump in her throat and followed Austin down a long corridor

"Let's find some seats," Austin said as he led the way, winding through the busy platform to the Grimsby Channel train.

The boxcars were modern and comfortable and could easily accommodate seven students walking shoulder to shoulder down the center aisle. Elena sat comfortably in a leather seat to the far left of the compartment as Austin scanned his Trademark into the side of the seat. A floorboard opened near his feet and Austin stowed their carrier bags. As he sat across from Elena, an Optivision screen flickered on, and a Telecaster reported a message about travel safety.

Soon, Pigg arrived with lipstick smudges on his cheeks. He tossed his carrier bag on the floor and flopped down in a seat next to Elena.

"Pigg, that shade of pink lipstick doesn't do a thing for you," Elena teased him.

Pigg rubbed his face, looking embarrassed. "Mom gets a bit *emotional* about good-byes." And then, fingering his neck, he said, "I think I have tonsillitis."

"You can't get tonsillitis, dimwit," Elena replied. "People are genetically engineered without tonsils. Even a two-year-old could recite that procedure to you."

Pigg pouted and said, "Well, I'm getting sick, anyway. Like, remember that time mom told me to come home early, but we'd been out playing too long...well, actually...you sort of forced me to stay out with you...and we got caught in the rain simulation? Do you remember that time? Well, I had sniffles for a week."

"You're not getting sick. You're just nervous," said Austin flippantly. He opened the top of a Peppers Fizzy beverage infusion and took a huge gulp. "Here," he added, taking out a cylinder container and giving it a shake. "Have a Rock Popper while you can."

"What do you mean *while I can?*" asked Pigg warily.

"We won't be able to eat foods like this on school grounds," said Austin. "They take all snacks when we arrive."

"No one told me that!" exclaimed Pigg, Then, looking thoughtful, he added, "Most of my snacks are cleverly hidden in my carrier bag, so I'm guessing they won't find them."

"You can't hide it from them," Austin laughed. "They go through all our belongings and confiscate anything they consider *contraband.*"

"You must be wrong," said Elena, looking dumbfounded. "Mom never said anything about contraband items."

"Well, Hannah probably didn't want you to flipout. The Initiation Memorandum on our Smartslates listed out all the items that we couldn't bring."

At that moment, Pigg leapt up. He grabbed his carrier bag off the floor and pulled his Smartslate from it.

"Oh, you mean the *Manual of Manipulation,*" said Elena, looking miserable. "I didn't watch that dimwit thing."

"How do you expect to get through school without knowing anything about it?" Austin asked, shaking his head at her.

"After I found out that I wasn't allowed to bring my own clothes because Grimsby wanted me to 'purge' my 'identity' I decided I didn't want to see anymore," Elena said grumpily. "Still, I can't believe we don't get to have candy for a whole year. It seems a little extreme, don't you think so, Pigg?"

Pigg, who hadn't really been listening because he was searching through Optivision screens, looked up and said, "What? Yes, I guess…Phooey! It says we can't bring any electronic devices."

He pulled the PocketUnit from his carrier bag and fumbled around inside his shirt for a moment.

"Good thing I sewed all these secret compartments into my clothes. I call it my 'body bubble' and I think I'll just go ahead and stash some of these snack bars, too."

"You didn't watch the *Manual of Manipulation* either?" Elena questioned him.

"Stop calling it that!" Austin rebuked her.

"I find it better to know the least amount of info about a hostile environment as possible," said Pigg.

"Hostile environment!" Austin exclaimed. "You sound as pitiful as Elena. It's not like we're going to prison."

"Austin, I don't care what you say," Elena said sassily, one cheek full of Rock Poppers. "A campus full of raging teenage hormones can only be described as a *hostile environment.*"

As Elena felt the train pull away from the platform, a female Telecaster with long blonde hair and a pretty face appeared holographically along the aisle.

"Welcome to Grimsby School of the Republic," the Telecaster said in a calm and soothing voice. "For all Level 1 students, your first year of school is sure to be informative and life-changing.

"For your safety, please remain seated until the signal for lunch to be served in the dining car."

Then, the Telecaster began to explain the check-in procedure for Level 1 students, but Elena was barely listening. She watched the hologram display in her window, secretly wishing that she could be sitting at whatever beach the holographic scene was depicting.

At last, the Telecaster said, "The Dining Car is now open for lunch."

Pigg leapt up and hurried down the train aisle. Elena watched him go, wishing that she could feel hungry. All she felt was a mixture of concern for her parents, fear over the fact that people could actually have their memories erased, and apprehension about the direction the train of her life was moving. Together, it was enough to make her feel that her head was about to explode.

"What are you stressing about?" Austin said, suddenly breaking into her thoughts.

"What?" Elena said distractedly. "Oh, nothing." She jumped up as if she'd been poked. "Come on, let's go see if Pigg has eaten everything in the diner."

As Elena and Austin walked through the train to the next car, she could sense a commotion at the front of the car even before she saw what was happening. Then, raised voices drifted down the corridor, but one much louder than all the others.

"Out of the way, *Big Ears*," yelled one voice.

Elena stood on tiptoes and peered over the tops of the heads in front of her. Pigg was standing in front of a boy with spiky black hair and brown eyes. He looked similar enough to the other boys with the same features, but there was a deep grimace set on his face.

"There's n-no need for n-name c-calling," Pigg stammered.

Elena heard the boy reply, "I wasn't name calling. I was pointing out a clear birth defect."

Elena felt anger creep into her chest. She started toward Pigg, shoving other students out of her way, but in the following moment a Humanoid entered the boxcar and spoke loudly, "Move along, young ones."

The fight broke up quickly, and the boys and girls began moving in and out of the dining car again.

"Come on, let's get back to our seats," Austin said in Elena's ear. "It'll be the quickest way to meet back with Pigg."

Soon after, Pigg found his way back to his seat looking pale and miserable.

"What did you do?" Elena said in an almost accusatory way.

"I didn't do anything to him. Somebody behind me tried to cut in line and shoved me forward into that boy. I tried to explain, but he got so angry. He looked just like your dad did that time I accidently lit the living room on fire. You'd think that Truman Ransom, above all people, would appreciate that some people have a tendency to be clumsy. I mean, he works with all those brainiacks in the United Republic office. It's not like those guys are so coordinated."

# CHAPTER 4

"Pigg, you're being picked on already and we haven't even gotten to school yet," Elena said, slumping down in her seat. "It's going to be a long year."

□ 5 □

# Grimsby School of the Republic

The Grimsby Channel continued on for another hour until, at length, it climbed out from the underground tunnel and into the artificially-lit school campus. In awe, Elena stared out her window at four gleaming skyscraper towers that stood like points on a compass, just like the resident towers in Atlanson. But, unlike Elena's home town, the buildings were separated by tall hedges that made her feel like Grimsby wanted to keep people out...or maybe lock people inside.

She could see that Grimsby was an extensive campus with groves and forests around the outer boundaries and landscaped lawns around the buildings. The entire left side of the complex was sectioned off as an athletic field where several groups of upper classmen were already exercising.

"Look at the ropes course," said Austin excitedly.

As the train slowed to a stop, all the other teenagers began to stand, eager to explore their new home. All except Elena who remained in her seat, looking out the window with dismay etched on her face. She couldn't manufacture a single feeling of wanting to get up from her chair.

"Come on, slow poke," Austin beckoned, as he tossed her carrier bag in her lap.

Elena shook her head slowly and said, "I think I'll just go back to Atlanson with the train."

Austin reached down, grabbed her firmly but kindly by the arm, and pulled her to her feet.

"Don't worry so much."

After Elena slung her carrier bag over her shoulder, Austin half dragged, half directed her through the multitude of other students getting off the train. As she stepped onto the platform after Austin, a gust of frosty air blew around them.

"It's freezing!" Elena said, her teeth chattering instantly. "Why is it so cold here?"

"Grimsby has a seasonal weather simulation," Austin replied. "Tomorrow is the first day of the new year and, in the *real world*, it's cold the first few months of each year."

"Oh really? Did you learn about that in the *Manual of Manipulation?*"

"Stop calling it that," Austin murmured.

"You think they could have mentioned something about bringing a coat to wear," Elena said insolently.

"You'll get issued a coat that goes with our uniform inside," Austin said.

"I miss warm weather already," said Pigg as the three friends passed through a gate with the words "Grimsby School of the Republic" engraved into the entire crest of the entrance.

Elena remembered thinking before they arrived that Grimsby would be uninspiring, but now, standing before the shining complex, she thought it was anything but uninspiring. As they walked up the sandstone colored sidewalks, surrounded by the perfectly manicured landscape that was offset by fountains with spouts of jumping water, she marveled at her new resident tower that featured both a triangular and partially rounded façade. Glass elevators on the outside of the building hurried up and down, no doubt delivering new students to their dormitories.

By this time, Pigg was so distracted that he didn't notice that there was a carrier bag lying on the sidewalk, directly in his path. He tripped over it and fell hard, spilling his own bag and scattering his possessions over the ground. Everyone around them laughed.

Elena sighed and helped Pigg to his feet while Austin started to pick up the fallen Smartslate, snack bars, and a hodge podge of trinkets.

"It's really nice of you to laugh," Elena snapped at the other Level 1 students as they passed. "And thanks for stepping on his stuff."

"Let it go, Lena," Austin said. "Pigg, are you okay to walk?"

Pigg's face was fireball red, but he nodded and walked along holding firm to Elena's free arm.

"The towers were modeled after the Petronas Towers in Kuala Lumpur," Austin said.

"There were only two Petronas towers," Elena grumbled.

"But the school needed four buildings," Austin explained. "What's the big deal? I thought you would find it interesting." Then, he leaned toward her ear and whispered, "Doesn't your dad have a book about this in his office? It's one of your favorites..."

Elena shrugged in a non-committal way, but really she felt a little rush of excitement. However, she pushed it to the pit of her stomach and said, "I bet they'll make us eat liver and eyeballs for dinner."

"Nah, they wouldn't do that. Would they?" Pigg asked nervously, looking around so quickly that his eyes spun wildly. "How come we have a view of mountains on one side and an entire ocean on the other?"

"Only the mountains are real," said Austin. "The ocean is a hologram."

"Put there to give us the impression of freedom," said Elena. "Which we don't actually have."

"Come on! We go this way to get our room assignments." Austin directed them forward again.

"You're awfully bossy today, Austin," Elena griped.

"Someone has to take over for you." Austin's grin stretched across his entire face. "You seem so traumatized."

Austin led Elena and Pigg to a crowd of students that were sectioned into a series of lines underneath a row of indigo colored awnings. The three friends were sorted by last name. Elena stood in her row feeling bitter as she watched Austin chat happily with some of the boys and girls in his line.

After waiting in line for what seemed like an hour, Elena reached the clerk's desk and was asked to scan her Trademark. Her information appeared holographically on an Optivision screen for the Humanoid clerk, and he scrutinized her face carefully, making her feel extremely uncomfortable.

Finally, the Humanoid barked, "Hold out your index finger."

As Elena presented her finger, the clerk touched it with a sterile looking cylinder. She felt a sudden prick and a sensation of pain.

"Ouch!" she winced, pulling her finger away and looking at the little dollop of blood on the tip. "What was that for?

"Blood sample for our records," he said vaguely as he deposited her blood sample into a box. "This building behind me is your resident tower. Take your Smartslate to the Media Lab to upload your room assignment, class schedule, and textbooks.

"Then, go to the Uniform Locker to be measured for your uniform," the clerk continued on dolefully. "Proceed to your assigned dormitories. Dinner will commence in the Mess Hall at 1700 hours. General Assembly will be held in your respective common areas at 1800 hours."

"You just said a lot of stuff that I didn't understand," Elena said earnestly. "Could you start again with the first thing you said?"

The Humanoid clerk gave her one last fleeting look and shouted, "Next!"

Feeling scandalized, Elena turned away and found Austin waiting for her.

"He stabbed me with a needle," she complained as Pigg also joined them.

"We're to go this way to the Grimvators inside our resident tower," Austin said, directing them with his finger.

"Excuse me?" Elena said. "What is a *Grimvator*?"

"It's like an elevator, except besides going up and down Grimvators can go frontways, backways, sideways, and slantways."

As they reached the front of the resident tower, Elena gawked at the building and marveled at the height. Austin had to physically push her through the front door. Inside, the foyer was stunningly beautiful, with shining floors and dozens of areas for relaxation.

The center of the building was hollow all the way up to a glassed ceiling several stories above them. Hundreds of windows looked out and down and, unlike the campus, the foyer smelled like fresh dill and cucumber water. The hallways on either side of the foyer were aligned with dozens of Grimvators.

Elena followed Austin and Pigg into a Grimvator with translucent doors and watched it fill up with students. Then, an Optivision screen appeared with the same holographic female that had appeared on the Grimsby Channel.

"This Grimvator has reached capacity," the Telecaster said in the same calming tone she used on the train. The doors slid shut and Elena felt a jerk slantways. "The Grimvator is a multidimensional transit system designed to maximize use of the building.

"You will find the different floors engaging and practical. The recreation lounge, pools, resident floors, Simulabs, Telepost Office, Instructor lounge, Media Lab, Uniform Locker, Mess Hall, and more are available with a touch of this convenient Optivision display.

"To get straight to your resident hall, simply scan your Trademark into the scanner niche." The hologram pointed to a scanner on the wall of the Grimvator. "This Grimvator is scheduled for the Media Lab where you will upload all the information you need to start your school year."

Elena felt the elevator come to a slow stop and the doors slid open silently. She followed the other students into a grand room, larger than any place she'd ever been, with the words "Media Lab" displayed on the wall above the entryway. Row after row of pupil stations and tables lined the space to make walkways. But there were also clusters of cushiony chairs and window-dimensionals where students could scan their Trademarks to access a searchable Optivision screen.

Austin moved toward one of the pupil stations and slid his Smartslate across the table to a half wall of glass that rose out of the center of it. Elena heard a little click as his Smartslate connected with a porthole.

"Come on," Austin said to Elena and Pigg. "We've got to upload our schedules and a syllabus for each class."

"Why do we have to do this anyway," Elena grumbled as she removed the Smartslate from her carrier bag and slid it across the table, also connecting to a porthole. "Wouldn't it have been easier if they'd just given us a Smartslate with our assignments already on it?"

"Yes, that would have been easier," Austin said. "But we're supposed to get to know where things are in the school, and we're supposed to be meeting new people. That's the whole point."

"I'm not ready to meet new people," squeaked Pigg. "I'm still having a panic attack about falling in the courtyard. Everyone was laughing. It was like the bad dream I had the other night about kids laughing at me for arriving at school without my clothes on." He looked away and said quietly, "I just couldn't cover myself or run quick enough to get away."

Elena wanted to laugh, but her own bad dream about arriving to school without shoes and the other kids laughing at her naked feet still haunted her thoughts.

"My Smartslate's done. How about yours?" Austin asked. As Elena picked hers up off the table he said, "Great. Let's see what classes we got."

When the class schedule appeared holographically from Austin's Smartslate, Elena looked it over and frowned.

"Three days during the week we have Advanced Historical Analysis and Advanced Phonology before lunch! And Theoretical Physics and Social Science after lunch! Are they trying to kill us?"

"But look," Austin said, trying to sound encouraging. "On these other two days it says Basic Training and Survival Skills. That's only two classes all day."

"That's not very comforting," Pigg interrupted. "Basic Training does not sound easy, and I'm fairly sure that any class where I'm required to have survival skills is going to be a disaster."

Austin smiled. "Look, we have a week before we have to worry about this, okay? So, let's just go get our uniforms and forget it for now."

Elena followed Austin and Pigg onto another Grimvator and watched Austin select "Uniform Locker" from the menu of options. When the Grimvator was full of students, the translucent doors slid shut and the elevator began to

GRIMSBY SCHOOL OF THE REPUBLIC

move backwards. As it climbed, descended, and slanted Elena caught glimpses of some of the other floors. One floor had exercise equipment and a lap pool with a waterfall. Another floor had a tavern with teens sitting at stools. She saw a series of Simulabs with students competing in boxing, karate, and tennis.

The other boys and girls hopped on and off the Grimvator at various levels, chatting merrily and laughing boldly. Everyone seemed to be having a great time, everyone but her.

At length, Elena stepped off the Grimvator into a long corridor lined with doors. She watched boys and girls swiping their Trademarks and entering and exiting stalls in a quick, consistent way.

"Um...where are we?" Elena asked, looking expectantly at Austin.

"We're at the Uniform Locker to get fitted for our uniforms."

"But, there are boys in here!" Elena said, feeling bewildered. "How can they expect me to change in front of a boy?"

"No." Austin laughed. "Just scan your Trademark into one of those doors and go inside. You'll see what to do after that."

Elena hurried into the nearest available door and scanned her Trademark. The stall door opened. She walked into a small room with a mirror and dozens of thin panels instead of walls. After the door locked behind her, Elena's face appeared holographically on an Optivision screen in midair. Then, laser lights appeared out of thin air and scanned her entire body, including her head and feet.

Once this was complete, a drawer popped open from the wall. Feeling suspicious, Elena leaned forward and looked timidly inside. She reached in slowly and began to remove several clothing items, including a high collared armorwear combat shirt, buckle breeches, combat boots, and a winter cloak.

After looking apprehensively at the mirror as though someone might be behind it watching her, Elena removed her shoes and clothes and pulled on her new attire. After everything seemed to be properly in place, the laser lights came on again and scanned her body once more.

Then, the Telecaster appeared holographically and said, "Elena Ransom, please remove the uniform and place it neatly inside the drawer. You may get dressed in your regular clothing. Your wardrobe will arrive in your room shortly."

"That was the weirdest thing ever," Elena told Austin and Pigg back in the hallway. "And those clothes are beyond anything I could have ever imagined."

"So..." Austin said, looking at her nervously. "Pigg and I have been talking, and we want to go meet our roommates before dinner."

Elena dropped her head and quietly said, "I guess I'll do the same. But you'll save a seat for me at dinner, right?"

"Of course we will," Austin laughed. "And don't look so pitiful. We're going to have an excellent year."

Elena sighed heavily as she, Austin, and Pigg hopped into another Grimvator. The three of them scanned their Trademarks into the Optivision panel and felt the elevator begin to move slantways. Soon, the screen flashed with the words "Firebird Girls," and the doors opened to a circular vestibule with cozy couches and a row of pupil stations sitting in front of a window that overlooked the mountains.

Austin gave Elena a little push, and she tripped ungracefully through the door into the vestibule.

"Thanks so much for that," she said to Austin sarcastically as the doors began to slide shut and he called, "See you at dinner!"

Across the room, a single door stood with the Firebird logo etched into the center. Elena scanned her Trademark against the scanner niche and it slid open silently. She peered in cautiously, but there was no one in sight, so she stepped over the threshold quickly.

The bedroom was comfortably furnished. A half dozen beds and a half dozen wardrobes lined the walls across the length of the room. This was the first time she would have to share a room, let alone with five roommates. At the apex of the room, a picture window looked out over the ocean.

Elena followed along down the row of beds to the third one on the left where her last name was inscribed on a nameplate in the shape of a Firebird on the footboard. The golden and red comforter on her bed and the pillow touching the headboard were all embroidered with the Firebird logo. She flung her carrier bag on the bed and heard the contents bang together.

Elena continued to the far side of the room and walked into the washroom where she saw a long row of sinks on one side and a row of shower stalls on the other side of the room. The Firebird logo was stitched into all the towels that were hanging on hooks along the wall, and it was also hewn into the sinks, the toilet seats, and showers.

"So, I guess they don't want us to forget that we're Firebirds," Elena said sarcastically.

Alongside the bathroom, a narrow hallway was lined with beautiful paintings. This hall led out to a veranda that overlooked a stunning courtyard that was filled with flowers. The porch was equipped with lounging chairs and a fountain of drinking water. Elena stood outside for a long while watching boys and girls enter and exit the courtyard below. She couldn't help but think that Austin was probably best friends with all his roommates by now.

By the time Elena arrived back in the bedroom the other five of her roommates had arrived, dressed in school uniforms and busily organizing their closets. As she walked back to her bed, she noticed a girl with platinum blonde hair sitting there. The girl was speaking animatedly to a girl with raven black hair who inspected Elena with cheerless eyes.

When the girl with blonde hair noticed Elena, her voice trailed off. The three girls were silent for a moment, surveying each other. But then, the blonde girl stood up. She was very tall for a girl their age and built for athletics, though she also had dainty features. And even though she looked a lot like all the other blondes with blue eyes, she had one of the most beautiful faces that Elena had ever seen. Her uniform was pristinely pressed and she had gloss on her nails and lips.

"Your hair is gorgeous!" she told Elena with a melodic voice.

Elena narrowed her eyes, not sure if the girl was being sincere.

"You're Elena, aren't you?" the girl continued.

"Yeah, that's me. How did you know?"

"Oh, I memorized the entire class list, including all the names of the kids in our Company." The blonde girl smiled pleasantly, and extending her hand, said, "I'm Abria Bowen."

Elena reluctantly shook it.

The girl with raven hair smiled wryly and said formally, "My name is Fergie Foreman. I am pleased to make your acquaintance."

Fergie shook Elena's hand rigidly.

"I suppose we're going to be suitemates," Abria said lightly, pointing to her bed just on the other side of Elena's bed.

Elena half smiled as Abria continued talking, completely unaware that Elena had no interest in talking to her.

"I've just been telling Fergie how cute the boys are."

"Were there no boys where you come from?" Elena asked dryly, intending her comment to dissuade Abria from talking further. She had no desire to become friends with a girl who could only talk about boys in just the first few seconds of meeting.

"I'm from the Galilee Province, and I assure you there were plenty of boys there. But meeting boys that are not from home is, like, exciting. You know?"

Elena turned around without a reply and rolled her eyes as she scanned her Trademark to open her closet door. It appeared that in addition to sleeping next to Abria she'd also be sharing a wardrobe beside her because the cheery blonde girl's closet door stood open and was already plastered with pink, purple, and sparkling things. Elena detested pink. She began to wonder if Abria, like Pigg, had used a body bubble to sneak these items into school.

"What's all that stuff on my bed?" Elena asked after she noticed that there were piles of polybags sitting beside Abria.

"Your clothes, silly," Abria said, her words laced with laughter.

Elena didn't like it when people laughed for no reason. She grabbed the first polybag and ripped it open a little too rough. A strange looking piece of plastic sprang from the package. Once Elena had unfolded it, she noticed that it had a hood on one end.

"What is this?" Elena exclaimed.

"It's a poncho," Abria said. "You know, for when it's raining outside."

Elena sighed. "That doesn't inspire any kind of confidence."

She opened another polybag that contained several high collared armorwear shirts, similar to what she'd tried on in the Uniform Locker except that these portrayed the Firebird logo.

"We'll let you get unpacked. But, you'll be eating dinner with us, right?" Abria asked in a singsong voice.

Elena hadn't thought about what she would say if anyone asked her about seating arrangements for dinner.

"Oh, I'll probably sit with my friend, Austin Haddock. We came from Atlanson together."

"Austin Haddock!" Abria squealed. "I met him when I was waiting in line at the first registration table. He was sweet looking. So, I guess we'll be joining *you* at dinner."

Elena stared blankly at Abria Bowen with her mouth half hanging open. She'd never heard anyone refer to her best friend as "sweet looking" before and wasn't sure she liked it.

"Well, I'm off to make myself presentable," the blonde girl said, skipping off toward the washroom.

Elena sat down heavily on her bed.

"Do not let her discourage you," Fergie Foreman said to Elena in an almost apologetic tone. "She does have good intentions at heart. One of the defining characteristics of her personality is a vivacious spirit."

Elena had barely noticed Fergie earlier because Abria had monopolized the conversation, but now she saw that her other roommate was about Elena's height and built much the same except that Fergie had remarkably seamless posture.

Elena decided to take Austin's advice to try to make friends and asked, "Did you know her before?"

"We grew up together in the Galilee Province," Fergie responded in a formal tone. "Not to worry, she shall grow on you."

"Yeah, like a fungus," thought Elena, and Fergie Foreman gave her a funny smile like she'd read Elena's mind.

## ▭ 6 ▭

## The Resident Advisor

After seven full minutes of waiting for the blonde girl to get out of the washroom, Elena begrudgingly walked with Abria Bowen and Fergie to catch a Grimvator that was descending backwards to the Mess Hall on the first floor. She noticed that Abria greeted every girl and flirted with every boy they passed the whole way to dinner. In comparison, Fergie Foreman was quiet, watching Abria with a serene glimmer in her eye. She was very poised and unassuming, taking in the surroundings with a simple smile on her face.

Elena was glad when they reached the Mess Hall. She left Fergie and Abria, who had started talking to yet another girl at the entrance to the dining room, and quickly wound around the plethora of tables until she found Austin and Pigg sitting at a table together.

She dropped down into a chair beside Austin and whispered, "Watch out for..." But she never finished the sentence because Abria had appeared at the table looking radiant and full of life.

"Hi again!" Abria said to Austin, her voice tinkling like crystal. "Remember meeting me from earlier?"

"Yes," said Austin with a bright smile on his face. He hopped up immediately and pulled out a chair for her.

Abria sat gracefully. "Glad you could join us for dinner."

"And I'm Pigg." He tried to stand to greet her, but he tipped over a goblet and water began to spread across the table. Before Elena could think about how they would clean up the mess, a Humanoid had arrived at their table. The robot mopped the water and replaced it with a new goblet and was gone before Elena could even turn around to say, "Thank you."

Abria laughed like a little girl and said, "Pigg! What a funny little name."

"Pigg is his last name," said Elena through gritted teeth. "And, Austin, I noticed you weren't tripping over yourself to pull out my chair."

Austin cut his eyes at Elena as if to say that she needed to be more polite and then, addressing Fergie, asked, "What's your name?"

Fergie sat straight backed into a chair beside Pigg and said her name so quietly they barely could understand her.

"Fergie Forman is her name," Abria informed the table. "She's introverted, but she's also the best study partner you'll ever meet. Plus, she is eternally patient with me." She laughed loudly, her voice tinkling again. "I gab so much you'd think she'd grow tired of our friendship."

"Yes, you'd think so," Elena said, rather rudely, but Abria Bowen didn't seem to notice. Her eyes were fixed on Austin.

"You must tell me all about Atlanson. I've only ever seen holograms."

At that moment, an unusually tall thirteen-year-old boy appeared at their table. He looked surprisingly like Abria, with just as beautiful a face.

"Abria," the boy said sternly. "Anne said that I could have the PocketUnit during the first quarter. It was in my bag before we got onto the train and now it's missing. What have you done with it?"

"I'm glad I'm not the only one that tried to sneak a PocketUnit in," Pigg whispered to Elena.

"Declan Bowen! Don't be so rude," Abria rebuked. "Join us and introduce yourself."

Elena was astonished when Abria had used her same last name when she referred to this boy. She had never known anyone to have siblings. By law, a family consisted of a father, mother, and one child. But Abria's brother was living proof that sometimes the law could be broken.

Declan seemed to suddenly notice the others sitting at the table because his demeanor changed instantly and he smiled coolly.

"I've met Austin and Pigg already; we're going to be suitemates this year. But, I haven't met this fiery red head," Declan said, sitting next to Elena and staring at her hair. He put his arm around her with ease, like he'd been doing it her whole life.

Elena thought he had a very charming demeanor, but shrugged him off and said curtly, "Did you seriously think you could sit down and start a conversation without even technically asking my name?"

Everyone at the table burst out laughing, including Declan who laughed the loudest.

"A sassy mouth to match that hair. Is she always this *friendly*?" Declan asked.

"Her name is Elena Ransom and, yes," Austin said. "She is always like that."

"That's okay," Declan replied airily. "So, any chance that scowl comes off your face at any point?"

Out of her peripheral vision, Elena could tell that his eyes were staring at the side of her head. She wished she could keep herself from blushing, but it was impossible, which made her blush even more. Plus, she couldn't even think to respond to his question because she felt it was too direct for a first meeting.

"The school probably took your PocketUnit," Pigg told Declan. "Strictly speaking we're not allowed to have electronics from the outside. They probably found it when they searched your things."

"It's so beautiful in here, don't you think?" Abria said, ignoring Declan and Pigg. But she didn't wait for anyone to answer before adding, "Honestly, when they said dinner was in the *Mess Hall* I was expecting inox steel cups and billycans."

Elena hadn't noticed before, but now saw that the tables were set formally as if they were seated in a fine dining restaurant. The floors were waxed to the point of cleanliness that she could see everything reflected on its surface. The arched ceiling was painted with mesmerizing frescos, like the kind Elena had once seen in a picture of the Sistine Chapel, with reds, greens, and yellows. Her cushioned chair was as soft as a pillow. The room smelled of baking bread and rosemary lemon roast chicken.

From the front of the room, there came a sudden commotion as a line of adults dressed in high collared, tailored uniforms marched onto a theater platform at the front of the room. An impeccably fit man with sharp, harsh features stepped to the center of the stage. His collar was higher and tighter than all the other adults, and he had a look in his eye that made Elena slightly unnerved. Based on looks alone, he didn't seem like a man that would like teenagers. He seemed domineering, a person you'd never want to argue with. He surveyed the room in silence until the last of the voices died away.

Then, he spoke with a commanding voice, "Good evening, students. Welcome to a new year at Grimsby School of the Republic. I am Headmaster Worthen Bentley. I sincerely hope you enjoy the feast this evening, as this will be the last time you are served a meal this year until the end of the year feast."

Elena leaned over toward Austin and whispered, "Last time we'll be served? Are we expected to grow our own food?"

"He just means that tomorrow we'll start self-service style eating," Austin said, not even bothering to look at her.

"What does that mean?" Elena asked Austin, feeling anxious. But Austin put his finger up to his lips and pointed back to the stage.

"Your Instructors are here," Bentley continued, turning briefly to the men and women standing behind him. "They have full authority to issue praise as well as punishment, so I expect they be treated with the utmost respect.

"After supper you will return to your dormitory common area for instructions from your Resident Advisor. I am pleased that you are here" — though, to Elena, he didn't look pleased in the slightest — "And hope you enjoy your Level 1 studies."

Headmaster Bentley turned on the spot and led the Instructors out of the room. Then, as though an enchantment settled on the room, hundreds of Humanoids entered the Mess Hall carrying trays of food. Family-style serving platters were set in the middle of each table, piled with roast chicken, succulent duck, and grilled beef tenderloin. Mounds of garlic-mashed potatoes, salvers of juicy cooked apples, and patches of green vegetables filled every inch of the table.

"Look at all this exquisite food!" Pigg looked like a wild animal as he pulled plates toward him. "I wasn't expecting them to feed us so well."

Elena felt a sudden rumble in her stomach and filled her plate. She hadn't expected to enjoy Grimsby in the least bit, but it was hard to be prejudiced when the beef tenderloin melted on her tongue and cinnamon butter poured out from the cooked apple as she cut into it.

Elena tried to enjoy the meal to its fullest, but Abria Bowen talked the entire time, asking questions but barely waiting for a response before offering a comment or opinion. Pigg offered a couple jokes, while Fergie watched tentatively, sitting so straight Elena found herself wondering if the girl had a rod for a spine.

Declan and Austin fell easily into conversation, and Elena learned from their discussion that the two blondes at their table were not biological siblings. Declan's parents had adopted Abria after her parents died when she was just a baby. Still, Elena had never known anyone with cousins. She got lost in her own thoughts wondering about how the Bowens' must have been one of the last families on earth to have siblings before the Great Drought. She made a mental note to be sure to ask her mom about it the next time they spoke.

After dinner, Abria and Declan Bowen walked on either side of Austin, talking to him like they'd been friends their entire lives. Elena couldn't get a word in edgewise so she trailed behind them with Pigg and Fergie Foreman in silence. They'd only been at school a few hours and she already felt lonely. The remnants of her life with Austin were being forgotten with every giggle from Abria's mouth.

They climbed onto the Grimvator and made the selection for the Firebird common area. When the doors slid open, they entered a courtyard that was lined with modern furniture, pupil stations, and lounging chairs. A rich red and warm golden banner, which bore the Firebird logo, was stretched across the wall. A hum of student voices reverberated off the walls.

Austin, Declan, and Abria moved easily around the room introducing themselves to the other Firebirds, but the idea of filling the minutes with mindless chitchat was exhausting to Elena. So, she stood with Fergie in silence, trying to think of something friendly to say, while Pigg was off in the corner of the room consulting his PocketUnit in a covert manner.

At length, a Telecaster hologram arrived and said, "Your Resident Advisor will arrive momentarily. Please wait here."

But, after the hologram left, the minutes ticked by slowly. Elena managed to chew off all the fingernails on her left hand into neat little rounds when she noticed that the chattering in the room slowed.

"Where is our Advisor?" Elena finally said to Fergie, feeling frustrated. "He should have been here by now, don't you think?" She folded her arms and pursed her lips together.

"Maybe we should try to find an Instructor," Declan said.

"We're not supposed to leave," Abria reminded him. "I'm sure it can't be much longer."

"But, we've had a long day," said Pigg, sounding tired. "I'm ready to go to bed."

"You whine like a little girl," said a curt voice from one side of the room.

Elena turned and watched as the boy with spiky black hair, who had called Pigg "Big Ears" on the Grimsby Channel earlier that day, appeared from behind a topiary that had obstructed him from view.

Feeling furious, Elena opened her mouth to speak but Abria called out, indignantly, "Excuse me! Some of us are, like, girls."

"There is no *excuse* for you, *Blondie*," the boy answered, making it a point to say "Blondie" like he thought Abria was a clueless dimwit.

At that remark, Declan crossed the room in two strides and said, "Don't speak to her that way."

While the black haired boy looked like he didn't like being told what to do, he also seemed to enjoy the threat. He smiled wickedly at Declan and asked, "Who made you the dialogue enforcement?"

Everyone else waited in silence, staring at the pair of boys who seemed on the verge of fighting. Elena felt a rush of excitement; she'd never seen a physical altercation. She was hoping to see Declan give the boy a bloody nose, but Austin stepped between them suddenly.

"Bowen, I'm sure our classmate is impatient to be excused, just like the rest of us," Austin said abruptly. He turned to face the black haired boy and said, "I think Bowen was just suggesting that you speak with a little more sensitivity to the girls."

The boy looked like he was about to retaliate, but a loud bang like a canon firing overpowered whatever he was about to say.

Elena spun around as a wild mess of hair and clothes came screaming toward the students on an antique motorbike. As the bike squealed to a stop, black smoke emitted from the pipes and a grungy looking young man scrambled off the back.

"What's up, dudes and dudettes!" the wild man yelled. "So, check it out. My name is Hartwell Hopper, but everyone calls me Hopper, and I'll be your Resident Advisor this year."

The fight between Declan and the other kid was completely forgotten as all the boys seemed excited to see the new arrival, and even Abria gave a little squeal of delight as the RA removed his weather-beaten jacket. But Elena surveyed him from top to bottom with her eyes narrowed in disapproval. She had been raised going to medical conferences and political functions. In her opinion, leaders were supposed to look dignified and regal. Hartwell Hopper didn't meet with her expectations in any regard.

For one thing, this man had wildly curly hair that was dyed every color of the rainbow. Under his jacket he had on baggy clothing instead of the proper uniform that all the other Instructors wore. He had a scraggly, long goatee and a repulsive silver ring through his nose, not to mention the fact that he was driving a non-environmentally approved vehicle.

"What that means," Hopper continued, "is that if any of you rugrats has a problem you can come to me and I'll help you deal."

Elena could hardly believe that this crazy person was speaking and could barely understand what was coming out of the senseless mouth. Furthermore, she did not understand the term "rugrats" but she was certain she didn't like it.

She looked to Austin for support, but he seemed to be just as enamored with the crazy beast as everyone else.

"So, first things first," Hopper said, pulling up an Optivision screen from his Smartslate. "We're gonna practice standing in formation for tomorrow's general assembly, which will take place each morning during registration this week and then each morning you have Basic Training once classes begin, kay?"

"Do you have any idea what this person is talking about?" Elena whispered to Austin.

Austin shrugged and smiled.

"Girls to the front and boys to the back," Hopper continued.

There was a lot of noise and shuffling as the boys and girls attempted to make a respectable line.

"Good job my peeps!" Hopper praised. "When I call your name, you say 'here' if you are present. Starting with the boys: Declan Bowen. Crosby Gamble, cool name, dude. Austin Haddock. Gribbin Pigg. Frankie Smiley, another cool name. Kidd Wheeler."

Elena looked quickly and saw that Kidd Wheeler was the black spiky-haired boy who she had decided was a troublemaker.

"Very cool, dudes," Hopper said. "We're gonna have such an awesome year. Now, for the laid-ez..."

He said the word 'ladies' like it was two separate words.

"Kate Bagley. Abria Bowen. Vivienne Castellow. Fergie Foreman, very awesome name. Olivia Nelson and..."

Elena knew that her name was coming next and she was not looking forward to finding out if her name was "awesome" or not.

"Elena Ransom. Totally righteous name, dudette," Hopper finished.

Elena was not sure what he meant by "righteous name" but she did not like being referred to in a slang term like "dudette."

"So, now that we know we're all here I want you all to take a good look around. This is your Unit. You'll work together during Basic Training, live together, and attend classes together."

Elena did not like the thought of being a part of a Unit that had a leader who looked so questionable.

—

80

"Our Unit is called 'Firebird' and likewise our emblem is the Firebird." Hopper threw one hand in the direction of the banner that was stretched across the wall. "This Unit is one of the most revered in all of Grimsby. Why? Well, first off we have the gnarliest dude as Commander. General Hannibal is a celebrated veteran and is a purdy awesome Instructor as well. He won't be teaching you this year, but he'll evaluate your individual progress and together as a Unit."

Hannibal. That name struck a cord in Elena's memory. Just a few nights ago she'd overheard her parents say that "Hannibal" would protect her at school.

"The second reason we're most revered is because this Unit always produces the most fearless competitors, the finest skilled warriors, and the most articulate students in all the school," Hopper continued. "I know you will do us proud."

Elena doubted that Hooper had ever made anyone proud before, and it was hard to imagine how anyone could ever take him seriously.

"So, this is how it's gonna fly for the week startn' tomorrow; you'll wake up, have breakfast and then have general assembly for an hour. Basically, you just need to remember how you're standing tonight and then stand the same way during assembly. After that, you'll spend the rest of each day taking various placement tests and going to the Medical Station to get blood drawn, vaccinations, and other fun stuff."

Elena's stomach jumped into her mouth at the mention of vaccinations. At registration she only had her finger pricked, and that hurt enough. She'd never had a needle shoved in her arm before and didn't really see the need for one.

"Now, can anyone tell me how many students are in each Unit?" Hopper asked, though Elena's mind was still racing with the thought of an enormous needle sucking blood from her arm.

Fergie's hand shot in the air.

"We have eager young minds this year!" Hooper smiled appreciatively. "Yes, Fergie Foreman."

"Six boys and six girls form a Unit," Fergie said formally.

"That's correct. Tomorrow, you Firebirds will meet our three sister Units. Can anyone tell me the names of our sister Units?"

Again, Fergie's hand shot in the air.

"Dude, Foreman is schooling you all," said Hopper lightheartedly. "Yo, Declan Bowen, do you know our three sister Units?"

"They are Falcon, Raptor, and Harrier, Sir," Declan answered mechanically.

"Yo, dude, don't call me *Sir*; it makes me feel old. But you are correct, those are the names of our sister Units. Together, the four Units make up a Company. Can anyone tell me..." But before Hopper could even finish, Fergie's hand was in the air again.

"Not to be rude, Sweetie," Hopper said to Fergie. "But it's only right that everyone gets a chance to answer. So, Austin Haddock, can you tell me the names of the three Companies?"

"The Companies are Aves, Animalia, and Maritime," Austin answered.

"And what is the name of our Company, Abria Bowen?" Hopper asked.

"The Firebirds are assigned to the Aves Company," Abria answered in a singsong voice.

Elena was beginning to feel like she should have spent some time watching the *Manual of Manipulation* after all and hoped that she wouldn't be called upon to answer any questions. She looked over and noticed that Pigg was sweating slightly; he also hadn't read the manual.

"That's right, Dude. You'll attend classes with the other kiddos in the Aves Company and eventually you'll compete with them against the other Companies for top marks in Basic Training. But you'll learn more about that as the days go on.

"I noticed that everyone uploaded their schedules to the Smartslates," said Hopper. "But try to memorize them this week because classes start a week from tomorrow, and the Instructors don't like tardy rugrats.

"Well, that seems to be it," he said, walking back toward his motorbike. "If you have any questions, get on the Grimvator and look for my name." After that, Hopper swung his leg over the motorcycle, kicked off and sped away.

After Hopper was out of sight, the Firebirds broke their lines and the courtyard filled with a buzz of voices again.

Austin hurried over to Elena and said, "That guy is so awesome!"

Elena did not look pleased. "I can't believe they allow him to look like that."

"What is it your dad's always saying? Never judge a book by its cover, Lena," Austin whispered.

"I hate that expression," Elena complained, rolling her eyes. "All the best books have the best covers. It's called *marketing*."

"I can't believe that *you* are judging him based on his appearance."

"Austin," Elena sighed heavily. "This morning I had to leave home, I got my finger stuck by a needle during registration, and I had to move into a room with five other girls, one of which will not stop talking long enough to catch her breath. Then, I witnessed you almost get into a fight with a nasty boy, and I met the most pathetic excuse for an RA that I think has ever lived. I'm a little overwhelmed so could you just not do the whole *I'm perfect* thing right now?"

"Don't fall apart now," Austin replied, trying to look sympathetic, though clearly still captivated by meeting Hopper. "I need you to be in a good mood tomorrow so we can get through our placement tests and medical assessment."

"Speaking of that, what's all this nonsense about vaccinations?" Elena asked. "Did my mom know about this?"

Austin laughed. "Of course she knew. She went to school here too, remember?"

"Where's the Telepost office?" Elena said. "I want to complain to my parents right now."

"You won't be able to. We're not allowed to speak with anyone outside school for the first two weeks while we're going through the 'conditioning phase.'"

Elena was outraged and her feelings must have appeared on her face because Austin said, "Let's just get through tonight, and tomorrow and we'll worry about everything else later."

"I think that's expecting a little too much from me," Elena grumbled.

"Stop flipping out!" Austin ordered. "And quit acting so snobby around Declan and Abria Bowen."

"Austin, we just met them and they're already acting so..." Elena searched for the right word and when she found it, she said it sourly, "Friendly."

"Friendly is good," Austin said.

"Friendly is intrusive," Elena replied, the edges of her words full of cynicism. "Plus, I already feel like you're leaving me out. That Abria girl dominates every conversation with her giggling and her annoyingly kind voice."

"Tomorrow is going to be just us, I promise," Austin said. "Come on, lights out is in ten minutes. We'd better get back to our rooms." He put his arm around her shoulder and directed her toward the Grimvators. "Tomorrow's going to be great. You'll see."

# ▭ 7 ▭

# A Long First Week

"Good morning, girls."

Elena heard the sound of birds chirping and water trickling. She opened a sleepy eye and could just see the outline of the morning Telecaster hologram, though it was quite blurry to her. Elena groaned and rolled over. She was exhausted, having unwillingly stayed up late listening to Abria ramble on and on about the hair color, eye color, and physical features of every boy she'd found attractive that day. She learned the hard way that covering her ears with her hands and pillow did not block out Abria's tinkling voice and giggles.

"Wake up, sleepy head," Abria sang, sitting hard on the edge of Elena's bed.

She was already dressed in her school uniform with her hair combed and a fresh coat of makeup painted on her face. Elena wanted to clobber her.

"I slept great. Did you? These beds are so comfortable. Well, you'd better get a move on. I heard that they are docking points off our personal scores for tardiness."

Then, the blonde girl pranced out of the room. Elena groaned and turned over. A pajama clad Fergie was sitting on the edge of her bed staring at Elena with an amused look on her face.

"That was merely the first alarm," Fergie said knowingly. "Two additional warnings are sent in each morning before we must be at breakfast. Abria's appearance is extremely important to her; therefore, she starts the day early. I would presume you have approximately twenty-seven minutes and forty-seven seconds more if you are able to sleep through the noise."

Elena considered herself a master sleeper, but she wouldn't be getting any more rest this morning with all the other girls talking and getting ready. Begrudgingly, she sat up and swung her legs over the side of the bed. The cold marble stone floor was not welcome to her bare feet, but she followed bleary-eyed after the line of girls heading toward the washroom.

After she was dressed, Elena and Fergie followed a group of students making their way to breakfast. They searched the foyer and joined Austin and Pigg in a long line of students waiting to get inside the Mess Hall. As they reached the door, Elena noticed that each child ahead of them submitted their Trademark on a scanner before proceeding through the entrance. When she scanned her forearm, a picture of her face appeared holographically on an Optivision screen.

Elena followed Austin to the food line where he retrieved a plastic tray from a stack and handed it to her, gesturing her to stand in front of him. She looked through a glass partition to a galley of Humanoid cafeteria workers and a series of hoses that hung from the walls. Elena watched a blonde-haired robot grab the handle on one of the hoses, and a gray colored goop issued from the mouth of the hose onto a plate that was then given to the boy in front of Elena.

"What do you think it is?" Elena whispered to Austin, her insides churning.

"I'm not sure, but move forward," Austin replied, pushing her a little.

The Humanoid standing behind the partition grimaced as Elena scanned her Trademark. Then, the robot read from an Optivision screen, "Elena Ransom, you tested positive for high amounts of glucose."

Elena's mouth fell open as she watched the robot place a white plate on the counter. Then, it reached for a hose that emitted an olive colored ooze when the handle was squeezed. When the plate was full, the Humanoid dropped the green gob onto her tray and said, "Off you go."

Elena walked blankly through the rest of the line and found an empty section of tables in the eating area. She sat heavily, inspecting her breakfast as Austin dropped into the seat next to her. He had a plate full of ginger colored slop. They looked at each other wordlessly for several moments.

"How do they know my glucose isn't normal?" Elena asked, but Austin only shrugged and shook his head.

"From the blood sample they took yesterday," said Fergie in a tone of formality as she eased into a seat at the table. Then, after seeing the looks of dismay etched on Elena and Austin's faces she added, "After our bodies are detoxified they will begin serving us a well balanced diet that will visually appear normal."

Elena ran her spoon through the porridge and watched it slide off the tip. "This is the most disgusting, pathetic excuse for breakfast I've ever seen."

"It could be worse," said Fergie, smiling subtly. "One of the other students received brown paste."

Elena looked around at some of the other students and noticed that none of them were eating what they were given in the food line.

"How can I eat this when all I want is an egg bagel with bacon and capers?" Elena asked.

"You'd better try," Austin encouraged. "You heard Hopper last night. We have to stand in formations this morning, and there is no telling when we'll get our next meal. Bottoms up!"

Austin shoved the orange goop into his mouth.

Elena put a little dabble of the green slime on her spoon and lifted it to her mouth. She took her bite slowly with her eyes closed and her nose pinched. The pleasant sensation of a luscious, ripened strawberry dipped in sweet cream filled her unwilling mouth. Her eyes popped open and she stared at her plate.

"Yum, pineapple," Austin said, smacking his lips.

"If it tastes so good why do they make it look so bad?" Elena asked Fergie.

"This week, our meals are served as a type of psychological experiment," Fergie answered after taking a big bite of her apple red slime. Then, using the end of her spoon, she motioned up to the mosaic drawn in the ceiling. "The ceiling is strewn with surveillance. They observe our reactions to color and texture and then record the length of time it takes each of us to decide to eat the meal and how long it takes us to finish the plate."

"Why? That's so ridiculous," Elena said, shaking her head.

"The school performs a series of procedures each day to examine and record our natural inclination toward varying circumstances. With this information, they will begin to develop profiles on each of us," said Fergie patiently. "This will not be the first or last time we shall be observed during mealtime."

This pronouncement made Elena extremely uncomfortable. If the school administrators were watching while they ate would they also be watching while she was sleeping, doing class work, and talking to Austin in private? And, what exactly did a profile look like? Did it affect their marks during class? She was nervous that her profile might already say that she was prone to moodiness brought on by change.

"How do you know that the school is testing us?" Elena asked.

"In addition to the Grimsby Initiation Memorandum, which was explicit about all the rules, regulations, requirements, and agenda, my parents were extremely forthcoming with details about the additional practices in the school."

Elena half wished that her parents had been equally candid in explaining things about Grimsby, though technically she felt that the less she knew the better. She debated internally for a few moments trying to decide if she wanted to ask Fergie questions about school that she really didn't want to know. Fortunately, Pigg arrived to distract her. He dropped down in a vacant seat at their table looking thoroughly disgruntled about the plate full of brown colored paste he'd be given.

"I think I'm going to be sick."

"It tastes alright," Elena tried to encourage him. "Go on, it's fine."

"Are you sure it's not poisonous?" Pigg apprehensively dipped his spoon into the sludge. "You know, it's like that time my mom served us something for dinner that looked like cabbage stew, and guess what! It was cabbage stew, and I felt sick for a week after I ate it. It's a good thing I brought snacks. I'll have to get back to the room to stock my pockets before general assembly begins."

"How did you sneak snacks past the baggage inspection?" Fergie inquired.

"I have a body bubble," Pigg said, but after seeing Fergie's curious look, added, "It's a body suit I created that goes on under my clothes. I can hide all kinds of things in the pockets and no one is the wiser."

Abria and Declan appeared suddenly at the table.

"I am *always* open to trying new cuisine," Abria said, her words laced with pretension. "However, I just want to mention that this slop is *not* part of any diet plan I've ever heard of."

Declan slid into the seat next to Elena and said, "Good morning, Sunshine."

Elena looked up sharply. "How did you know to call me that?" she asked, feeling startled that he'd used the nickname reserved only for her dad.

"What do you mean? Abria said that you didn't seem like a morning person so I felt the nickname was appropriate." Declan's smile stretched ear to ear.

Elena replied with a sullen look on her face.

"I'm determined to get you to smile at me by the end of today," Declan said. Without hesitating, he scooped a spoonful of yellow paste into his mouth and kept on smiling.

Pigg watched him in awe. "You're so brave. You didn't even smell that first."

Declan shrugged and put more in his mouth. "Food is food, and I'm starved."

"I beg to differ," Elena said. "I've read about some ancient cultures that considered insects a fine meal. I'd rather die than eat a grasshopper."

"If it was covered in chocolate I might, like, eat it over this stuff," said Abria.

After breakfast, Elena gathered with the one hundred forty-four Level 1 students from the Aves, Maritime, and Animalia Companies on an exercise field for general assembly. The campus was simulating miserably cold weather and a gloomy skyline, so Elena huddled close to Austin, Pigg, and Fergie while they waited for their Unit to be sorted.

"Why do they have to make it so cold," complained Pigg, burying his hands in his pockets. "They *could* always simulate warm weather."

"Part of the requirement for human development is to become accustomed to a wide range of varying obstacles, including changing weather patterns," said Fergie in a reserved tone.

"Fergie, do you always speak so...you know," Elena began, "properly or formally or whatever?"

"I developed an extensive vocabulary when I was very young," Fergie said. "I suppose it never occurred to me to speak in a normal, teenage vernacular."

"The weather condition never changes in Atlanson," Pigg said, dismissing Fergie and Elena's conversation. "It's always a beautifully, perfect day." He looked around covertly and then asked, "Does anyone have anything to eat?"

"We've just finished breakfast!" Elena squealed. "Besides, I thought you were going back to get a snack."

Pigg pouted at her and replied, "You know I have low blood sugar. Plus, I don't see how we can call that slop *breakfast*. It would have been better to eat those awful granola protein bars that Mom makes me." He began to compulsively scratch his neck. "I hate this uniform. It's so tight, and I didn't have time to modify it before we came out here today. I just can't see how this day could get any worse and it's not even 0800 hours yet." But he suddenly looked up, startled. "Did you hear that?! It was my stomach growling. Being cold all the time makes me want to eat."

"Then, what's your excuse when it's warm?" asked Elena.

But Pigg didn't even have a chance to answer because Abria squeezed herself into the middle of their circle and said, "It is so cold out here that my hair is frozen to the back of my neck." She took a moment to whisk her hair up in a bun on the top of her head. "Declan and I were just over there scoping out our competition in the other Units."

"They have some big guys in that Raptor Unit, but I didn't see anyone else that looked intimidating," Declan said, as he joined them. "Especially not when we have little Miss Sunshine in our Unit. If looks could kill, Elena could have all the other Units begging for mercy by the end of the week."

Elena smiled a little, catching Declan's attention at once. "A smile! I knew I could get one out of you today."

A horn blast interrupted their conversation. Elena saw a man dressed in a military style uniform climb onto a dais that was slightly above their groups. His hair was cut closely to the scalp, but a walrus mustache grew down his face onto his neck. Hopper scrambled up behind him, wearing an un-tucked shirt and his rainbow hair was bouncing around his shoulders. Elena took a moment to chastise his clothing under her breath.

Over the next hour, the Units were sorted and Hopper read through all the names from an Optivision screen. The assembly was extremely tedious. Elena practically froze as she waited. She was dressed warmly, but it wasn't enough to block out the glacial wind chill. She spent her time imagining a long list of complaints to tell her parents during their first Telepost meeting.

At length, a booming voice called out, "Good morning!"

Elena looked up to see the man in the military uniform with the walrus mustache standing before them.

"I am General Hannibal," he said with a voice that sounded like sandpaper rubbing against a boat hull. "This is the standard formation for general assembly that you will attend two days each week before Basic Training.

"During Basic Training you will learn to work together in your Unit. You will be stretched to the limit during this class and will eventually be expected to perform beyond your current abilities. I am confident that each of you will excel under Major Marshall's instruction." Hannibal pointed to a man standing to his right who had more frown lines etched in his forehead than Elena had ever seen. "You are dismissed to your placement tests."

Elena hiked with Austin and a few other members of the Firebird Unit back to their resident tower and followed a line of students through the academic entrance and into a classroom. The room walls were high and white and crafted specifically for holographic learning. Instead of pupil stations there were seats that pulled down from the walls and a working-top that folded out from the seats.

Elena took a seat beside Austin and waited nervously while Hopper gave the Aves Company directions for the preliminary placement test. She was not generally good at taking tests. Sure, she could ace a history exam, but that was her best subject; any other test put her stomach in knots.

Elena looked at Austin and he mouthed, "You'll be fine."

She tried to relax. Elena had already bitten off most of her fingernails waiting to meet Hopper the night before, but there was just enough thumbnail on her left hand to keep her preoccupied while Hopper said, "In a moment, an Optivision screen will activate on your desktop. Do not feel burdened with an urge to cheat because every single test is completely different.

"This exam does not have a time restriction. However, it should not take you longer than three hours. Okay, dudes, good luck."

The lights in the room were lowered and an Optivision screen appeared, hovering midair above the desktop. Elena scanned her Trademark against it and a list of questions appeared. She skimmed the first few questions to see what she was up against. But, as it turned out, the test was nothing more than a series of puzzle solving riddles and critical thinking questions.

Answering the questions seemed easy to her, so she advanced quickly through the test. Minutes stretched into an hour, and then two. Elena felt so confident that she didn't even check her work after she'd finished the test. After she'd closed the session out, the Optivision screen disappeared and that's when she noticed that Austin was already gone. She found him waiting for her in the hall.

"That was easy-peasy," said Austin, smiling.

"Yeah," Elena agreed. "I actually feel really good about my answers."

As the other Level 1's began to finish their exams, the hallway started to fill up, so Austin motioned for Elena to follow him away from the chaos. As they turned down a nearby hall, Elena heard a voice yell, "Get out of my way, *Big Ears!*"

Elena saw Kidd push Pigg up against the wall. This was the second time she'd seen this boy abusing Pigg and she'd had enough of his mouth. Without pausing to think, she hurried down the hall and marched up to Kidd with Austin hard on her heels begging her to calm down.

"Don't push him," she shouted at Kidd.

Kidd hadn't noticed Elena approach, but was roused by her sturdy command and turned to face her. He looked down on her, but she stood rigidly, not afraid of him. He surveyed her stubborn face and then smiled slyly.

"This is none of your business, *Freckles*." Kidd said the word "freckles" like Elena had been cursed with a hideous disease. "Someone with a face like yours should be quarantined so the rest of us are kept safe."

Several of the girls around them giggled. Elena's face turned a violent shade of red. She felt like she wanted to punch him in the face. But just as she was beginning to feel ashamed of her appearance, she could hear her mom's voice in her head, *You're special to your dad and me. Being unlike the other children is what makes you extraordinary.* Elena's heart swelled with confidence and a second later she had calmed.

"It is clear by my appearance that my mom taught me never to be ashamed of what I look like." Elena said this loud enough for everyone in the hallway to hear. "What is unclear, *Wheeler*" — she spoke his name like it was a sour footnote — "is why your mom was ashamed of how *you* look, because I can see the scars from where your freckles were removed, even though they are practically naked to the human eye."

Kidd was instantly silenced as the hall erupted in a torrent of laughter. Elena gave him one last look of loathing and then turned on her heels and strutted away.

Austin ran to catch up and scolded her. "You shouldn't have said it, Lena. You shouldn't behave in a way that is beneath your character."

Austin always had a way of making her feel guilty about her outbursts. He was right, but Elena didn't want to admit it so she kept her mouth shut.

"Well, I thought it was, like, the greatest thing I ever saw," Abria said, as she joined them. "Did you see the look on his face? Serves him right, pushing Pigg like that. He obviously has, like, no manners. Wait until I tell Declan! He'll be happy that someone stood up to that horrible boy."

"You handled that brilliantly," Fergie said, also coming up beside them; Pigg was with her, looking red-faced, but satisfied.

Elena was only half listening. A sickening fury had built in her chest. She decided that Kidd Wheeler was the enemy and she was willing to do anything in her power to make sure that he'd regret being in the Firebird Unit.

"Do my ears really stick out that much?" said Pigg, sounding troubled while groping the sides of his face with both hands.

"No," Austin said firmly. "Wheeler's just trying to make you feel bad about yourself. Don't let him."

Austin led the way to a Grimvator and they started sideways through the building. It was then that Elena realized they were going to the Medical Station where she'd be unnecessarily poked and prodded. She felt a sudden wave of panic again.

Once inside Medical, a Humanoid ushered Elena and Austin into different directions. The robot took Elena's height, weight, and body mass index. Then, the Humanoid performed a comprehensive physical exam, including laboratory tests, chest x-rays, pulmonary function testing, audiograms, heart stress tests, vascular age tests, urinalysis, vision test, blood pressure, pulse, and respiratory rate.

After Elena's respiratory examination, she was given a bioenergetic assessment that utilized a computerized instrument to measure the energetic patterns of each organ in her body to detect if she had any neurotransmitter imbalances, digestive disorders, immune system deficiencies, or emotional stressors.

For the rest of the week, Elena was subjected to a wide array of assessments. She was given an achievement test to measure intelligence, which was essentially a series of verbal and non-verbal tasks that relied on eye–hand coordination. She was required to complete puzzles, assemble strange objects, and identify images in a series of patterned substances.

One day during the week, she was given a neuropsychological test that was specifically designed to measure a psychological function that was linked to a particular brain pathway. Elena was also given a personality test to assess her attitude and feelings about specific events, cultures, and social advancements.

At the end of the week, Elena dropped into a chair in the Medical Station lounge thinking that she was finally finished with all her tests. But then, a severe looking Humanoid called out "Elena Ransom" from behind the desk across the room.

Elena thought seriously about running for the door, but the robot was staring at her expectantly, so she stood up and trudged helplessly toward the desk. When Elena arrived, the robot held up a long needle and said, rather gruffly, "Hold out your arm."

Elena couldn't stop herself from blurting, "You can't honestly think I'm going to let you stick me with that?"

The Humanoid gave Elena an unsympathetic glare, but said nothing, so Elena continued on, "My mom is a Healing Pediatric Surgeon, so you should know that I am fully aware that I don't need vaccinations of any kind. Now, I've been here all week being tested and probed and I'm pretty sure you have enough info about me. I've had enough!"

"I can have you strapped to a seat with your mouth muzzled if you try to fight me on this. Now, you can either stick out your arm and we can do this the easy way or we can do this the hard way," the robot replied mechanically.

Elena did not feel that these two options were acceptable. However, she did not want to be the only person in the room gagged and bound to a chair, so she reluctantly submitted her arm. The needle pierced her hard and she screamed out in pain.

"Ouch! I guess you skipped the day in nursing school when they taught the delicate needle insertion technique."

The Humanoid gave Elena one last fleeting look, and hollered, "Kate Bagley!"

## 8

## A Challenging Day

After a long week that felt like a month, Elena's placement tests, physical exams, and vaccinations were finally complete. The first day of the new week dawned bright and early with Elena anticipating what her new classes would be like. She hurried down to breakfast alone and saw that Austin and Pigg were waiting for her outside the Mess Hall. Pigg was already chewing on a snack cake; Elena laughed and rolled her eyes.

"Don't look at me like that," said Pigg defensively as he followed Austin and Elena into the Mess Hall. "I'm really nervous about today, alright? Remember the time that we had that exam to determine if we were ready to move to the twelve-year-old class? I stayed up late the night before the exam to help Mom reformat the entire house for my grandma's visit and I didn't even get a chance to study. In the morning, I was so tired and nervous that I would fail, I ate the entire casserole that my mom made for Gran. Then, I was so sick that I up-chucked all over my pupil station. I'm just trying to avoid a situation where I overeat and get sick."

"That's the truth," said Austin. "He's been eating since he first woke up."

"What are you going to do when you run out of food?" Elena asked.

"Oh, Mom promised to send me stuff to hide around the room as soon as we're allowed to receive parcels from home. With her help, I won't go hungry," Pigg explained.

At breakfast, Elena enjoyed a crumpet with egg whites, tofu bacon, and avocado emulsion, which she was told would help increase brain function. She managed to avoid getting into a discussion with Abria about the best way to part her hair by listening to Austin and Declan talk about the performance abilities of some of the boys from the other Units. But soon, a bell sounded, signaling the end of breakfast, so the Firebirds abandoned their table and walked along the Grimsby halls to their first class.

"You're walking too fast," Elena grumbled as she struggled to keep up with Austin's lengthy stride.

"Sorry," Austin said as he slowed. "I'm just a little excited to see what it's going to be like."

As they continued down the hall, Elena noticed a group of girls looking at her intently and then began to whisper behind their hands.

"What are they looking at?" Elena whispered to Austin, sounding uncomfortable. "Do I have something in my teeth?"

"It's your hair and your freckles," said Austin, rolling his eyes. "I heard some of the girls talking about how *different* you look."

For the first time in her life, Elena wished she had a hat. Knowing that people were gossiping about her made her feel anxious. But then, she also felt ashamed that she was concerned about her looks. Her parents had always taught her to be proud of her unique, distinctive features.

"Let's sit with Abria, Fergie, and the others," said Austin as they entered their first classroom.

As Elena pulled a seat down from the wall, she noticed that Kidd Wheeler was sitting at the very back of the room. He glowered at her as she turned and sat down. She accessed the desktop from the side of her chair and set it over her lap.

Pigg plopped down in the seat next to Elena and said, "I can't wait for lunch."

"Got a smile for me yet, Sunshine?" Declan asked as he dropped into the seat on her other side.

Just as Elena was beginning to blush, she felt a sudden prickly sensation on the back of her neck as a thick, deep voice filled the room.

"*In the beginning.*"

Instructor Booker, their Advanced Historical Analysis Instructor, had entered the room. He was tall and broad with crew-cut black hair and bushy black eyebrows.

"There is much debate on when and how the world began. In the long years of historical evidence that we've acquired, we know that theologians promoted the Antediluvian period, the period of time between Creation, when the deity called 'God' created the world, and a world-wide flood. And the long years of scientific research will tell you that the earth is millions of years old and that human beings evolved from great apes.

"However, in this class, it matters not what theories we may have about how humans got here. We will focus on facts that research analysts collected from ancient writings and combine those facts with archaeological data that was recovered and tested by experts. You should take out your Smartslates to take notes."

Taking notes hadn't even occurred to Elena, but she joined with the other students in putting her Smartslate on her desk. From the side of the Smartslate, Elena removed the Pointer, a utensil that would enable her to write, as Booker cŏntinued lecturing.

"One of the first indications of life comes from the Fertile Crescent, between the years 8000 and 5000 BC." As Instructor Booker spoke, the lights dimmed and the high, white walls filled with a map of the earth and section of land with two vibrant blue squiggly lines cutting pathways through a piece of land called Mesopotamia. Several sighs and gasps echoed through the room as the boys and girls surveyed the hologram. "The Fertile Crescent was located between the Tigris and Euphrates rivers.

"About 3000 BC a nation of people called *Sumerians* created the first civilization in the heart of the Fertile Crescent."

Instructor Booker went on to explain about polytheism, Sumerian farming, primitive pictograms, Cuneiform writing, accounting procedure, ziggurat architecture, and city building architecture. As he spoke, the entire room filled with different Optivision holograms of the details he described to them. He looked almost supernatural in the ethereal blue-green light of the different screens.

Elena looked around the room expecting to see the other students looking as overwhelmed as she felt, but they were all dutifully writing on their Smartslates and were clearly enraptured with Booker's lecture.

"Pottery was plentiful in the Sumerian culture, and the forms of vases, bowls, and dishes were diverse. They had jars for honey, butter, oil, and wine. Stone tablets were used for writing purposes. Daggers with metal blades and wooden handles were worn, and knives, drills, wedges, and saws were used.

"Common dress included feathered head-dress and necklaces or collars made from gold. Beds, stools, and chairs were used, along with fireplaces, chimneys and fire-alters. Sumerians also loved music and used it as an important part of religious and civic life."

Eventually, he told them about the Sumerian use of slaves, who worked as weavers, pressers, millers, and porters. Booker told them that potters decorated with cedar oil paints and that Sumerian masons used alabaster, ivory, iron, gold, silver, and carnelian. And finally he covered a wide-ranging belief system of idol worship, gods, and poems that included mythological artifacts such as the Tablets of Destiny and religious cosmology.

Elena scribbled notes as fast as she could, but she'd only ever had just a few handwriting lessons in her entire life. Writing seemed completely senseless to her, plus the Pointer felt odd to hold, and the constant motion to create letters hurt her hand. So, when class ended, she felt it was appropriate to start complaining to Austin as they left Booker's classroom.

"That was brutal. He talked for almost two straight hours without drawing breath. I don't know how I'll survive the rest of this day."

"When are we supposed to eat again?" asked Pigg. "I'm starving"

"My fingers are killing me," said Austin, massaging his hand.

"I don't think I can listen to anymore lectures today, and we've only had one class," Elena said as they walked down the hall and entered a classroom that looked very different from the first. Pupil stations were organized in a grid style pattern.

"Why do we have to learn a new, like, language?" Abria asked as they all took seats together on the front row.

"Learning to speak in foreign dialects will help expand your ability to remember information that is studied throughout each school year," Instructor Niva announced as she entered the classroom in a whirlwind of energy, her black hair billowing around her shoulders. "However, we will begin Advanced Phonology by studying the cultures that invented language and writing. Take out your Smartslates and access the first chapter."

Elena opened an Optivision screen from her Smartslate and pulled up the first chapter of their Advanced Phonology textbook as Instructor Niva began to lecture.

"The Sumerians were one of the first civilizations to create writing, which is known as Cuneiform." Niva opened several Optivision screens around her and Elena saw strange symbols appear, hovering in midair. "Our goal for learning the symbols of the Cuneiform text is that you each will come to understand the art of language in its fullest extent."

Elena followed along with the textbook and made notes on her Smartslate using her Pointer. She scrawled the symbols as best she could, but they still never looked exactly right to her.

"Approximately two thousand years after Cuneiform, the Phoenicians originated the alphabet by creating uniform symbols to explain distinct sounds," Niva continued. "This pioneering effort contributed to many new languages, including what would eventually become Hebrew, Aramaic, and Arabic. We will begin studying the Sumerian pictographs and Phoenician alphabet to help us gain a better understanding of language."

In the end, just as the bell rang to indicate that it was time for lunch, Instructor Niva set a homework essay about Cuneiform text. Elena followed the rest of her class toward the Mess Hall, dragging her feet slightly. Her hand hurt, her head was spinning, and her ears were ringing.

"I'm exhausted and we haven't even eaten lunch yet," she complained to Austin, collapsing into a chair at the lunch table with her tray full of food that she didn't even feel like eating. "And my fingers are throbbing in pain."

"Mine, too," Austin admitted, flexing his hand. "I can't believe we already have homework."

Elena observed him with an amused look on her face. "Are you still happy we came here?"

"Yes," Austin murmured. "It's just, I don't understand why we can't use the Optivision from the pupil stations instead of Pointers and Smartslates. Writing by hand seems like such a waste of time."

Elena looked down at her lunch plate feeling thoroughly defeated. She didn't care how good the mangolicious tilapia, wakame brown rice, and spring grilled vegetables were going to taste; she was in a bad mood, and nothing could fix it.

"That was, like, the most grueling five hours, like, ever," said Abria glumly, dropping into a seat at the table. "My fingers, hands, and wrists are killing me."

"I'm so hungry!" Pigg exclaimed. As he sat down, Elena noticed that quite a bit of food was already missing from his plate.

"Dude, Niva spits when she talks," Declan said, taking a brief survey of the food on his plate. "I'm still wiping my face."

This pronouncement sent Elena into a fit of uncontrollable laughter, mostly because she was overly exhausted. The others joined in briefly, but then they spent the rest of lunch eating in silence, except for an occasional outburst of refreshed chuckling.


By the time Elena reached her next class, she was feeling a bit better. The bell had barely rung when a peppy voice floated into the room.

"Understanding astronomy and physics and how it relates to you is a vastly important skill in life."

Elena turned to see an average looking woman with short, spiky blonde hair enter the room. She walked to a polished desk at the front of the room, her spiked heels clicking against the tile floor.

"My name is Instructor Copernicus and you are in AstroPhysics, in case you didn't know. The study of Astronomy is one of the oldest academic disciplines," the Instructor went on. "Even the earliest civilizations that we have record of applied mathematics with the study of astronomy. Physics is both significant and influential because advances in its understanding have translated into revolutionary and pioneering technologies.

"To understand astronomy, mathematics, and physics, we must understand the intricate details of how numbers work into equations. This will be the most important skill you will possess."

Elena was very doubtful that understanding numbers was the *most* important skill she would possess and even more doubtful that she would learn to understand equations of any kind, especially since Pigg sat several seats away and there would be no possibility of cheating. Plus, her head already felt so full of new information that it felt like it might explode.

"By 4000 BC, the Sumerians developed a complex system of metrology, resulting in the creation of arithmetic, geometry, and algebra," Copernicus said as she scrawled an algorithm in midair on an Optivision screen. "From 2600 BC onwards, the Sumerians wrote multiplication tables on clay tablets, and they were the first to use a type of slide rule in astronomical calculations. They were also the first to find the area of a triangle and volume of a cube."

Elena wrote the algorithm onto her Smartslate as fast as she was physically able as Copernicus talked for an hour straight about algorithms, decryptions, and the knowledge they would gain from astrological, mathematical, and scientific study.

Elena looked around often to make sure she wasn't the only person not understanding a word of the lecture. Abria was picking at her nails and running her fingers through her hair; Declan looked like he was sleeping with his eyes open; Fergie actually had her eyes closed peacefully. Only Pigg and a couple of the other students scribbled fiercely onto their Smartslates, looking mildly interested in what Copernicus taught.

Elena began to bite her fingernails, feeling hopelessly unintelligent. She'd barely understood two words the Instructor had said and felt sure she'd never be able to pass the class.

"I was hopelessly lost," Elena told Austin quietly as they left the classroom.

"We'll get the hang of it eventually," said Austin, grabbing Elena's carrier bag off her shoulder and slinging it on his back. "Did you see Fergie sitting with her eyes closed!"

"Yeah. Apparently, she'll be learning AstroPhysics through osmosis," Elena laughed.

"Come on," said Austin. "We'd better get our coats since we've got to hike across the freezing campus for our next class."

"Yeah, I don't understand why we can just have Social Science in here," Elena said.

However, when she, Austin, and Pigg started out across the lawn and circled around the last resident tower she saw right away why the class wasn't inside their building. A gigantic, geodesic glass dome covered an entire field.

"What is that?" said Elena.

"A Hydroponic farm." Fergie had appeared to Austin's left. "The farm grows all the food for the school."

Elena entered the vestibule of the dome; it smelled fresh, like cucumber salad in the springtime. She walked along the hallway with her other classmates and into an endless room of clear tubing that was secured to the ceiling and walls. Plants sprouted from every tube. Pathways paved in brick wound through the building with small streams of trickling water and dozens of Optivision pupil stations.

When they reached the end of the brick walkway they found Instructor Emerald standing atop a bucket. His greasy black hair was smoothed back against his head and a black goatee grew on his chin. Elena thought she heard Abria whispering to Fergie about how dreamy he looked in his lab coat as the Instructor beckoned the class forward with his hands and said, "This year, we're going to plant a farm!"

Emerald hopped off the bucket. "We have discovered through excavation that the ancient Sumerians had advanced techniques of land cultivation, mono-cropping, and organized irrigation through the use of shadufs, canals, channels, dikes, weirs, and reservoirs. Therefore, using their methods, we are going to produce foods similar to what they would have, such as barley, chickpeas, lentils, wheat, dates, onions, garlic, lettuce, leeks and mustard. The foods we grow this year will be used in our school meals. Isn't that exciting?"

The whole class was silent and Elena rolled her eyes at Austin. Instructor Emerald went on speaking as though his class were the most interesting in the history of time.

"The Sumerians were also skilled at animal husbandry." "Therefore, we will also be raising cattle, sheep, goats, oxen, donkeys, and pigs."

Pigg suddenly clutched Elena's arm and squealed, "Animals are dangerous!"

"No animal farming today though," Instructor Emerald said, and Elena felt Pigg's grip relax. "We need to get started on our crops."

Emerald divided Elena into a group with Austin, Pigg, and Abria. He gave them a plot of earth that was floating over a body of water and a sectional tray of seeds to plant.

Abria talked the entire time about growing up in the Galilee Province and how they had an aptitude for growing plant life and how she, herself, had a green thumb. Austin was friendly and gracious, assuring Abria that it was good Emerald had put them in a group together since he and Elena had no idea about plants. Elena kept her mouth shut. Admitting that Abria could be good at anything besides gossip was stretching a little too far for her.

After the first full day of classes, Elena wasn't sure she'd be able to do it again. Although, it was helpful that all the classes were being taught on the same point of human history, Grimsby classes were faster paced and more strenuous than any schooling she'd had at home.

She hardly spoke during all of dinner and went straight back to her room instead of going to the Media Lab to start on her homework with the others. Tired and cranky, she collapsed into bed, falling asleep quickly.

The next morning, Elena lay in bed struggling to feel conscious. Her hands ached and her shoulders were tense from sitting hunched over in the hard desk chairs the day before. With a wave of panic, she remembered that Basic Training would begin right after lunch. She'd heard that the class was a hardcore workout, and she felt that her muscles weren't up to the stress.

CHAPTER 8

"Why do they make us write, like, everything?" Abria's voice rang in Elena's ears as she opened her eyes.

"It is believed that handwriting helps develop kinetic reasoning skills," Fergie answered. She was still in bed with the blankets drawn up around her.

"I don't even understand what that, like, means." Abria laughed girlishly. She was sitting on the edge of Fergie's bed wearing long sleeves under the high collared armorwear shirt and trousers with laced up combat boots. A bomber jacket was sitting in her lap. Her hair was in a loose ponytail, and there was fresh gloss on her painted face; she looked as though she'd been awake for several hours. "How many times have I told you that you have to speak in layman's terms when you talk to me, Fergie?"

Fergie smiled patiently and said, "I mean, it helps with coordination."

"Do they have something that can help me do better in Physics because I'm hopelessly dimwitted about that?" Fergie laughed mechanically as Abria looked over and noticed that Elena's eyes were open. "Oh, good, you're awake."

"It's kinda hard to sleep with your mouth going," Elena grumbled. "Are you always going to be this energetic in the morning?"

"All signs point to *yes*," Abria giggled. "Here's your gear for Basic," She rambled on, tossing a brown-papered package on the foot of Elena's bed. "They delivered it last night but you had already gone to bed. Better bring your bomber jacket and wear your combat boots today; it's supposed to be fr-eeez-ing."

Abria hopped up and rushed back into the washroom.

"I need to ask for a new rooming assignment," Elena sighed as she grabbed the package and removed an under armor shirt that matched Abria's and a pair of trousers. She dressed quickly and joined Abria and Fergie on the way to the Mess Hall. Austin, Declan, and Pigg were already eating by the time they arrived at the table.

After a filling meal of whole grain cereal, scrambled eggs, and toast, Elena followed a procession of students to a sterile room that was equipped with a series of inox workstations. Hopper was sitting with his feet propped up on his desk. His hands were rested behind his head, and he was humming rather loudly.

"Come in, come in and choose anywhere you'd like to sit," Hopper said as he jumped up to greet them.

Elena followed Austin to a table in the center of the room and joined Pigg, Fergie, Abria, and Declan as the rest of the Firebird Unit filed in and sat at the table beside them.

"Welcome to Survival Strategies. The first part of our mornings together will be learning how to survive in the wild; this instruction includes medical training, basic food prep, and water procurement. Then, we'll spend the last part of our time together doing practical instruction."

Hopper walked around the class as he spoke; Elena wished that he wouldn't. His rainbow colored hair and baggy clothes were extremely distracting to her. Plus, the whole class seemed like a waste of time. Why were they learning how to *survive in the wild* when they all lived within the civilized, dome cities?

Fortunately, Hopper taught in a way that was easy for Elena to understand. He lectured the first hour on the basics for survival in any situation; like needing shelter, food, and water. Then, they had a short recess, which included a lesson on how to make a snack mix with nuts and berries. As they ate this snack, Hopper led them in a classroom discussion on the Sumerians' use of tools and weapons.

"So, in review," Hopper said, as their class was coming to an end. "What are the most important things to remember if you find yourself alone in the..."

Fergie's hand was already in the air, so Hopper called on her.

"Vanquish fear, adapt to your environment, and remember your location," said Fergie.

"Good job, Foreman. You Firebirds better take notice of Foreman," Hopper said to the class. "She's the girl with all the answers."

◻ 9 ◻

# The Drill Instructor

At lunch, everyone spoke excitedly about Hopper's teaching and how they looked forward to his next class, except Pigg, who was distracted by the small lunch portion they'd been given. He had already drained his soup bowl and was picking through the nuts and raisins on his salad.

"I'm going to be starving in twenty minutes," Pigg grumbled.

"In reality, at the rate our bodies burn calories during physical exertion, and based on the caloric intake of this meal, I would estimate that you will burn through your lunch by the time we have walked out to the training field," Fergie said formally.

"We're not supposed to eat too much right now," Elena said. "It's our first day of Basic. They don't want people puking all over the field."

"How can they expect me to exercise on so few calories?" Pigg looked completely miserable. "Good thing I have a snack cake."

He reached into his shirt and retrieved a packaged bar. After one quick rip, the package was off and the bar was in his mouth.

"I'm just, like, totally nervous about having class with the other Units," Abria said. "I've tried to meet as many of our other classmates as I could, but you still never know what people are like until you see them under pressure."

"We're not going to have time to socialize during Basic," Declan said, rolling his eyes. "I doubt Marshall will let us talk at all. I heard that he once made an entire Unit do lunges all afternoon because *one* kid spoke without permission."

"What's that?" Pigg said, his mouth filled to the point that it wouldn't close. "Who are you talking about and what is a *lunge?*"

"I'm talking about our Drill Instructor," Declan said patiently. "I've heard that he's a real maniac and that most kids cry at some point or another during the first quarter of his class."

This news made Elena extremely uncomfortable. She felt anxiety grow in her chest as she pulled on her bomber jacket and marched with the Firebirds out to the far side of the campus where large, square patches of lawn were broken by paths of hard pressed gravel. She noticed chin-up bars, leg and arm weight stations, anchor cylinders, and press benches. But, before Elena had time to even worry about what they'd be using all this equipment for, the entire Aves Company was called into formation for the reading of the names.

After roll call, the fierce looking man Elena had only seen once before, when Hannibal had introduced him as Major Marshall, stepped to the front of their uniformed lines. His hair was cropped so closely to his scalp that he looked bald. His thick, black eyebrows were creased together, and deep frown lines were set in the corners of his mouth and cheeks. He surveyed them silently for a few moments and then launched into a verbal assault.

"I am certain that this is the most pathetic group of trainees that has ever walked the Grimsby halls. Now that I've seen you, I do not have high expectations for optimum performance. However, while you are in this class you will learn to be fierce and vigilant," Major Marshall barked.

Elena felt numb from shock. The Instructor had just hurled insults at them without having a reason.

"I am Major Marshall. I expect you to call me Sir or Major. Is that understood?"

At this question, Elena wasn't sure how to react. Perhaps it was because Marshall was so intimidating, or perhaps it was because he had demanded they answer so quickly, but hardly anyone answered.

"When I ask you a question you reply 'Sir, yes Sir' or 'Sir, no Sir.' Is that clear?" Marshall barked fiercely.

"Sir, yes Sir," the Company replied in unison.

"We will begin each training session with stretching." As Marshall spoke, several faceless holograms in the shape of people appeared in front of the class. "You will obey every command you are given, and you will perform to my standards or you will receive discipline."

Without warning, the holograms began to yell commands and stretch in unison. The Firebird Unit caught on quickly and began mimicking the holographic movements. They started with a hamstring routine, push-ups and pull-ups, and then moved quickly into a circuit workout. After this, the Company was expected to do crunches, sprints, and a cardio workout.

Even Elena, who had benefited from Hannah's physical education training, was having a difficult time keeping pace with the rigorous routine. Her muscles were screaming in pain; she could literally feel them tearing. Her red curls were a frizzy mess, and the sweat from her forehead was dripping into her eyes making it nearly impossible to see. She noticed that most of the other Level 1's were barely able to do even some of the simpler exercises.

As the students struggled through, Marshall viciously attacked them: screaming in faces, shouting orders, and issuing insults. The more he yelled, the less patient Elena felt. What could Marshall honestly expect on the first day of class? Most parents believed that mental exertion was more important than physical exertion, so most teenagers had barely learned to run much less exercise. Plus, they hadn't even stopped for water or rest. Elena's face burned and her heart pounded with revulsion at every comment he made.

After a while, Elena realized that the Drill Instructor's booming voice had localized into one area. To her left, she could see that Marshall was bent close to Pigg as he struggled to do a simple push-up. It was true that Pigg was hopelessly clumsy and physically feeble, but all the same, she felt that Marshall was being too harsh.

"You are weak!" Marshall bellowed into Pigg's face. "Push harder."

Pigg was red faced, sweating, and shaking so hard that he kept losing his balance. Elena was beyond feeling uncomfortable watching the whole spectacle. What was Marshall's problem? And then, Elena noticed tears streaming down Pigg's cheeks.

"That was the worst class in the history of time!" exploded Elena, as she stormed down the hall toward the Mess Hall after Basic Training was over.

Austin was walking quickly behind her trying to keep up. "Lower your voice."

"I won't lower my voice!" said Elena furiously. "He had no right to treat Pigg that way."

"It's his job as the Instructor."

Elena stopped dead in her tracks, feeling irate, and rounded on Austin. "Are you defending him?"

"No, I'm saying that we can't do anything about it. He's the Instructor."

"Well, I can't stand it!" she screeched, flailing her arms. "I'm going to say something about his attitude problem."

"Don't do that," Austin said seriously. "You'll make it harder on all of us. Not to mention the fact that you could get in trouble."

"That pitiful excuse for a human being shouldn't be allowed to yell at the students like that, especially since most of them haven't had any physical education training before," she argued.

"You're acting crazy. Let's get some dinner and try to calm down," Austin said reasonably.

After Austin and Elena got their food, they joined Pigg and Declan at a table. Pigg's face was still blotchy red, but the tears in his eyes were gone.

"I'm starving!" he said, but not really to anyone in particular as he shoveled food into his mouth.

"Where are Fergie and Abria?" Elena asked Declan.

"Abria was crying so hard after Basic that she had to go get cleaned up. Fergie went to help."

Elena looked down at her plate, anger boiling up again.

"Dude, Marshall is a hard core loony," Declan said woefully.

"Yeah. I swear, when he was staring at me today, I felt a little flesh melt off my face," Pigg added.

And suddenly, all the pinned up rage Elena felt was replaced with the thought of Pigg's face melting off, and she smiled in spite of her anger.

"Marshall is tough," Austin said in agreement. "But we have to make an effort. We don't want our Unit to fall behind the others. The Firebirds are the best. We need to model that for everyone to see."

Sometimes, Elena hated that Austin always knew the right thing to do.

■■■

The first two weeks of Grimsby passed by quickly. After their second Basic Training class, Elena's muscles, joints, and bones were in a constant state of screaming in pain. She began to literally hobble around the school because she wasn't able to walk properly. And she wasn't the only one.

"I have muscles in places that I didn't know about," she grumbled to Austin almost every day. "And just when I think my body is starting to feel better, we have another workout with Marshall and I feel terrible again."

The Firebird Unit had been expected to perform beyond their abilities. In addition to the regular stretches, Major Marshall had added new exercises like a metabolism booster, bicep curls, stationary cycling, and stationary rowing. Elena was beginning to feel desperate about the workload in class and the physical strain on her body until, finally, the day came when she was allowed to speak with her parents.

Early in the morning, Elena hopped onto a Grimvator alone and selected "Catacombs" from the Optivision screen. The elevator slanted upwards, then to the side, and eventually it began to descend. When the doors finally opened, she stepped out onto an eerily vacant hallway and hiked to the backside of the building.

At length, Elena came to a hallway lined with doors, each with a light indicator above the frame. If the light was red that meant the room was occupied, but if the light was green that meant the room was available for holographic contact. The entire Telepost office was lit to green, except the farthest door on the right at the end of the hall. She chose the first door she came to, scanned her Trademark in the scanner niche, and entered a small, white-walled room.

When the door closed behind her, the room slowly morphed into the comforting space of her kitchen back home. Her parents were cooking breakfast together, and so it took them a moment to realize that Elena had joined them.

"Oh, honey!" Hannah said fondly. "How are you doing?"

"Horrible!" Elena stated. "Do you see this face? Does this look like a well-rested, happy-go-lucky face to you?" She used her finger to pick at her skin. "Do you see these eyes? I never sleep because I have one of the most talkative roommates in the history of mankind. The classes are giving me a complex, and my Pointer is giving me a callus. I mean, just look at my poor, swollen fingers."

"Oh, things must be bad," Truman said in a semi-sarcastic tone. "All her nails are gone and her cuticles are infected."

"It can't be that bad," Hannah started, but Elena held up her hand.

"Mom, please, I haven't even begun to start complaining about my new living situation. Did you know that I was going to have to share a washroom? Also, there is the daily onslaught of classes and homework, followed by Basic Training class that is taught by a dimwit who makes the other students *cry* while we're exercising. I can barely concentrate because I spend my time imagining how I could use one of those karate moves you taught me on him."

Elena could tell that Truman and Hannah were trying to look sympathetic as she ranted, but she became frustrated as she watched them eat the blueberry pancakes that she traditionally made with her dad every week.

"Look at you, eating your yummy little breakfast while I'm here suffering," Elena stated in a rather rude tone. She folded her arms over her chest. "I can't believe I'm here."

Elena saw Hannah give Truman a look of pity mixed with trepidation; it was the same face she'd seen the night before she packed up and left for Grimsby. Her mom was worried again, and Elena's complaints were making it worse.

"Elena," her dad said seriously. "You are trying to do your best, aren't you?"

This was the moment of truth...truth that was going to be ignored for a greater purpose.

"It's not all bad," Elena said, and she rolled her eyes to make the sudden change from grievances to positives seem a little more plausible. "Austin and I are always together. And I'm fed well. But the best part is that, now that I'm through the conditioning phase, I can see you both whenever I want. I guess I just miss you."

Success. Hannah's face relaxed into a smile.

"We miss you too, Sunshine. Just remember," Truman said. "You will get out of Grimsby only what you put into it."

Elena smiled at them both and said, "Well, gotta go now...there's a line outside the door."

Kisses were blown back and forth between time and space. Then, the room faded back to white. Elena stepped into the empty Telepost office hallway, but the silence was just what she needed to sort out her thoughts. A time would come when she would sit down with her parents and be honest about her feelings about school but, for now, it would have to be enough that she could see them. At least, she could take comfort in the fact that they were safe.

As the days stretched on, Elena had homework from every class every single night. Fortunately, Austin excelled at Survival Strategy, and Pigg had a knack for AstroPhysics, so that made homework a lot easier to get through. And since Elena was good at Advanced Historical Analysis, she was happy to share her knowledge.

They gathered together each night in the Media Lab to do their homework. Eventually, Declan, Abria, and Fergie began to join them. Elena learned that Abria and Declan surpassed them all in Social Science, and that Fergie was uniquely exceptional at Advanced Phonology.

"I really feel like I'm about to have a brain hemorrhage," Elena complained on one such evening as a miniature holographic image of Instructor Niva walked up and down the Media Lab pupil station reciting part of the transcript fromtheir last Phonology class.

"Yeah," Abria agreed. "Like, who else here feels like they have no idea what they're doing?"

Everyone raised hands, including Fergie, which Elena was surprised to see.

"You're lost too?" Elena asked Fergie. "I don't believe it. You always seem like you know what you're doing."

"I feel that I comprehend the majority of our classes. However, for what I know there, I seem to lack in Basic Training."

Elena sighed deeply and said, "At least you haven't had to run laps yet. He made Kate Bagley run laps because her boot was untied."

"Marshall is determined to, like, kill us all," Abria chimed in. "It's wrong for him to be so hostile just because someone can't do a proper chin-up or can't run a mile in less than, like, eight minutes."

"He's the Instructor for a reason," Austin said, after re-plotting the road on his cartography map for the third time. "He wouldn't be if he wasn't effective at this job."

"How are you measuring effectiveness?" Declan asked skeptically.

"Every class we have gets better. Most of us are growing stronger and performing better. The majority of the Company is scoring fairly well," Austin said.

"He may be effective, but he's not likeable," Elena said emphatically.

"Yeah, last week he put two students in the hospital wing for, like, heat exhaustion," Abria said. "I don't even see how it's possible to get heat exhaustion when it's, like, freezing outside."

Elena felt her ears grow warm. Major Marshall was getting harder and harder on the Firebirds and her sister Units. Her hostility toward him had steadily grown over the weeks. The Drill Instructor spent a total of eight hours screaming at the Level 1's during their exercises. Even though some of the Level 1's had not improved much in Basic, most of them had developed enough endurance to last through the exhausting work without too much faltering.

However, a few days later, Elena finally had enough. The Firebird Unit was attempting to run a battlement endurance obstacle course for the first time. Marshall was being particularly severe, chastising people for untucked shirts and skinned knees, even though it was nearly impossible to crawl through tunnels and leap over walls without having some kind of uniform malfunction.

As the Firebirds reached a point where the Units were required to come together in formation and be inspected, Marshall approached Pigg looking dumbfounded. Pigg was particularly red in the face. He had a bruise under his eye, and the knuckles on both his hands were bleeding slightly. But then, tears began leaking out of the corners of his eyes.

"Are you *crying*?" Marshall yelled in Pigg's face. "You may not cry in this class. If you're going to cry you should remove yourself from my presence."

At that moment, Elena finally reached her breaking point. She called out, "Don't yell at him!"

"Who said that?" Marshall screamed, trotting his way down the line of students.

Elena looked at Austin who shook his head ever so slightly, but she had a feeling that if she didn't confess they'd all be punished for her outburst.

"I did, Sir," Elena said pompously, sticking her chin in the air.

Marshall stood in front of Elena, towering over her, and then bent to put his face directly into hers. They made direct eye contact for a few breathless moments.

"What makes you *think* you can lead this class better than me?" he yelled, spitting in her face as he spoke.

"I don't deserve to be yelled at," said Elena stubbornly. "And neither does Pigg."

"I will yell this day and every day as I see fit to train everyone in this class," Marshall said, his eyes bulging.

Elena's face burned red as she stated, "You *will* step away, or I will make you step away."

"Lena, no," Austin hissed under this breath.

Elena used the half-second that Marshall was distracted by Austin's voice to drop to the ground and side swipe the Drill Instructor's feet, just as her mom had taught her so many times before. At least, she *tried* to swipe his feet out from under him. But, her foot stopped dead at his ankle, and the Instructor simply looked down at her for a moment with rage in his eyes.

Then, Marshall grabbed her by the top of her arm and lifted her easily into the air.

"How dare you strike me!" Finger shaking, Marshall pointed to the far end of the training field. "Run! Run until *I* am tired."

Elena wasted no time getting away from him. She took off around the training arena, pacing her steps as Hannah had always taught her. She had no intention of wasting energy and giving Marshall the satisfaction of knowing that he'd beaten her down.

Elena tried to concentrate on her breathing, but the air was so cold that soon her throat began to burn and her nose began to drip. She ran until the field emptied of all classes. She ran during all of dinner, through study time in the Media Lab, and during the Simulab modules she knew the other students would be doing to help them relax after their hard day. She ran until dark.

At length, Marshall came onto the field and signaled her to come over. She came to him, panted a few quick breaths, and then stood at attention.

"I am ready to retire for the evening so you may stop for now. But when you return to this class you will run again. And you shall run every class until I crush your spirit."

Elena was happy to run instead of stand before his ugly face.

"It would be my pleasure, *Sir*," Elena said a little too indignantly and, unfortunately, Marshall noticed.

Marshall surveyed her stubborn face for a long moment and then said, "On the other hand, I believe there might be a better use for your time."

She did not like the look on his face.

"Next class, you will lead the Firebird Unit in exercises."

Elena could see where this was going and felt frightened, but hardened her face so he couldn't see the fear behind her eyes.

"And for every Firebird who does not perform to my liking, you will receive their punishment."

"Sir, yes, Sir."

"You are dismissed."

Elena trotted away. When she was sure she was out of Marshall's sight, she stopped and leaned heavily against a wall outside her resident tower. Her lungs felt like they were on fire. Her mouth felt dry and her throat scratchy. Her entire body shook from weakness and she felt dizzy with hunger.

When Elena finally made it back to the hall of Grimvators, Austin was waiting for her.

"I know what you're going to say," she said, sounding tired. "But can you save it until tomorrow? I'm exhausted."

"Would you meet me out tonight?" Austin asked, pushing one of Pigg's snack cakes into Elena's hand.

Elena was so stunned that she wasn't receiving a lecture that all she could think to say was, "We have a curfew. We can't leave our rooms after lights out."

"Sure we can. Just sneak out to the side porch from the washroom hallway. I'll meet you there."

"Austin, there is surveillance everywhere."

"Just go to the porch and you won't be seen. I promise."

Elena surveyed his face and then said, "Alright, give me about thirty minutes after lights out to make sure everyone is sleeping."

Elena was tired, but felt elated at the thought of sneaking out with Austin just like they had always done at home. At half past lights out, she pulled on her boots and headed out to the hall through the washroom. Austin was waiting for her on the porch as he had promised.

"Come on," Austin said, arching his leg over the side of the porch railing.

"What are you doing?"

"Climbing down the side of the building," said Austin lightheartedly. "The walls were built with crevices, so just mind your footing and follow me."

Elena looked timidly over the side of the building and watched Austin for a moment, but it appeared that he was moving easily down the side of the building. She swung her leg over and followed him down. Elena was surprised that the building lent itself to climbing, almost as easy as a stepladder. It only took a couple minutes to reach the courtyard below.

"How did you know to do that?" Elena asked.

"Hush," Austin said, looking around. "Follow me."

Austin led Elena to the edge of the courtyard where he walked in the shadow of the farthest wall.

"Where are we going?"

Austin smiled and said, "It's a surprise."

He continued on. Darkness spread out around the absolutely silent campus except for the small dots of perimeter lights in the distance. They hurried beyond the schoolyard and through the orchard to the edge of the school boundaries. Then, Austin took out a hololight and led Elena down a steep hill.

"You do realize that I have been running all afternoon," Elena complained.

"This is worth it."

At length, Austin stopped in front of a myriad of trees that were covered with creeping plants. He grabbed a handful of foliage and yanked it back to reveal a steel plated door. The Firebird emblem was etched directly in the center of it. Elena felt a prickling on the back of her neck. For some reason, seeing the secret Firebird logo out in the woods made her remember her dad talking about the Firebird Disc.

But, a moment later, all was forgotten as Austin pulled down a steel lever, and there came a loud scraping sound of metal on metal. Then, he heaved the door open and stepped inside. Elena followed with her mouth partly open in astonishment.

The space behind the door was an apartment of sorts. The main hallway led into a wide, circular room. On one side, there was a stainless steal kitchenette, an island cooking station with a half dozen high-rise stools, and also a six-top table with chairs. Metal bunk beds lined another wall. A cluster of cushiony chairs surrounded an Optivision pupil station in a circular fashion.

"It's called the *Firebird Station*. Isn't it awesome?"

Elena was pleased and exclaimed, "How did you ever find this place?"

"Hopper told me about it. He seemed to think that you might need to blow off a little steam after lessons with Marshall."

"Why would he tell you about this place for me? He knows I don't like him."

"Why are you always so suspicious of everyone?" Austin asked dismissively. "Hopper said that this station was home to a communications officer before the school was first built, but that it has long been abandoned and no one should bother us here. He also said we couldn't tell anyone else about it."

Elena didn't really think much of Hopper, but it was hard to dislike him now that he'd given them a safe place to hide away from everyone else.

"This is amazing!" she gushed, walking around.

"Come sit down and take your shoes off." Austin indicated the chairs in the living room with his finger.

Elena plopped down into one of the cushiony seats and unlaced her combat boots. Her feet were screaming in pain and were covered over with angry, red blisters.

"I broke into the infirmary earlier to steal medicine for your feet," Austin said, removing a bottle of ointment from his shirt and the Suturand from his pocket. "I figured your feet would ache after all the running you did today."

"Why didn't you just ask for the medicine?"

"You have to be examined before they give out medicine of any kind, but I figured you would need this tonight," Austin said.

"How did you manage to break in to the infirmary?"

"Pigg used his PocketUnit to hack into the security system. I was free and clear for one whole minute. Did you know that he wrote all those programs from scratch? It's a little scary how smart he is."

"This school is turning you into a rebel," Elena said, pleased that Austin was not following the rules like he always did at home. "Did Pigg help us escape tonight?"

"Actually, it was Hopper who told me about the gaps in the surveillance. He monitors the school at night sometimes."

Elena looked at the red blotches on the tops of her feet. "What are they?"

"They're called 'blisters.' They're like burns caused by forceful rubbing," Austin said, using his laser wand to gently cut open each blister. "It's only the seventh week of school and you're already in trouble."

"Are you surprised?"

"I'm surprised you lasted this long."

Elena smiled boldly. "Remember the first fight we got into together?"

"Yes, we were ten and playing at the park when that boy tried to bully me," Austin said fondly. "The result was a black eye and bloody nose if I remember correctly."

"Mom made me sit in the corner for a week." She smiled reminiscently.

"Lena, you can't go fighting the whole world just because you don't agree with something. Think about what your dad would say."

They were quiet for several minutes. As Elena watched Austin's steady hands heal her feet with the Suturand and ointment she thought about her dad. Truman would be disappointed to find out how she'd behaved. He would have challenged her to think about Marshall's class logically and come up with a solution that didn't involve an emotional reaction. He didn't seem to understand that it was nearly impossible for her to be level headed about things that made her angry.

"Marshall is going to make me lead the class in exercises," Elena said softly, revealing the anxiety she felt in her voice. "And if anyone messes up, I'll be punished for it."

Austin sat in silence.

"I know, I know," Elena sighed. "I shouldn't have lost my temper. But you saw how he was torturing everyone."

"Since when is *yelling* considered torture?"

"He shouldn't talk to us that way. It isn't right," she said indignantly.

Austin continued working on Elena's feet without a reply. She stared at him; Austin was always even-tempered, just like Truman. She was jealous of his demeanor.

"I feel like a juvenile delinquent."

"Me too." Austin smiled. "Let's form a club."

Elena broke into a fit of giggles, but almost as soon as she started, a worried frown caught her face.

"Hey, we'll let the Firebirds know that you're leading the class and make sure everyone does their best," Austin said, trying to comfort her.

## ⌑ 10 ⌑

# The Firebird Station

Elena startled awake the next morning with an unfamiliar hollowness she'd never felt before. Her stomach had gone past the point of grumbling to completely empty. She could tell instantly that it was early, long before the first Telecaster holograph would arrive to notify the Firebird girls that it was time to rise, because Abria was still asleep. She knew the Mess Hall wasn't open yet, but she dressed and hurried down so she could be the first in line when it did.

By the time Austin, Pigg, and Declan arrived at the table she'd already finished raisin bread, key lime yogurt, orange slices, pancakes with gooseberry jelly, banana bread, a spinach cheese omelet, and French toast with cream. And now, she was fingering her way through a large plate of deviled eggs.

Declan observed her with an amused expression on his face. "I haven't seen you look this ravishing in the morning before. Did the shower run out of shampoo, or something?"

Elena quickly wiped her mouth, feeling sure that it was smudged with breakfast, and thumbed her fingers through her hair.

"I guess I was a bit hungry from all the running yesterday. I actually haven't even looked in a mirror today."

"We can tell," Austin joked.

As the Mess Hall began to fill, Elena heard whispers from the other boys and girls about how *abnormal* she was for fighting with an Instructor. She felt her face growing warm and frowned at the toast on her plate, wishing that she could be anywhere else in the world.

After catching the distressed look on her face, Austin leaned toward her and whispered, "What's wrong?"

"I can hear people whispering about me, and about what happened with Marshall," she replied and noticed that she caught Declan's attention.

Austin looked around, not bothering to be covert about it, and then said, "It's not like you to care what people say about you, right?"

Elena couldn't think of how to reply. She certainly shouldn't care what other people thought, and she certainly wasn't sorry for her actions. All the same, she didn't necessarily like them talking about her.

"Ransom, you were brave yesterday." Declan had put his face directly in front of her to distract attention away from a set of gossiping girls. "Sticking up for Pigg showed strength of character."

"I really appreciate it," Pigg added after scooping scrambled eggs into his mouth.

"I couldn't decide how I wanted to do my hair," Abria said brightly as she slid into one of the chairs at the table. "What are we talking about?" she asked as Fergie took the seat beside her.

"How awesome Ransom was for challenging Marshall yesterday," Declan said.

Abria smiled and her voice tinkled like crystal as she said, "If I hadn't been so tired I would have burst out laughing when you tried to take him out. Oh, the look on his face was just too funny."

"It's the last time I'll be able to stick up for someone during Basic," Elena said. "Marshall is making me lead our exercises, and if anyone falls behind I'll get the reprimand."

"That won't be a, like, problem," Abria said lightly. "We'll just tell the others that you're leading the class. Everyone will do their very best."

---

"That's what I told her," Austin said while spreading orange relish on a piece of crispy toast.

"I can't work any harder," Pigg complained. "I think I had a heart attack after our exercises yesterday."

"Or..." Declan grinned like a cat, "we could each take a turn trying to drop Marshall during Basic. It would take his mind off you pretty quick if he had a mutiny on his hands this early in the year."

Elena wasn't sure why, but this cheered her up a bit. Taking turns trying to attack Marshall was a ludicrous idea, but funny just the same, especially since Pigg looked a little queasy at the idea.

Suddenly, a Telecaster hologram arrived at the table. "Elena Ransom, report to General Hannibal's office."

Dozens of heads in the Mess Hall turned toward the Telecaster, and everyone around her table gave Elena a startled look. She slid slowly from her chair and stood.

"See you later."

Elena walked numbly down the hall, entered a vacant Grimvator, and selected "General Hannibal" from the list of options. When the doors opened again, she stepped into a foyer and a Telecaster asked formally, "Are you Elena Ransom?"

Elena couldn't even speak, so she just nodded her head.

"General Hannibal is waiting," the holograph said. "You may proceed."

Elena swallowed hard and stepped through a door on the other side of the room. Hannibal's office was in pristine condition; the furniture was uniform and the artwork was sharply angled. He was standing behind a gleaming desk with several Optivision screens open in midair above it.

Now that she was standing in his presence, he seemed very tall to Elena, and his walrus-like mustache was distracting. His military uniform was immaculate and tailored perfectly to his broad shoulders. His salt and pepper hair complemented his handsome features, strongly pronounced chin, and enormous kindhearted eyes.

"Miss Ransom, welcome," Hannibal said genially, though in a deep, expressive tone. "Please come in and sit."

He indicated a chair across from his Optivision station, which Elena took quickly.

"I know your parents very well." Hannibal spoke fondly as he sat in the chair behind his station. "Your dad was one of the brightest minds I ever taught. His precision and attention to detail earned him the highest markings in Basic Training in the history of the school. Did you know that?"

"No, Sir," Elena replied, looking down at her hands folded in her lap. She knew that Hannibal was evaluating her. She felt her face grow warm with embarrassment. "He doesn't speak much about his time here."

"He is too modest," Hannibal replied, smiling as he used the tips of his fingers to access one of the Optivision screens.

Elena's picture and profile information materialized above the table. Hannibal's eyes scanned the information slowly and then pushed the screen to one side of his desk where it hung in midair. Then, he accessed another screen where Elena was forced to watch a projection of herself trying to side-swipe Marshall.

"I'm curious how a student with superb marks, in just these few weeks of school, would act out so violently during Basic Training."

"Violently?" said Elena with a pitch in her voice she didn't recognize.

"You attacked an Instructor. A good Instructor."

A grimace appeared on Elena's face. "I suppose our definition of 'good instructor' is different."

Hannibal did not smile or frown at this pronouncement, but he made a face similar to the one her dad might make when she gave him a sassy remark.

"Miss Ransom, you may disapprove of Major Marshall's methods, but he *is* a good Instructor. Your dad, in particular, excelled under his instruction, as do most trainees."

"You mean the Level 1's who don't die of heat stroke or exhaustion?"

Elena knew she was being rude, but Hannibal remained calm and his smile friendly. It aggravated her.

"He yells at us. He's rude. He...he makes people cry," she stumbled over her words. "He's a bully."

"Yet, you are the one who struck him."

That was a fair point. Elena had tried to attack Marshall. But, didn't it count that she was trying to defend her friend? She was not the type of person to regret outbursts that she deemed reasonable, but she was finding it hard to justify her behavior under Hannibal's gaze.

"You have a distinct advantage over most students that take Basic. You already have the physical stamina to withstand almost every challenging exercise. On the contrary, most of the other trainees will have to be pushed beyond their limits in order to develop the muscle mass it will take for them to pass the class. They need support from the stronger students. Students like you.

"If the Firebird Unit fails Basic Training as a whole, the entire class will be held back from moving forward to the next level of training," said Hannibal. "Can you not see that your cooperation and submission in class is ultimately best for everyone in your Unit?"

Elena had not realized that the entire class would be held back if they failed as a Unit. She began to bite the remaining fingernail on her left thumb. As she started to wonder what he could possibly have meant by "submission in class" it was as if Hannibal read her mind.

"Submission does not mean you're weak. It is a choice in humility: putting the Unit's needs above your own personal agenda. You can choose to participate in class and use your gifts to help the other students without the attitude, or you can be rebellious and watch the class fail."

Elena felt this did not leave her with much choice.

"Do not allow Major Marshall's behavior to control your actions. Control yourself and then you will be able to effectively impress your viewpoint in class."

As Hannibal stood from his chair, Elena also stood. He walked around his desk and placed his hand on her shoulder in a very fatherly way. "I trust that you will make a wise decision based on sound judgment and accountability."

Elena left Hannibal's office feeling true regret, an unusual feeling for her. She suddenly felt determined to suppress her behavior in Basic. She didn't want to hold everyone back. Also, she was hopeful that her punishment with

Marshall would be bearable because General Hannibal had not raised his voice once, nor had he been unkind as he spoke to her about her behavior. She couldn't help but feel hopeful that Hannibal had put in a good word for her to Marshall.

However, as the Firebird Unit gathered for Basic Training the next afternoon, it was immediately apparent that Marshall had not forgotten his punishment for Elena and that he was not planning to take it easy on her.

"Elena Ransom," Marshall called out, wiggling his finger to summon her forward. "I believe you are in charge today."

Elena stepped out of line and, with her chin held high in the air, walked pompously to the front of the class, though her heart pounded anxiously against her ribs as she noticed that some of the Harrier, Falcon, and Raptor students had looked over; their stretches were still being led by holograms. She looked out at the Firebirds and noted some of the curious looks, too, but stood at attention until Marshall gave her permission to begin.

"Today we start with full body stretching, and then we'll move into the standard routine," Elena shouted confidently. "We'll begin on my mark. Three, two, one, mark!"

Together, the Firebird Unit moved in unison on Elena's command, advancing through the series of customary exercises. Marshall walked between the ranks, monitoring the progress. As Elena led, she shouted encouragement to her comrades.

"Nice lines, Nelson; Good job keeping in step, Pigg; Bowen, impressive upper arm strength."

But Marshall scowled, looking only for the flaws.

"Bowen, you're out of formation. Ten laps for Ransom," Marshall barked loud enough for the whole class to hear. "Foreman, you're not doing those push ups correctly. Add five more laps for Ransom. Pigg, you shouldn't be sweating so much, we're not even half way through the lesson. Ten more laps for Ransom."

As Elena commanded, she kept a sharp ear out for how many laps that Marshall was assigning to her. And while most of the students were working hard to try and spare her from running, it seemed that Kidd Wheeler was trying to get her as many laps as he could. Normally, he performed above adequate, but today Elena heard Marshall calling him down often.

"Wheeler, you're looking sluggish. Add five more for Ransom; Wheeler, you're slacking on the chin-ups. Five more laps for Ransom; Wheeler, you're never going to learn the correct marching patterns if you keep talking to Smiley. Add ten more laps for Ransom," Marshall rattled off.

For two straight hours, Elena led the class. After she finally called out the last few reps, she instructed the class to stand at attention before Marshall. Then, she stood at attention once more, sweltering underneath her long-sleeved armorwear shirt and feeling tired while Marshall inspected their lines again.

"It seems that Ransom has quite a bit of running ahead of her for the rest of the day," Marshall said with pleasure in his voice. "Units are dismissed."

Elena hung her head as Austin approached her and said, "You did a great job!"

"Not good enough," Elena said somberly. "He gave me so many laps. I'm going to miss dinner, homework, and Simulabs again."

"That wasn't your fault," Declan said, joining them, followed closely by Pigg, Abria, and Fergie. "It was Wheeler mostly. He was slacking off on purpose."

"Yeah, that was totally, like, unfair," Abria added, then dabbing her forehead with her sleeve, said, "I am sweating like a pig."

Pigg looked at her and raised his eyebrows. His body armor shirt was wet straight through while Abria looked as if she had barely perspired.

"It's just an expression," Abria said to Pigg in an apologetic tone.

Elena felt a strange twinge in her stomach. Abria was on one side of her speaking in waves about how unfair Marshall had been; Fergie was on the other side telling Elena they would review her exquisite class notes later that evening so she wouldn't get behind on her homework; Declan was making a quippy remark about how he could fill all Kidd's combat boots with mud. And then she realized. The strange sensation she had was the recognition of friendship that was developing.

Her spirits felt uplifted until Kidd approached and smirked, "Hey, Freckles, you'll be running laps every night until next term if I can help it."

Declan stepped forward and balled his fist. "Move along, Wheeler."

"Lookie here," Kidd growled. "Bowen's defending his girlfriend."

"Wheeler." Austin spoke authoritatively. "Walk away or I'll get Marshall."

Kidd rolled his eyes and turned to walk away, but yelled back, "Don't be such a boyscout."

Abria put her arms around Elena's neck and said, "I, like, totally hate that guy."

Elena smiled, feeling for the first time how strangely nice it was to have people besides Austin supporting her.

Yet, weeks later, Elena's rapport with Marshall had not improved, and she was running more and more laps after each Basic Training class, which severely cut into her studying time, not to mention the Simulab time that all the other students were able to have.

Abria and Fergie were faithful to bring meals to their common room, and the Firebirds took turns helping her finish homework in the evenings. Declan was especially thorough with Emerald's homework; even though he was opposed to taking good notes in other classes, his notes from Social Science were surprisingly detailed. His tutoring was expressive, funny, and insightful, though sometimes his captivating personality could irritate Elena.

"You know," he said in a reflective tone, "I've never tutored anyone in my life, let alone a beautiful girl like you."

Elena rolled her eyes. "Take it easy. I don't want to vomit on my Smartslate." Declan laughed loudly. "Maybe you should go try that line on one of the girls at that table."

Elena didn't even have to point; the table across the room was filled with girls making covert, and some not covert glances, at Declan and Austin.

For several weeks now, a few of the girls from the Harrier and Falcon Units had started following Austin and Declan around the school. They giggled often as the boys passed them in the hallway, a few of them had asked if they could join the Firebirds for lunch, and one girl was caught sneaking a little too close to the boy's locker room.

Elena rolled her eyes again. "I don't see how you can stand all the attention."

"Why? Because it's positive attention, and you prefer negative attention?" Declan asked. "Let's be honest, you've drawn more bad publicity to yourself than I have attention from silly girls."

"Good point," Elena said.

"Oh, that reminds me, what would you say to doing a fencing Simulab with me on day six?" Declan said. "I promise I'll go easy on you."

"Oh, puh-leese," Elena said. "Like you could ever actually beat me in Simulab."

"Care to find out?"

"Okay, enough with the back and forth trying to prove which one of you is superior," Austin said suddenly. "Time to get back to work. We've only got an hour left before the Media Lab closes. Plus, Elena and I still have to go over Survival Strategy."

■ ■ ■

As the third month was coming to an end, Elena's classes seemed longer somehow, but it may have been because she'd been working so hard during Basic Training. Plus, the class workload was steadily increasing to prepare the students for their exams, which Fergie informed them were meant to assess how much information they had retained in the first quarter of school. Elena could only assume that Fergie had learned about the exams from the Grimsby Initiation Memorandum, but she had no desire to look it up herself so she smiled politely and said nothing.

As often as she could, Elena spent time in the Telepost office visiting with her parents. Truman had been angry when he first learned about her outburst with Marshall, but now that several weeks had passed, her dad spent most of their time together encouraging her and telling her funny stories. Her mom asked many questions about Elena's classes and about the pressure she was under. She tried to be vague with Hannah about how stressed she actually felt and saved her true feelings for Austin to deal with when they were alone.

On the days Elena felt beyond overwhelmed, Austin would pack up their homework and dinner and take her down to the Firebird Station for quiet.

However, the undisturbed atmosphere wasn't the only draw. After several weeks of visiting the Station, they'd discovered some very interesting features.

First, there was a room with the words "Research & Development" scrawled above the doorframe. This room was filled with a hodgepodge of electronic toys that Elena was sure only Pigg would appreciate. There was also an entire wall of nothing but various types of weapons that Elena had only seen in books. Some of the weapons were ancient, like two-handed swords, double bladed throwers, t-handled knives, leafed spears, bronze shields, and battle-axes. But there were also modern looking weapons, or at least Elena assumed they were weapons though she didn't recognize them from anything she'd seen before.

Elena and Austin also found a communications panel with a series of logos similar to the Firebird logo, but each with its own unique markings.

"Look at all these symbols. Do you think there could be more places like this on campus?" Elena asked.

"Possibly," Austin replied. "But what could the school need all these bunkers for?"

Elena only shrugged, feeling that Grimsby might have more secrets than she really cared to know.

Another room was filled with canned food, warm and cool clothing, cleaning supplies, sleeping bags, rollaway cots, and gallon after gallon of water. And yet another room was stocked with tactical vests and packs, hololights, and various crates of survival equipment.

"Do you think Hopper brought all this down here?" Elena asked Austin one afternoon as they were picking through the room. "Or do you think it was left by the communications officer?"

Austin shrugged and smiled. "Hopper does seem crazy enough to have done something like this."

But the most intriguing discovery was made on their twelfth visit to the Firebird Station. Elena had been exploring a tunnel that looked like it had been carved out of solid rock. When she reached the end, her breath caught in her chest. She'd arrived at a vast, limestone cave that had been converted into a hangar.

"Austin!" she cried, and he came running.

Together, they stepped onto a platform and overlooked an enormous cavern, hand paved landing pad, and a massive hovercraft with the word "Independence" painted on its side. They walked down forty stairs to reach the main landing pad and stood for a while staring at the hovercraft. The Independence was tall enough to scrape a thirty-foot ceiling, but the cave was so immense that Elena couldn't even see where it ended.

"Ready to try to get inside this thing?" Austin said finally.

"Absolutely!"

Elena set off in one direction around the Independence and Austin the other. Circling the entire hovercraft took quite a while. When they met back up, neither of them had seen even an inkling of a door.

"I guess this adventure will have to wait for another day," Elena said, looking around, still completely in awe. "Really neat cave though."

"I think we should tell the other Firebirds about this place," Austin said as he thumb the scar on this chin in an absentminded way, though Elena knew that it meant he was thinking hard about something.

"What?" Elena sounded flabbergasted. "What would be the point in that?"

"It would be fun to have them here, don't you think?"

"No. I like it just us."

"But, Pigg used to hang out with us in Sector 7. Besides, I thought you liked Fergie, Abria, and Declan."

"I do. It's just...Abria talked my ear off for thirty minutes yesterday about the dire state of her nails — *They say we can't paint our nails, which I think is just ridiculous. So, I brought this clear polish'...blah, blah, blah...*" Elena mocked Abria in a voice that sounded jarringly similar.

"Bringing more people here will ruin my sanctuary. And let's face it, with all the changes I've had to endure and all the punishment I've been blessed with," she continued on sarcastically, "I deserve some peace and quiet with the one person who gets me."

Austin only shrugged, looking disappointed.

❑ 11 ❑

# The Gauntlet

The first day of a new week started fast and furious. Every Instructor was
giving the Firebirds extra homework and essays so they would be prepared for
the first quarter exams that would take place the following week. The students
had covered approximately five hundred years worth of history, including the
Sumerians' contributions in writing, astronomy, and mathematics; The Old
Kingdom of Egypt and the building of the Great Pyramids at Giza; The Indus
Valley Civilization being the first to develop a system of uniform weights and
measures; The Minoan history in overseas trade; and the Mesopotamian wars.

Instructor Booker, in particular, was being exceptionally hard. He assigned
the Firebirds a five page, hand-written chart of items that could be covered on
the test and told them they could join him after classes for tutoring and
discussion if they had additional questions.

And, likewise, in the other classes the Firebirds were required to plot maps
of the development of human civilization, interpret hieroglyphics, record
notations and equations of the astronomical findings from the beginning of
history, and itemize crops that were grown in each culture and agricultural
system.

By the fourth evening of the week, Elena felt exhausted as she found Austin and Fergie at a Media Lab workstation. They had been working on homework for several hours while she'd been running laps for Marshall.

"I don't think I'll ever be ready for our exams," Elena grumbled, but Austin barely looked up from the notes he was taking. She scanned her Trademark into an Optivision screen and examined the list of her homework as it displayed holographically above the pupil station.

"Look at all this work I have left from yesterday!" she complained, feeling harassed. "Phonology took me a lot longer than it should have and now I have all this AstroPhysics to catch up on. And did you read all those pages Booker gave us? I didn't even realize we'd studied that much history. I'm already tired and this will take hours."

"I wish I could help," Austin said as he closed out the Optivision screen he was using. "But I have to go see Bowen and Pigg about our AstroPhysics lab."

"You're just going to leave me here!" Elena whined.

"It's not like I can help with AstroPhysics anyway. You're not in my group," he replied.

"I could help, if you want," Fergie offered.

Austin nudged Elena in the shoulder and said, "See you later."

"Would you like to begin with Phonology?" Fergie asked as Austin walked away.

Elena accessed the Advanced Phonology homework on the Optivision screen. As Fergie explained the features of each pictograph in a simplistic way, Elena jotted down answers on her Smartslate. They worked through Phonology so quickly that Elena had almost finished by the time Abria arrived.

Surrounded by a couple boys who were vying for her attention, Abria crossed the room without even noticing Elena or Fergie, She appeared to be telling a story by the way her arms moved and her face contorted. Then, she sat in a comfy chair, and the boys sat on either side of her. Elena noticed that she often flipped her blonde hair with her glossed fingernails as she was talking.

"She attracts attention wherever she goes," Fergie said passively, her eyes still scanning the Optivision screen.

Elena hadn't realized she'd been caught staring at Abria. "Don't you ever find it annoying?"

Fergie looked at Abria with a half smile and said, "Everyone possesses an aptitude that is uniquely their own. Abria's gift is establishing relationships with people. It is a mark of distinguished character that Abria is able to appreciate the best qualities in people and exploit their strengths instead of focusing on their weaknesses."

Elena did not like hearing this excuse for Abria's flirtatious behavior and felt like arguing, but it seemed that Fergie was not disconcerted by her narrow-minded opinions of Abria.

"Let us analyze you for a moment," Fergie continued. "Your strength is your ability to be loyal to your friends no matter what it costs you. I choose to focus on the fact that you came to Pigg's defense in Marshall's class instead of concentrating on the fact that you are self-righteous and clearly struggle with trust issues."

Elena wasn't sure if she wanted to punch Fergie or hug her. Fergie had spoken about her faults in a gentle but matter-of-fact, non-threatening way. Elena admired her candor.

"We're going to be life-long friends, I can tell," Elena told her.

Fergie smiled knowingly and said, "I suppose one of us should inform Abria that it is time to complete our group work for AstroPhysics."

■ ■ ■

On the first day of the third week of the third month, the Aves Company gathered in Booker's classroom to begin their first quarter exams. Elena pulled her seat down from the wall as Booker said, "In a moment, an Optivision screen will activate on your desktop. Do not feel burdened with an urge to cheat because every single test is completely different."

Then, the lights in the room were lowered and an Optivision screen appeared, hovering midair above the desktop. Elena scanned her Trademark against it and a list of questions appeared. As she looked over the first screen, she realized that the other Firebirds had made perfect study partners because all the questions were familiar from their review.

After Elena's last exam was finished for the day, she gathered with the other Firebirds at a table in the Mess Hall to enjoy dinner. Tonight, Grimsby served a duck and foie'gras terrine with black pepper poached pear topped by fresh walnuts. Elena figured the exquisite meal was some kind of reward for the students finishing their exams.

As Elena was getting ready to bite into her white chocolate cheesecake with raspberry sorbet, Major Marshall's voice filled the room.

"I know you've finished your exams today, but don't get comfortable!" barked Marshall's holographic image that was coming from an Optivision screen at the front of the room. "Tomorrow you are required to take a practical exam for Basic Training. After dinner, proceed to the Uniform Locker to collect your gear."

"He really knows how to ruin a person's appetite," Pigg said, slamming his fork down on the table. "I'm not going to be able to enjoy cheesecake the same way again."

"I'm so, like, nervous about this exam," Abria said.

"Me too. Marshall barks everything he says," Elena complained. "It doesn't inspire any kind of confidence."

"What do you think happens if we fail?" asked Pigg

"I guess we won't be able to move on to the next phase of training," Austin said.

Elena swallowed hard, wondering how she was ever going to sleep with so much anxiety building in her chest.

"This is your standard issue rucksack!" Marshall barked at the Firebirds the next morning as they waited for their exam to begin. "You wear it across your back and snap it in front of the chest."

Elena picked up a rucksack and began to strap it to her body.

"Each pack is equipped with a medical kit, canteen of water, a length of rope, a fire starting kit, flare gun, rain poncho, and a variety of other items that may prove helpful during your exam."

Elena leaned toward Austin and whispered, "I hope they didn't give Pigg a flare gun."

"For your exam," Marshall barked, "you are required to run the Gauntlet for the first time. The Gauntlet is an obstacle course designed to challenge your physical stamina and your Unit cooperation.

"This course includes running, climbing, jumping, crawling, and balancing elements to ascertain your endurance. You should be prepared for these obstacles based on the training you've had so far. You will also be evaluated on Unit problem solving skills.

"Keep in mind that each Unit will be required to complete this exam within a three hour time limit. I will be coming around to choose a Lieutenant for each Unit. For today only, your Lieutenant will choose a strategy and then assign the advancing formation to each student. The Lieutenant will make decisions for the entire Unit during this exam."

Marshall set off around the individual Unit formations, barking off random names. Elena looked around at the other Firebirds and considered each person individually. They had all improved greatly during the first quarter on the exercises and endurance training and, as a result, each seemed fairly qualified in his or her own way to lead the Unit; except Pigg, of course, who would more likely guide the Firebirds off a cliff before taking them to the end of the Gauntlet. But even Pigg would be preferable to Kidd, the only person she absolutely did not want to lead the group.

She was hoping Marshall would choose Austin to lead because he seemed the only person truly qualified for the job. He was well liked among the other students, he was firm but fair, he had one of the top marks in the class, and he had a suitable amount of leadership skills that could lead the Firebirds to victory.

Suddenly, Marshall was standing before the Firebird Unit. Before Elena could blink he called out, "Kidd Wheeler."

Elena's cheeks burned red in an instant. How could Marshall choose Wheeler? He was the last person she would have picked, and it seemed she was not the only person who felt this way because as soon as Marshall called his name out, there was a low murmur of disapproval from her comrades.

"We can't change the fact that Wheeler is Lieutenant," Austin told Elena, Declan, Abria, and Fergie when they had all come over to complain as they waited their turn to run The Gauntlet. "I know that no one likes him, but we need to respect him as the leader."

"We can't follow him!" Elena said fervently. "We'll have a mutiny in the Unit before we get half way through the course."

"Yeah, he is such a total, like, dimwit. No one will listen to him," Abria added.

"Austin," called Pigg, who was just joining them because he had been retying his boots after Marshall scolded his appearance. "I'm not going to be able to make it back here in one piece if Wheeler leads. He hates me." He began obsessively scratching his neck. "Is anyone else itchy? This collar is choking me."

"Stop messing with it," said Austin, pulling Pigg's hand away. "And give me your flare gun right now."

Pigg looked offended, but pulled the gun from his bag and handed it to Austin, who placed it in his own bag.

"Listen, we want the Firebird Unit to pass the exam, right?"

Elena and the others gave a mutter of agreement.

"Marshall said Wheeler is the leader for today only," Austin continued. "We can handle this."

Feeling bitter but in agreement, Elena turned from Austin to stand in the line behind the other students waiting at the entrance to The Gauntlet. Then, she noticed that Kidd was calling the Firebirds together in a huddle.

"I'm going to divide us into formation now," Kidd said.

"We haven't even seen the exam yet," Elena remarked. "Don't you think we should wait until..."

"If I wanted your opinion I would ask for it," Kidd said rudely.

Elena crossed her arms over her chest as he called out the directions for the exam. But, unfortunately, either Kidd was ignorant or he didn't pay attention to the skill level of the individual Firebirds during endurance training. He arranged all the stronger students to advance first and left all the weaker students to come after.

"He put all the weak students in the back," Elena whispered to Austin the first chance she got.

"I know," he whispered back. "Listen, I don't know what we're going to be up against in there, but I bet there are areas that are designed to cause confusion. If necessary, we'll fall back in the ranks and help the weaker kids. Just don't let anyone else know that you're breaking ranks, alright?"

"I thought you said we should listen to Wheeler."

"That was before I realized he was a complete dimwit at tactical analysis."

Elena smiled broadly and Austin, catching her look, said, "Sorry. I shouldn't have said that."

"No, it's thrilling for me to see you like this."

Then, Marshall was suddenly calling the Firebirds to the entrance to the Gauntlet.

"The course is a mile in that direction," Marshall told the Firebirds, and he pointed to a long road stretched out in front of them. "When you arrive at the beginning of the course you may begin your exam. We will monitor your progress. If you have not returned within the three-hour time limit, the Firebird Unit will fail the exam. Dismissed!"

Kidd called the Unit together and instructed them to jog. In very little time, Elena and the Firebirds reached the edge of a grassy knoll that looked down over a vast arena where students from several other Units where struggling to get through the series of obstacles. At her feet, Elena noticed four ropes knotted to anchors in the ground and realized that they weren't standing on a grassy knoll, but on top of a rappelling tower.

The ropes led out over the edge of the tower where she observed a wall of wood descending to a muddy patch on the ground. Beyond that stretched a track of pressed dirt that was obstructed by climbing walls, puddles of muddy water, ropes and nets, and ringed holes to jump.

"Elena," Pigg muttered, clawing at her arm and looking down over the battlement. "No one said anything about a rappelling tower."

Elena felt dread surge through her body. She knew that Pigg had a fear of heights, but it had never actually mattered before. However, as they stood on the edge of The Gauntlet, Elena felt her confidence plummet. This was certainly the worst exam she could imagine for Kidd to lead. She knew that, as a team, they weren't strong enough to get through the entire course.

"Let's get going, Firebirds!" Kidd called out. And before the others had time to react, he had rushed forward, grabbed one of the ropes, and was quickly out of sight, rappelling down the tower.

"Great leadership," scoffed Elena as she and Austin circled around some of their frightened looking team members.

"Who here is afraid of heights?" asked Austin, and Elena noticed that Kate Bagley and Frankie Smiley's hands rose along with Fergie and Pigg. "Each one of you needs to partner up with someone who is not afraid of heights and descend on ropes next to one another. Got it?"

Then, Austin grabbed Fergie's hand and led her to the rope, saying, "You're coming with me. Don't look down. Just come to the edge, pick up the rope, and put your feet in front of you. Concentrate on the movement of your feet jumping against the tower the entire way down and we'll be on the ground in a minute."

A few seconds passed as everyone got situated, but finally all the pairs had grouped together and the Firebirds began making progress down the rappelling tower. Elena could hear Austin giving Fergie instruction and encouragement.

She followed his example and shouted helpful tips to Pigg as they progressed down the tower next to each other. The rope was rough and hard to grasp without it cutting her hands, but in a few minutes they were safely on the ground standing in front of Kidd, who looked furious.

"What took you so long? And why are you out of formation?" he shouted as the last couple people were descending the tower.

He said it generally to everyone, but it was Austin who answered. "Some of us are afraid of heights. Try to allow time for insecurity and developing..."

"I didn't ask for a lecture or your opinion," Kidd barked. "Everyone get back in formation and let's get going!"

Before the last Firebird had touched the ground from the rappelling tower, Kidd was already hurtling toward their next obstacle, a twenty-foot climbing wall fitted with grommets. He reached the wall and began to climb without waiting for anyone else.

At that moment, a rain simulation program began. Thunder crashed, lightning struck, and fat drops of water began to pelt Elena in the face.

"Oh, perfect!" Elena screamed over the thunder at Austin. "This is going to make it so much easier!"

"Rain ponchos on," Austin hollered to everyone.

Elena removed the poncho from her carrier bag and was immediately grateful for the hood that kept the rain out of her eyes. But, then she heard Pigg let out a small moan as he looked at the wall.

Without speaking, the Firebirds coupled with the person who they helped down the repelling tower and began to ascend the climbing wall, placing their hands and feet on the grips that had been positioned in various intervals on the wall. Climbing the wall proved to be tough, slippery work in the rain.

Elena's arms and legs burned while the tips of her fingers strained to hold tight to the grips. By the time Elena had reached the top of the wall her whole body was slightly shaking. She suddenly realized how heavy her carrier bag felt.

The top of the wall had a short platform that declined to elaborate netting that was hung with rope ladders. Kidd was half way descended on the nets before the last Firebird even arrived at the summit of the climbing wall.

Declan flexed his fist as he looked down at Kidd. "When we catch up with him you're gonna have to hold me back because I might punch him in the face."

"You'll have to wait your turn," Elena said with rain dripping off the end of her nose.

Declan smiled at her. "You know, the rain poncho really suits you."

Elena rolled her eyes as Austin hollered, "Let's get going."

Again the Firebirds pursued the Gauntlet, partnering up to help encourage one another, and doing it all without Kidd's help or direction.

The tangle of nets led them down to a field of ringed holes that they were forced to jump through. Pigg was hopelessly clumsy, falling so often that he scraped holes in the knees of his pants.

Then, Elena came to the edge of a sea of water that was thick with mud. Far ahead of them, Kidd was struggling so much in the sludge that he was finally forced to slow down.

"This would be a good time to take off our rain ponchos," Austins suggested.

"But, it's still raining," Abria argued.

"Do you see Wheeler?" Austin continued. "He's stuck in that lake of mud. I bet it's harder to move with the poncho on. Keep yours on, if you like," he added as he pulled his over his head and discarded it on the ground.

Elena removed her poncho and followed Austin into the pit of mud. Soon, all the other Firebirds were in the muck and mire, moving at an extremely slow pace. Without warning, the rain simulation ended and a bright sun streamed down on them.

"Ewe, I got mud in my hair," squealed Abria while flapping her hands like a bird flaps its wings.

Declan wasted no time grabbing Abria and tossing her unceremoniously over his shoulders. Elena watched him struggle to carry her to shore. And then, quite suddenly, her foot caught on something hard and she felt a strange sensation.

Elena paused for a moment then whispered, "Ok, yes, I'm definitely sinking."

"Austin!" she screamed. "I'm sinking."

"Me too!" Pigg cried out.

Elena turned the best she could and saw that Pigg had already sunk up to his chest.

"Why didn't you say earlier?" Elena shouted at Pigg.

"I just thought I had stepped into a hole, or something," Pigg said. "It didn't occur to me that I could actually be sinking until I saw you start going too. Austin, I'm really not excited about drowning here, so I hope that you have some kind of plan or suggestion for how to get out of this."

Austin looked around and Elena could tell that he was assessing their situation. Not one Firebird had made it to the shore on the other side of the quagmire, but Kidd and Declan, who was still carrying Abria, were the closest.

"Bowen and Wheeler, when you've reached the shore, grab the rope from your packs and throw it out to us," Austin said. "We've got to get Ransom and Pigg out of this pit."

An eternity of time lapsed while Kidd and Declan attempted to get close to the shoreline. Elena wished she'd had a fingernail to nibble, but everything was covered in mud. Kidd made no sound as he finally struggled onto the shore, but Declan grunted loudly as he hoisted Abria up and tossed her beside Kidd.

In the meantime, Austin had instructed the other Firebirds to join hands in a chain fashion. From the shore, Declan tossed his rope to Crosby Gamble, who gave the end to Frankie Smiley and on down the line. The entire process was slow, but eventually Vivienne handed Austin an end of a rope and he gave it to Elena.

She turned briefly as she was being pulled and noticed that the mud around Pigg was up to his chin. His arms were raised above his head. When Elena was steadied, she extended the rope out toward Pigg, who looked grateful as he grabbed the end.

"My pack was drowning me so I dropped it," Pigg said in a small voice. "You think we'll get points taken off for that?"

"Don't worry about that now, Pigg," Elena told him. "Let's just get out of here."

Eventually, all the Firebirds waded out of the swamp and sat panting on the shore.

"On your feet, Firebirds," Kidd shouted suddenly. "We're wasting time."

"We've barely had a chance to catch our breath!" Elena said angrily.

"We're going right now!" Kidd hollered.

Elena and Pigg grasped arms and clumsily tried to stand as they slipped on the mud that coated their clothes and boots. Together, they followed the other Firebirds to a series of low rope swings that were strung on wooden scaffolding.

"They expect us to swing from rope to rope now that we're caked in mud from head to foot?" Elena said with astonishment. "Impossible!"

"Over here," said Austin, pointing to a precipice that was off the beaten path. "There's water spilling off the rocks. If we could wash off some of this mud, maybe we could make it through the ropes course without having to stop again."

"Out of the way," growled Kidd, as he marched resolutely to the water and began washing his boots and hands.

Elena was now struggling to remain patient, but Austin's calming presence was effective in the face of their adversary, and she waited with the other Firebirds to take her turn splashing in the water.

Once everyone was somewhat cleaned off, the Firebirds returned to the ropes course and evaluated the first set of obstacles. From the jump site, it appeared that they would have to go one at a time, zip-lining across a ravine on a rope that was dangling from a metal shaft. After they arrived at the landing zone on the opposite side of the ravine, they would have to return the rope back across the metal shaft so the next student could cross.

One at a time they started to cross. Of course, Kidd insisted on going first. Then, Crosby and Olivia followed him and made it safely. But Abria swung poorly during her turn and missed the mark entirely. She lost her balance and fell twenty feet, screaming the entire way, before smacking the ground. When she landed, Elena heard an explicit crack.

Austin reacted first, hurrying down the rampart with Elena hard on his heels. However, while Austin was on his knees by her side Elena stood over them feeling astonished at the amount of blood that flowed hard and fast down Abria's breeches into her boot.

Austin ripped open her pant leg. A part of Abria's shinbone was piercing through her skin. Seeing Abria's bone made Elena's stomach churn. Her insides began to scream for her to run away, and she began to panic about what they should do next. Should they run for help? Should they wait for someone to come get them? What, oh what, could they possibly do for Abria out in the middle of the Gauntlet?

Austin removed the Suturand from his pocket and activated the scanner. An Optivision screen appeared, and Elena saw the shattered bone from the inside of Abria's leg materialize.

"Abria has a compound fracture. I can't stop the bleeding with my Suturand alone," Austin was saying, somewhere far off in the distance of Elena's awareness. "Lena!" As Austin spoke her name, she snapped back to reality.

As Elena watched Austin strip off his outer shirt, she turned and screamed at Declan, "Bowen, get down here to help us."

She dropped to her knees and held Abria's shoulders as Austin tied his shirt around the top of her knee.

Declan had just reached Abria's side as Austin said, "I suppose I could set Abria's leg, but she'd probably pass out from the pain."

Abria let out a groan at the thought. Declan held her hand with a look of terror on his face.

"I guess we should do what you think is best."

Austin looked around steadily and then, finding Kidd still standing at the top of the ramp, and yelled, "Wheeler, what do you want us to do now?"

Kidd stared at them with a dumbfounded expression on his face.

"Dude, wake up!" Declan hollered, but Kidd only blinked, looking petrified. He turned to Austin, looking desperate. "What do we do now?"

Austin assessed their position, and then commanded with the force of a veteran general, "Bowen, Gamble, and Smiley, start making a stretcher using our rain ponchos. We're carrying Abria back to school."

"That's over a mile hike from here," said Pigg with full panic in his voice.

"Which means we need to hurry," Austin said calmly. "Abria, I'm not going to set your leg out here, but I'm going to steady it with my pack and reinforce the tourniquet I've already tied above your knee. It's going to hurt but we have to do this."

Abria screamed in pain as Austin readied her leg for transport. Then, Declan lifted Abria gently and placed her on top of the makeshift stretcher. The Firebird boys lifted Abria and marched her up the ramparts along the sides of the Gauntlet course with the girls behind them, toting the remaining rucksacks.

Then, a hovercraft appeared out of nowhere. Marshall stepped from the vehicle, looking surlier than ever.

"Set her down and move away!" he barked.

The Firebird boys set Abria down gently, but before Elena could blink, she was lifted into the vehicle and was carried away.

Then, Marshall rounded on the Firebirds and screamed, "How could you have let this happen, Wheeler? Stand before me at attention," He added to the rest of the Firebirds. They quickly took their places, forming straight rows. "And, why did you fail to use your flare gun to signal distress?"

As the Firebirds took their positions, Elena felt glad that (for once) the Drill Instructor was yelling at someone that she utterly despised. She smiled a little waiting for Kidd's excuse.

"It was Austin Haddock, Sir," Kidd said, standing rigidly. "He refused to obey the formation I chose for the mission, he broke ranks, and he encouraged the others against me."

Elena felt blood boil in her ears.

"That's a lie!" she shouted. "Wheeler left us all behind to go through the course. We were just helping our teammates the way he obviously should have been."

"Ransom," Marshall said sharply. "I don't remember asking for your input."

Elena felt mutinous, but she caught Austin's eye and held her tongue.

"Haddock," growled Marshall. "What do you have to say for yourself?"

"Sir, it is true that I broke ranks and failed to obey orders," Austin replied. "No excuse, Sir."

Marshall surveyed them all with disgust in his face. Then, he barked, "The Firebird Unit has failed the first quarter exam. A remake exam will be given tomorrow at 0600 hours. You are dismissed!"

With that, Marshall stomped away leaving Elena seething in his wake.

## ❑ 12 ❑

## The Eavesdrop

Days later, Elena was still brooding over the disastrous Gauntlet run. To make matters worse, Austin didn't seem bothered that Kidd hadn't supported them during or after the exam, or that Marshall gave the Firebirds a failing grade, thus forcing them to run the Gauntlet again. At least they passed the second time around, but she was still irritated that none of the other Units had to repeat the course.

The hint of spring coaxed Elena and Austin outdoors, where they walked shoulder to shoulder around campus. Elena and Austin argued the same conversation they'd had several times, but which never ended to her satisfaction.

"I shouldn't have broken ranks," he said in an almost apologetic tone. "We were given orders and were expected to follow them."

"But," Elena objected. "Some of the Firebirds wouldn't have even made it down the rappelling tower without your help."

"That may be true," said Austin. "But, how would you feel if I had been leading and Wheeler did that to me, or you for that matter?"

"You would've never been a dimwit like he was in the first place," grumbled Elena. "You already know the strengths and weaknesses of each person in our Unit and you would have put us in formation correctly. And don't you deny it," she added, after noticing signs that he wanted to object to what she was saying. "You and I both know you would have done a better job."

Austin shrugged. "It doesn't matter now, does it?"

"You know what else?" Elena said, not giving up the fight. "Marshall said we'd be monitored throughout the exam. They knew we were in trouble, so why did he get so upset when he found us?"

"Marshall said the correct protocol was to use the flare gun, remember?" Austin said. "We disobeyed a direct order."

"But disobeying that order may have saved Abria's leg," Elena pointed out.

That was true. Abria had been taken straight to the Medical Station. The Healing Surgeon said that she could have lost the leg completely if Austin hadn't tied it off and immobilized her. The medical staff set her leg with an orthopedic implant to help support the damaged bone. Then, they wrapped it in a surgical shell while it healed.

Once they'd been allowed to see Abria, all the Firebirds (except Kidd) went directly to the Medical Station to sit around her bed. Elena noticed that the room looked almost identical to the ones at the hospital where her mom worked. Abria's bed was structured with the latest medical advancements that provided optimum efficiency to the surgeons. Each holographic screen measured a different vital organ and there was one monitor specifically overseeing the healing progress of her leg.

Abria couldn't have been more pleased with her injury because it came with a steady stream of concerned visitors giving her plenty of attention.

"It's great to have one whole week without classes, or Pointers and Smartslates," Abria was telling Declan just as Elena and Austin were coming in to see her after their walk. "I'm doing my nails and putting on my dancing shoes. Well, I mean, once I get out of this, like, bed." She laughed, and then added, "Oh, hey friends!"

Declan helped Abria sit forward after she'd greeted Elena and Austin. Then, he fluffed up some of her pillows.

"What should we do on our day off tomorrow?" he asked. "I heard a lot of the older students say they were planning to go to Harleston Village for the day."

"I wish we could go," Abria said. "I heard there is a shop that sells a lipstick that tastes like cherry flavored bubble gum!"

"Dude...boring!" said Declan loudly, and Abria rolled her eyes. "Actually, I was sort of hoping to get Ransom on the Judo mat. It's the one Simulab that I've gone completely undefeated in." Then, he slid his arm around Elena. "You see, I know that you're a little behind because you haven't been able to practice as much as the rest of us, so I thought I'd take advantage of you."

"Are you sure you'll have time to fit me into your schedule?" Elena said.

"Huh?" Declan asked.

"You always have a group of girls following you down the hall...writing 'I heart Declan Bowen' on their Smartslates. I bet there'll be a line of girls waiting to get you in the ring."

Declan flashed a toothy grin. "Can I help it that I am a fine specimen?"

"Technically, your parents had you engineered to look this way, so 'no' you can't help it," Elena replied.

"Sounds like someone's jealous."

"In your dreams, Bowen," Elena said curtly.

"Let's go right now, if you think you can manage it," Declan challenged her.

Elena looked at Austin and he smiled. They'd practiced on the Judo Simulab in Atlanson for years, not to mention the fact that Hannah had given them physical training in the art of karate. She felt confident that she could break Declan's winning streak.

"Alright," Elena said. "Let's go right now."

"Oh-wa! That's going to be your first Simulab here, like, ever!" Abria squawked. "I miss everything fun."

"You don't miss everything fun," Declan said. "We can wait if you want us to."

"Does that mean you're backing down already, Bowen?" Elena provoked.

Declan smirked at her and shook his head.

"Go on," Abria sighed. "No one else should have to suffer just because I'm locked up in here."

---

Elena, Declan, and the others grabbed a Grimvator slantways to the Simulab. When they arrived, she gasped. The room was massively deep with dozens of simulated activities spread out along the walls and down the center, making up rows and aisles of kick boxing rings, judo mats, karate floors, hand-to-hand combat halos, wrestling mats, and obstacle courses. But it seemed that word had spread quickly that she and Declan were planning to have a competition because none of the other gaming zones were being used. Instead, dozens of boys and girls lined the walls around the Judo Simulab. Elena pulled her red curls back into a clasp as she approached Declan.

"Are you ready for this, Bowen?"

"You know I am," Declan said, his smile causing girls all over the room to sigh.

Elena stepped onto the simulation floor and pulled on the Transmitter, a suit exclusively designed for enhancing the gaming experience. When Declan's suit was securely fastened to his body, a holographic gaming projection of Elena and Declan appeared inside a matted ring in front of them.

As the timer counted down ten seconds, Elena and Declan's holographic projections stared at one another. Then, a buzzer sounded and Declan immediately lunged forward at Elena. But she, having sharp reflexes, dodged his advance, and he fell heavily into the boundary of the simulation.

"Ouch!" Elena said derisively. "You might want to slow down and concentrate before you advance, Bowen, or you'll just use up all your energy before the first round is even over."

"That's good advice, Ransom," Declan said, circling around her. He'd adopted a lower stance and was clearly looking to strike again. "Maybe you could talk a little more about my strategy. Your mouth is mesmerizing."

This statement caught Elena completely off guard and she flinched slightly, but it was enough to give Declan an edge. He lunged forward again. With one swift motion he'd grabbed Elena and flung her over his shoulder, flipping her down to the mat. Her holographic projection turned red and a point lit up on Declan's scoreboard.

As the game reset for round two, Austin came up beside Elena and said, "I can't believe you let him distract you. Concentrate. You can beat him."

"I know, I know," Elena replied through gritted teeth.

The bell sounded for round two and Elena tried to circle around to the right, but Declan moved in, forcing her to the left. Then, their simulated arms clasped and Declan moved in swiftly for another flip, but Elena used his body weight against him this time. She extended her left leg its full length and attacked him with a karate lunge. This caught him completely off balance and Elena was able to roll him to the ground in one swift motion. Declan's simulated mass turned red and a point lit up for Elena.

Cheers rang out from the Firebird girls and from the other students who had lost to Declan in the Judo Simulab before. But Elena also heard several scoffers and hecklers from the crowd, no doubt coming from Declan's admirers.

Austin gave Elena a nod of approval. "Well done. Just one more and you'll be the new champ of this game."

Elena felt more confident than ever as she squared up against Declan for the third round. However, just before the bell sounded Elena noticed something odd. In her peripheral vision, she saw Declan adjust the transmitter glove ever so slightly on his right hand. As she began to contemplate this, the bell sounded, but it was too late for her. Declan had her flipped before she even had a chance to prepare for the assault.

Declan threw his hands up in the air and cheered. Then, he tossed the Transmitter suit on the floor and approached Elena with a glowing smile.

"It was a superb effort, Ransom, even better than most of the boys. Keep practicing and maybe one day you'll beat me."

"Don't be so smug, Declan," said a voice tinkling with laughter.

Elena turned to see Abria striding toward them.

"How are you out of bed?" Elena called to her. "You don't even have a limp."

"I don't know what they do in that Medical Station, but it's magic. I told them that I wanted to get out of bed to see you Simulab, and they just made it happen." Abria giggled and pushed her hip against Elena's in a playful way. "My leg doesn't even, like, hurt."

"It's not magic," Austin said seriously. "After they set your bone they reinforced the break with nanobandages, a process of fusing together the bone marrow in such a way that it would be impossible to fracture that point in your body ever again. It's actually a technology that was pioneered by the original D.E.S. labs that invented the use of Humanoids in modern society."

Abria simply smiled at him dreamily and said, "And I had so many, like, visitors."

Elena rolled her eyes at Austin.

"So, what do you say, Ransom?" Declan said, talking over whatever Abria was beginning to tell Austin about her many admirers. "Want to try kickboxing?"

First quarter break flew by quickly. Elena kept busy with Simulabs and homework until second quarter classes were back in session. The Firebird Unit had passed all their exams and advanced on to the next phase in their education, which didn't actually feel any different to Elena except that the weeks of intense schoolwork were beginning to pay off, as she felt less ignorant.

"During the second quarter we will study the five hundred years between 2500 and 2000 BC," Instructor Booker told the Firebirds after they'd gathered for his first class.

"We will journey to the Middle Kingdom of Egypt and also discuss how the Akkadian empire was bound together by roads and therefore included a regular postal service. Also, we'll study a ruler named Sargon who established the first known empire, we shall study the Bronze Age, the Harappan civilization, and the life of a man named Abraham who eventually became known as 'father' to three of the worlds largest religious groups.

"But today, we'll start with one of the earliest urban settlements in the world. Around 2600 BC, Mohenjo-Daro was built in the country of Pakistan in the middle of the flood plain of the Indus River Valley. Let's take a few moments to observe the culture that was developed here."

Instructor Booker activated a group of Optivision screens and before Elena's eyes, the country of Pakistan in the Middle East appeared and also a schematic of the town of Mohenjo-Daro. As he continued speaking, layer upon layer of the city was built, forming a perfect holographic model.

"Mohenjo-Daro was fortified with towers to the west of the main settlement and defensive fortifications to the south. The city was a street-grid of rectilinear buildings, planned to house around thirty-five thousand residents."

After this, Booker broke the class into groups and had them design a schematic of a central marketplace, with a large central well so that households could obtain water from smaller wells. Elena read a paragraph from the text about how houserooms were set apart for bathing and that underground furnaces were used to heat the water for it.

During Elena's next class, Instructor Niva said, "In 2500 BC, scribal schools flourished throughout the Sumer regions. They took pride and care with the written word.

"Around the year 2330 BC, an intimate culture between the Sumerians and the Akkadians included widespread bilingualism. We will continue our study in these ancient texts in order to gain a complete understanding of linguistics."

Then, for the first time, Instructor Niva said, "I'm grouping you into threes at random. Once you're in your group, I want you to translate the Akkadian alphabet from session seven. You will observe the pictograph symbols; one member of the group will verbally describe the characters so that the other two can sketch them."

Before Elena even had a chance to hope that she was in a group with Austin, Niva placed her at a pupil station with Frankie Smiley and Kate Bagley, who both had blonde hair and blue eyes.

"I'll draw." Kate offered. "I have a thing for it. Niva is picky about the technique for forming the characters so we should probably all try drawing."

"But Niva said that one of us is supposed to describe the characters verbally," Elena said.

"Yeah, I heard her say that, but drawing the characters properly might be on the next exam," Kate said practically. "Wouldn't you like to get some extra practice in now?"

Elena looked from Kate to Frankie as if to ask what he thought, but the boy simply shrugged his shoulders.

"What's wrong with you?" Elena said bluntly to Frankie after realizing that she'd never heard him speak before. "You the silent type?"

"Honestly, you make me nervous," Frankie replied, staring at Elena's hair. "Is that all your real hair?"

"Of course it's her real hair, dimwit," Kate said impatiently. "It's not going to bite you, so let's get to work."

Elena spent the rest of class fielding curious looks from Frankie Smiley and being told by Kate Bagley how to draw the Akkadian characters in exactly the correct fashion.

Elena was so grumpy after their group work that she felt thankful that Copernicus didn't split them into groups during AstroPhysics after lunch. Instead, the Instructor lectured about how early cultures identified celestial objects with spirits, and how the first professional astronomers were priests and that their understanding of the "heavens" was seen as "divine." They also learned that Sargon the Great established a library with the first collection of astronomical observations and terrestrial omens.

In Social Science, Instructor Emerald continued teaching the class about the Akkadians by describing their dependency on agriculture systems, including irrigated farmlands of southern Iraq and the rain-fed agriculture of northern Iraq.

"Harvest was done in late spring and during the dry summer months. Extraordinarily, these civilizations had already mastered the art of raising animals," Emerald said as the Optivision screen filled with farmlands and images of animals. "Nomadic Amorites would pasture their flocks of sheep and goats to graze along irrigation canals. As payment for this, they would have to pay a tax in wool, meat, milk, and cheese to the temples, who would distribute these products to the bureaucracy and priesthood."

After Emerald's lecture, he assigned Elena to work in a group with Vivienne Castellow and Olivia Nelson, who both had black hair and giggled so much during the rest of the lesson that Elena found it hard to answer the lecture review questions that Emerald had assigned.

"What's going on with all the group work today?" Elena asked Fergie as they entered their room that evening.

"Learning to work as part of a group is one critical element of a well-rounded education." Fergie replied.

"Well, it's really uncomfortable," Elena said as she removed her combat boots.

Abria flopped down on her bed and said, "You know what your problem is? You're too cautious when you meet or have to deal with new people. And, your knack for impatience does nothing to help your personality."

Elena scanned her Trademark into the wardrobe door and pulled out her pajamas. "Oh, I guess you expect everyone to be as friendly and chatty as you? Not everyone has a need for constant, dramatic behavior. Plus, I don't see you saying anything about how introverted Fergie is."

"Being introverted is not the same as being unapproachable," Fergie said. "Abria is attempting to indicate that you usually rise to create conflict instead of choosing to greet new people with docile kindness."

"Yeah, I have all these flaws...blah, blah, blah," Elena grumbled.

"At least we have Hopper tomorrow," Abria said. "And class with Marshall has been better."

Elena did feel relieved by this fact. For her, the best part about second quarter was the fact that Marshall had stopped having her lead class and had also ended the "torture by running" that Elena did in the afternoon, leaving her free to eat dinner and finish her homework early so she could relax or do Simulabs with all the other students. Soon, Elena was enjoying Basic Training so much that she was making one of the top marks in the entire Aves Company.

And so, the weeks stretched on pleasantly enough that Elena stopped going to the Telepost office each day to complain to her parents. She had learned the unique expectations that each of her Instructors required and was able to participate more during the practical application of their lessons in class.

Fergie taught her an efficient method of planning out her homework so it didn't pile up overwhelmingly. Declan and Abria kept Elena active in the Simulabs; they even teamed up sometimes in triples tennis with kids from the other Units. But still, her favorite time was spent in the Firebird Station.

One evening, while Elena was at the Station doing her homework, Austin arrived looking harassed. He dropped into a chair near her, slightly out of breath.

"I looked for you everywhere!"

"I had so much work to do and Abria was going on and on about the importance of maintaining a certain amount of style, even though we have to wear uniforms that all look the same," Elena complained. "I needed the kind of quiet time that only the Station can offer. Why?" she asked after catching the intense look on his face. "What's up?"

"Wheeler was caught going to Harleston Village over first quarter break. I heard that they are talking about kicking him out of school."

"Oh, I hope he gets expelled." Elena took a moment to stretch her arms. "That would make my whole year so much better."

"Aren't you even curious what he was doing there? Everyone else was."

"Not really," Elena replied, consulting the Advanced Phonology text on her Smartslate.

"I'll tell you anyway," Austin said. "They said he was flying in a race."

Elena was not intrigued, but in view of Austin's interest in the subject she said, "I didn't know humans could fly. He must be a mutant. That would explain his cheery personality."

"He was operating in a *hovercraft race* and actually won!"

Elena yawned. "Why does anyone care what that dimwit does?"

"Oh!" Austin had caught a glimpse of the time. "We've got to get going if we want to make it to our rooms by curfew."

Darkness had fallen over the entire forest as Elena and Austin headed back to the school. The night was springtime cool and was mostly silent until they were almost back to their resident tower. Then, suddenly, two voices called out of the stillness and echoed through the courtyard.

Elena gasped and stopped so suddenly that Austin had to pull her quickly into the shadow of one of the buildings. They crouched silently and listened until Headmaster Worthen Bentley and Hopper came into view. Even in the fading light the Headmaster looked intimidating. Elena felt a chill run up her spine.

"Whitlock has just returned with the Alpha Manuscript," the Headmaster told Hopper.

Hopper looked thoughtful for a moment and asked, "Have you had a chance to look it over?"

"Only briefly. We took it straight to the Vault for analysis," the Headmaster replied. "It appears that Haddock's father was an Enforcer for the Oligarki. This manuscript is written in his handwriting throughout."

Elena's mouth fell open. Headmaster Bentley and Hopper were talking about Austin's father. They'd used the term "Oligarki." What did that mean?

"I will need your expertise to decode and interpret several of the notations. I find it peculiar that some pages are blank. But the one thing I am most concerned with is learning the location of the Firebird Disc. The manuscript does not overtly discuss its handler; therefore, finding it will prove to be a challenge."

Elena's head began to spin out of control with questions. There was that name again. Firebird Disc. She remembered her dad talking about it to his diary. She knew he was trying to keep it safe. Elena wondered desperately why everyone was searching for this Disc. And, if Truman Ransom knew where the disc was, why wouldn't he give it to Headmaster Bentley?

"This manuscript is our top priority now," the Headmaster said. "I want to know what's in that book. And I want the Amulet found as soon as possible. I have waited too long for it already. I am certain that once we locate the Amulet it will lead us directly to the Firebird Disc."

Headmaster Bentley and Hopper began walking again. "I will leave the Alpha Manuscript in the Vault for you to do your research."

"How much time do we have?" Hopper asked.

But what the Headmaster said next was lost as the two men walked further away from where Elena and Austin stood. Austin backed into the wall and slid all the way down to the ground.

"What was that all about?" Elena whispered, joining him on the ground.

"I don't know," Austin said. "They were talking about my father."

"Yeah, that's weird! And what does *Oligarki* mean?"

Austin was silent for a few moments, running his thumb over his chin.

And then he said, "I need to see that Alpha Manuscript so I can know for sure if it belonged to my father."

"So, you'll just ask the Headmaster Bentley if you can look at it?"

"Are you insane? He told Hopper about the manuscript in confidence. I can't admit that we were eavesdropping."

"What if we ask Hopper? He told us about the Station. Maybe he'd tell us about this too." Elena suggested, but Austin was already shaking his head. "But what can we do? It's not like we can find this Vault thingy and break into it." She laughed, but Austin looked serious. "Austin, I know that you want to know about your father but...I can't believe we're even talking about this!"

Austin hung his head. "Does that mean you won't help me?"

"Of course I'll help you," Elena said without even thinking about it. "I'm just surprised that you want to lie and manipulate the system with the intent of burglarizing school property."

"Well, when you put it that way it sounds horrible." Austin looked guilty for a moment, but then Elena had also never seen him look so determined. "I just have to find out what happened to my father."

But, as it turned out, trying to find the location of the Vault in the school was impossible. For several days, Elena and Austin searched the Media Lab archives for historical records of the school to see if they could find structural specifications, blueprints, or even a basic floor plan of Grimsby, but found nothing. They even researched archived articles during the time Austin's father was at Grimsby. And then, painfully, they read articles about his father's disappearance to see if there were any clues, but after weeks of searching they weren't any closer to discovering where the Vault was located.

## ¤ 13 ¤

## Into the Tunnel

As the fifth and sixth months slipped away, Elena's class load was steadily increasing again. The Grimsby campus simulated spectacularly warm weather, the kind that made students want to sit outside for a picnic, run up and down a rugby field, or swim in the lake. But, with second quarter exams only days away, Elena felt completely unprepared and therefore couldn't enjoy anything, much less the weather.

The long hours of studying were daunting and left her feeling exhausted each evening. In fact, she and Austin had spent every spare moment of the week studying that they hadn't been able to return to the Firebird Station, and Elena could tell that Austin was getting anxious about not having the opportunity to research the Vault.

Secretly, Elena was glad that she had a break from thinking about the Vault, especially when Marshall stood up during their next class holding a vest that was covered with pockets, zippers, and clips.

"These are a standard issue tactical vest," Marshall explained. "They are equipped with a medical kit, canteen of water, a hololight, flare gun, rain poncho, and a variety of other items that may prove helpful as you run the Gauntlet today."

At this news, Elena physically relaxed. The Firebirds had run the obstacle course during their first quarter exam. And, even though they'd failed it, they were the only Unit that had been on the Gauntlet more than once. Therefore, she felt extremely confident that her Unit would do really well this time on the course.

"Today's class includes running, climbing, jumping, crawling, and balancing elements to ascertain your endurance. You will also be evaluated on Unit problem solving skills. This will be a timed exercise. *Use your flare gun* if you get into trouble." Elena noticed that Marshall looked pointedly at Austin. "The Lieutenant for this exercise will be chosen at random."

Marshall stood in front of an Optivision screen and Elena watched it flicker with the faces of the different students in the Firebird Unit. Finally, the images stopped rotating and a girl's face appeared holographically in midair on the screen.

Marshall called out, "Firebirds! Your Lieutenant today is Kate Bagley."

Elena knew that Kate was competent enough to lead them through the Gauntlet, but she was mostly relieved that Kidd Wheeler wasn't in charge.

Minutes later, the Firebirds hiked the mile out to the Gauntlet, but when they arrived, Elena realized instantly that she'd been naïve to think that the obstacle course would be the same. She stood on the edge of the grassy knoll and looked down a vast arena of sludge.

Instead of a rappelling tower, there was a muddy slide, forty feet down into a pit of brown water. Beyond that, there were over-under logs placed over a grimy ditch and, after that, a screen of wire hung low over a field of mud. Then, some type of mountain was obstructing her view of the rest of the course.

"Now, that is unpleasant," Pigg grumbled. "I thought the last Gauntlet was bad, but this is way worse."

"Yuck!" Abria squealed. "I'm totally going to get, like, mud all over."

Kate Bagley tucked a strand of blonde hair behind her ear and said, "Firebirds, who has a fear of getting dirty?"

Abria and a couple of the other girls raised their hands.

"Technically, I'm really afraid of drowning in mud," Pigg whined.

"Okay," Kate continued firmly. "So, let's pair off the way we did in the first exam so we can help each other out, agreed?"

There was a murmur of agreement.

"We can't afford any mistakes. We've got to prove to the Aves Company that the Firebirds are in this to win. Let's get going!" Kate ordered as she led the way down the slide.

Elena suddenly felt impressed with Kate's take-charge attitude. She sat beside Pigg on the edge of the hill and watched a few other Firebirds glide down into the pit below.

"This time," Elena told Pigg, "if you feel like you're stuck, or sinking, or drowning tell me right away, okay?"

Pigg nodded, looking green.

Then, Elena pushed off from the top and slid quickly down into the pool of mud at the bottom. It was thicker and slimier than the sinking pond from their first exam. Elena looped her right arm through Pigg's left arm and together they struggled to get to the shore on the other side.

After that, they came to a series of logs where Elena watched Kate Bagley alternate slipping over and under the logs through muddy water. This was particularly challenging for Pigg who was naturally clumsy. Every time he crawled over one log he'd lose his balance and splash down heavily onto the ground below. But eventually, Elena was able to help him all the way across.

Next, they came to a screen of wire suspended low over a field of mud.

"We're going to have to crawl on our bellies," Elena told Pigg.

Pigg groaned loudly. "Can I have some water first? I think I swallowed some mud on that last obstacle."

"Hurry up," Elena replied, the edges of her words impatient as she waved Austin and Fergie ahead of them.

Finally, Pigg seemed ready and they crouched together under the screen of wire. Crawling was extremely difficult and time consuming due to the bulky tactical vest that was zipped on Elena's chest. Often, she felt it snag against the wire or she felt the wire pull on her hair. Pigg was also having a lot of trouble, and Elena had to stop frequently to help him get untangled.

At long last, they reached the other side and Elena stood up, arms shaking and feeling like she might be sick. Mud covered absolutely every part of the front of her body and her hair felt matted and heavy.

"I think that was at least forty feet of, like, crawling," Abria said wearily.

"How are we supposed to get over that?" Kate Bagley called out.

Elena realized that they were surrounded on all sides by a mountainous formation. She didn't see ropes or grommets or anything else that might help them climb up the side of the hill.

"Look! There's a hole," Declan said, pointing at the mountain. "Do you think that's our way out?"

Kate took the hololight from her vest and shined it inside the mouth of what appeared to be a tunnel.

"I can't see anything. Haddock, what do you think?"

Austin stepped forward and peered into the entrance. "I don't know."

"Could be a trap?" Pigg squeaked.

Austin looked deep in thought for a moment and then said, "Not a trap, but maybe a physiological experiment. It's a small, dark hole with no indication of how long it is."

Kate examined them mountains all around them again and said, "Well, clearly we can't climb out of here and we can't go back. So, we've got to go through. Anybody afraid of enclosed spaces?"

Pigg was the only one to raise his hand, but Elena wasn't surprised. He was afraid of almost everything.

"Okay, Pigg," said Kate. "The rest of us will go first with lights on. You come next to last with Smiley, Nelson, and Ransom so there are lights on each end, okay?"

Elena watched Kate and Austin crawl into the hole on hands and knees, one after the other, with hololights gripped in one hand. Then, the other Firebirds followed until only she, Pigg, Frankie, and Olivia remained.

"It's our turn now, Pigg," Elena said slowly.

"Olivia and I will follow behind you," Frankie added."

"While you're in there, just think of something pleasant," Elena suggested.

"I have been trying to create an algorithm for my PocketUnit that would help me disable the surveillance around the school kitchens."

Elena smiled. "That's perfect. Just think of that."

Elena crouched down and helped Pigg fit the hololight to his vest so he wouldn't have to hold it in one hand. Then, she watched him crawl into the hole and she scurried in after him.

It was absolutely the smallest space that she'd ever been inside in her entire life. She could feel the top of her vest scraping against the roof of the tunnel and the only thing she could really see was the bottom of Pigg's boots.

Elena quickly lost all sense of time. Her knees and arms were soon burning in pain and her forehead was slick with sweat. She was also finding it extremely difficult to breathe in the condensed air and thick smell of mud.

After a while, or maybe it had been three days, Pigg's boots stopped moving.

"Why did you stop?" Elena asked breathlessly.

"Well...um...there's a fork in the tunnel, but I don't see where the others went."

"What!" Elena hollered, her temper rising quickly. "Austin!" She screamed.

"Austin! Declan!" Pigg yelled. "Is anyone there?"

Elena waited silently, but she didn't hear a reply.

"Why have we stopped?" Frankie asked from behind her.

"The tunnel splits off ahead," Elena called back to him. "Pigg, how is the tunnel forked?"

"It goes straight, and right, and to the left," Pigg said nervously. "Any guesses as to which way we should go?"

"Yes, I know exactly where we should go," Elena said derisively. She was close to feeling panicked. She was, after all, trapped with Pigg in a place where they didn't have a clear sense of direction. But then, her head cleared suddenly; they were all covered in mud. "Pigg, do you see any mud smeared down any one of the tunnels?"

"Mud is smeared down all three tunnels."

Elena felt her confidence plummet. If they couldn't follow the trail of mud, how would they ever find the other Firebirds? But then, Elena heard her dad's voice in her head, *"Why is it okay when we fail, Elena? So, we can learn how not to do things."*

"Pigg, just go straight. If we take the wrong path, at least we'll know where we made our mistake."

But, as it turned out, going straight didn't help them one bit. The tunnel began to fork and twist every few feet. After the third time they'd unwillingly turned, Elena could not remember how to get back to the first fork in the road. Plus, the tunnel slowly began to incline, making it even more difficult for her to breath.

"I've got to stop, Pigg," Elena said breathlessly. "I need to rest and have some water."

"Thank goodness!" Pigg said wearily. "I was only going because I knew you were behind me. I'm glad you need a break."

Pigg stopped crawling and laid out flat on his stomach, groaning in pain as he did. As Elena spread out on her belly, she realized why he'd moaned so loudly. She felt a blast of pain shoot up and down her arms. Her knees felt on the verge of collapse.

"Nelson says that it's hard for her to breath," Frankie called from behind Elena.

"I think I saw a breathing apparatus in the front zipper pocket," Elena called back. "See if she can get to it."

"How long do you think we've been in here?" Pigg asked, his voice echoing down the hollow tunnel.

"I'm just going to take a guess and say one hundred years," Elena replied.

"Good guess," said Pigg. "Fortunately, I put some snack cakes in my body bubble before we left our room this morning." Elena watched him roll slightly and struggle for a moment. "I guess zipping the cakes into my front chest pocket wasn't the best place for them. Ahhh...got it."

Pigg handed a snack cake back to Elena.

"Thanks, Pigg," she said gratefully as she unwrapped it quickly and stuffed some in her mouth.

"What if we're in here forever?" Frankie asked.

"We won't be stuck forever," sighed Elena. "Grimsby wouldn't want to explain to our parents that we died during Basic Training."

"But, we could be stuck in here long enough to make us all go insane," Pigg said.

"That won't be too much longer for me," Elena said. "But it's comforting to know that we'll be crazy together."

She heard Pigg and Frankie laugh.

"I wish we knew where the others went," Frankie called out. "They're probably all on the other side of this thing wondering where we are. I bet they took the short, easy route and we've been crawling around for ages."

Elena took a big gulp of water and said, "We should get going. Who knows how much longer we have."

But soon after they'd started crawling again, Pigg exclaimed, "I see a light ahead!"

Pigg somehow managed to crawl a little faster and soon Elena could see the light also. Elena breathed a sigh of relief.

But, then Pigg stopped rather abruptly and said, "I can't see the ground on the other side of the tunnel."

"What do you see?" Elena asked.

"Blue sky," Pigg said anxiously. Then, he shimmied forward a bit more. "Oh geez! Elena, we're high above the ground. That must be at least a twenty-foot drop. I don't see a ladder or anything. How are we supposed to get down from here?"

"Stay calm," Elena said, dropping down to her belly. "Lay flat, I'll hold your ankles, then I want you to stick your head out as far as you can and tell me if you can see anyone on the ground."

Pigg obeyed her directions. Then, Elena heard him shout, "Austin! Kate! We're over here." He arched his head back toward her and said, "It's going to be okay. I see Austin down there. He'll know what to do."

Moments later, Pigg said, "Okay, Austin wants me to lean out the entrance and grab hold of the side of the mountain. Then, I'm supposed to climb down the rock crevices. He promised that they'll catch me if I fall. Could you just grab hold of my ankles until I feel like I've got a good grip on the rocks? I don't want to fall to my death."

Elena smirked and shook her head. "Sure, I'll hold your ankles so you don't fall to your death."

Very slowly, Pigg inched his way through the end of the tunnel and Elena held firm to his feet until he told her to let go. As Elena shimmied to the mouth of the tunnel, she covered her eyes with her hands and felt an immediate headache because of the blinding light.

"Lena!" Austin shouted. Are you okay?"

"Yeah, I'm perfect," Elena said sarcastically. "This is the best obstacle yet."

Austin smiled at her. "Okay, then, easy does it out of the tunnel and onto the rocks."

When she finally reached the ground, Austin scooped her into his arms.

"You were a little worried about me, huh?" Elena said as she rubbed her eyes again.

Then, she noticed dozens of different tunnel mouths sticking out from the side of the hill; some of them were high off the ground and some of them were low.

"So far, it seems that all the different passages lead to the outside," Austin said. "Kate and I came out over there, and several of the others came out of that tunnel, there. We're still waiting on Bowen and Castellow, but I think we'll finish. Now, it's just a race against the clock."

In the distance, Elena could see an Optivision screen with a clock that was counting down the last minutes of the exercise.

"I think we all have to be together to stop the clock," Austin said. "A few of us tried to stop it ourselves, but it just keeps ticking down."

Elena felt nervous watching the time tick away. Her left thumb found her mouth and she began to chew the nail.

"So, if they don't get outta there soon we'll fail after all that."

"Don't worry," Austin said in an assuring way. "They'll make it on time."

But, after another full minute ticked down from the clock, Elena's nerves were more strained than ever.

"I wonder if there is something we can do. I mean, we could try calling down some of the lower tunnels to see if…"

"Look!" Austin shouted. "There's someone there!"

Elena saw Vivienne's head appear from one of the lower tunnels. Behind her came Declan. The Firebirds didn't waste time greeting one another, but took off running for the clock, holding their Trademarks out to scan as quickly as they could. Once the last Trademark had finally been entered, the clock stopped ticking and Major Marshall's face appeared on the screen.

"Firebirds, you've completed today's assignment. Your scores will be posted later this evening. Dismissed!"

Elena slumped to the ground, gasping for breath and hoping that they'd never have to do that Gauntlet again.

# ✿ 14 ✿

## The Proposal

On the first day of the third week of the sixth month, Elena and the other
Firebirds began the second quarter exam schedule. She chewed the pinky nail
on her left hand clean off as the Optivision screen materialized with the exam
questions for Advanced Historical Analysis. In the weeks since school began,
Instructor Booker's class had become her favorite. At first she thought this was
because it dealt with proven facts, but her dad reminded her during one of their
recent Telepost visits that her love for history really stemmed from all the
years she'd spent reading from his vast library.

However, knowing that she'd soon have to sit through the Phonology and
AstroPhysics exams made Elena especially nervous. Fergie had tried to teach
Elena an easy way to memorize what all the symbols meant for the Phonology
exam, but it took her a really long time to remember how to decipher them. For
AstroPhysics, Pigg had tried to show Elena an easy way to determine how
numbers were used to read constellations and specific integers for building
equations, but she felt like she kept mixing up the order of the digits.
Therefore, by the time Elena sat for those two exams, she didn't have any
confidence that she'd answered enough questions correctly to pass the exam.

Fortunately, Instructor Emerald had her develop an ancient agriculture system holographically for her Social Science exam. Elena created her simulated diagram with confidence and ended well ahead of the time restriction.

However, Hopper's exam was a lot more comprehensive than Elena would have guessed. She entered a simulated environment where she was forced into situations that tested her knowledge of survival techniques. In addition, she had to assemble a tactical pack from a room filled with seemingly random objects. Finally, she was forced into a space where she experienced unpredictable weather conditions.

"Hopper's exam just about killed me," Elena told Austin as they hurried off into the woods toward the Firebird Station before the other Firebirds had even finished their tests. "What did you do when the rain simulation started and you were asked to build a fire?"

"I tossed a poncho over my head and used the fire starter on the extra pair of socks that I packed from the utility room," Austin replied.

"Oh, that was so smart. I wish I'd thought to bring extra clothes," Elena said jealously. "I didn't pack anything like that."

"Why? What did you do?"

"Oh, I was lame," Elena said. "I wasted time looking for a part shelter under a tree where the rain wasn't so heavy. Then, once I realized that everything was too wet to catch fire I took off my outer shirt and lit it up. It just didn't burn very well because it's made to withstand flame."

"How was your shirt dry enough?"

"Oh, I was wearing a bomber jacket that kept everything dry underneath."

"Still, you got a decent fire started, right?" Austin asked as he opened the Station door.

"I guess it was fine," Elena said dismally as she passed over the threshold into the Station. "It just seemed pitifully small compared with what I'd been practicing lately in Hopper's class. Especially since I was able to start a bonfire with two sticks and a pile of brush in his last class."

Elena dropped tiredly onto one of the bunks off the living room as Austin opened an Optivision screen from the main pupil station. She watched him flip through a familiar looking set of frames.

She closed her eyes. "How do you have enough energy to look through that stuff right now? We've had exams every day this week."

"I really think the info about the Vault is right here somewhere. I know I can get to it, even though I don't know how. But if I keep going I know the right answer will come."

"I doubt that," Elena said pessimistically. "We've been over it and over it for weeks and still aren't any closer to solving the riddle of the magic Vault."

"That's not entirely true," Austin said patiently. "At least now we know where we don't need to keep looking."

"Yeah, yeah..." Elena said dismissively. "I'm still too tired to look at that today."

"Rest then," he encouraged her. "I'll let you know if I come across anything that seems important."

Elena laid her head back, thinking about how persistent Austin had been looking for the Vault. She was still relieved that they hadn't found anything yet. If they'd found something, he would have expected her to start working on a plan for finding it and then somehow getting inside. And, quite honestly, it was all she could do to keep up with her homework so she could take exams.

Before Elena had any awareness of the time, Austin was shaking her awake.

"Hey. Glad you could take a nap, but it's almost dinner so we should get back."

"I don't want to go back," Elena replied, rolling her back toward him. "I'll just eat one of those prepackaged dinners that Hopper has back in that pantry. He has a million of them so he can't miss just one."

"Come on," Austin implored, poking her in the side. "We'll be missed."

Begrudgingly, Elena crawled off the bunk and began to walk back toward the resident tower with Austin. The afternoon was warm, but the trees gave them shade, and there was a soft breeze blowing through the forest. Austin held his Smartslate in hand and was reading out some of the questions he'd written about the Vault when suddenly Elena heard twigs snapping. Declan appeared unexpectedly from behind a tree.

"Hey!"

Austin scrambled to put away his Smartslate as Fergie, Abria, and Pigg also appeared in their path.

"We were just curious where you two go all the time. There can't be much but trees out here."

"Oh, hey..." Elena was trying to sound casual, but she noticed a twinge of guilt in her voice. "We were just out for a walk."

"We have noticed that you both are preoccupied lately," Fergie said. "We are beginning to feel excluded. Is that not correct, Pigg?" She looked at Pigg hopefully.

Pigg looked down at his feet and shuffled nervously. "You always let me tag along back home. Like, remember the time you two were first building the skate-park and Austin asked if I could come along. Elena, you were skeptical at first, but it turned out that I was good at..."

"We mean to express," Fergie interrupted in a formal tone, "that we know you have been doing research for non-educational purposes."

Elena noticed the eager, but disappointed looks on each of their faces.

"We're friends, aren't we?" Abria added. "You can, like, trust us."

Elena and Austin looked at each other for a couple long moments, talking with their eyes. She could tell that Austin didn't want to reveal every detail of what they were working on and she knew the reasons, but they both knew that they needed help to find the Vault because all their efforts had failed. Finally, Austin opened his mouth.

"A few weeks ago Elena and I overheard a conversation that the Headmaster and Hopper were having. We think it had something to do with my father, who disappeared on an expedition for his job when I was two."

"What about your, like, mom?" Abria asked.

"She died during childbirth," Austin replied quietly.

"The Headmaster was talking about a collection of papers hidden in a Vault," Elena interrupted so Austin wouldn't have to talk further about his mother. "So, we've been trying to locate this Vault to see if we can get inside to find out more about Austin's father."

"But there isn't much history about Grimsby's campus on the central processing unit," Austin said. "We haven't even been able to locate blueprints of the school or even a suitable map."

"How have you been researching?" Fergie asked, sounding nervous. "You haven't been using the school mainframe, have you? Because someone would be able to trace your research."

Austin looked at Elena meaningfully. They'd been doing the research on the Optivision screen at the Firebird Station, which they assumed was not traceable by the school, but they really had no way of knowing that for sure.

"Lena, I think it's time to show them," Austin said abruptly.

"Austin," she hissed, shaking her head.

"Show us what?" Declan asked.

"Nothing," said Elena hastily.

But Austin had already started to answer. "We have a secret *place* we'd like to show you."

"I don't know," Pigg said warily. "Elena gets into trouble a lot. Remember what happened with Marshall? She's going to be expelled soon, I just know it."

"Thanks for the confidence, but this isn't like that, dimwit," Elena said curtly. "We're not doing anything to get us expelled...*yet*."

"I want to see this place," Declan pressed.

Elena rolled her eyes and sighed as Austin proceeded to lead Pigg, Declan, Abria, and Fergie back through the woods. They stomped on overgrowth and wound through the trees without speaking until Pigg let out a small squeak of fear.

"Oh, it was just a tree branch that brushed against my arm," said Pigg nervously. "I thought maybe some kind of creature jumped out and grabbed me."

Eventually, they came to the myriad of trees that were covered with creeping plants. Austin grabbed the handful of foliage and pulled them back to reveal the steel plated door with the Firebird logo. He pulled open the door and

Declan, Abria, and Pigg, stepped over the threshold with their mouths wide open. Fergie simple looked as though she were mildly impressed.

"It's called the Firebird Station," Austin said. "Make yourselves at home."

Declan, Abria, Fergie, and Pigg set off in different directions while Elena watched Austin open an Optivision screen in the main living room.

"I can't believe you brought them here," Elena complained to Austin in a low voice.

"We need help with the Vault," Austin said, and she could tell by the look on his face that he was desperate. "It was time to tell them."

Elena sighed deeply. "I guess I should go make sure Pigg hasn't broken anything."

She found Pigg and Fergie in the Research & Development room.

"Look at these awesome macrobinoculars," Pigg exclaimed. He was holding a pair of identical telescope looking objects that were mounted side-by-side. "These can display several distance ranges and are equipped with night-vision. And they show the distance, velocity, and measurement of any object that you set the sights on!" He sounded completely thrilled

"I found something very interesting here!" Fergie's tone was oddly excited as it echoed around the room. She stepped out from behind a row of shelves holding a leather band with a faceplate attached to it. "This is called a Broadcaster. It was a device of intelligence and means of communication that was last used over eleven years ago."

Fergie pushed a button on the side of the Broadcaster and a tiny object the size of a drop of water shot from it. Then, an Optivision blue screen appeared holographically in midair. "This small, round device is called a *Touchdot* and it can perform over twelve million tasks."

"A-maz-ing!" Pigg said, grabbing for the object. He turned it over and over in his hands. "It even has a touch pad key board. Are there anymore?"

"Yes, in fact," Fergie said. "There are a dozen Broadcasters and each one has Touchdot capabilities. I also noticed tactical vests and suits and a plethora of supplies that would keep us alive for many years down here."

Pigg hurried away from them and to the back of the room where Fergie had come from.

"The most important aspect of this Broadcaster is that the Touchdot may allow us a way to hack in to the Grimsby's central processing unit without being detected," Fergie said.

Without a word, she took her newly acquired Broadcaster and hurried back out toward the living room. Austin smiled to greet her, but she completely ignored him and walked straight toward the Optivision pupil station in the main living area. Elena watched the Touchdot fly into a scanner niche. A holographic operations center appeared instantly in the middle of the room.

"Very interesting," Fergie mused. "This Touchdot does not possess a serial number, which means that it is not connected to any orbiting satellites. I wonder where the information is stored so that it can be accessed on this terminal. Nevertheless, I propose that we attempt to use this device to see if a Vault does exist at the school," she said confidently. "Then, we can ascertain if we are able to gain admittance to such a Vault."

"You mean, you want to help us?" Austin asked her.

"Naturally," Fergie said plainly.

"I do, too," Declan added.

"You see," Austin said, looking at Elena. "I knew it would be good to bring them here."

He smiled broadly at her, but she simply rolled her eyes.

■■■

On the first week of the seventh month, the third quarter of school began with the Grimsby campus simulating the kind of heat that could melt the makeup off Abria's face. Elena's classes started at an enthusiastic pace. The Instructors seemed rested from break and launched into their lesson plans with such momentum that Elena felt like it was the first day of school again.

When the second quarter ended, Elena had felt overwhelmed by the amount of information they'd learned from 2500 to 2000 BC: Sargon the Conqueror, Ancient China, the Mohenjo-Daro urban settlement, and the Kingdoms of Egypt. Nevertheless, when Instructor Booker announced the syllabus would cover the five centuries between 2000 and 1500 BC during the third quarter of school she felt positively flabbergasted.

"Are they trying to kill us?" Elena complained to Austin after they'd sat through Booker's lecture and summary of the syllabus that would cover the era of the Amorite kingdom and their conquest of Northern Mesopotamia, the Minoan and Mycenaean civilizations in Ancient Greece, the fall of the last Sumerian dynasty, the end of the Indus Valley civilization, and the Shang Dynasty instituted in China.

"I don't know," Austin said, looking tired. "But it feels like it."

"My brain can't fit another five hundred years."

The next class wasn't any easier. As Instructor Niva described the Proto-Sinaitic Alphabet, Elena felt like her head would explode with information overload. And, in AstroPhysics, Copernicus began to explain the use of numbers and astronomy during the Shang Dynasty, but to Elena, he may as well have been speaking Chinese for all she understood.

Fortunately, Social Science was not as difficult. Instructor Emerald had already created a compare and contrast diagram of the different agriculture techniques in the Minoan civilization and the Shang Dynasty. Both cultures had farmed wheat and barley and raised sheep and pigs. However, it seemed that the Greeks were skilled at cultivating grapes, figs, and olives. They also grew poppies, imported pomegranates from the Near East, domesticated bees, and imported cats from Egypt for hunting purposes.

"I'm thrilled to tell you that we'll be learning how to press olive oil today!" Instructor Emerald said excitedly. He always acted like his class was the most interesting of all Elena's lessons; she couldn't help but smile at his simple-minded optimism.

"I saw that smile," Declan said to Elena as the students broke into groups to begin working at the olive oil presses that were aligned toward the far end of the hydroponic farm. "Let's press some olive oil together." He flashed her a toothy grin.

"I don't want to press oil with you," Elena said sassily.

"Oh, come on. I'll even let you use the millstone. Emerald said that the person doing that job would get extra credit."

Elena rolled her eyes and sighed. "There's something about how nice you are that nauseates me."

Declan laughed at her genially. Then, he leaned forward and whispered, "It's okay to accept kindness sometimes, Ransom."

Elena shook her head and watched Declan saunter off to another group. Then, she joined Austin, Pigg, and Fergie at an olive press.

"Pigg and I have done some preliminary searching for the Vault during our visits to the Firebird Station," Fergie was telling Austin in a hushed voice. "The Touchdot and Optivision station have been extremely helpful in accessing data. However, the Grimsby central processing unit is —"

"A tough cookie to crack," Pigg interrupted her, as he spread olives on the press. "Speaking of cookies, did anyone bring a snack?"

"It will take longer than we originally anticipated to circumvent the security system," Fergie said.

"Elena and I appreciate your help, no matter how long it takes," Austin said.

"Now, on to more important things," Pigg said. "I noticed a large pantry of dried foods in the Station. Do you think Hopper will mind if we dip into his emergency stores?"

"What makes you think the food is for an emergency?" Elena asked, as she helped Austin turn the millstone.

"There is no reason for him to have that much food stashed away unless he's one of those crazy people prepping for the apocalypse."

Austin and Elena both laughed.

"Knowing Hopper, he just might be one of those people."

Later that day, after dinner, Elena walked with the other Firebirds to the Media Lab to finish the homework that Hopper had given them about the military strategies of Ancient Greece and the Amorite Kingdom. On the way, Elena was only vaguely listening to Abria gossip about one of the Raptor girls getting a fungal infection because she was watching Austin and Declan, who seemed to be engrossed in a serious conversation only a few feet in front of them. She wanted to hurry forward to escape Abria until she said something that provoked Elena's attention.

"So, I was like, 'Don't talk to me like that,'" Abria said, explaining her most recent encounter with Kidd to Fergie. "And he was like, 'I can talk to you however I want, Blondie.' And then, I was like, 'Oh, how original to call me

Blondie.' And then, do you know that dimwit said he could think of another name that started with a 'b' that also isn't original. Then, Declan appeared at my side looking surly. You know how he gets around Wheeler. Honestly, I don't think Declan is going to settle down until he gives him a good punch in the nose."

In between this entire monologue, Abria hadn't failed to say "hello" to every person they saw and, quite often, was even able to throw out polite comments about a girl's cute hair style or a boy's sweet dimples.

"Abria," Elena said as Declan and Austin crossed into the Media Lab ahead of them. "How can you talk that long without drawing breath?"

"Oh, it's a gift," said Abria cheerfully. "I learned it from Declan's mom."

"And another thing," Elena went on. "Why are you always so friendly? I mean, you talked to absolutely everyone we saw on the way here."

Abria flipped her hair away from her face. "People tend to have a better day when someone has taken the time to acknowledge that they exist."

"But, what does that matter to you if people have a better day?" Elena asked.

"Gee wiz, Elena!" Abria sounded exasperated. "What does it matter to you that I give people a little happiness in their day? I mean, what's the point of living if you can't pass on a little kindness to a fellow human being?"

"Gag me," Elena said, sticking her finger in her mouth and pretending to vomit. She dropped into a vacant seat beside Austin and complained, "I know we're supposed to be doing stuff for Hopper, but I have so much homework in Physics. Have you seen where Pigg's gone off too?" She looked around expectantly. "He's the only one who can help."

"I think he stayed behind in the Mess Hall," Declan said offhandedly. Then, he turned his attention back to Austin. "Anyway, as I was saying, those Raptor boys are maniacs. Oscar Hunter has basically taken over the whole Unit by force and the rest of them just follow along behind him. I've heard that he's just as cruel as Marshall, expecting all the Raptors to perform a certain way during classes and Basic. Plus, he's been a complete bully in the Simulabs, especially with the Harriers. He actually taunts some of the other students at certain modules until they get frustrated enough to leave. What are we going to do with him?"

"Why do you even care what he does with the Raptors?" Elena asked.

"Because next year we'll start having class with them," Declan replied. "I think it's best to try and get the situation under control before that happens."

"Successful leadership requires sacrifice sometimes," Austin said in a serious tone.

"Sacrifice? I hope you're not suggesting that we just give in to his bullying."

"I'm suggesting that we *appear* to sacrifice our desires in order to study our opponent, learn his weakness, and exploit his strengths for our own agenda," Austin said.

Elena smiled at Declan and said, "And that's why Austin should always be the leader of the Firebird Unit."

## ≎ 15 ≎

## Lieutenant Haddock

The third quarter of school pressed on at a rapid pace. The Grimsby campus simulated the steamy, hot weather that Fergie said was apparently *normal* during the seventh month of any given year. So, Elena spent most of her time indoors and only ventured out when it was required for Basic and walking to the hydroponic farm for Emerald's class.

Emerald was in the middle of teaching the Firebirds how farmers and herders traveled south from Ethiopia and settled in Kenya, Africa. Elena stared at a holographic map of the massive continent feeling absolute awe at its size.

Instructor Niva focused most of their class on writing script from ancient China during the Bronze Age. Elena found this to be exhausting work, especially since they were also expected to continue their writing and speaking studies of India during the Iron Age.

In Copernicus' class, Elena had a little easier time following the Instructor as she showed them the oldest surviving astronomical documents from Babylon because Instructor Booker had spent his entire lecture that same morning discussing the rule of Hammurabi in Babylonia and the many achievements that were accomplished during this reign.

As always, Hopper's class continued to be the best. He'd already taught the Firebirds the basic psychology of survival, how to make an improvised compass, and how to use the sun, shadows, moon, and stars to determine location. They'd also done a series of classes on survival kits, survival rationing, herbal medicines, lifesaving techniques, and rucksack construction.

But today, Hopper taught them about the environmental factors that contributed to the success or failure of surviving in the wild. He taught them how to properly insulate their clothing with objects found in nature, build a basic fire, cook an easy meal, procure water in an unpredictable environment, and construct different types of shelters based on debris found in the wilderness.

"I just can't get the hang of this!" Pigg gasped, sounding frustrated as the Firebirds attempted to construct a shelter using only rope and a flimsy tarp.

"I don't see why we're forced to do this anyway!" Elena said, sweating as she tried to keep her piece of the tarp from slipping off a jagged stick. "It's pointless to learn how to build a shelter in the wild."

"Do you realize that you say that every single time we have a practical lesson with Hopper?" Austin said.

"Yeah, it's not like we'll ever use the, like, military tactics he teaches when we're sitting in lecture, but you listen with all intensity to what he says," said Abria.

"Yeah, but that has historical value," Elena countered. "This is just pointless busywork. Come on, Pigg, back me up."

"I heard that he's going to teach us about plant edibility, and how to use plants for medicine," Pigg said nervously. "Does anyone besides me think it's not a great idea for me to be around possibly poisonous substances?"

"I wouldn't worry about that yet, Pigg," said Declan. "I'd be more worried about dying in Marshall's next class. Apparently, it's going to be some kind of practical in a field of battle."

"Where did you hear that?" Elena asked, the edges of her words splintered with anxiety.

"Oh, I overheard Oscar Hunter talking about it with the Raptor Unit," he replied.

"Hunter is a dimwit," Abria said. "How can we trust anything he, like, says?"

"I don't know," Declan says. "But for some reason he seems to know a lot about the classes and about Basic. Maybe he knows someone from the older Levels that has gone through all this."

Just as Elena was beginning to contemplate how unfair it would be if Oscar was getting help from someone else, Hopper's class was over and she hurried to lunch with her friends. But, she was completely distracted thinking about what Marshall's next class would be like that she barely noticed the time pass and soon enough she was standing in a hallway while the Drill Instructor barked orders at them.

"Gather around, gather around! Our lesson today is a significant test of skill. And, you Firebirds will be competing directly with the top score of the Falcons, Harriers, and Raptors, though they will compete against you from another classroom.

"The door behind me," Marshall jerked his thumb behind his head, "is a holographic training room. Moments after you enter, the room will simulate seven square miles of the preliminary Grimsby Field Course. Your mission is to choose a strategic plan, plot a route, and then advance through the training course. Your objective is to get through in the shortest amount of time with the least amount of wounds or causalities."

"Casualties?" Pigg whispered earnestly to Elena. "He doesn't really mean someone could die, does he?"

"No, it's just a game, dimwit," Elena whispered back.

"In a moment, you will be fitted with a target vest and may choose a weapon," Marshall continued, indicating a long row of racks that were stocked with identical black vests and weapons that looked like pistols.

Elena had never held a gun of any kind before. How could Marshall send them into a room and expect any decent results if they'd never had this kind of training, especially with Pigg in the room?

"The vests are laser censored. If your vest is shot, a casualty point tallies for your Unit. If executed properly, you should be able to make it through the course without getting anyone on your team shot.

"And for goodness sake, Pigg, don't shoot your teammates because that automatically disqualifies you from finishing the training exercise," Marshall said cruelly, and Pigg hung his head. "The acting Lieutenant will be chosen by collective vote of your peers. After you have chosen a Lieutenant, collect your gear and then return to your formation. You are dismissed to vote for your Lieutenant."

The Firebirds had barely joined together when Kidd said, "I think I should do it."

"Too bad no one likes you enough to vote for you," said Elena sharply.

"It doesn't have anything to do with popularity, Freckles. It has to do with top marks in Basic and Survival," Kidd said.

"Then, you are unable to submit your name for the position," Fergie said earnestly.

"Why is that, Brainiack?" Kidd asked.

"Although your marks in Survival Training have been superb, your performance in Basic Training during the first quarter was abysmal."

"What?" scoffed Kidd. "You mean when *Freckles* was teaching the class?"

"Precisely," Fergie replied.

"Not to mention the fact that you totally lost your nerve the first time we ran the Gauntlet and couldn't lead us to the end of the task," said Elena viciously.

"I didn't lose anything," said Kidd, growing red in the face. "I briefly hesitated."

"The only conclusion that can be determined," continued Fergie as if there had been no interruption, "is that Haddock has received the highest marks and is therefore our leader."

Elena burst out laughing as Kidd's mouth fell open.

"Show of hands for Haddock," Fergie polled.

Every hand flew into the air before Kidd could make another sound or motion.

"The Firebird Lieutenant has been chosen," Fergie said matter-of-factly. "We are pleased for you to lead us, Haddock."

Austin nodded and said, "Firebirds, back in formation."

Elena grinned as she and the Firebirds hurried over to the racks to obtain their gear. She noticed that Kidd moved rather slowly and had a grimace on his face, which made her feel even happier. Elena slipped on her vest, chose a laser pistol, and rushed back to formation, feeling eager to start the simulation with Austin as their leader.

"Have you chosen a leader?" Marshall barked as the Units came to formation.

"Sir, yes, Sir," the Firebirds responded. "Then, Lieutenants, you are free to discuss your plans with your Units."

As Marshall turned away, Austin wasted no time getting the Firebirds together.

"Wheeler and Bowen, take the two front lookout positions; Ransom and Gamble take the offensive front; Smiley take the left wingsite and Nelson take the right; I'll take the officer's position in the middle; Abria, Foreman and Pigg, take the defensive back; and Bagley and Castellow, you two take the rearsite."

"Why do I have to be in front?" Kidd asked, clearly disappointed with Austin's choice.

"Coward," Elena said bluntly.

"Because," Austin interrupted, "as Fergie already pointed out, you are *second* best. Plus, you aced your marksman training exercise."

"So, I'm being punished because I'm good?"

"Strategically, it is best for our team."

"You mean, as long as he doesn't screw it up," Elena said to Abria and Fergie, who smiled.

"I heard that!" Kidd barked, looking fierce.

"I said it loud enough so you could hear me," Elena answered, turning toward him and making a face.

Kidd looked as if he was about to punch her, but Austin said firmly, "Listen up, Firebirds! We're not running this course individually. I've put you in these positions to exploit your unique qualities. I demand team cooperation." Then, Austin turned specifically to Kidd and said, "But if you have trouble taking orders you can sit it out and accept a fail for the day."

Kidd looked as though he might retaliate, but turned to his classmates instead and said, "You weaklings better not hold me back."

A moment later, Marshall called the Firebirds to the front.

"Remember your objective?" he asked Austin.

"Sir, yes, Sir."

Marshall stepped aside and the Firebirds went into the classroom, which morphed instantaneously into an ominous night sky. Elena felt a surge of panic as her eyes adjusted to the sudden darkness. Lanky trees grew all around them and the forest floor was covered with a mossy texture. It was also unbearably warm, so she took a moment to knot her hair.

"This is so, like, weird," Abria said.

"You know what's weird," Pigg whispered in a weak voice. "This gun in my hand."

Austin didn't seem confused by the abrupt change in scenery. He reminded them quickly of their positions, made sure that everyone felt confident, and then ushered the Firebirds forward with their hololights aloft. As they entered the vast expanse of the simulation, some of the terrain required them to change course so they could navigate ravines and cliffs without loosing footing or separating the team. But, overall, the Firebirds moved easily through the field training course, meeting very few obstacles.

"Something seems wrong," Austin said finally, calling the Firebirds to a halt.

"Why?" asked Crosby Gamble.

"There aren't enough obstacles," Austin said. "Marshall said that we would be competing directly with the other Units, but so far our biggest struggles have been terrain. I haven't seen a single member of any of the other Units."

"We should be thankful," said Vivienne Castellow. "Marshall has finally given us an easy class."

"Since when has Marshall ever been easy on us?" Elena said darkly.

"We should have been attacked by now, or something," Austin said thoughtfully.

"I agree," Declan said. "But what does it matter? We've still got to get through the room in the best time."

"I know we need to keep going, but something just feels...not right," Austin said thoughtfully.

"I say let's keep doing what we've been doing and take things a little slower," Kidd said. "It's dark, but manageable. Bowen and I can get a little ahead so we can alert you if we see anything."

"That's a great idea," Austin said graciously.

Elena watched Declan and Kidd head off into the darkness between the trees, then turned to Austin and said, "I know you're trying to get on Wheeler's good side, but them going on ahead may not be the best plan."

"We've got to try something," Austin said. "I haven't seen any way out of here. We have nothing to give us a sense of direction. Basically, we've been following how the terrain is laid out. And since we haven't seen any of the other Units there is nothing left for us to try. Wheeler's suggestion wasn't a bad one. And, before the end of this, I may let everyone take a turn at suggesting how we get out of here."

Austin turned toward the rest of the Firebirds and said, "Alright everyone, fall in behind me."

Elena eased into the darkness with her Unit feeling slightly uncomfortable about what they could encounter in the woods. But Austin had made a fine point. They did have to keep going because they had no other options.

As the minutes stretched on and the simulation was still quiet, Elena began to feel more confident about the darkness and their progress. But suddenly, Declan and Kidd appeared from just beyond the trees to their left and signaled for the Firebirds to take a defensive position. Elena hurried to duck under a canopy of hanging trees with the others, their weapons at the ready.

"What is it?" Austin whispered to Kidd, who was listening intently without speaking.

Moments later, Kidd said, "It's a girl screaming, 'Help me! Please!' over and over again."

## ◻ 16 ◻

## The Vault

Austin stood slightly and looked around.

"Bowen and Wheeler, scout ahead to observe. Only to observe. Report back as quickly as you can."

The two boys rose from their positions, abandoning their front lookout posts, and hurried off into the wilderness. Frankie Smiley and Olivia Nelson rose and swiftly took Kidd and Declan's positions, while Elena and Crosby turned out toward the darkness that spread through the wilderness.

Minutes passed. In the darkness, it felt like an eternity to Elena, and the sounds of the forest did nothing to help her confidence. She chewed off two fingernails before Declan and Kidd returned, panting for breath.

"There is a girl at the bottom of a ditch over there," Kidd whispered, "She says she's from the Raptor Unit and that she fell and broke her leg, but they left her so they could finish the course."

"That sounds like something Hunter would do," Elena said scathingly, thinking about all the awful things Declan had said about Oscar Hunter from the Raptor Unit.

"Did you check her leg?" Austin asked.

"No. She was pretty far down in the ditch," Declan answered, wiping sweat from his brow. "Besides, you told us to see what was up and come straight back."

Austin looked deep in thought for a moment and then said, "We can't help her. We've got to keep moving. We're not safe here."

"Safe?" Kidd scoffed. "We're in a classroom."

"She could be really hurt," Abria said, twisting her hair through her fingers. "We should at least go and, like, check."

"That's not our objective," said Austin sternly.

"But we can't just, like, leave her out here."

"Yeah, doesn't leaving a Unit member behind go against some kind of moral code, or something?" Crosby Gamble said.

"Our task is to complete the course unscathed and in the least amount of time. We were not tasked to pick up stragglers," Austin said logically.

"She's not a straggler. She's injured," said Abria.

"She's not on our team. If she was one of our own we would help her." Austin seemed to grow more patient and sensible as the conversation continued.

In contrast, Elena was getting impatient with the debate.

"This is not a democratic vote," she said bluntly. "We chose Austin to lead us so we need to listen to him."

"Yeah, dudes," Declan added. "We're wasting time arguing here."

Austin motioned with his hand for everyone to get back into formation and they obeyed. With another hand motion, the Firebirds left the tree canopy to continue the field training exercise.

An hour later, Elena began to see daylight on the horizon. Then, quite suddenly, she stepped through the darkness into the light of the room that had morphed back into a white-walled space. Marshall was there to greet them. He barked at them to get into formation and wait in the hallway.

Soon, the Raptor, Harrier, and Falcon Units returned from the simulation and joined the Firebirds outside the classroom. After everyone was present, Marshall stood before the class looking surly and annoyed.

"Firebirds!" Marshall barked. "You were the *only* Unit who didn't pick up an injured person in the field. Why?"

"Sir, I instructed the Firebird's to follow your direct orders." Austin raised his voice proudly. "You made it clear that our objective was to return our Unit unscathed and in the least amount of time."

"That is absolutely correct," Marshall replied. Then, looking at the other Units he said, "The injured person in your simulation was a deliberate hoax. The Firebirds are awarded the top score for the day. Dismissed!"

As the Unit broke apart, most of the Firebirds rushed forward to congratulate Austin on his presence of mind and leadership. But, Elena watched Kidd stalk away without saying a word to anyone. She also noticed that they received a lot of nasty looks from the Raptor Unit, but she didn't care. They'd won, and now everyone knew that Austin was the best Lieutenant in the Aves Company.

■■■

Days later, Elena was still feeling elated over the great work the Firebirds had done in Marshall's simulation. The fact that the Firebirds were the only Unit to complete the course without diverting from the main objective had apparently made Oscar Hunter more extreme than ever. And, since then, she'd noticed that Austin and Declan had been spending a little more time together, huddled over minuscule Optivision screens in the Media Lab.

"What are you doing?" Elena asked finally, after catching the pair of them for the third time.

"Declan and I are reviewing the play back of how the other Units performed during the last class in Basic."

"What for?"

"We've started doing this after every class with Marshall," Declan said. "We even went back to the very beginning of the year so we can learn more about who we're competing against and who we'll have to work with during our Level 2 studies."

"Have you learned anything good?"

"Just that Oscar Hunter is a really bad leader," Austin said, rubbing his eyes tiredly. "During that last exercise he sent two of the Raptors toward the injured girl and then set off with the rest in a different direction so they could finish the exam."

"I bet he got bad marks for doing that," said Elena.

"You know," said Declan. "You should really sit down with us sometime to review all this."

"How will I ever find time for that?" Elena scoffed. "I've been busy trying to study for our exam. Or have you forgotten that we somehow have to remember how to record the decline of the entire Harappan civilization, the fall of the last Sumerian dynasty, and how the Israelites entered Egypt again after two years of famine?"

At that moment, there came a commotion on the other side of the Media Lab as Fergie and Pigg entered and tripped over one another trying to get to Elena.

"We have extraordinary news," Fergie whispered, though she was slightly out of breath from running. "We have successfully achieved full access to Grimsby's central processing unit. We can finally complete our strategy for admittance to the Vault!"

Declan jumped up to go find Abria while Elena and Austin hurried to the Firebird Station with Fergie and Pigg.

"When we originally retrieved the archived records that were available on Grimsby's mainframe we could not locate the Vault as we studied the schematic of the building," Fergie said formally.

"Then, last night it hit me," Pigg interjected. "The school had to have an original schematic of the building stored virtually on the global server, and I could find it using my PocketUnit."

"What's a *global server*?" Austin asked.

"It's a place where they keep absolutely all data in existence," said Pigg. "Actually, I accidently found the global server that one time I was trying to fix the Ransom's Optivision screen. I nearly burned the living room down and Elena's dad was…let's put it this way…I still can't walk down the hall at night by myself to use the bathroom because he was just that scary." He laughed nervously at the memory. "Anyway, while I was plugged into Elena's house server, I found an archaic piece of software that stores confidentiality files from the past one hundred decades. But it was built behind an unhackable security interface that has never been challenged."

"Unless you have my abilities," Fergie said.

"And me," Pigg added hastily. "You couldn't have done it without me."

"Right you are," Fergie said, smiling at Pigg. "We found a routing program in the terminal at the Firebird Station that we determined was untraceable. From this program we realized that we could hack the confidentiality files."

"Elena, remember how I told you about the portal cipher I designed so we could cheat during class in Atlanson?" Pigg did not seem embarrassed by this admission of unethical behavior, but Elena's face turned red with shame. "Anyway, Fergie and I accessed the portal and were able to walk right into the confidentiality files. The best part is that it's completely untraceable. I mean, again, at least I'm ninety-nine point nine percent sure, give or take a couple point percentages based on the technology that's been developed in the past few months of us being at school."

"Look what we found."

Fergie approached the Optivision screen and accessed a holographic schematic of the original Grimsby campus. Elena watched a piece-by-piece model of the building as it was being constructed. Then, there was a list of architect names, designers, builders, and details about the campus, resident towers, and acreage of the training fields.

As they were studying the schematic, the door to the Station opened and Declan hurried in with Abria hard on his heels.

"It took me forever to find her," Declan complained.

"Some of us have a very active social life," Abria said defensively. Then, she noticed the schematic and frowned. "Couldn't you have, like, waited?"

Fergie took a moment to repeat everything she'd just said so that Declan and Abria could get caught up, and then she indicated a spot on the map with her finger. "You see this area over here? The scans indicate that this section of Grimsby has a distinctive amount of oxygen levels circulating."

"Meaning what?" Austin inquired.

"It means they either have sensitive materials stored there or someone is building a bomb," Fergie said.

"That's a cheerful thought," Declan said.

"The bomb theory was mine," Pigg spoke up. "Because, see this dark spot," he pointed, "that room is made from material to withstand a blast of explosives. We'll have to get beyond that to get inside the Vault. But that's not even the worst news. The bad news is that it's located in the Catacombs, *inside* one of the Telepost stalls."

"The one that's always out of order?" Elena questioned, and both Pigg and Fergie nodded their heads.

"Why is that, like, bad news?" Abria asked.

"Because they have a billion surveillance monitors down there. So, we would be seen at every corner of the hallway. Not to mention the fact that this particular Telepost door is locked from the inside," said Pigg.

Elena looked over the schematic and frowned. Then, she shared a worried look with Austin.

"So, it's impossible to get inside unnoticed?" Austin asked.

"Nothing is strictly impossible when dealing with technology," Fergie said. "However, it will be extremely difficult."

"Austin, I still don't understand why you just can't ask the Headmaster if you can see the manuscript. It was written by your father, after all," said Pigg timidly, though he had a hungry look in his eye. He seemed to be teetering on exploring his hacking abilities and not wanting to get into trouble.

"The Headmaster told Hopper about the manuscript in confidence," Austin said. "Clearly, if he is keeping it locked up he's not about to tell me what's in it." He paced the room once and then looked serious. "Listen, I'd like to try to get inside the Vault, but we could get in so much trouble. Anyone want to back out?"

Pigg's hand slowly rose from his side, but Elena grabbed it and bent his thumb back until he screamed in pain.

"I say, let's go for it," Pigg said with tears in his eyes.

"So, where do we begin?" Elena asked Fergie eagerly.

"First, Pigg will hack into the security terminal and reformat the surveillance in the Catacombs. We will do this while people are going to and from lunch."

"We're going to miss lunch?" Pigg groaned.

"In fact, I want you to hack this from the Mess Hall so it does not seem so suspicious. Everyone would notice if you did not attend a meal," Fergie told him. Then she turned back to Elena and Austin, "Then, you two will get to the Telepost stall and I will unlock the door for you remotely. Unfortunately, we have no idea what is behind the locked door. However, the Vault is here," Fergie indicated with her finger again, "Merely steps away from the Telepost door. And, the best we can tell, it is not guarded by another locking mechanism."

Fergie handed Austin and Elena each a Broadcaster.

"Wear them on your wrist so we can communicate. Once you are inside the Vault, locate the manuscript and release the Touchdot. The dot will scan each page of the manuscript and store it so we may download it later to the Optivision screen here."

"This is so awesome, Fergie and Pigg!" Austin praised. "You've both done excellent work."

Fergie gave him a rigid smile, but Pigg looked very pleased with himself.

"When are we going to do this?" Declan asked.

"Tomorrow."

"*Tomorrow*!" Elena exclaimed. "Don't you think we should have a few more days to go over this plan again, maybe even do a few practice runs?"

"This is a simple plan and can be executed with minimal effort. We should complete this as soon as possible," Fergie said.

"I agree with Fergie," Austin said. "The less we stress about this the better."

With this final word from Austin the matter was settled. Instead of arguing for more time to prepare, Elena resigned herself to stress about the Vault burglary in private. In fact, she was so nervous the following day that she answered a question incorrectly during their next Advanced Historical Analysis. And, during Phonology, Instructor Niva told Elena that her classwork was sloppy and she needed to start again.

By lunchtime, Elena was absolutely distracted as she followed Austin down to the vacant Catacombs. When they reached the Telepost office door that was out of order Austin activated his Broadcaster and said, "We're in position."

A moment later, Fergie's holographic head appeared on his wrist and said, "Proceed."

And Elena could only assume that Fergie had somehow managed to unlock the door because it suddenly slid open silently. Unlike the other white-walled stalls that Elena had visited, this room was pitch black. She and Austin stepped forward into the darkness, and then the door closed behind them.

"Um...lights," Elena said into the darkness. And, it was as if she'd said a magic word because the lights turned on quite suddenly.

Elena seized Austin's arm and gasped. They were standing on a ledge over looking a vast, sand stone ravine. Jagged canyon rocks spread out in all directions and the depth so extreme that it would have been impossible to cross without days of climbing.

"I'm not technically afraid of heights," she said as a cool breeze rose out of the ravine and circled around the ledge, blowing red curls around her face. "But I'm genuinely terrified about falling to my death."

Austin looked around attentively, thumbing the scar on his chin. Elena was at a loss, but she could tell that he was using every sense to figure out what they should do next.

"It's not real," he finally said. "It's a simulation."

"Are you sure? It feels pretty real in here to me," Elena said. "And it's not like we have a second chance once we step off this ledge."

Austin looked at Elena square in the face.

"This canyon can't actually be here. This Telepost office is in the middle of the school. There's no place for a chasm like this to actually exist."

Elena knew he was right. Without speaking, they held hands and stepped together off the ledge and onto a firm floor. The room did not change, but they continued on, walking across the gorge in midair.

"This is the weirdest feeling," Elena said. "I feel like we're going to fall any minute."

Austin nodded, looking serious as Fergie's head appeared holographically on his Broadcaster.

"This is quite extraordinary," said Fergie. "You are inside a simulation that is being created by your fears."

"That means," Pigg's head appeared on Elena's Broadcaster. "The room is actually *reading* the fears from your brain! Can you believe that?" He sounded awe-struck. "It's the most amazing technology that I've ever seen in a program."

"Yeah, it's really fantastic," Elena said sarcastically.

Quite suddenly, the simulation completely changed and they were surrounded on all sides by stiletto snakes, pitvipers, spinytail lizards, goliath birdeater tarantulas, and scaly gavials. Elena immediately shut her eyes and squealed.

"I can't move!"

"It's not real, Lena," Austin said reassuringly. "It's just a simulation."

"I don't care. I'm terrified," Elena stammered. She could feel that she was now sweating through her shirt. "I literally can't move. You go on, I have to go back."

Elena felt arms wrap around her and was then hoisted in the air.

"I'm not leaving you here alone, and I'm not going on without you. You don't need to be afraid. I'm with you."

Elena kept her eyes shut tight, thankful that Austin was not afraid and that he was willing to carry her.

At length, Elena felt Austin stop suddenly.

"Lena, before you open your eyes. I need you to remember two things." He set her down gently. "One, no matter what happens, don't let go of my hand." Austin slipped his hand into hers and grasped firmly. "Also, remember that this is a simulation, and the most important objective at this point is to get out of here."

Elena nodded and opened her eyes. The sheer terror of what she saw shook her to the core of her being. A group of bloody corpses littered the floor, but they weren't just any people. It was everyone she knew and cared about. Her parents' bodies were there, along with Austin, Grandpa and Grandma

Haddock, and Pigg. The perimeter of the room was outlined with mirrors so that the dead were reflected all around, with no visible entrance or exit.

"Lena, take a deep breath and tell me what you see," Austin said.

Elena tried to inhale, but it was impossible. She began to tremble all over and squeaked, "Austin, what do you see?"

"Everyone I love is dead on the floor. Do you see anything else?"

Elena felt so confused. Why did he keep asking her what she could see? Wasn't it enough that she was experiencing one of her worst fears in life?

"There!" Austin yelled, pointing far off at something. "Did you see that? Over there, it's a door."

Elena followed his finger to the wall of mirrors, but she could only see the reflection of the people she loved. She kept staring until her eyes hurt.

"I can't see anything," she said impatiently.

"That's okay," Austin replied. "I know where we need to go."

Austin led Elena through the room and, quite suddenly, a door appeared as if from thin air.

"Fergie," he called into his Broadcaster. "We've found a door. Can you open it?"

Before Fergie could even speak, the door opened with a swish. Beyond the door was an enormous room lined with rows of white cabinetry. Several long rows of Optivision stations sat in the center of the room, each holographic screen analyzing data. Laser beams were scanning several oddly shaped items that Elena had never seen before.

Elena and Austin walked and walked, until they came to the farthest corner of the room where they noticed a book suspended in mid-air. Special lights and lasers surrounded it from above and beneath, like it was being examined.

"That's my father's handwriting," Austin whispered.

"Fergie," Austin said into his Broadcaster. "The manuscript looks like its being inspected by some sort of lasers or lights."

Fergie's holographic image appeared on his Broadcaster. "I was not expecting the possibility that it would be in the process of being analyzed while we were also trying to scan it."

"Oh, perfect!" Elena blurted. "Now she tells us."

Fergie looked liked she was busy doing something. Then, she said, "In three point seven seconds, reach your hand into the middle of the lasers and pull the manuscript toward you."

Hand trembling, Austin reached forward and pulled the manuscript away from the lasers. Elena and Austin stood silently for a few moments, scarcely daring to breath. But nothing happened, so he set the book on the table and flipped to the front page. The Touchdot shot from Austin's Broadcaster, and Elena saw an Optivision screen open. Then, a beam of light began to scan the page.

Austin turned page after page of the manuscript until it seemed that all the pages had been copied. Then, he returned the manuscript to the inspecting lasers and Elena heaved a sigh of relief.

She and Austin eased back through the Vault and back through the ironclad door. The room that had simulated corpses was now a white walled space. As they arrived back at the door of the Telepost stall, Elena couldn't help but admire the technology. What had seemed like hours on the journey to the Vault was in reality only minutes when they went back through.

"Do you hear that?" Austin asked, freezing as the stall door opened.

Elena stopped to listen and heard the sound of thick, pounding boot steps echoing from down the hall.

"You must not get caught standing in that doorway." Fergie's head had materialized holographically on Austin's wrist again. "Initiating the diversion."

At that moment, a loud siren sounded off through the halls. Austin grabbed Elena by the hand and led her into one of the other Telepost rooms.

"How are we going to get out of here?" Elena groaned into her Broadcaster at Fergie.

"Stand by," Fergie said.

"*Stand by?*" Elena grumbled to Austin. "My heart feels like it's gonna through my chest and all she can say is 'stand by?'"

"The nerve of that girl," Austin said sarcastically.

"I'm glad one of us is taking this seriously."

"Overreacting to stress is not the same thing as taking something seriously," Austin pointed out. "I think this has been a successful mission. Think about where we are. If anyone catches us down here they'll think we've been Teleposting."

Fergie's head appeared on the Broadcaster.

"I had to reactivate the surveillance to the live feed and activate the diversion I created to distract Major Marshall away from the Telepost office. I believe it is safe for you to exit the Catacombs now."

## ▢ 17 ▢

# News from Home

"How did you know where that door was back there?" Elena asked Austin much later as they tromped through the forest toward the Firebird Station. "Because all I could see were dead bodies."

"I don't know, exactly," Austin said. "I was looking intently at the mirrors and suddenly there was a rippling effect on one of the mirrors. It was almost like the simulation was failing in some way. Then, I could see through it to the door."

Elena was curious to know more, but they'd just entered the Station and saw that Fergie was waiting for them. Austin handed her the Broadcaster from his wrist. Elena watched the Touchdot fly from it and load into the Optivision pupil station automatically.

A holographic image of the Alpha Manuscript appeared and she watched Fergie flip several of the pages. Each page was filled with writing, but some of the text was not in a language that Elena recognized.

"Sorry to disappoint you, but it appears that this book is incomplete," Fergie told them after she'd reviewed the entire document. "Many of the pages are blank, and some of it is written in a language that I do not understand."

"What does it matter if there are blank pages?" Elena asked.

"Commonly, in cryptology, a person would leave blank pages as a indicator of writing that is hidden."

"Do you mean to say that those pages could have text, but it's invisible?" Austin asked incredulously.

"Precisely," Fergie replied.

Elena felt disheartened. She had expected that after they had the manuscript all Austin's questions would be immediately answered. She was weary and the only thing she could think to make herself feel better was to see her parents.

The Telepost office hallway was quiet as usual and Elena was thankful that she didn't have any interruptions. When she entered the warmth of her family kitchen she breathed a sigh of relief.

"You look tired, Sunshine," her dad said as a greeting. He was sitting at the table with Hannah, who was looking just as radiant as ever.

"I am tired," Elena conceded. "I would never have imagined that school could be this hard, or exhausting."

"How are your grades?" Truman asked.

"I'm a genius," Elena yawned, and was happy to see that her comment made Hannah and Truman smile. "Actually, I read mathematic texts the same way I read ancient Akkadian. When I get to the end I think, 'Well, there's no way I'm ever understanding that.' So, don't be surprised when you see those grades."

"And how are things with Marshall?" Hannah asked, looking concerned.

"We've reached a suitable arrangement," Elena replied. "He still acts like a radical tyrant, but I've decided to mask my passionate dislike for him behind a plastic smile. I channel Abria Bowen for inspiration. It's working really well."

"Ah, playful banter," Truman said. "The sign of a healthy and happy teenager."

Elena smiled, and then realized something out loud.

"I would have never thought it possible to be happy here at school while I'm away from you, but I am."

Her dad and mom moved closer to Elena's space. They couldn't actually touch her, but their loving arms moved around her hologram.

"We're so proud of you," Hannah said. Her hand reached up to seemingly stroke Elena's hair.

"Only one more quarter to go and then you'll be home for a visit," Truman said. "Your mom and I can hardly wait. The house has been so quiet that it seems unnatural."

"Oh, it can't be that quiet," said Elena. "You still have Tiny."

"Yes, but we can turn her *off*," Truman laughed.

Elena laughed, too. Feeling their unconditional acceptance, even if it was from afar, was just the encouragement she needed. Secretly and selfishly, she was thankful that she didn't have to feel like Austin, who had so many questions about his father and no one to answer them.

■■■

In the next few days, the students at Grimsby were in panic mode getting ready for their third quarter exams, which covered yet another five hundred years of history. Elena spent every day and night after classes prepping a detailed timeline for the Amorite conquests, studying the historical significance of the Minoans in Ancient Greece, reviewing the records from the First Babylonian Dynasty, and following the ancestral progression through the Shang Dynasty in China. The frenzy of studying caused a more than usual crowd of students to flock to the Media Lab each day.

"Oh-wah! Every seat is taken," Abria said after Elena followed her into the Media Lab one particular afternoon. "I just need one of those plush chairs if I'm going to get any studying done." She looked disgruntled for a moment, and then exclaimed, "Oh look! There's a cute guy in that chair. I'll go persuade him to move."

As Abria moved off in one direction, Elena and Fergie set off in another through the low buzz of noise as students quizzed each other. Eventually, they found Declan and Pigg studying together at a table.

"Hey ladies, we saved you seats," Declan said, standing to pull out their chairs.

"Where's Austin?" Elena asked.

"Hello to you, too," Declan said. "You'd think you could be a little more appreciative. We did have to beat others away from stealing these seats."

"Oh, thanks for the seats," She replied distractedly as she opened an Optivision screen. "Do you know where Austin is?"

"One track mind, this one," Declan said to Fergie, who smiled and sat down rigidly. "Hopper called him into a meeting. He'll be here soon."

Elena selected the Historical Analysis lecture notes from the options and gazed at them absentmindedly. Even though she knew she needed to study, she couldn't get her mind off their most recent classes with Marshall. If their exam in Basic was even half as hard as their lessons had been lately she felt that it was impossible to pass unless Austin was their leader. But how could they make him the leader if the Lieutenant was chosen randomly?

Just as she decided she would sit down with him to talk strategy, she startled and looked up to see a that Telecaster had arrived at their table.

"Elena Ransom," the hologram said. "Report to the Headmaster's office immediately."

Fergie and Declan eyed her and shared a wary smile.

"Do you think they found out about our little break-in?" Elena whispered.

"We broke into the Vault ages ago," Declan pointed out. "Why would they bring it up now?"

Elena shrugged and slipped her Smartslate into her carrier bag. Her mind was racing as she climbed onto a Grimvator and started sideways toward the Headmaster's office. She could be in trouble for anything, really. Plus, she and Austin had snuck out so much past curfew they could have been caught on surveillance by now.

Suddenly, Elena realized that she didn't want to be expelled from school. She'd spent so much time complaining about the work load, Marshall giving her a hard time during Basic Training, and Abria's incessant talking that she hadn't even realized that she actually liked Grimsby. She had grown fond of her Instructors and loved spending time with her friends. Her friends! She actually had friends. Fergie with her honest words and the hours they spent studying together; Abria's friendly, unassuming personality; Declan's toothy grin and Simulab challenges. She was going to miss them.

—

CHAPTER 17

Elena knocked lightly on Headmaster Bentley's door hoping not to be heard, but then it slid open abruptly. The Headmaster was sitting at his desk, an imposing figure with an unfriendly face and a high-necked collar that made even Elena feel suffocated. This was the first time she'd seen him up close.

His face was perfectly framed with a strong jaw, and his features were so precise that they looked like they were stenciled on. Elena remembered feeling welcome and warmth the first time she'd entered Hannibal's office, but the Headmaster's office was rigid and formal, with his behavior almost mechanical.

Hannibal was standing to the right of the Headmaster, and Hopper was standing to the left. Elena knew that something was very wrong, especially as Austin turned toward her from the chair in front of Bentley's desk. They were all somber with grave expressions.

"Miss Ransom, please come in and sit down," Hannibal said kindly.

"This is it," she thought, trying to swallow the growing lump in her throat as she took the seat next to Austin. She would just have to convince the Headmaster to let her stay, but images of the coming expulsion and her parents' disappointed faces flashed across her mind. She could feel the Kairos bumping against her pounding heart.

"Miss Ransom, this is difficult to say," Hannibal began slowly, looking her in the eye. "And under the circumstances might be more appropriate coming from a family member, but it is not possible." He paused for a moment and then said, "We have received word that your parents have been killed in an accident."

After the words came out of Hannibal's mouth, the room filled with a deafening silence. Elena could not understand what he'd just said. Austin reached for her hand, but she pulled away.

"Excuse me?" she coughed, blinking back tears that burned her eyes.

"It happened earlier today," Hopper spoke softly. "Their Speedster collided with a pedestrian transport vehicle. It was quick. They didn't suffer."

Elena scanned the room with her eyes without moving her head. Hopper and the Headmaster were looking at the floor; Hannibal was looking at her with pity in his face. Austin reached for her hand again.

The Headmaster moved his arm, almost robotically, and accessed a holographic image. "It appears that custody has been granted to Mr. and Mrs. Stephen Haddock."

Elena was only partly registering what he'd said. A mistake had been made. She had plenty of years left with her parents. She suddenly felt a swell of emotion, thinking about her mom's laugh and the way her dad called her "Sunshine." Without speaking, she stood up from the chair.

"We understand that you are upset," Hopper said, moving toward her. "We've made arrangements for you to..."

But what the arrangements were, Elena never found out. She took one last look at each of them and then bolted out the door. She ran down the hall and jumped onto the first Grimvator. The box seemed to move slowly, suffocating her, and there was an unfamiliar ringing in her ears.

When the Grimvator stopped, she burst through the doors into the main foyer and gasped for air as if she'd held her breath the entire way. The fresh air made her momentarily dizzy. But then she ran out the front doors. She hurried across the courtyards and fields, around the edge of Grimsby's boundaries, and through the tangled trees.

Hours passed as she jogged through the forest. Hannah's face was forefront in her mind. Her mom had always been so loving, generous, and graceful. Elena thought about all the times they had run together, and the talks and laughing late into the evening when her dad had to work late. Her dad. Elena's heart swelled until she thought it might burst as she remembered Truman. He was always telling her something important, always reading to her and asking her questions to make her think.

The sun was setting, but she continued on. Anytime Elena felt tears, she ran harder, burning off her emotions, disappointed expectations, and her uncontrollable loneliness. Soon, it would be too dark for her to see, but she didn't care. She felt a stabbing pain in her heart that she'd never had before. Half conscious and half numb, Elena pursued the forest with an unrelenting, unrestrained furor.

Just before darkness consumed every inch of the forest, she found her way to the Firebird Station. Elena stopped finally, panting as she glared at the open door where Austin was leaning against the doorframe.

"I brought some dinner for you," he said like he'd been expecting her for quite a long while. "Come, eat and drink." He didn't reach out for her this time, but turned and walked inside.

Elena's mind did not want to enter, to be consoled, but her feet moved her forward until she collapsed heavily in her favorite chair. Austin handed her a flagon of water and she took several loud gulps. And then, there was silence, the space filling up with feelings that were felt between friends; feelings that did not need to be expressed with words. She could not eat, but took the plate that Austin offered her and stared into it, her suffering beyond overwhelming.

"So, this is how it feels," Elena gulped at last, a single tear creeping down her cheek. "To lose both your parents."

Austin sat next to her and put his arm around her shivering shoulders.

"There can be no consolation in this life for the loss of a parent," he said, so quietly that she barely heard him.

At his words, the loneliness she felt engulfed every part of her being. Elena began to sob on his shoulder, cries of desperate grief, sounds she'd never made before. And once she started she was unable to stop.

"Did you," she finally managed to say, "stay with the Headmaster after I left?"

"Just briefly."

"Did he mention..." she started, though she hated to ask, "where their bodies are being kept?"

"Lena, they didn't find bodies," Austin said somberly, drawing her closer. "Your parents were incinerated on impact."

At his words, a new wave of despair entered her heart. She would truly never see them again. Death had consumed every part of them. As she cried, she suddenly began to feel sleepy. The room seemed fuzzy and her eyes were blurry.

Hours later, Elena awoke with a start, feeling achy and thirsty. She sat up on her elbows and looked around. Her dorm room was oddly vacant. She rubbed her hands over her face, trying to recall the last thought she had before she went to bed the night before. And then, a wave of panic flooded her heart as she remembered the news that Headmaster Bentley had given her.

The bedroom door slid open silently and Austin suddenly appeared, carrying a tray of food on his arm.

"Morning," he said, coming close to her.

"What's the matter with me?" Elena said rubbing her eyes because her head felt fuzzy.

"Don't be mad," Austin replied. "But I figured it would be hard for you to sleep last night, so I put a sedative in your water."

Elena sighed. "So, I'm not remembering that wrong, then? My parents are dead?"

Austin nodded, his expression so distraught that Elena's heart ached even more.

"You need to eat," he said. "We're leaving in an hour for Atlanson."

Elena accepted the piece of toast he handed her and began to nibble, feeling numb.

"Where is everyone?"

"In class," Austin said. "We've been excused from taking the third quarter exams for now, although that doesn't really matter right now, except I didn't want you to worry about it. Abria packed your rucksack." He indicated her carrier bag on the floor. "Pigg's gonna meet us on the train."

Elena nodded, but didn't speak again until an hour later, as she stood on the Grimsby Channel platform. Pigg wrapped his arms gently around her neck.

"I'm really sorry," was all he could manage to say.

Elena closed her eyes as Pigg and Austin took seats on either side of her. As the train pulled away from the station, a new wave of sorrow swept over her. She was going home to a memorial service for her parents. Life would never be the same again.

"I'm so hungry today," Pigg said grumpily. "I think I'll go check to see if they plan to open the dining car for us."

Pigg leapt up and made his way for the next car. Elena watched him, feeling bitter that she didn't feel hunger. She couldn't feel anything except her heart breaking to pieces.

She gazed vacantly at the window and said, "I'm really gonna miss them."

"Me too," Austin replied, reaching for her hand. "You can cry. I won't tell *anyone.*"

Elena hiccupped a laugh. She'd cried so much already that it was almost senseless to cry anymore, but fear and anxiety rushed through her blood. Tears spilled down her cheeks as she rested her head on Austin's shoulder. As she sobbed, he wiped her face with the sleeve of his shirt.

"It's just," Elena managed to say between gulps of air. "I'll never see them again. It feels so lonely just saying it out loud."

"It's not fair that they're gone."

"I'm afraid to be *without* them."

"I know. But you won't have to be alone," Austin said in a soothing tone. "You'll stay with me."


Elena, Austin, and Pigg stood at the front door of her apartment for a full three minutes in silence before she actually scanned her Trademark and the door to her house opened. She stepped inside cautiously, as if she expected to encounter an intruder. Everything was silent and seemed so vacant. She held the Kairos in her fingers.

"Tiny," she called out hoarsely. "Tiny?"

Elena waited, but the Humanoid didn't come.

"Where could she be?" Elena wondered aloud.

Suddenly, a loud beeping noise sounded and Pigg fumbled through his pockets. "Sorry, sorry." he apologized profusely, pulling out his PocketUnit. "I wrote a Sensory Skulk application for my PocketUnit. It basically collects electronic activity readings from anywhere, like your house, your bathroom, the classroom...you know. I had it set on alarm mode, but I'll just turn that off now."

Elena felt tired just hearing Pigg speak. She sighed deeply and closed her eyes. "Could you leave me alone for a while?"

"Sure," said Austin, squeezing her shoulder. "I'll be right down the hall."

As Austin and Pigg turned to leave, the front door slid closed and Elena's feet carried her straight to Truman's office. She stood in the doorway a long time looking around. The room felt unwelcoming, like her dad's essence left when he died. Even the smell of his cologne had vanished.

Eventually, she stepped over the threshold and curled up in the armchair across from his desk. Her mind raced. Soon, Grandma Haddock would come check on her and give her details of the memorial service. Soon, Elena would have to endure a hundred people telling her how sorry they were about her tragic loss. Soon, she would have to begin packing up her old life to make way for the new.

But at that precise moment, she wanted nothing more than to talk to her parents one last time. She wanted to feel her mom's fingers running through her hair. She wanted to hear her dad tell one of his goofy stories. Fast and furious tears spilled down her cheeks. And, it was through her blurred vision that Elena noticed the family film diskettes stacked in rows on Truman's oaken shelves.

For as long as she could remember, Elena and her parents had spent one night each week watching family films together. Truman had been somewhat of a passionate filmographer, capturing all of Elena's major milestones. The films were stored on translucent diskettes, which fit into the scanner niche of any of the Optivision stations that were around the house for holographic projection.

Elena felt a small smile catch her cheeks. She *would* be able to see and hear her parents again because she had all the family films from her birth. She rushed over, grabbed as many of the diskettes as she could hold, and placed them on her dad's desk. She loaded one of the disks into a scanner niche that was built into the framework of the desk.

She expected a recording of her last birthday to appear holographically in the center of the room, but nothing happened. Disappointed, she loaded another disc, and then another, but none of them worked.

Elena turned the disk over in her hand and noticed something very strange. Her dad's insignia was missing from the bottom right corner. Truman had coded the outside of every diskette with his family crest, but none of the files Elena had pulled were marked.

She went back to the bookcase and pulled more files down, but none of them were marked either. Frantically, she tore every file from the shelves and checked each one, discarding them chaotically on the floor. When she was finished, she sat heavily back in the chair. Someone had been in her house. Someone had taken her dad's diskette files and replaced them with fakes. But who would break into her home? And why?

Elena sprang from the chair, and hurried over to the elaborate bookcase that stretched the entire wall behind her dad's desk. She pushed back the third emblem from the left. Scarcely daring to breathe, she inserted her finger into the hole behind the emblem. A moment later, a portion of the bookcase swung away from the wall, revealing the secret library.

Elena approached the desk across the room, blinking away tears as she opened a concealed panel. Her dad's diary lay there just as she hoped it would be. She looked at all the strange symbols on the front and remembered how her dad had entered a code to lock it. Feeling discouraged because she didn't know the code, she pulled the diary from the compartment.

However, at the touch of her fingers, she heard a small click of a lock. Feeling astonished, she opened the cover and read the words: *Ransom Dossier*. She turned the pages quickly.

Part of the book was filled with parchment, and detailed notes in her dad's handwriting. On the front and back cover there was a display screen with a keyboard of letters, digital symbols, and cryptic markings. Elena was at a loss for what the symbols meant, but she was sure of one thing: her dad wanted her to have this diary.

She flipped through the book again and noticed a mostly blank page, except for one peculiar marking that looked like her Kairos. She ran her index finger over the top of the marking and was surprised to see that ink began to fill in the blank spaces on the page until finally, a long letter written in her dad's handwriting appeared.

My Sweet Sunshine,

My desire is to explain to you all that is about to happen, but alas, I am not able to do so in this letter. I do need to tell you the most important aspects of our situation in the hope that you will be kept safe from those who mean you harm.

Elena, I am not a classified agent for the Chancellor. In truth, I am a Guardian. My specific job description is not important, but it is important to say that I am an emissary for a faction called the Renegades. We are actively trying to eradicate a ruler named Imperator from his supremacy over the human race. Imperator is in control of all the domed cities, and his control extends into other parts of the world, as well.

The Ransom Dossier is a book of my research for the Renegades. It also contains a database of evidence that I have furtively collected in an attempt to remove Imperator from power. I am not the only special agent assigned to this task. Dozens of officers are working on this case, protecting precious artifacts and finding clues.

Imperator is actively searching for Renegade agents and their children, but I changed our identities long ago, so you should be safe the rest of your life.

I know that this time will be confusing for you, but your safety is my top priority. You must stay in school. Grimsby is one of the only places where you will be truly safe. Your mom and I have also given permanent custody of you to Austin's grandparents in the hopes that you will be protected when you are away from school.

I will only ask one thing of you — please hide My Dossier in a safe place that only you know. And Elena, no matter what happens, do not try to interpret my Dossier.

Your mother and I are deeply sorry that we won't be there to watch you grow up, but we know you will make us proud. I love you, Sunshine. Don't ever forget you are loved.

Elena read these last words from her dad several times through. Then, she left the library and placed the diary on the desk in her dad's office. She accessed an Optivision screen, and it hovered in midair above his desk. She read through several of the last screens he'd worked on before he died. She wasn't exactly sure what she was hoping to find. Maybe a clue as to what she was supposed to do next? Truman Ransom's final words to her about doing *nothing* seemed ludicrous.

"How are you feeling?"

Elena looked up, feeling frantic, as Austin entered the room.

He looked around the demolished office and said, "I don't think that destruction of property is one of the stages in the grieving process, but if it works for you..."

Elena didn't say a word, but sank heavily to the floor atop a pile of the diskettes.

"What's the matter?" Austin asked, sounding alarmed. "You look awful."

"I have to tell you a secret," Elena said, but then she added, more for herself, "I can't let them get away with this."

"Let who get away with what?" Austin asked.

"My parents didn't die in an accident," she replied, holding up her dad's journal.

"Huh?"

"My dad was working to remove Imperator from power," Elena stammered. "Don't you get it? My parents were murdered by *him*." She handed the dossier to Austin. "Look at this and tell me if it reminds you of anything."

He began to flip through the book, and his eyes wide with disbelief.

"It's similar to the Alpha Manuscript!"

Elena nodded and then rubbed her index finger across the Kairos symbol on the otherwise blank page. She watched Austin read the letter that Truman left for her. An expression of understanding passed over Austin's face. They stared at one another for several tense moments. And then, an incessant pounding came from the front of the house, causing Elena to jump.

She started for the front room and noticed Pigg on the surveillance monitor.

He was bouncing up and down on the balls of his feet, banging his fists against the door.

After Elena scanned her Trademark, Pigg burst through the entrance and exclaimed, "You have to come! I have an *emergency*...a food emergency."

"A food emergency?" Elena said, looking puzzled. "That doesn't even make sense."

"Pigg, we're tired right now. Can we help you with your emergency later?" Austin said briskly.

"No! I need you right now," Pigg insisted. "Please don't make be beg, because I'm not above begging at this point, but I really don't want to get down on the floor and hurt my back or my knees or my face. You know, in case I trip while going down and fall over incorrectly..."

Elena sighed and rolled her eyes at Austin, then said, "I'm fine. Let's just go see what he's talking about."

Elena tucked the Ransom Dossier into a rucksack and the three friends left the resident tower and hurried down to Sector 7 where Elena felt a rush of familiar pleasure as she sat down inside their crudely built clubhouse.

"Remember how I told you about the Sensory Skulk?" Pigg asked, holding his PocketUnit up for them to see.

"I thought you said you had a food emergency," Elena said skeptically.

"I just said that to get you out of the house because you two never listen to me when I'm being calm and rational. Like, remember the time..."

"Pigg!" Austin half yelled. "Tell us why you dragged us down here."

"Okay, okay," said Pigg, waving him down. "So, just a bit ago I was in my room and the Sensory Skulk kept making strange noises. I just figured it was malfunctioning so I started searching its memory module when I noticed it had registered a strange frequency coming from our building. Well, that really didn't make sense to me, so I researched the frequency and it was unregistered, which means that it can only come from an organization that has advanced technologies. So, I started analyzing the frequency and suddenly I heard you two *talking*."

Elena stared at Pigg, not comprehending a single word he said.

"Your house is bugged!" Pigg blurted.

"Excuse me? It's what?" Elena said.

"Bugged," Pigg repeated, but since she still didn't look as though she understood, he added, "It means that someone put electronic devices in your house to listen to every conversation. They can hear everything that is said inside the apartment."

"Who's *they*?"

"Well, that's the question, isn't it," said Pigg, consulting the PocketUnit. "Someone clearly wants to know what's going on inside your house, but who?"

Elena and Austin shared a deeply significant look. She knew exactly who wanted to hear what was happening in her house.

"Oh, goody," said Pigg derisively, and looking a little offended. "You two already have a secret about this, don't you? I'm always the odd man out."

"You're not odd," said Austin.

"Never mind that now," Elena said urgently. "Pigg, what are we supposed to do about the bug?"

"I'm working on that," said Pigg, who then hastily checked his watch. "I've got to go or Mom's going to have a conniption fit."

And before Elena or Austin had a chance to say anything more, Pigg was hurrying down the corridor to the Sector 7 exit.

# ▭ 18 ▭

## Disclosure

The following day, Elena sat on the edge of the guest bed in the Haddock house dressed in a black dress and shoes. She couldn't remember the last time she'd been in a dress, but the petticoat was itchy. Austin sat with her, holding her hand.

"Time to go, dears," Grandma Haddock called out from the front door.

Elena followed Austin gloomily through the house. Grandma Haddock had spent the previous evening decorating everything with flowers for the reception after the memorial service, but the cheery colors did nothing to improve her spirits.

They left their resident tower and made the journey to the Cathedral. The service felt oddly formal, as Elena imagined her mom picnicking on the lawn in the park. Or perhaps it would have been better to have the memorial in her dad's secret library, surrounded by hundreds of books he loved. The Reverend recited a sermon of sorts, sharing kind words about her parents' work and life. It meant less than nothing to her.

At the reception, Grandma Haddock forced Elena to greet everyone that came through the door. She'd never been to a funeral reception, but it was a strange sort of quiet loudness. The room was a buzz of whispered voices talking about a new extension added to a home; a recent bad hair cut at the new salon on Peachtree Street; a baby that was born; an investment deal that profited a lot of money. All Elena could think about was how she was an orphan now and that these were not her people.

"I've got to get out of here." Elena told Austin after she'd finally been able to get him alone. "Can we *please* go to Sector 7?"

"Sure, let me just grab my rucksack," Austin said.

"I'm coming, too." Pigg arrived at Elena's side. "I've got something to show you."

Once inside the clubhouse in Sector 7, Pigg removed a translucent square diskette from his pocket, and declared, "This is the sound track of your life."

"What's it do?" Elena asked.

"It makes fake noises. I just slip this beauty into the Optivision niche in your living room and," Pigg clapped his hands in triumph, "we have the shower running, people talking, and the sound of cooking in the kitchen, among other things. This way, when you're home from school the people on the other end of the bug will think you're being normal."

"What if they have surveillance in the apartment?" Elena asked. "Won't they be able to *see* that I'm not in there?"

Pigg made a face like he hadn't thought of that. Then, he sighed and mentioned something about going back to the drawing board. Before Elena could blink, Pigg was headed off back through Sector 7, no doubt going back to design something suitable for Elena's apartment.

"I'm glad he's on our side," Elena told Austin. "But sometimes he's a little spastic."

Then, she began to feel dizzy thinking about all that she'd discovered in the past few hours. Her house had been raided, her dad's files had been stolen, her house had been bugged, and whoever was listening on the other end knew that she knew about Truman Ransom's secrets.

"Our parents *were* murdered by Imperator," Elena said slowly. "He was searching for my parents. And my dad's dossier proves that he was working against Imperator. Your father must have truly been working against him, too. I wish we knew who he was or how to find him."

Austin sat down heavily in a chair. "I wonder if my grandparents know if Imperator killed my father? I guess it's not like I can ask them."

"Imperator must want us alive for some reason," said Elena.

"Why do you say that?"

"He has some kind of surveillance in my apartment so he heard me tell you about my dad's job; yet, we're still alive. If I were him, I would have beat the door in to capture us," said Elena. "I can't take the Ransom Dossier back to my house."

Austin considered this for a moment and then said, "Let's leave it down here and then get it before we leave for school."

Elena nodded.

"When we get back, I'll hide the Dossier in the Firebird Station. No one will ever find it there." She rubbed her eyes in frustration. "This is so confusing. I'm so mad at him."

"Who?"

"My dad," Elena said through gritted teeth. "Why didn't he leave me some better clues, or some idea as to what I should do next?"

"He doesn't want you to do anything next," Austin said. "He said so in the letter."

"Yeah, but he knew me. He knows that I would figure out they didn't just die in an accident and that I'd want to do something. You know I *have* to do something."

"Of course I know that. I feel that way, too. Maybe we could tell Hopper about the dossier. He knew our parents. Maybe he knows something about all this," Austin suggested. "We'll talk to him as soon as we get back."

Elena fiddled with her nails and, feeling tears well up in her eyes, nodded curtly.

On the seventh day of the week, Grandpa and Grandma Haddock escorted Elena, Austin, and Pigg back to the Grimsby Channel. Grandma Haddock made Elena promise that she would Telepost if she felt like she needed anything. She resisted the urge to ask if she could have her parents back.

Hours later, as the train pulled into the station at Grimsby School of the Republic, Elena wished for nothing more than to return home and curl up in her dad's study.

"I'm going to put my stuff away and find something to eat," said Pigg the moment they stepped off the train. "Austin, do you want me to take your rucksack to our room?"

"Yeah, thanks," Austin replied, handing his bag over to Pigg, who scurried away quickly. Then, turning to Elena, he asked, "Are you sure you want to do this?"

Elena looked at him somberly and nodded.

"Alright," Austin said. "I'll go get Hopper and meet you in a bit."

After Elena arrived at the Firebird Station, she searched a long time for the perfect hiding spot for the Ransom Dossier. She considered putting it inside a piece of furniture, under a cabinet in the kitchen, and behind one of the shelves in the Research & Development room. She finally settled on a crevice of hollowed out rock just to the left of where the Independence sat motionless. She found a loose stone to place over the mouth of the crevice and then stood back to admire the camouflage.

When she was certain that no one else could ever find it she returned to the common room and noticed that Austin was just arriving with Hopper behind him, looking serious.

"Elena, I'm glad to see you. Have you eaten?" he asked, gesturing to a bag he was holding in his right hand. "I brought some toast and cheese and..."

"My parents were murdered," she interrupted him.

Hopper stood very still, unblinking, so it was impossible to tell what he was thinking.

Austin looked at Elena and said, "Good job easing him into the conversation."

Elena simply stared at Hopper, unmoving.

"Hopper, Elena *thinks* that a ruler of some kind, named Imperator, murdered her parents," Austin explained further, "because her dad worked for the United Republic."

Hopper surveyed them both with curious eyes. Then, he walked over to one of the chairs and flopped down in it like he had done it many times before.

"Elena," Hopper said gently. "I understand that you are upset."

"I'm not upset," she lied.

"But your parents died in a collision. I saw the news report. You can watch it if you want."

"I don't care what the report said. My parents were murdered, and I'm going to find out why." Elena took a deep breath. "Look, we already know about the Renegades, my dad's work, and Imperator so you can't trick us. But you *can* help us."

Hopper stood up and paced, his curly locks bouncing off his shoulders. Then, he sat down heavily in the chair again. He considered Elena for a long while, and she stared back at him.

Finally, he spoke in an earnest tone.

"Dudes, I could totally get fired for talking to you about this, but I know how hard it is to lose a parent. Look, Grimsby is not *exactly* an educational school."

Elena felt confused, but tried not to react. She cut her eyes at Austin, but he looked just as puzzled as she felt.

"It's more like a *training facility*."

"Training?" Elena said, her voice betraying the composure she was trying to portray. "For what?"

"For resistance against Imperator."

Elena sat down, waiting for him to explain more.

"For about twenty years now, Grimsby has trained teens to become adults that are capable of using their skills to one day overthrow Imperator and his army. You learn this more each year you are here, although this is all done in a subliminal way," Hopper explained. "It's one of the only ways we have to protect our culture from complete invasion."

Elena sat motionless as a sense of understanding began to swell in her mind. She thought back to the classes she'd taken over the past year. The Basic

Training and survival techniques had been interspersed with mental conditioning, historical preparation, and strategic development. And though the other classes seemed normal, she realized that she was being educated in matters of social customs, global translation, and cultural etiquette.

"This isn't coming out right, dudes," said Hopper after observing their confused faces. "I should start at the beginning."

Hopper positioned himself on the edge of the chair with his forearms resting on his knees.

"Around 2200 A.D. there was a world wide famine. It was brought on largely by the shift of the earth's position in the galaxy. Earth had increasingly gravitated closer to the sun, thus changing the temperature of the ocean. Eventually, this caused extreme weather conditions throughout the globe. Water sources began to evaporate and there were long periods of drought.

"People everywhere were scared and starving, so it was proposed that a World Government be created to help dispense the basic necessities of life.

"Twelve Judges were elected as the leaders of the new world government. They were given supreme power over everything and everyone on the earth. Every person was required to become a *World Citizen*." Hooper used finger quotes to accent. "Everyone thought it would be so great: global division of wealth, international healthcare, universal religion, worldwide law...global life. No one guessed that it would be the ultimate demise of the world's economy."

"Why would that ruin the world's economy?" Austin asked. "It seems like it would be helpful to be a world citizen, especially during famine."

"That's what our ancestor's thought, too. But creating a world without poverty and suffering takes a lot of money. The Twelve Judges imposed exorbitant taxes on the wealthy people to pay for the poor. Then, they skimmed whatever they wanted off the top."

"But that's wrong," Austin said.

Hopper shrugged and said, "Every government from the beginning of history has stolen from its people. The people in power steal from the citizens to get wealthy and then oppress the nation they have sworn to protect."

"So, what happened next?" Elena asked, eager for more of the story.

"Eventually, the money ran out. There were too many mouths to feed and not enough people contributing to the bank." Hopper laughed bitterly. "So, they did the only thing they could do. Genocide."

Elena gasped and clapped her hand to her mouth.

"One of the Judges, Imperator, convinced the other eleven that in order for the human race to survive they would have to create one master, perfect race of people. Together, the Judges launched the largest attack on human life in history.

"They started the process over twenty years ago. First, they created a new regime that they called *Oligarki*. They developed hundreds of thousands of android soldiers, called Droidiers, weaponized them, and convinced the world that having robot soldiers would create peace throughout the world.

"The Oligarki spent years slowly disposing of humans through accidents, food supply contamination, and petty civil wars so that they would have time to build the domed cities for the lucky 'chosen' ones.

"Hannibal and a few other people, including your parents, realized what was happening. So, Hannibal began to change Grimsby's curriculum so that he could train you kids for the resistance.

"Then, a little over ten years ago, the domes were complete and the Oligarki could finally enact their plan. They infected people with the Kearney Virus, a lethal disease that is spread through basic human contact, like breathing. Within three months, half the world's population was dead.

"The majority of the people who were miraculously immune to the virus were rounded up and executed by the Droidiers.

"Then, with the world's population reduced to just half a million people, Imperator had the other eleven Judges executed. Imperator declared himself supreme ruler over the earth.

"The people who survived were sent to live in one of three cities that were built to hold humans: Atlanson, Galilee Province, and Crowfield Plantation. Then, Imperator destroyed all the historical records that he didn't want studied by humans, making sure to destroy anything pertaining to the genocide so that future generations wouldn't know what happened."

---

"But, how could they disguise a genocide like that? People must have known what was going on and remembered it?" Austin said.

"Ever heard of the *Great Drought*?" Hopper asked.

Elena and Austin nodded their heads.

"There was a drought, yes, but it wasn't severe," Hopper explained. "The Great Drought is a cover story for the truth. Imperator created the lie to explain why people had to go live inside the domes. He *said* it was protection against the wide spread disease that had killed all those people. And, since earth's resources were diminishing because of the sun the people didn't complain.

"After that, Imperator gave a speech that was broadcast to the new cities, relinquishing his power. He described a new government called the *United Republic*, which gave power back to the people. Then, he introduced the newly appointed Chancellors of each city and said they would help maintain law and order."

"If he relinquished his power, then why..." Austin started, but Hopper interrupted him.

"Imperator *said* he relinquished his power to the new city states, but in truth he kept the Oligarki forces under his control. And after the Droidiers secluded people in the domes, Imperator was guaranteed ultimate control over the entire human race, secretly holding everyone in slavery to his power."

"I have been living in Atlanson all my life and I'm not a slave!" Elena yelled.

"You're not?" Hopper questioned. "Are you sure about that?"

Elena's brow furrowed and she shook her head stubbornly.

"Have you ever used your Trademark before?" Hopper said with bitterness in his voice that Elena had never heard before. "Have you ever gone to the store and spoken with a hologram? Have you ever used public transportation?

"All of those technological advances exist for Imperator's personal use, so that he can know what everyone is doing at all times. He even controls the birth rate through Healing Surgeons, like your mother. Most men and women are forcibly sterilized after one live birth is recorded. But sometimes, nature finds a way. The Healing Surgeons are required to dispose of any other babies against the parent's will."

"My mother would never do that!" Elena shouted, feeling hot in the face.

"No, no, calm down," said Hopper. "Hannah didn't murder babies. That's *why* she became a Healing Surgeon, so she could save them.

"Since the law states that each family can have only one child, Hannah kept women who had second pregnancies under hospital quarantine. Then, she sent the newborns to safe colonies outside the domes where they would never receive a Trademark implant."

Elena suddenly remembered her mother's words: *Sometimes people do jobs in life that aren't perfect in order to bring some decency to the wrong that is being done.* She felt suddenly foolish and sick to her stomach.

"What are *safe colonies*?" asked Austin.

"They are pockets of people that miraculously survived the genocide. They live outside the domes in secret cities around the world. They can't be tracked because they don't have Trademarks."

"This is a great history lesson, and all," said Elena abruptly, "but what does all this have to do with my parents' murder?"

At this, Hopper stood and helped himself to a glass of water, looking as if he didn't want to say any more.

"Tell us about the Renegades," Austin asked suddenly.

"Ransom, your dad was one of the key Renegade leaders. We built communication bases, like this Firebird Station, all over the globe to keep in secret contact with each Renegade group.

"When the global economy finally failed and the mass executions started, your parents adopted aliases and went into hiding so they could continue leading the rebellion against Imperator.

"Eventually, Imperator discovered that there were rebels. He won't rest until he has put down all the Renegades and their children. It's unclear whether or not Imperator knows your names, but we have a plan in place to send you into hiding in case your safety is jeopardized."

"Wait...if all this history was erased, along with everything that incriminated Imperator, how do you know about it?" asked Austin.

"The Renegades kept the true records written in a series of secret diaries. Each Renegade had their own dossier that included an entire historical archive, plus any extra research they worked on individually."

"What's the research for?"

"The Renegades are searching for a way to remove Imperator from power using unique artifacts."

"What artifacts?"

"Well, for instance, at the beginning of term Hannibal told me there was a special student in the Firebird Unit. He said that the kid's parents were Wardens for the Oligarki. A Warden was the highest level of secrecy job you can get, except, these parents were also Renegades.

"This couple had created an Amulet, something that was supposed to be instrumental in helping us remove Imperator from power, but no one knew where it was hidden. Hannibal told me that I was supposed to protect this kid," Hopper finished.

"Who?" Elena almost demanded.

"Declan Bowen."

Elena gave Austin a significant look.

"Declan's dad, Charles, passed intelligence and classified documentation from the Oligarki to the Renegades." Hopper let out a deep sigh. "When Grimsby gets new students each year, the selection of each Unit is supposed to be random. But your selection was not. The twelve of you were specifically assigned to the Firebird Unit."

"Even Wheeler!" Elena ejected, sounding revolted.

"Well, once in a while you get a bad omelet," Hopper said dismissively. "But my point is, you each serve a very specific purpose, and that's why you were assigned to Firebird."

"What purpose is that?" Austin asked.

"I don't know. I'm not even supposed to know that you were all hand selected to be Firebirds. I actually found out by accident," Hopper replied.

"But, how is an artifact supposed to remove a ruler from power?" Elena scoffed.

"I don't know," Hopper admitted. "I don't know what the artifacts are for, or how many there are, or why it's all secret. I just know what Hannibal and the Headmaster have told me."

Austin paced the floor for a few moments and then turned to Hopper and asked, "What should we do?"

"I can't recommend that you do anything," Hopper said, standing to stretch. "You are at Grimsby so we can keep you safe from Imperator."

Elena pouted, feeling mutinous.

"But..." Hopper grinned from ear to ear, "fourth quarter break is coming up soon. A person could find out where this Amulet might be. And maybe this Amulet could help explain why certain murders have occurred.

"Also, there is a beautiful hovercraft in the back room that should work. A hovercraft that is untraceable," Hopper continued conversationally. "I know it's untraceable because I helped build it."

"But we can't get inside," Austin said.

"Oh, that's easy," Hopper said dismissively. "Did you dudes find the Broadcasters?"

Elena and Austin nodded.

"Well, each Broadcaster has a Touchdot with a key to the Independence inside." He stood and stretched. "However, I have to warn you, taking that hovercraft would be highly reprehensible behavior, and may warrant an expulsion from Grimsby if such a person were to get caught."

Hopper made his way toward the Station door and said, "Sorry to lay all this on you and leave, but I have a feeling you two have a lot to discuss."

But Elena and Austin didn't talk. They immediately grabbed a Broadcaster from the Research & Development room, and hurried through the narrow hallway into the hangar toward the Independence.

Austin held the Broadcaster up toward the hovercraft, and said, "Let's see if this really works."

Elena watched a Touchdot shoot out toward the hovercraft. Then, an Optivision screen appeared in midair. She and Austin searched through several files.

Finally, he said, "I think this is it."

At that moment, a staircase automatically unfolded from one side of the hovercraft. Elena and Austin smiled at one another as they raced to the top of the stairs.

"Wow!" Elena breathed as the entered a grand atrium with a dozen hallways leading away from the door. It was a difficult decision, but they determined it was best to search the hovercraft together.

Winding quickly around the halls they found a command bridge, a wing of dormitories with adjoining washrooms, a galley with ample table seating, a cargo bay stocked with dozens of crates, an engine room, an observation lounge, an extendable docking port, a room of exercise equipment, and a vehicle distribution center with rescue evac-shuttles and a dozen hover-rickshaws.

"We'll have to ask Declan about the Amulet that Hopper mentioned," Austin said after they'd explored the Independence to the fullest extent.

"What if he doesn't know anything about it?" Elena asked as they climbed the stairs out of the hangar.

"Then, we'll get Fergie and Pigg involved to see if we can do some research on the thing."

"I don't think we should tell them *everything* Hopper told us. It would only frighten them, especially Pigg. And, I don't want to tell anyone about the Ransom Dossier."

"That's your secret to tell," Austin said plainly. "How about this? We'll tell them a shortened version of what Hopper said. You know, just enough for them to see how important it is for us to know more about the Amulet."

Elena nodded. For the first time since the death of her parents, she felt a deep sense of stillness. Even though they were both orphans, she and Austin were making plans for their future. To her, this meant that she didn't have to succumb to depression, but she could choose to move forward into what would become her life without her parents. She realized she still had a purpose, something extremely important to live for. Revenge.

# Working with the Enemy

Later that afternoon, as Austin and Elena sat in the main apartment of the Firebird Station, the door opened and Pigg, Fergie, Declan, and Abria arrived looking sad.

"We heard what happened to your parents," said Fergie sullenly. "We are grieved for your loss."

Elena felt a dull, stabbing pain in her chest. She blinked quickly and swallowed hard. "Oh yeah…thanks."

Abria surveyed Elena's face, but when she didn't say anything else, asked, "Aren't you, like, upset? I know my parents died before I could technically remember them, but if they'd died now I would be totally devastated."

"My parents didn't die," said Elena angrily. "They were murdered."

Elena and Austin took turns telling their friends portions of the story Hopper had told them, but they left out details about the Oligarki and how the Renegades are still being hunted by Imperator. They spent most of the time talking about how Imperator was looking for an artifact called an Amulet. Finally, Elena and Austin added some theories and ideas about what happened to their own parents.

When they were finished, Elena looked specifically at Declan and said, "So, we were wondering if we could speak to your parents about this Amulet that Hopper told us about?"

Declan gave Abria a significant look and then were silent for a moment.

"We wouldn't ask unless it were very important," Austin implored, after seeing the looks of distress on their faces.

"You won't be able to talk to them," Declan stated.

"Declan's parents have Katatonia," said Abria, wiping a tear from her cheek. "They're never fully conscious. When we go see them, they just sit and stare." Fergie reached out and put her arm around Abria's shoulders. "They're at an assisted living facility back home."

At this statement, something snapped in Elena's brain. She had a distinct memory of a medical journal in her dad's study, which wouldn't have been significant had it not been for Elena's grandmother who had pioneered developments in the human brain. Grandma Ransom had discovered how to reconnect or transplant nerve endings in the brain that had been previously damaged. This research allowed medical professionals to cure a variety of autoimmune disorders, bipolar disorders, schizophrenia, and Katatonia.

"His parents can't have that disease," Elena blurted. "It's impossible!"

Abria shrugged and said, "That's just what the doctors say."

Elena looked swiftly at Austin, but the look on his face told her to keep her mouth shut.

"Declan and Abria live with my family in the Galilee Province," Fergie stated in a formal way.

"Kenneth and Anne Foreman agreed to take us in after Declan's parents went to hospital," Abria sniffed. "We could always ask them more about our parents' condition."

"No, that's fine," Austin said soothingly.

"We can't ask my parents," said Declan suddenly. "But I think I know a way we could find the Amulet." He looked at Abria and smiled. "We could go home, to the apartment in New York City."

"New York City in the *United States of America?*" gasped Elena.

Declan nodded, and Elena and her friends sat in stunned silence.

"Are you, like, crazy?" Abria said to Declan. "What makes you think…"

"Listen, looking at the Alpha Manuscript brought back a lot of memories for me. I remember my dad writing in a book like that."

"You never told me that," said Abria.

"I didn't know it was important before now," shrugged Declan.

"Wait a minute," Austin interrupted. "Are you saying that your dad had a diary and it may still be in your apartment in New York City?"

Declan nodded again. "And that the diary may tell us how to find the Amulet."

"People are forbidden from entering the United States," said Fergie.

"Even if it wasn't forbidden, how could we even get there?" Pigg said.

"We have a perfectly good hovercraft in the hangar. Maybe we could break into Grimsby's central processing unit to take the maps we need to get there," Elena suggested.

The members of the Unit stared at Elena with their mouths agape.

Pigg coughed a little and with eyes watering, said, "Just choking back the vomit." Then, he held up a finger as if asking them to wait.

"We can't download something off the school's server. We would totally get, like, caught," Abria stated.

"No way," said Declan. "We broke into the Vault and haven't been caught."

"But that didn't involve us *stealing* something off the server. We only *looked* at blue prints of the school. We *would* get caught if we tried to take maps," Pigg said.

"We could use a rogue agent worm," Fergie suggested to Pigg.

"What does that even, like, mean?" Abria asked.

"In short, it is an imitation worm that would deceive Grimsby's central processing unit into *thinking* that it is functioning like normal," Fergie continued. "Then, we would be able to download any information without detection."

"Pigg, does that sound like it could work?" Elena asked intently.

Pigg tried to avoid looking directly at Elena. He pursed his lips together and twiddled his thumbs while Austin examined Pigg's face.

"Look, Pigg, if you don't want to help us, you don't have to, but please tell us if you think Fergie's idea can work."

Pigg looked at Austin for a moment and then said, "Yes, it can work. But you'd need a very clever, high-tech worm written specifically for the mainframe that you'd be using."

Everyone, except Pigg, looked around hopefully to one another.

"If this works, we could actually get to New York!" Elena said, feeling elated. She had a suspicion that once they found the Amulet all their questions would be answered. And, she would know how to get revenge for her parents' murder.

"But isn't it nearly, like, a thousand miles to Manhattan?" Abria asked.

"In fact, it is more than one thousand seventy-five miles," Fergie corrected.

"May I be excused now," Pigg asked timidly.

Elena stood in front of him with eyes narrowed, and said, "Pigg, I swear, if you don't help us I'm going to pull all your toenails out one by one and then make you eat them."

"Ewe, that's totally, like, gross," Abria said.

"You can't do that," said Pigg, sounding skeptical, but then he turned to Austin and in a half whisper, asked, "She couldn't really do that, right?" Austin shrugged and looked away so he could hide a smile.

"Listen, it's one thing to break into a little school Vault. But trying to get to New York City is truly dangerous. It is *illegal* to go into the United States of America. We could be arrested, held without trial, tortured, not to mention the fact that we could be killed. Besides, Austin said I didn't have to help you."

"I don't care what he told you! You *are* helping us." Elena was yelling, but she didn't care.

"Lena, calm down," Austin cut in, grabbing her by the arm. "We'll leave the decision up to Pigg's conscience."

Everyone stared at Pigg until he was red in the face.

"Fine!" he finally exhaled. "But if we get caught, I am going to say this was your idea and I was coerced against my will."

After Pigg agreed to help, Elena felt confident that inserting a rogue agent worm into Grimsby's central processing unit would be easy work for Fergie and him.

However, their plans were put on hold because Elena, Austin, and Pigg had to take the third quarter exams that they'd missed by leaving school early for her parents' funeral. Plus, Instructor Booker sat them down to review the fourth quarter syllabus that they'd missed during their makeup exams.

"During the fourth quarter we are going to study the five hundred years between 1500 and 1000 BC." An Optivision screen with a timeline lit up above Booker's workstation. "You will remember the Indus Valley Civilization that began around 3300 BC and encompassed most of what was known as Pakistan in the twenty-first century."

"We learned that in the first quarter of school," Elena recalled.

"Precisely," said Booker. "This quarter we will study the collapse of their civilization in 1300 BC. We will also see how the Shang Dynasty flourished and ended in 1046 BC and the Kingdom of Kush in 1070 BC, which was an ancient African state developed in the Nile River Valley.

"Instructor Niva will discuss the content of the 1258 BC agreement between Ramses and the new Hittite king at Kadresh. The treaty was recorded in two versions, Egyptian hieroglyphs and Akkadian cuneiform.

"Instructor Copernicus will lecture on the mathematical equations that were used by the Egyptians during this period. And, Instructor Emerald wants to examine Phoenicia from 1550 to 300 BC. The Phoenicians had an enterprising maritime trading culture that spread across the Mediterranean during this era. They traded by means of a galley, a man-powered sailing vessel. Therefore, he is going to teach you about their seafaring achievements and the textiles they traded. You'll learn to harvest crops so you can simulate selling them by maritime trade.

"Instructor Hopper will lecture you in the Dorians' invasion of Ancient Greece, the end of the Mycenaean era, the New Kingdom of Egypt, and the Shang Dynasty in China."

Elena looked at Booker and couldn't help but feel slightly overwhelmed by this lengthy summary. However, later that evening Fergie presented all the notes that she'd taken during their classes and said that she'd help Elena with any of their studies. She couldn't help but feel appreciative.

In fact, Elena studied with Fergie a lot during the fourth quarter, and they were almost always alone. Elena had stopped going to the crowded Media Lab and preferred to sit in the silence of the girls' common room while she studied. In the evenings, as she was lying in bed, Elena took to absentmindedly fiddling with the Kairos while thinking of her dad and trying to figure out why his letter had specifically told her to not interpret the diary even though he'd left it for her to keep safe.

During free time on the weekends, she met with her friends at the Firebird Station to discuss their plans for getting to New York City. Fergie and Pigg had successfully, and without detection, downloaded the maps to New York from Grimsby's mainframe. Therefore, most of their time was spent working on details for the trip.

Declan and Abria studied the maps with Fergie so that they could give an approximate guess as to where their old apartment building was located. Austin sketched out different scenarios of what they might except once they were outside the domes. And, Pigg was put in charge of stocking the galley because he had expressly volunteered for the position.

As Elena helped him stock the pantry she noticed he'd brought dry cereal, powdered milk, cheese, crackers, bread, sausage, raisins, peanut butter, rice, trail mix, energy bars, chocolate, coffee, and tea.

"How did you get all this food?"

"Some of it I've taken from Hopper's stores in the Station. But, also, I've been sneaking into the kitchen every night with Austin and Declan," Pigg said. "I have enough here to last us four weeks, just in case anything happens and we can't get back. I refuse to starve to death or resort to cannibalism."

Elena smirked. "What's inside all the other cabinets?"

"Oh, the galley was already stocked with billycans, cooking utensils, and light weight base camp equipment. So, we should have everything we need."

They worked steadily until one afternoon, as they were all sitting in the command bridge on the Independence, Declan said, "I hate to point out the obvious, especially now that we've done all this work, but these plans don't really matter because number one, we don't even know how to get the hovercraft outside this cave."

"Actually, Pigg and I found the passcode to open the wall." Fergie quickly sat down in the navigator's chair and opened a holographic screen. With her face illuminated in blue, she selected a few different icons.

Suddenly, the floor began to vibrate under Elena's feet. She watched in awe as the rocks along the eastern wall began to swivel in a circular motion until eventually a hole appeared large enough for the Independence to pass through with room to spare. She felt that it was a truly marvelous achievement in engineering.

"That's wonderful, but you didn't let me finish," Declan said sarcastically. "We don't have anyone to operate the Independence, unless you also know how to fly."

"I can't believe we didn't think of this before!" Elena exclaimed, feeling foolish.

"Actually, I've been thinking about that quite a bit," Austin said. "We really need an experienced pilot for where we want to go." Then, with a meaningful look at Elena, he added, "You know what we have to do."

A look of dread passed over her face and she grumbled, "I'd rather eat all the mud in the Gauntlet."

Abria looked from Austin to Elena and then asked the others, "Does anyone else know what these two are, like, going on about?"

Fergie, not looking up from the Optivision screen that was hovering above the Touchdot, said, "They want to go ask Wheeler if he would be willing to drive us to New York City."

"No," snapped Elena. "Austin wants to go ask Wheeler if he'll drive us to New York. I want nothing to do with that."

"Elena, we know he can operate a hovercraft."

"We don't know if he can really fly the thing," Elena retaliated. "We only know that he was suspected of operating a hovercraft in that race in Harleston Village. Even if he really was there, I doubt any of the vehicles in that race were as big as the Independence."

"It can't hurt to go ask if he can operate one," Declan said.

"It could actually hurt a lot: our pride, our nerves, our secrecy. We risk
*everything* by including him on this." Elena folded her arms over her chest,
internally grumbling over the fact that her friends were encouraging some kind
of liaison with the boy she most despised in the world.

"Well, he scares me," Pigg interjected, his eyes scanning his PocketUnit.
"And he seems really dangerous, so it could be a liability to have him come with
us."

"Thank you, Pigg. You're the only one making any sense," Elena said.

"Lena, you know we at least have to ask," Austin said in the voice he used
often to point out that he was right.

"Well, I'm not going to be the one to ask him," Elena said stubbornly. "So,
you'll have to figure that out between the five of you."

She looked reproachfully at Austin, who said, "Actually, I think only Abria
and I should go. Anyone else might just annoy him too much." He looked at
Elena sympathetically and said, "Just wait here. We'll be back soon."

After Austin and Abria left, Elena rounded on Fergie and said, "I know that
you're going to say something profound about me needing to find something
good about that dimwit, but don't even try it. My mind was made up about him
a long time ago."

"As a matter of fact, I rather agree that he is a dimwit, and I wish we did not
require his services. But it seems we may be unable to proceed without him,"
Fergie said practically.

"You're not going to try and convince me that he has some kind of
redeeming qualities?"

"Would it matter if I did?" she asked, surveying Elena with an interrogating
look.

Elena felt exposed, as she often did when Fergie challenged her way of
thinking, and was relieved when Pigg interrupted.

"He put me head first in the toilet last week."

Elena gaped at him. "Why didn't you tell us?"

"He said if I told anyone he'd hang me by my toes from the rafters in the
Mess Hall," said Pigg, trying to make an excuse. "You know how much I hate
heights."

Elena sat in angered silence as they waited for the others to return with Kidd. An hour passed before the door to the Station opened and Austin and Abria arrived with Kidd following behind them, looking mildly interested in his surroundings.

"How did you talk him into coming with us?" Elena whispered to Austin, as she watched Kidd roam around the Station.

"We had to bribe him," replied Austin.

"What did you pay him with?"

"The hovercraft."

"What!" Elena exploded. "You just gave it to him?"

"He's the only one who can operate it. We had no choice."

Elena felt enraged as she watched Kidd strut around the Station. To her, he was an unwelcome beast. The others stared at him in silence. Kidd seemed to take pleasure in the fact that everyone was uncomfortable with his presence.

"It smells like stale bologna and feet in here," Kidd commented, as he leaned up against one of the kitchen counters. "So, where's this hovercraft? My fee for being your pilot is based on the condition of this craft."

"Right. Follow me," said Austin.

He led Kidd down the hall to the hanger in the back of the Station and the others followed slowly behind them.

"Wow!" Kidd blurted, rushing forward to touch the hovercraft. "This is a Romulus Shuttle, a forced propeller hovercraft. This is a beauty!"

"Wheeler, can you at least tell us if it will operate?" Austin asked.

"Give me a minute and I'll see," he replied gruffly.

Kidd climbed the stairs into the Independence. He took a long time inspecting every gadget, gear, and wire. Once in a while, Elena heard him gasp or laugh out loud in disbelief, and once he blurted, "This beauty has a steering column! Most ships only have an onboard guidance system."

Over an hour passed before he finally approached Austin.

"The Independence is in fine condition and I will accept it as payment. But, like I said, this ship gets its main controls from a private satellite. So, you won't have any navigation system, observation usage, communication structure, or weather guidance analysis, unless one of you geniuses has a satellite to link to."

"This will not present a problem," Fergie said, as she set a strange looking contraption in front of Kidd that was part sphere and part square with mirrored wings and shiny disks. "This is an Orbitor. Pigg and I have been rebuilding it for the hovercraft. When we are outside Atlanson, we will launch it into the atmosphere and derive our navigation from it."

"*Outside* Atlanson?" Kidd queried. "Where exactly do you want me to take you?"

"To New York City in the United States of America," Austin said.

Kidd stared for a full seven seconds and then said, "Did I just hallucinate or did you say you wanted to go to New York City?"

Austin nodded.

"Every time I talk to you people you either irritate me or say something completely unintelligent," Kidd said, rubbing his hands over his face in a way that indicated he was annoyed. "Perhaps you zoned out in kindergarten when the Instructor was explaining the reason why all livable cities have a dome, so let me enlighten you. The dome was built to protect humans from harmful elements. Have you never heard of a little catastrophe called the Great Drought? That event made it impossible to live outside the domes. The sun causes all kinds of health problems, plus there's barely any breathable air left. Also, the exits to the dome exteriors have twenty-four seven surveillance. In other words, for those of us who look confused," Kidd said, looking over at Abria. "It's impossible to get out."

"Few objectives in life are technically impossible," Fergie said. "Challenging and complex, yes, but not *impossible*."

"Oh, really, Brainiack?" Kidd scoffed. "How exactly do you plan to get outside without anyone noticing?"

"I'm surprised you don't know this, Wheeler, since you obviously come from the sewer," said Elena viciously.

"We're going to use the drain channel," Austin said. "The channel is primarily used for taking waste from the cities and allowing crews access to the outside for maintenance. Fergie and Pigg are going to design some kind of a camouflage so we can get out and back in without being detected."

After a brief silence, Kidd said, "I suppose that could work."

"Does that mean you'll help us?" Austin asked.

"Fine. So, who's the leader of this mission?" Kidd asked, his voice sodden with cynicism.

Elena's eyes narrowed in disgust as Austin asked, "Why does it matter?"

"While we're out in the land of the unknown, I just want to make sure that I know who to blame if a bad decision leads to capture, torture, murder, or cannibalism."

At this, Pigg leaned toward Elena and whispered, "Please tell Austin that we don't want him along."

"I'm the leader," Austin replied. "But we'll make decisions democratically."

"What? *Freckles* isn't going to be the leader?" Kidd said rudely, looking at Elena with a smirk on his face. "She did such a fine job leading our Basic Training exercises."

Elena felt like punching him.

"Wheeler, let's get one thing straight," said Austin authoritatively. "We already paid you for your services. So, you will treat everyone with respect or we'll find someone else to come along with us."

"I'd vote for that," Fergie said quietly.

"So, what should we, like, bring with us?" Abria asked, trying to distract attention away from the growing hostility in the room.

"We can't be sure of the climate, so we'll pack carefully with sensible clothing and shoes," Austin replied.

"So basically, no cosmetic bags, Blondie," Kidd said.

"There you go again," Declan said, standing up to get in Kidd's face. "Do you want to come or not?"

Kidd backed away from Declan and nonchalantly inspected the side of the hovercraft. "I'll come."

"Then, let's make that your last sarcastic remark," Declan said, building a fist.

"I am unsure that is a practical demand," Fergie whispered to Elena.

"Fergie, let's show them what we've done," Pigg said quickly.

Fergie and Pigg led the others to the Research & Development room. The walls were aligned with cabinets that Elena hadn't paid much attention to before, but Fergie reached inside one and removed a black suit and a multi-pocket vest.

"Pigg and I have our entire wardrobe planned. We designed these suits and tactical vests. They are fire resistant, water resistant, and are designed for optimum comfort."

"The tactical vests are light weight," Pigg added excitedly, grabbing it from Fergie's grip. "Each vest can hold a canteen, a change of clothes, and it's equipped with a light-weight parachute. But, most importantly, there is an entire compartment specially designed for storing food. See?" He unzipped one of the pockets. "This was my idea."

"With how much food you eat it's a miracle that you don't, like, gain any weight," Abria said, almost laughing.

"It's not a miracle when we've all be genetically altered to make sure we all have the same appearance," Elena said bitterly while thinking about how Imperator had imposed the laws that forced them to all look the same.

"So, we're going base jumping in New York City, are we?" Kidd interjected loudly.

"No," Elena said coldly, "But you never know if someone might *accidentally* fall off one of the skyscrapers."

"We did not create a suit for you because we did not know you were coming," Fergie said. "But we will get to work on it."

"Can't wait," Kidd said drably.

"Where did you, like, get all this stuff?" Abria asked.

"The Research & Development room was stocked with all the supplies we needed," Fergie explained. "Pigg and I simply made the required enhancements."

She gave them each the leather band with round faceplate.

"These are Broadcasters and should be worn on the wrist at all times. It will be our only means of long-range communication. Pigg wrote a program for the Touchdots and his PocketUnit that would allow us to track one other via Trademark."

Fergie opened an Optivision screen from the Touchdot and Elena watched it hover in midair.

"If you would each open an Optivision screen from your Touchdot then we will scan our Trademarks here," She indicated a place on screen, "on each device. This way we will always be able to track one another in case we are separated."

"I'm not scanning my Trademark in there!" Kidd said firmly.

"Why are you coming again?" Elena barked at Kidd.

"I want the hovercraft. This seems like an easy enough job to get what I want. That is, *if* I can tolerate *you people*."

"Maybe instead of coming with us you could go fly in one of those illegal races again and actually get expelled from school this time!" Elena half screamed. "Obviously your last attempt wasn't good enough."

Kidd smiled sinisterly. "I won't have to race again if I take you to New York. That's illegal enough to last me a lifetime, and I can take that satisfaction to the detention center with me, which is where we'll go if we get caught."

A few tense moments passed after this statement. Elena began to feel that they were truly making a mistake. If Kidd found the journey an adventure of a lifetime then surely they must be doing something dreadfully wrong.

Over the next few weeks, the Firebird friends spent as much time as they could at the Station making final preparations for their trip. Elena devised a lie to tell each of their parents so that no one would worry while they were gone.

Austin and she would explain to Grandpa and Grandma Haddock that she was still depressed over the loss of her parents (which was technically true) and that they'd like to go stay with their friend Fergie Foreman over break so that Elena wouldn't have to deal with the pain of being home. Pigg was instructed to tell his parents that he'd be staying with his best bud, Declan Bowen. Declan and Abria agreed that Fergie would ask her parents if the three of them could stay with Austin to help him comfort Elena in her time of grief.

When all this was settled, Elena swallowed her distaste for Kidd and walked out to the Independence to ask him what lie he'd need to tell his parents. She was not surprised to find him working on the command bridge inside the hovercraft.

Kidd had spent most of his prep time studying the hovercraft avionics. He often checked and rechecked the communications, navigation, flight control systems, collision-avoidance systems, aircraft management systems, radar and sonar, electro-optics, life support, altitude control, guidance systems, thermal control, and hyperdrive.

"Excuse me, Wheeler?" Elena said rather softly. She still hoped that she wouldn't need to talk with him.

"What is it now?" said Kidd gruffly. He was working underneath one of the Optivision lab stations.

"We've all made up excuses…or I should say *blatant lies* about where we'll be on fourth quarter break. I just came to see if you had something in particular you'd like to tell your parents?"

"No."

"Well, Austin and I are going to say…"

"What I mean," Kidd said impatiently after appearing from under the table, "is that I don't need to tell anyone anything about where I'm going."

"Oh," Elena said, her brow furrowing. "Why not?"

"That's none of your business, Freckles."

"Look, Wheeler," Elena said with irritation in her voice. "We're all in this together now, so…"

"Let's get one thing straight," Kidd barked. "We're not in this together. I'm being paid for my services. That doesn't include chitchat or personal anecdotes about my family life. Got it?"

"Fergie needs everyone to gather around the planning table." Declan had appeared. Elena wasn't sure how much of their conversation he'd heard, but from the annoyed expression on his face she guessed he'd heard everything.

Elena nodded, still feeling offended by Kidd's rude behavior, and followed Declan through the hangar and into the main Station quarters. The other Firebirds were already sitting around a holographic image of the drain channel exit near the underground entrance to Atlanson.

"Glad you could join us," said Fergie eagerly. "I was explaining again how we still have a problem with detection. The city exits have surveillance, but are observed at all times by machines. This means that the central processing unit will accept commands from my Touchdot, but if it observes the Independence it will take note of the craft and register a warning. I was planning to inform the central processing unit that we are performing maintenance to the outside structure. However, we do not possess a maintenance vehicle, thus making our exit problematic."

"If only we could be invisible," Elena grumbled.

"Invisible!" Pigg cried out, slapping his hand to his forehead. "Why didn't I think of that before? Elena, you're a genius."

"Obviously I'm not as smart as you because I have no idea what you're talking about."

Fergie jumped in excitedly. "We could use a Masquerade."

"That's what I was thinking," Pigg said.

"Yo, Brainiack and Big Ears. You want to fill the rest of us in on your little brain hemorrhage?" Kidd said.

"Wheeler, give the name calling a rest, will ya?" Austin said.

"A Masquerade is a device that utilizes a series of visual elements to bounce one image off another," said Fergie.

"And what does that, like, mean?" Abria asked.

"It means that we can project the landscape around us back onto the outer part of the ship, thus making it invisible," Fergie replied.

"Anyone looking in our general direction would think they were just looking at a street or a building, or a stretch of highway," Pigg said. "More importantly, we'd be able to project the image of a maintenance vehicle onto the outside of the Independence. There's a Masquerade in the Research & Development room. I'll see if it works."

Elena felt a sudden tightness in her chest. The trip to New York was coming together really well. Soon, they'd be leaving the confines of their homes and venturing out into the unknown. Her dream was coming true.

# ❑ 20 ❑

## The Final Exam

"I can't believe we've been here an entire, like, year already."

Elena looked up from the Optivision screen that was hovering above her Smartslate and stared at Abria, who was twirling her hair absentmindedly through her fingers.

"Do you guys think I should, like, cut my hair?"

Elena shook her head, feeling frustrated by the distraction. It was the first time that she'd ever studied over breakfast, but it was the first day of fourth quarter exams, so Elena was eager to cram any last information that she could into her head before Booker's test began.

"You know, you'd think they could set up this schedule differently so we didn't have to take tests on two *thousand* years of history in three days," Declan said gloomily as he looked up from his Smartslate.

Two examinations had been scheduled each day for the first three days of the week. This morning, the Firebirds and her sister Units would take Booker's exam in the morning until lunch time and then Instructor Niva's test on Phonology in the afternoon.

"If we have studied sufficiently we should have no trouble completing our exams with satisfactory scores," said Fergie.

After a year of knowing Fergie, Elena still couldn't understand how she could talk and concentrate on reading at the same time. Then, Elena looked at Pigg. She felt too anxious to eat anything but toast, but he had so much food in his mouth that he was continually on the verge of choking. Declan was whispering dates and events under his breath and Austin was sketching a tactical plan on his Smartslate.

"I'm mostly worried about the oral examination during Phonology. I mean, it's one thing to have to answer questions about the symbols, but it's quite another to try and speak in the...Austin," Elena said wearily after looking at his work. "We don't even have our Tactical exam for two more days."

"This isn't for the exam," said Austin, not pausing to look up from his Smartslate. "It's for, you know, something else."

Elena felt a sudden jolt of nervous energy about the upcoming trip to New York City. It was so far from home. What if they had trouble? What if someone got seriously injured? What if they couldn't get home for some reason? She wanted to learn more about her parents' work and the reason for their death, but not at the expense of her friends.

But before she could dwell on it, the bell sounded for the end of breakfast. The Firebirds made the short walk to Booker's classroom, and Elena sat tensely in her pupil station, tearing off some fingernails from her left hand with her teeth.

However, once the Optivision screen opened with her exam, she noticed that the questions were designed to help lead her through the hundreds of years of curriculum in an efficient way. Each question built on the previous one to promote a well-rounded, complete timeline of historical events.

Later that afternoon, Elena sat in her Advanced Phonology exam feeling nervous again because it was her hardest subject. Fergie had quizzed her on hundreds of vocabulary words, and they had practiced speaking to one another in different dialects for the oral part of their exam, but the test questions didn't build on one another as they had in Advanced Historical Analysis. In fact, she got stuck with the Akkadian language, her least favorite, so Elena finished the exam feeling that it hadn't gone well.

And it didn't help at all when, the next morning, Elena opened her AstroPhysics test for Instructor Copernicus and she realized that she'd again have to answer questions about the astronomical observations and terrestrial omens from the Akkadian Empire. She didn't take it as a good sign that she had to reread the second paragraph of the first question several times before she comprehended its meaning.

However, by the time Elena arrived at her Social Science exam she felt that all her harder exams were over. She easily answered questions about the demographics in Phoenicia, and she was able to describe their economy, trade route innovation, language and literature achievements, and their basic culture.

On the third morning of the week, Hopper asked Elena to draw a regional map of the Fertile Crescent and outline the rise and fall of three major civilizations from the first century. She began with ease, recalling details from Booker's exam to help support her map, but she was soon distracted by thoughts of what might be on the final exam of the day.

Elena wasn't sure why, but she literally feared the Basic Training examination. Perhaps it was because she had no idea what to expect, or it could have been because she now knew that any preparation they did was, in truth, training to defeat Imperator. She wondered how much of their exam would secretly be committed to preparing for his demise. Marshall's speech before the exam did nothing to comfort her fears.

"For your exam, your Unit will complete a field exercise that will challenge your physical strength, aptitude, and mental intelligence. One student from each Unit will be chosen at random to lead during the exam."

Elena held her breath while the Optivision screen flashed through a catalog of faces. Finally, it stopped and Marshall called out, "Austin Haddock is the Lieutenant for the Firebird Unit. Now, move on to collect your gear for the exam."

Elena rushed toward Austin, giddy with delight.

"I'm so happy it's you! It would have been awful to follow Wheeler into the exam. This is such a huge relief."

Austin was smiling, but not in a prideful way. "Come on." He threw an arm around her shoulders. "Let's go see what gear we need for this mission."

Elena and Austin arrived at an assembly area and found a table filled with black tactical vests. She picked through the pockets carefully and found a plastic poncho, one extra armorwear shirt, a water purification kit, one canteen of water, a first aid kit, a firestarter kit, a warning whistle, and a small hololight.

"Anyone else, like, nervous that there's a water purification kit in this vest?" Abria had joined them already wearing her vest. "I had to pull my hair up because this vest is so high on my neck. You know, I think I'll speak to the person that, like, designs these things and see if we can't come up with something that's a little more flexible for girls to wear."

Elena smiled and pulled her vest on, zipping it up and adjusting the straps until it fit perfectly.

"Firebirds!" Marshall barked. "Attention at the front."

Elena and the others moved together in forming lines.

"Lieutenant Haddock, are you ready to begin?"

"Sir, yes, Sir."

"Then, step this way through the door to begin your exam," Marshall instructed.

"What are my orders, Sir?" Austin asked.

"Your only order is to step through the door," Marshall said.

Elena swallowed hard and followed the other students through the door into their exam. They had entered the white walled classroom, but it wasn't until the entire Unit was inside that Elena realized how small the room dimensions were. She was pressed up against the tactical vest in front of her and someone was pressed up against her vest from behind. She was standing shoulder to shoulder with Fergie and Abria and she wasn't even able to move her arms. Then, the lights went out and a wall of glowing, green hieroglyph characters appeared.

Austin didn't even hesitate before giving out his first commands. "Foreman, what do you see?"

Fergie studied the wall carefully with her eyes.

"These appear to be Mesopotamian pictograms and cuneiform from around 2500 BC," she replied respectfully. She took a moment to scan the characters again. "We are observing some form of puzzle. Perhaps when we solve the puzzle we will know what step to take next."

"Anything to get out of this room," Austin said.

"I am unable to see the entire wall because of my limited range of motion. If I could have more room, I think that would help."

But suddenly there came a commotion from one side of the room. Several of the students were murmuring, and a feeling of panic filled up the already tight space.

"What is going on over there?" Austin said loudly.

"Pigg's gone to the floor and is pulling at his vest," Frankie Smiley called out. "Says he's claustrophobic."

"I can do some, like, cognitive therapy with him," Abria offered to Austin. "Hopper taught us a little bit about it during first quarter, and I was so interested in the topic that I asked him to give me some lessons after, like, class."

Austin looked very pleased to hear this.

"You boys along the back wall, lift the girls onto your shoulders to make more space in the room. And Frankie, tell Pigg we're sending Abria over."

Immediately, Elena could tell that girls were being hoisted into the air because the room felt a little less confined. She watched Abria's blonde head bob through the crowd. Then, she could hear Abria's tinkling voice talking in a soothing way.

"Hey Pigg, it's Abria. Can you open up your eyes a sec and focus on my face? Terrific. Now, let's get your vest off. That's good. Now, close your eyes and focus on my voice. We're not actually in this room. We're at school in a simulation. So, let's go somewhere else in your mind. Tell me about your most favorite food to cook…"

But how Pigg answered this question was drowned out by Austin's voice.

"Fergie, can you give me a status update on interpreting the pictograms?"

"I almost have all the individual characters translated. After we do, it is simply a matter of arranging them in the correct sequence," Fergie said. "Then, I believe we simply touch the icons in that pattern."

"Any idea what happens after that?" Austin asked.

"It is counterproductive to make assumptions at this point about what lies ahead of us, especially when we have not managed to decode the wall."

Austin nodded. "Point taken, keep going."

As it turned out, decoding the wall was a long, arduous process. Crosby Gamble and Olivia Nelson had come to Fergie's side to try to help her assess the wall. However, even though most of the pictograms had been determined within the first few minutes, there were plenty of characters on the wall that Fergie and the other two disagreed upon.

And, even though some of the boys were able to endure longs periods of time hosting a girl on their shoulders, the room began to feel small again. Elena's legs began to cramp from standing so perfectly still in one spot.

"If you can shimmy out of your vest I'll hold it for a while," Declan suddenly whispered in Elena's ear.

"No, I'm fine," Elena lied.

"Then, could you hold my vest for a while because I'm exhausted."

Elena looked at Declan with disgust and then noticed the playful grin on his face. She smiled and relaxed.

"I wish I'd paid more attention in Phonology so I could help," Declan said.

"Save your energy," Elena said dolefully. "As we've been standing here I've determined a few things. First, this exam is *not* going to be like any of the others. Also, I'm almost certain that each of us will be challenged academically based on what subjects we're best in and, most unfortunately of all, this is going to take a lot longer than any of the other exams."

"Listen up!" Austin shouted. "Form a row as close as you can to the back wall. Foreman, Gamble, and Nelson are going to enter the code."

Elena squeezed against the wall and watched Fergie press the first pictogram in the sequence. The character turned from green to red, but after that nothing happened, so Elena hoped that was a positive sign.

Then, Fergie, Crosby, and Olivia began to press the symbols along the wall in a slow, steady pattern. Twice the Firebirds were forced to construct a human pyramid in order to reach a cuneiform character that was higher up on the wall. Pressing all the codes in sequence seemed to take an enormous amount of time, but the moment that Fergie touched the last pictogram in the puzzle the holographic wall vanished and they all stumbled out.

Elena didn't have a second to be grateful for the impeccable skill shown by Fergie and the others because they'd entered their next task. They were standing in some kind of antechamber that was dark and had an astonishing representation of a galaxy moving around the walls, ceiling, and floors in such perfect motion that it was impossible to tell up from down. Planets, moons, stars, and constellations were displayed in a beautiful symphony of colors and light.

"How's Pigg?" Austin called out.

"Abria is helping him stand," Frankie Smiley called from somewhere Elena couldn't see. "He'll be alright."

Quite suddenly, a pedestal rose from a collection of stars. Austin stepped forward, and Elena watched him pull a paper-like object from a translucent box. He unfolded the paper tenderly and examined it for less than a second.

"It's a map," Austin said loud enough for everyone to hear. "Bowen, you're our best cartographer. I need you up front."

Elena watched Declan move toward Austin.

"Firebirds, hold the corners of the map stretched out so that Bowen can see the full picture," ordered Austin.

Elena obeyed at once, as did the others. After the map was entirely unfolded, it was nearly six feet wide. She held her hololight above the map to help everyone see better and noticed familiar terrain that they'd studied in Survival Strategies, but there were also many differently shaped symbols and notes that were written in cuneiform and Mesopotamian pictograms. She waited patiently as Declan and Austin reviewed the map.

"The map details our objective," Declan said. "However, the beginning of our course for this exam is not marked. Apparently, we'll need to read the stars, planets, or constellations to find our bearings."

"Which means you're up, Pigg," Austin said, clapping him on the shoulder. "You need to decipher the mathematical equation that will get us to the correct constellation patterns that lead us out of this void. If we begin in the wrong location then it's possible that we'll never reach the end of the exam, so you have to know for sure before we proceed."

With a blank stare, Pigg swallowed hard and his brow broke out in a sweat, but Austin laid a confident hand on his shoulder.

"Take your time, study the map for context, and we'll consult before we make our next move."

Elena could tell right away that this room was going to be much harder to decipher than the first room with the wall of hieroglyphs. For one thing, this room was changing; the stars, gasses, and planets were in constant motion. But, to Elena, the more pressing issue was that the Firebirds now had space to spread out, and spread they did. Some of the students had already strayed so far from the map that Elena could no longer see them.

Austin was busy consulting the map with Declan so Elena stood in between them and said firmly, "I need a word."

Austin seemed astonished when Elena interrupted them, but after noticing the look on her face he immediately stood off to the side with her.

"Austin, you've let them stray too far," Elena said. She was extremely anxious, but she tried to keep her voice calm. "I can't even see where some of the others have walked off. What if there's like a black hole or something in here."

Austin grabbed Elena's arm in an understanding and appreciative sort of way and then called at the top of his voice, "Attention, Firebirds! Everyone front and center for assembly right now, over here, near the map. Elena Ransom is in charge of sound off."

Slowly but surely, Elena saw the members of their Unit coming together in formation. She could see them clearly, but she called their names loudly and listened to the affirmations as the students replied to her. She was almost finished confirming that everyone was present and accounted for when she called out "Fergie Foreman" and didn't hear a reply.

"Fergie Foreman!" Elena called again. She stepped into the middle of the formation and saw an empty space where Fergie usually stood. "Fergie! FERGIE!" She was screaming now, but she didn't care. "Has anyone seen Fergie Foreman?"

But it was as if her question vanished in the vastness of space. She looked around at the other boys and girls and noticed that some of them displayed a vacant expression.

"Austin! Austin! I can't find Fergie and look!" Elena pointed at the others and Austin stared into their faces.

At Elena's command, Kidd stopped what he was doing and looked around at all the vacant faces.

"What's happening to them?" Kidd asked.

"They're being lost to the space," Austin whispered as he began to thumb the scar on his chin.

Elena knew that it meant Austin was desperate. He needed answers that he didn't have, but she couldn't see how spending time contemplating would help them in this moment.

Elena was practical. History was her favorite subject in school and she solved problems with facts. And the only physical data they had was printed on the map. She looked down at it, searching every square inch for something, anything that looked familiar to her.

She saw plains and fertile agricultural land. Then, her eyes found and followed the Tigris and Euphrates rivers into the Persian Gulf. And written in the sandy plains near the city of Babylon was the word *Ammurāpi*. Suddenly, the pictographs and cuneiform writing on the wall that Fergie had helped decipher was beginning to make sense.

"The kinsman is a healer." Elena had whispered, but Austin heard her.

"Yes, go on!" Austin said excitedly.

"*Ammurāpi* is the Akkadian word for Hammurabi, the sixth king of Babylon. He was most famous for writing two hundred and eighty two laws that were eventually called the 'Hammurabi Code.' But, more importantly, he was the first king during the Old Babylonia Period of history. During that time, stone tablets were inscribed, documenting the application of mathematics to the variation in the length of daylight over a solar year."

Elena and Austin arrived at the conclusion at the same time, and she saw a look of relief cross his face.

"Pigg! According to the constellations we've been given, calculate the length of daylight as would have been done in the Old Babylonian Period."

After Austin's request, barely a minute passed when Pigg pointed to a grouping of stars in the cosmos. Austin approached the constellation and pressed his palm against it. At first, nothing seemed to happen. But then, a maritime blue planet appeared in deep space. The stars began to spin faster and faster; the planet eased closer and closer.

Elena grew dizzy watching all the movement and shut her eyes until Declan screamed, "We'll be crushed!"

Elena's eyes popped open and she could scarcely believe it, but the blue planet had come so close that it looked as if it would land on top of them. She reached out and grasped Austin's hand, feeling certain they were about to meet their end. But the end didn't come.

Elena was falling through time and space, the planet absorbing the Firebirds into it. Then, the simulation changed and Elena was suddenly standing in the middle of a fertile valley with the Firebirds still in the same formation as she'd left them.

"That was totally, like, awful and I don't even want to finish this exam," Abria said loudly.

Elena looked around quickly and found Fergie standing quite a way from the others. She hurried over and hugged Fergie around the neck.

"Are you ok?"

"Yes, I am fine. My apologies," Fergie said. "I thought I had discovered one of the constellations we needed, but as I pursued it I was drawn into an area where I could not return. I could hear you and see you, but you could not see me."

Elena sighed. "Just try not to wander off again. If I lose you then I'll be forced to interpret Abria all by myself."

———

CHAPTER 20

Fergie smiled and walked with Elena back to the others, who were beginning to spread the six-foot map across the ground.

She took a moment to assess their surroundings. The Firebirds were standing on a hill overlooking a river and a walled city. The city was vast and impressive, with hundreds of buildings and a mountainous ziggurat.

"Firebirds! Sit under that tree over there and rest," Austin ordered as he pointed to a clump of foliage off to their right.

Elena was just about to pull off her tactical pack when Austin whispered in her ear, "Lena, I need a word."

As the others walked for the tree, Elena stayed at the map and Austin said, "We need to regroup."

In the daylight the map looked much different to her. She could see cities dotting the Tigris and Euphrates rivers; there were boats in the Persian Gulf harbor; she saw a tree standing alone in the desert; there was a mountainous region with strange looking animals. It was perfectly clear that there were many different targets on the map.

"Based on the script about Hammurabi," Elena said. "I think we're in the Old Kingdom of Babylon circa 1700 BC. But, the rest of the map is a giant riddle. How do we decide where we need to go?"

"We're going to have to ask for help," said Austin. "Do I have your support even if what we decide as a group doesn't work out and the others turn on me?"

Elena looked at him steadily. "You *always* have my support."

"Pigg! Foreman! Abria! Bowen!" Austin called out. "Front and center."

Moments later, their friends arrived and stood with them around the map; it was the first time Elena could ever remember that she felt grateful to be working in a group.

"We need help trying to decide where to go next," Austin said. "Will you help us study the map?"

Everyone looked down, and Elena watched her friends scan the map carefully with their eyes. Fergie was first to speak about the pictograms that were present on the wall in the first room they'd been in; Pigg was good at pointing out the details of how the constellations corresponded to particular points on the map; Declan was helpful in detailing the risks of each route based on the terrain. Once Austin had all this information, he talked with Abria briefly about the mental condition of the members of the Firebirds.

Then, with one last sweeping look of the map, Austin said, "We're headed toward the tree in the desert, here between the Tigris and Euphrates. But first, we're all going to sit down to have some water and a snack."

Pigg was already seated and pulling out a snack before Austin had even finished. The rest of the Firebirds joined them, and Austin carefully explained the details of what they'd be doing. As he spoke, Crosby Gamble and Kate Bagley began to make head coverings from the extra armorwear shirt that was stored in their tactical vest.

After everyone rested, Austin called the Firebirds to attention and they assumed a marching formation. At first, conditions were favorable for walking, except for the blisteringly hot sun. They moved along at a steady pace for an hour.

But then, a small sandstorm blew around them making everything difficult to see. There was absolutely no place to take shelter, so the Firebirds came together in a huddle, pressing up against one another with heads bowed toward the center. Elena kept her eyes shut tight and her nose down the collar of her shirt to try and keep the swirling sand from getting up her nose and in her mouth.

After the sandstorm calmed, Olivia began to complain that she had heat cramps, Pigg said he needed water and something to eat, while Vivienne asked if they could find a spot to rest.

"I'm pretty sure I'm having hallucinations," Crosby Gamble added. "Unless everyone else sees the pink camel standing over there."

Even Elena, at one point, thought she saw her parents running toward her from a distance.

At length, Elena began to see something on the horizon. As they marched closer, the shape began to take a specific form. And then, Elena could finally tell that a tree was growing out of the desert floor. She couldn't see a water source, but the tree was the widest and tallest she'd ever seen. Beautiful green leaves bloomed around plump ripened fruit. But easily, the best part about the tree was the shade that was all around the base.

"It's a mirage," Kidd said skeptically.

"It's not a mirage," Austin said. "The tree is on the map. We've found it! We can't be more than a mile away. Come on, we can do this."

Austin's rallying voice seemed to be what everyone needed and their pace picked up considerably.

In due course, Elena was a mere step away from the tree. She reached her hand toward the lush green, but then had to shield her eyes instead. A bright white light had pierced through the tree and blinded her so severely that it took a couple moments before she could that she was now standing inside a white-walled classroom. A murmur of outrage and distress filled the room.

# ▭ 21 ▭

## Outside the Dome

"You led us the wrong way!" Kidd shouted into Austin's face. "Why else would the simulation just turn off like that?"

"We've failed!" Olivia Nelson cried out. "After all that, we've failed."

"We haven't failed anything!" Elena blurted, her temper rising. "We don't even know what happened."

"It's not a big secret, Freckles," Kidd said. "Marshall told us months ago that the simulations are designed to turn off anytime we make a mistake. We've failed! I can't believe this!"

"Just calm down," Declan said loudly in Kidd's face.

"You calm down!" Kidd said, pushing Declan away from him.

Kidd Wheeler didn't even have a second to blink before Declan punched him square in the face. He fell back into the students behind him. He was getting up to fight back when a loud whistle filled the room.

"Firebirds will get into formation this instant!" Austin yelled after pulling a whistle from his mouth.

As Elena walked to her row, she could tell that some of the other students were moving rather reluctantly. But, Austin stood proudly, his command unwavering.

"We are *not* going to fight!" Austin stated after the lines had been formed. "We worked together on this exam so we're not going to point fingers now. Decisions were made in the best interest of everyone. Good decisions that are not going to be misdirected because of fear. We don't know what has happened, but we are going to stand here and wait patiently until we're informed about what to do next."

Silence filled the room, making Elena extremely uncomfortable because her mind began to fill with troublesome thoughts. Austin had done an impeccable job of leading them, but the exam had been stressful and annoyingly confusing at times. Making a mistake at any point during the exam would have been very easy to do, and one wrong decision did mean that they'd failed the exam.

Just as Elena was beginning to worry that someone had forgotten them in the simulation, the door to the white-walled room opened. Marshall stood in the doorway, calling them outside. They filed one by one into an atrium.

"Stand at attention!" Marshall barked. He stood before them looking irritated. "Firebirds! Congratulations. You have received top marks for this examination."

By the next day, all the grading for the year had been finished and their scores were posted. Marshall had explained that the last sequence in the Basic Training simulation where the scene changed instantly from the tree back to the white-walled classroom was specifically designed for the student in the position of the Lieutenant; to make sure that he or she could maintain control of the Unit when faced with exam failure. Because Austin had managed them well, the entire Aves Company had excelled on the fourth quarter exam and all received a passing grade.

"I'm so glad school is over for a while so we don't have to suffer under any more of Marshall's absurd and tricky assessments," Elena told Austin as the walked to the end of the year banquet in the Mess Hall.

In addition, the Firebird Unit ranked among the finest in the school, just as Hopper had hoped at the beginning of the year. The student rankings had been published by Unit and Company and, to Elena's surprise, she was marked third in her Unit, after Austin and Kidd, and seventh in the entire Aves Company.

But most surprisingly, as long as the first part of the school year had seemed, this last part was hurtling by with the speed of the Grimsby Channel. She wanted to enjoy the end of the year banquet with her friends, and the awards ceremony for top scores and ranking performance, but Elena could think of nothing but New York, and how she and her friends could be making a huge mistake in going there.


On the morning of departure day, Elena watched a simulated sun rise above the mountain as she sat in the girl's common room. She had been unable to sleep well during the night. After tossing for an hour, she decided to get up at 0500 hours to rehearse the plan again.

First, she would board the Grimsby Channel with Austin and Pigg. She would exit the train separate from the other two, with Pigg going first, and make her way down to the Firebird Station. Then, they would follow the Grimsby Channel to the sewer access tunnel from Atlanson.

She couldn't help but wonder if this plan could actually work. When they had planned the exit strategy as a group it made complete sense, but in the quiet of the common room it seemed beyond juvenile to the point of being ludicrous.

At breakfast, Elena sat with her friends in virtual silence. She noticed that Kidd was eating alone at a table. She pushed food around her plate, feeling unwell, and wondered if he would betray them.

Austin seemed to feel the tension at the table at once.

"Everything's going to be fine," he told them in a confident voice. "We've planned a good trip. We're smart enough for this."

An hour later, Elena said a quick "good-bye" to Declan, Abria, and Fergie as they climbed onto the train going toward the Galilee Province. Then, she followed Austin and Pigg on board the Grimsby Channel that was headed toward Atlanson. They selected seats near the middle of the boxcar where students were still stowing luggage and finding seats. Then, Pigg said something about going to the dining car and left abruptly.

"Well, I'm off to the restroom," Elena said, standing very stiffly.

Austin leaned forward and wiggled his finger at her, indicating that he wanted her to come close to him. She put her ear close to his lips and he whispered, "Relax, Sunshine."

Elena couldn't even smile; she just rolled her eyes and eased down the aisle and back onto the platform. Plenty of students were still sorting baggage and standing in huddles saying goodbye. Elena walked casually but purposely between students until she reached a grouping of trees just beyond the railway track. She ducked behind a tree trunk and heaved a big sigh.

Then, she peeked out from behind a branch. No one had seemed to notice her leaving. She'd imagined this escape many times before, except in those scenarios she was trying to get back home to her parents, and her heart was never hammering so hard that it felt like it would explode through her rib cage.

Elena ran as quickly as she could to the Firebird Station, feeling anxiety growing in her chest with every step. When she arrived in the hangar, she stopped for a moment to take the Ransom Dossier from its hiding place between the rocks. Then, she stuffed it quickly into her carrier bag and ran for the hovercraft steps.

When she arrived on the command bridge, Elena saw that Kidd was already sitting in the captain's chair with a command module accessed. So, he hadn't betrayed them, but she still wasn't exactly thrilled to see him. Fergie sat in the navigator's chair to his right. Out the window, Elena could see that the door leading out of the Firebird Station into the train tunnel was already open. Then, she noticed Abria and Declan were standing near the door talking in low voices.

"What's going on?" asked Elena, feeling slightly panicked.

"Pigg's not here yet," Declan replied, as Austin appeared at the door to the hovercraft.

"What?" asked Austin, sounding slightly alarmed. "He left the train before I did."

"Our mandatory departure is in four point six minutes," Fergie said.

"We're not leaving without Pigg!" Elena said firmly.

"Freckles, we have to consider the possibility that the little weasel skipped out on the mission," Kidd said. "He didn't want to come in the first place."

"If anyone here is a weasel it's you!" Elena spat angrily at Kidd. She looked at Austin for support. "He'll be here."

Elena could tell that he was considering their options, but he finally said, "Yes, we'll wait for Pigg."

A slow minute ticked by in silence. Then, there was a commotion coming from down the hall as Pigg appeared at the door, sweating and covered in dirt. He heaved a bloated bag through the door and fell clumsily onto the bridge.

"Where have you been?" Elena half screamed as she and Austin grabbed him under each arm to help him up.

"I hid this bag in the forest so I could pick it up on my way here. But it's so heavy with food that I tripped and fell down the hill trying to get here on time."

Austin sighed and Elena rolled her eyes.

"I think I twisted my ankle," Pigg whined. "And don't give me those looks. We don't even know how long we'll be gone."

"You packed the galley with enough food for a month!" Elena said impatiently. "You organized the whole room."

Pigg just shrugged, his face red with shame, as he took the command chair behind Fergie.

Fergie shook her head and turned to Kidd. "Prepare for departure."

Kidd took a long drawn breath and said, "Here we go."

He pushed a couple icons on the Optivision screen. The hovercraft jerked forward. Elena felt the vibration of the hull scraping against the wall. She and Abria crashed heavily to the floor while Austin and Declan swayed dangerously.

"That was brilliant," said Declan sarcastically, dislodging his shoe from underneath one of the seats.

"I was not responsible for calculating the depth of the hull to the floor," Kidd said as if no mistake on his part had been made, though the tips of his ears were blushing.

"Let's get belted in, okay?" Austin said, helping Abria and Elena off the floor. He led them to passenger chairs where they took seats and clipped on belts. "One more time, Wheeler."

The hovercraft moved forward slowly down a gloomy tunnel with a dozen front facing hololights giving off an eerie green glow. Lichen covered walls flickered in and out of view. The ceiling was so low it felt as though the top of the hovercraft would scrape it at any moment.

"Wait until the Grimsby Channel passes," Fergie said, "We do not want to interfere with the train."

"Are you sure that Masquerade thingy is working?" Kidd asked Fergie with uncertainty in his voice.

Fergie was quiet for a moment as she pulled up a screen from her Touchdot. Elena saw an image appear that looked like a maintenance vehicle, but she knew that it was really the outside of the Independence that had been disguised.

"Quite certain," replied Fergie.

Moments later, the Grimsby Channel flashed by them. Kidd moved the hovercraft forward through the gateway, into the tube for the train, and accelerated.

They followed the Grimsby Channel tunnel for a long while. Elena remembered that their ride to school had displayed scenes of towns and farmland out the window, but the actual tunnel was made of dull cement block. She felt like she was inside a cave with walls all around and no exits. This did nothing to ease her anxiety.

Elena bit all the fingernails off her right hand by the time Fergie shouted, "We have arrived at the maintenance tunnel."

Fergie used the Optivision screen feverishly.

"Bend to the left," she told Kidd and he obeyed.

This tunnel led them to a massive access gate that was covered with a "Do Not Enter" sign.

"Any unauthorized personnel will be subject to arrest," Kidd read off the largest sign posted squarely in the center of the door.

"I am informing the maintenance data control system that we will be performing repair services to the structure and require access," Fergie said while entering something into her Touchdot.

A minute passed and nothing happened, but then the door slowly opened. Elena suddenly felt a rush of appreciation for Fergie's abilities as Kidd drove the hovercraft through the access door. The light coming from the other side of the tunnel was temporarily blinding, but as Elena's eyes adjusted, her breath caught in her chest.

The vibrancy of authentic color was overwhelming to Elena's senses. The terrain was rich with a soft palette of greens and gold. Pale sapphire water canals outlined the vast expanse of amber plains. The sky was maritime blue, like a picture she'd once seen of the clearest ocean waters, and there was not a cloud in the sky. And though the dazzling tawny sun hung so close that it seemed she could touch it, all the colors seemed wrong to her.

"Austin..." Elena breathed. "It's more beautiful than I could have ever imagined."

She turned toward him, but he wasn't looking out her window; he was transfixed on something that she could scarcely understand.

Rising above the hovercraft on all sides was the eminent Atlanson dome, stretching farther into the sky than she could see. Elena stared with her mouth open, completely mesmerized. As the Independence moved farther away from the home she'd known her entire life, Elena marveled at the sheer size of the dome and wondered how people could have created such a magnificent structure. Dozens of questions cluttered her mind, and she wished that her parents could be there to answer her.

"I think this should do, Wheeler," Fergie said after Atlanson had finally vanished on the horizon. "I will step out now to launch the Orbitor."

"Don't you want to put on some protective gear before you go outside?" Pigg asked Fergie nervously as the hovercraft came to a stop.

"According to the Touchdot, the oxygen levels outside are perfectly healthy. I should be fine."

"But what about the harmful effects of the sun? Your skin could melt off, or you could get skin cancer, or boils, or..." Pigg tried to warn her, but Fergie held her hand up to calm him.

"Solar output is only a couple degrees above the output two hundred years ago. I will be perfectly safe."

Elena then watched Fergie exit the Independence and rigidly march several paces from the hovercraft. She set the Orbitor on the ground and then lifted her Touchdot. After a moment, the Orbitor began to smoke. Then, it shot from the ground like a rocket. Fergie returned to the command bridge smiling.

Kidd looked over the navigation instrument panel and frowned. "Your Orbitor isn't working."

"I thought I explained that it would need time to clear the earth's atmosphere?" Fergie said. "I know it is challenging for you, but be patient."

Elena couldn't help but smile.

"That means we're flying in the dark until it starts working," Kidd complained. "We should drive out to the shore and follow the coast down to New York."

"A course over land was decided for its ease and safety," Fergie stated.

"But it'll be harder to plot a course over land without a navigation system, especially if the terrain has changed," Kidd argued.

"The Orbitor will function," Fergie stated. "Give it time."

"Wheeler, we have a good plan," Austin said. "To change it now would add extra uncertainty to this trip. Keep using the onboard compass until the Orbitor starts working."

Kidd gave a snort of displeasure and then said, "And people wonder why I hate working in groups."

"No one wonders that," said Elena honestly.

The hovercraft moved steadily over the next few hours. Elena spent the majority of her time curled up in one of the chaise lounges staring out the window. Austin sat next to her, and they talked quietly, marveling over the insanely beautiful forests of green trees and networks of untouched waterways.

The wide open spaces were dotted with clusters of abandoned towns that were overgrown with weeds and buildings that were crumbling. Neighborhoods were filled with abandoned vehicles, and city streets were littered with broken grocery store windows and office buildings with peeling paint.

"Look at the animals!" Elena screamed when the Independence disturbed a healthy looking herd of coffee colored reindeer and a flock of multicolored birds. "I thought animals were extinct."

She watched in awe of this undiscovered world and felt betrayed by her upbringing. The land was fertile, the animals were thriving, and there was absolutely no sign that a drought had taken place.

Long after the Orbitor had started working, and Pigg had prepared lunch for everyone in the galley, Elena felt tired. She selected one of the cabins on the lower level of the Independence and settled on a bunk bed. She opened her carrier bag and pulled out her dad's diary. She ran her fingers across the cover and then opened the Ransom Dossier so she could read the letter her dad had written.

Then, she stuffed the Dossier under her pillow and settled down. And, the moment her head touched the pillow, she was running with a herd of bison in a lush meadow. She was barefoot, and the soft ground was pleasing. She paused beside a refreshing lake and gazed at the mountain that was reflected on its glasslike surface. Birds were singing in the glade, rabbits hopped to and fro, deer grazed in a nearby pasture, and the trees were bending in a soft breeze.

A lamb appeared in the thicket, and Elena gasped. The majestic creature was flawlessly white and trotted toward her in a determined sort of way. She knelt to the ground, feeling that she needed just one touch. But it looked at her and said, "We're here." Elena felt confused as the ground shook below her. "We're here." The lamb said again. "It's time to wake."

"We're here!" said Austin. He had been shaking Elena to try and get her to wake up. "We actually made it to New York!"

## ❑ 22 ❑

## A City in Ruin

Elena hurried to the command bridge and stared out at the city of New York that was approaching ever closer. A bright, orange sun illuminated the magnificent skyscrapers. The city suddenly felt like a frightening place to Elena, and her fear seemed to be contagious as her friends began to mumble and shift nervously.

"Fergie, could you check the thermal graphs again?" Austin asked. "Just to make sure there isn't anything *hostile* in our way."

Fergie launched into action at once, clicking away on her Touchdot.

"Oh shoot!" Abria cried suddenly, causing Elena to jump a mile in her skin.

"What is it? What's the matter?" she anxiously asked, looking timidly out the window.

"My hair looks terrible!"

Elena turned to see that Abria was examining her reflection in one of the gleaming side panels that decorated the walls.

"Are you seriously worried about your looks right now?" Elena screeched.

"If we're going into hostile territory we might as well look good doing it," Abria replied, brushing a comb through her hair.

"You're totally unbelievable," said Elena, sounding exasperated. "Everyone else is flipping out and you're worried about your hair!"

"Quiet!" said Kidd sharply as the hovercraft eased closer to Manhattan.

Minutes later they were hovering between the skyscrapers, scarcely daring to breathe. Wild grass grew along the abandoned streets and between the decaying buildings. Posters were peeling from the sides of filthy buildings and stained billboards, while hundreds of electronic ads blinked sporadically as they died. There was a vacancy about the metropolis that was unnerving.

Kidd steered the hovercraft down Broadway being careful not to crash into the piles of belongings left by the evacuees over a decade earlier. They came to several crudely built barricades and had to detour off their route, creating some confusion. Declan stood beside Kidd and Abria stood on the other side of Fergie. On the control panel, a holographic map of Manhattan displayed, but Elena soon realized that Declan and Abria weren't entirely sure where their resident building was located.

They drove aimlessly for a while until Kidd asked impatiently, "Does any of this look familiar to you?"

"Yeah, there's my favorite tree," Declan replied sarcastically. "Don't you think we would have mentioned if we noticed anything familiar?"

"We already told you," Abria added. "We left New York when we were two-years-old."

At this point, Fergie tried to say something, but Declan interrupted her. "This is hopeless."

"Just following your directions, Genius," said Kidd rudely.

Abria looked intently out the window. "I have a really bad feeling that something horrible is about to happen."

Again, Fergie tried to speak, but Declan cut her off. "Nothing bad will happen as long as we stay together. Now, what can we do to help us remember where the resident tower is?"

"I don't know." Abria sounded tense for the first time. "We're lost."

"We're not lost," said Declan, trying to smile. "We're in New York City, definitely somewhere in New York City."

"Yo, Blonde and Blonder," said Kidd loudly to Declan and Abria. "I think Brainiack here has something to say."

Everyone stared at Fergie who looked at Abria and stated, "You said that you think you remember seeing water from your window?"

Abria nodded.

"Wheeler, set a course toward Battery Park. We will circle around the apex of the island until we find the building."

But, as it turned out, it was difficult to navigate the ruins of 2291 New York. Truman had once shown Elena pictures of New York City during its prime years and had told her stories about how glamorous the city had been. This city of rubble was beyond disappointing. Some of the buildings had been demolished and pieces were lying in the streets. Plus, small forests and fields of grass had grown up between some of the boulevards.

At long last, Kidd was able to pull the hovercraft through a row of skyscrapers and Abria exclaimed, "That's it! That's our building!"

She was pointing to a predominately blue building with an outer structure that looked like the mast of a ship and its sail. The three-part exoskeleton of the building had a pair of tuning fork masts that appeared braced against the sea winds.

"It's spectacular!" said Declan, clearly awestruck.

Austin moved to the front of the hovercraft and peered out the window. "Fergie, do you need to disengage the Masquerade before we leave the hovercraft?"

"No. Pigg wrote a program that will allow us to keep the Masquerade on and also enter and exit the Independence. As long as we remember the general vicinity of where we park the door will open with the use of my Broadcaster or Pigg's PocketUnit."

"Fantastic!" said Austin. "Wheeler, put her down over there, across the street from Bowen's apartment building."

As Kidd moved the hovercraft around, Elena noticed that Pigg's face, neck, and ears were splattered with a thin layer of white paste.

"Pigg!" Elena said sharply. "What's that stuff on your face?"

"It's sunscreen. I mixed it up at the hydroponic farm before we left."

Abria let out a giggle, though it sounded nervous instead of its usual cheerful tinkling.

"I don't want to get sunburn, age spots, actinic keratoses, actinic cheilitis, or skin cancer," Pigg said defensively.

"Focus people!" Austin looked impatient. "I want Bowen and Wheeler to advance on the building first. Then, Abria, Pigg, and Fergie will follow, and Elena and I will trail behind." He slung a carrier bag over his shoulder. "Pigg, you got that Sensory Skulk alert set on your PocketUnit, right?"

Pigg nodded.

"So, let's get our gear and go," Austin said.

Elena followed Austin down the hall to the Research Lab where he gave a tactical vest to each of the Firebirds. After Elena checked the supplies in her vest, Declan and Kidd led the way out of the hovercraft into absolute silence.

The scent of the place was unlike anything Elena had experienced. The crisp air was filled with salt and concrete crumbles baking in the sun. The buildings around them were either boarded up or had smashed windows, and there was an overgrowth of green plants crawling up the walls.

Fragments of ruined buildings and shattered glass crunched beneath Elena's feet as she climbed over the littered terrain. Finally, she reached the outside of the blue building and stopped with the others who stared up at it with uncertainty.

"Now that I've seen this place, I'm not sure I really want to go inside," Pigg said.

"We've got to go in," said Elena enthusiastically.

"Not all of us are as brave as you," Pigg said feebly.

Elena looked around at her comrades; Kidd was sweating slightly, Declan and Abria were looking at their feet, Fergie was consulting her Touchdot again, and Pigg was watching the walls. Austin was the only one making eye contact.

"Is Austin the only one going in with me?"

Silence followed her question for several long moments.

"I suppose being eaten or tortured to death would be preferred over running away like a coward," said Declan at last.

"Speak for yourself," Pigg said quietly.

"Come on," Austin said, pursuing the front door. "Do you remember which apartment was yours?" he asked Abria.

She closed her eyes. "We were near the top floor, red door with the number four seven zero three."

The Firebirds moved slowly through the mildew stained lobby to a corridor with disabled elevators. Water trickled down the walls and plants grew up from the floor.

"Look at the staircases," Austin said, pointing to opposite ends of the elevator corridor. "Let's each take a staircase and meet on the forty-seventh floor."

"You want us to walk up forty-seven flights of stairs?" Kidd exclaimed.

"You can run up, if you think you can manage it," Elena said, giving Kidd a sarcastic little smile, which he returned with a roll of his eyes.

Then, Austin and Abria set off up one staircase while Elena, Pigg, and Declan started up the other. Climbing the steps proved a dangerous venture, as portions of the stairs were crumbling and other parts were almost unmanageable due to the wreckage from walls that had been blown apart. Pigg especially had a hard, clumsy time trying to manage the hike.

"You know," Declan said after the third time they'd stopped to catch their breath and drink water, "I've been thinking we should make this our vacation home. We could come here when we're on breaks from school."

"That's a great idea," Elena said sarcastically. "I've always wanted a vacation home without running water, electricity, or proper transportation."

They continued on, pursuing the stairs with as much purpose as they could muster. Elena finally reached the forty-seventh floor out of breath and sweating like she never had in her life, her curly hair sticking to the back of her neck. She collapsed on the ground, panting for breath.

Suddenly, Abria burst through a door at the end of the hallway with Austin and Fergie, and eventually Kidd coming in last. Without a word, Abria approached apartment number three and noticed that the front door had been broken down. She stepped over the smashed door and walked inside. Elena followed and saw that the first room was a cavernous living area with windowpanes stretching across one entire wall and an impressive view of the city and of Upper Bay. All the glass from the windows was gone and there was a soft breeze wafting through, blowing around scraps of paper.

Without speaking, Abria and Declan walked straight across the room and down a hallway.

"Let them go," Austin said to Elena as she tried to follow. "See what you can find down that hallway. Pigg, check the kitchen. Wheeler, check the back rooms. Fergie, come with me."

"Let me set the Touchdot at the front door first," Fergie said as the Touchdot shot from her Broadcaster. "Pigg wrote a program that will scan any area. It will take images from the apartment so we can ascertain if there are any clues that we are unable to see with our eyes. Then, it will relay any information to Pigg's PocketUnit."

Elena watched the Touchdot fly off with its laser lights inspecting the walls and floors. Then, she set off down a hall and found an office through the first door on the left. As she entered, she was astonished to see that it was very similar to her dad's office back home, except that dust had settled on the floor and the overturned furniture. A familiar, elaborate bookcase stretched across the entire back wall. The shelves were oaken and embroidered with rounded emblems. Elena hurried forward and checked the third from the left emblem, but it did not move like the one in her dad's office.

Feeling discouraged, she turned and noticed a vast library of shelved books that, unlike her dad's, were not hidden in any room. Elena moved slowly, picking her way through the book titles. Then, she came to a shelf of Opticals, each image showing a different scene: a happy couple holding two babies; the same family with a six-month-old boy and girl; a first birthday party cake smashed on all their faces.

Elena looked carefully at each image and was examining them so closely that she didn't notice the overturned chair at her feet. She tripped head first into the bookcase, putting her hands out for support; yet, she crashed heavily to the floor, pulling several of the Opticals and books with her.

"It's like I'm Pigg or something," Elena said under her breath as she rubbed out the pain shooting through her left knee.

She looked around arbitrarily, but then her heart skipped a beat. Elena reached among the pile of debris that she pulled from the shelf and picked up a photograph. An actual *photograph*. She'd only seen one other in her entire life.

But this particular snapshot was extraordinary. Her parents were featured standing shoulder to shoulder with a group of other couples. Austin and Pigg's parents were in the picture, as well as Declan's parents (who Elena recognized now that she'd been in the office). Eight other couples were also in the picture though she did not recognize them.

"I found Charlie!" Abria called from down the hall.

Elena startled, but then stuffed the photograph in one of her pockets and ran down the hall expecting to find a man standing with Abria. Instead, she found a nursery that had been completely untouched except by the dust of time. A mural of a carousel graced one entire wall, and on another wall stood twin beds, dressers, and organizer shelving filled with books, games, puzzles, and riding toys. Abria was standing near the closet door clutching a stuffed toy horse to her chest; she had tears in her eyes.

"What is it?" asked Elena, as Fergie and Pigg entered the room with Austin and Kidd coming behind them.

"Declan's dad hid this toy horse in here before we left," Abria said. Declan moved to put his arm around her shoulders. "I never thought I'd see it again."

From inside the stuffed horse, Abria pulled a cylinder contraption with numbered keys that encircled the entire outside like a casing. Without hesitation, she handed the object to Fergie.

Fergie examined the device carefully, turning it over in her hand. "This is called a Cryptext. This fragment of encryption was created over a hundred years ago."

Pigg hurried over and said, "It can't be!" He snatched it from Fergie's hand. "Wow! This has a voice identification module, a code entry function, and a storage compartment. This is very rare."

"Does anyone else know what they're, like, talking about?" Abria asked.

"A Cryptext is like a puzzle," Fergie began to explain. "This cipher requires two keys to solve the code. This box is the first key, but another key is required to decrypt it."

"What's the other key?" Declan asked.

"It could be any number of variables…a lyric, a name, even a riddle," Fergie replied. "We have no way to know."

Suddenly, a loud beeping noise echoed around the room.

"My Sensory Skulk is picking up a foreign transmission!" said Pigg, looking startled.

Pigg used his PocketUnit to open a holographic screen. Elena gasped as she saw two electronic signatures appear on the hologram.

"That's the transmission from Fergie's Touchdot at the front door," Pigg whispered.

Austin held a finger up to his lips and then used a series of hand signals to tell the others to take a defensive position. Elena couldn't hear a thing, but she watched the two figures ease down the hall toward the room they occupied. A feeling of foolishness washed over Elena as she realized, for the first time, that they had come to New York without any kind of weapons. What had they been thinking?

Declan and Abria took positions on either side of the nursery room door just as the two cloaked figures hurried into the room, brandishing weapons on their arms. Declan grabbed the barrel of the first weapon, ripping it away from the intruder. He slung it around, knocking the intruder to the ground where the hood flew back and revealed a man with a color of skin that Elena had only seen in books.

Meanwhile, Abria lunged forward and caught the other intruder by the arm. She used his body to support her weight as she swung around and tilted the cloaked man off his center of gravity. In one swift motion, she whipped off her tactical vest and looped it around one of his arms. She pulled tight and propelled her body back around the cloaked figure, wrapping his other arm as she went.

The man seemed confused for a moment while she was doing all this, but then he began to struggle against the bonds. Abria kicked him square in the chest and he stumbled back a couple steps, losing his hood. She pulled a small can of hair product out of her pocket and shot the man square in the eye. The man screamed, as the arid substance burned his face. Abria knocked him to the floor and then took a moment to brush her fingers through her hair. Everyone stared at her with dumbfounded looks.

"Whoa! Karate Chop Blondie," said Kidd, looking at Abria with a mildly impressed expression.

"I've been taking that Judo Simulab at school." Abria shrugged.

Pigg expanded the Optivision screen to six different viewing screens, and Elena saw electronic signatures of figures in the stairwell, combing the hallways, and converging on the building.

"We need to get out of here!" Austin hissed.

"Yeah, right!" said Abria. "Do you see how many guys are down there? We'll never get out of here, like, alive."

Elena looked around, feeling hopeless until Kidd yelled, "Do you guys trust me?"

"Of course we don't trust you," Elena shouted. "What a stupid moment to bring that up."

"Excellent point!" Kidd said. "Follow me."

Kidd hurried down the hall with the others following closely behind. He ran to the shattered window in the front room, and said, "We're jumping out the window."

"*What?*" Elena said incredulously.

"Big Ears said these packs have parachutes, right?"

"Yes," Pigg replied hesitantly.

"If we jump out this window we can parachute back to the Independence."

"No way!" Pigg said flatly, backing away from the window. "You're not getting me out that window."

"It seems risky..." Austin started to say, but Kidd pressed on.

"Worse than getting caught?"

But there was no time left to argue. Elena could hear boots marching down the hall outside the front door. In one brief second, Kidd lunged forward and grabbed the straps on Elena's vest. The next moment, she and Kidd were hurtling out the window at top speed. Then, he yanked the ripcord on her pack. She felt a jerk as her parachute caught air. Above her, she could hear Pigg screaming all the way down.

Elena's feet crashed onto the ground and she crumbled up in a heap. Pain shot from her ankles up through her spine, and she rolled over groaning.

"Ah! I twisted, like, both my knees," Abria said from somewhere close by.

"I'm pretty sure I broke both my legs," Pigg cried out in pain.

Elena pushed herself into a sitting position and, after seeing Kidd, shouted, "Don't ever throw me out of a building again!"

"Come on," Austin yelled urgently as he struggled to pull Elena by her arms. "We've got to get out of here."

"Austin, there's no way I can stand," Elena said weakly, but it didn't matter; it was already too late.

People wearing cloaks advanced on the Firebirds in a military style formation from every direction. Elena felt strong hands close in around her arms, and she was lifted to her feet. Her ankles and legs seared with pain. She almost slumped to the ground again, but her captor held her with such force that she was unable to move. Elena felt a surge of genuine fear. How were they going to get out of this?

# ▫ 23 ▫

## The Refugees

"Unhand me this instant!" Elena screamed defiantly, even though she could feel her heart pounding in her ears and her legs about to crumple beneath her. She boldly yanked her arm out of her captor's grip. But another hand was on her in an instance, grabbing her harshly to keep her from falling over.

"Search them," came a deep voice from under the hood of the one who held her.

The other figure holding Elena patted down her sides and legs.

"You will let us go this instant!" she ordered.

"You have a big mouth for someone so small," said the man holding her. "Why would we let you go?"

"You have no right to hold us," Elena preached. "We are here on direct orders."

"Orders?" questioned the man, his voice thick with disbelief. "Who would send teenagers into a forbidden territory?"

"That's none of your business!" Elena spat.

The man released his grip on her and tore the mask away from his face. Elena was momentarily startled because the man had caramel colored skin and a tattoo of black ink etched in his face.

"If you refuse to answer my questions, I will instruct my men to torture your friends," the man said earnestly, as he peeled back his hood to reveal wildly thick, black hair. "To death if necessary."

Elena heard Pigg let out a gasp of distress.

"Perhaps we could negotiate our release," Austin said calmly. "We have food and supplies in our hovercraft."

In response to this, a shroud was shoved over Elena's face. Then, she was pushed from behind and was forced to stumble forward upon the rubble beneath her feet.

"Take it easy." She growled several times at her captor as she was marched along in blindness. "We've just come out of a building, and the landing wasn't exactly pleasant."

Eventually, Elena tripped and almost fell as her foot came off what felt like a stair. She felt more steps under her feet until finally she came again to solid ground. That's when a strange noise filled her ears; it was a loud, constant beat interspersed with melodic tones.

At length, she was forced to sit. The shroud was removed from her face. The man with caramel skin was sitting in front of her atop a throne of sorts. She noticed that Austin, Pigg, and the others had been placed in chairs beside her. The walls of the room were shabby, but richly ornamented with carpets, drapes, and tapestries. Priceless artwork, sculptures, and furniture worthy of any museum filled the space.

The man with caramel skin picked up a long, wooden stem with a small bowl on the end and stuffed a strange wad of brown leaves into it. Elena watched him strike a match and ignite the leaves. He took a long draw on the pipe stem and blew several rings from his mouth.

"So, let's talk," the man said. "You're obviously the leader." He pointed the tip of his pipe at Austin. Then, he looked at Elena. "That would make you the aggressive, impetuous side-kick."

Elena wanted to be offended, but it was technically the truth. "Guess you have it all figured out."

"Let's start with your names," the man replied. "You there." He pointed at Pigg. "What's your name?"

Pigg simply squeaked. Then, his eyes rolled back in his head and he slipped sideways out of his chair, collapsing heavily to the floor. Elena tried to move toward him, but she was forced back into her chair.

"Let me help him!" she yelled at the caramel skinned man.

"Your friend seems a little overwhelmed by his surroundings. My people will tend to him. He will be fine," the man replied.

Elena watched some cloaked figures pick Pigg up off the floor and carry him to a lounge chair.

"We can sit here all day," the man said as smoke billowed from his nose. "Or you can start by telling me your names."

"May we have your name first?" Austin asked politely.

Elena didn't think that this was the appropriate time for friendly chitchat. She looked around to see if there was a way out of the room, but was surprised when their captor said, "My name is Fallon. And this is my humble abode." The man named Fallon spread his arms out with pride. "I think I can guess who you are."

Elena highly doubted that, yet she felt intrigued.

"Austin Haddock, Declan and Abria Bowen, Kidd Wheeler, Gribbin Pigg, Fergie Foreman." Fallon looked specifically at Elena. "And I've been wanting to meet you for a very long time now, Elena Ransom."

Elena's mouth fell open.

"Your dad has been giving us aid for many years. I am glad to finally meet you because Truman talks about nothing else but you."

Elena felt a lump growing in her throat. The fact that they were captured fell away suddenly; nothing else mattered except that this man had mentioned her dad by name. Perhaps Fallon did not know that he was dead.

"How did you know?" Austin began to say, but Fallon said, "Forgive me, but Hopper told me to expect you all."

"Hopper!" Abria exclaimed.

"If you knew we were coming, then what was the charade for?" Austin asked.

Fallon smile genially. "I hope you'll forgive me for that. Hopper told me that you are just out of your first year of school. He asked me to make it a little challenging for you."

Suddenly, Pigg gasped loudly and sat up so quickly that Elena was sure he must be dizzy.

"When do we eat?" He sounded somewhere between dream world and reality. Slowly, his eyes slid into focus and he seemed to realize that he wasn't dreaming. "Ohhh..." he breathed as his shoulders sagged forward and he lay back gingerly.

"What are you doing in New York?" Austin asked.

"We live here," Fallon said. "Come on, I'll show you."

Fallon leapt up and grabbed Pigg off the lounge chair. Then, with Pigg's arm slung around his shoulder, the man with caramel skin led the Firebirds out of his dwelling and into an underground transportation station. A network of over a dozen metrorail tracks lined the entire hub.

The metrorails had been converted into homes and businesses, forming a makeshift neighborhood. Then, Elena gasped as she saw a wide assortment of people in varying sizes, shapes, and colors. Old men with wrinkled skin sat around, chatting in clusters. Grandmothers held babies on hips while young children with different colored hair and skin played with kicking cans. Teenage girls were chasing toddlers and young men were training with weapons.

"Elena," Pigg whispered, grabbing her arm tightly. "I've never seen such a tall woman before; she must be over six feet tall! And did you see that man over there? He looked like he was maybe four feet tall. And that guy over there is wearing spectacles. I thought spectacles were an urban myth. Do you suppose they're cannibals?"

"I'm positive they're not cannibals," Elena replied.

"How do you know?

"They would have eaten you by now. Now, seriously, stop pointing," Elena murmured, lowering Pigg's hand with hers.

But she continued ogling at the diverse assortment of people as they followed Fallon through the tunnels. He was definitely leading them somewhere specific because they twisted and turned, fighting their way through the crowds of people. Fallon was very friendly, calling everyone by name. Elena was impressed with the running water fountain, clean air gardens, and open-air markets.

As they stopped to look at a wheel that was being churned by water, a younger looking man and an older looking woman shuffled over to Elena. The man laughed and rocked side to side not really looking at her in the eye. The woman gave her a hug saying some words that Elena could not understand. Between the two, they were completely violating her personal space. She felt somewhat frightened until Fallon shooed them away.

"Duke and Duchess," Fallon said as he watched the pair stroll away. "Very sweet, simple-minded folks, though. They're adults to be sure, but only have the skills of a small child."

At that moment, Elena heard the noise again: the constant beat interspersed with melodic tones. She covered her ears with her hands and asked Fallon, "What's all that noise?"

Fallon laughed. "It's music."

Elena was a little taken aback as he led them to an ensemble of people sitting in a circle; one man was beating his hand against a piece of skin that was stretched over a shell, keeping a fast paced pounding noise; a woman was blowing air into an open tube while her fingers worked a series of tone holes; another man was striking a wooden instrument that was strung with strings; there were several people holding various items that jingled and jiggled. Others danced around them, everyone enjoying a jolly celebration.

And that's when Elena saw it, a massive fir tree decorated with colored lights, candles, ornaments, garland, tinsel, strings of cranberry, and a golden star perched at the top.

"What's going on here?" Elena asked Fallon. "And why is that tree all decorated?"

"We're celebrating the holidays. You know, Hanukkah and Kwanza, and Christmas is in just six days."

Fallon explained the distinctions between the holiday traditions and festivities that they celebrated. Then, he showed them the difference between the wooden fiddles, bongo drums, and acoustic guitars. Elena was absolutely mesmerized by the music. She lost complete track of time listening to the violins, guitars, flutes, trombone, and — her personal favorite — the trumpet playing together in perfect harmony.

"Are you alright?" Austin asked her after catching a glimpse of her face.

Elena hastened to wipe tears from her cheeks and smiled. "I've never heard anything more beautiful in my life."

"Fallon, why don't we have music in Atlanson?" Austin asked.

"Ah, music is the ultimate form of human expression. You people in the domed cities are controlled down to the air you breathe," Fallon said bitterly. "There can be no true freedom until the government is destroyed."

"What do you mean we're not, like, free?" Abria said loudly over the music.

"As long as Trademarks exist you will be a slave to the system of constant surveillance," Fallon said, looking at Abria with a mixed expression of pity and amusement. "For instance, you are not allowed to think whatever you wish. You are given a life which you must live, void of basic human possibility."

"It sounds as though you believe we live in ignorance," Fergie said in a very un-Fergieish sort of way.

"Because you've never been allowed a chance to know anything else," Fallon pressed, though when he saw the look of doubt on their faces he added, "Take a look around you. What do you see?"

Elena looked and saw skin color of every kind. She saw people communing together with music and a variety of food, each dressed in their own style of clothing. She saw a variety of craftsmen and artisans unique in their expressions. Elena saw freedom.

"Funny-looking clothes and hair styles," Abria said flippantly. "But what I'm mostly concerned about are all the different, like, smells going on around here."

"Open your eyes, Abria Bowen," Fallon challenged. "Ask yourself, why does Imperator seek to ensure that you all look exactly the same? Why are you isolated from the rest of the planet under lock and key with no hope of leaving the domed cities? Why are your citizens so willing to accept a ruler that seems to give freely, but is really taking with both hands?"

"You make our world sound, like, awful," said Abria defensively. "It's really not so bad where we live."

Fallon looked Abria squarely in the face and asked, "But is it good?"

Elena looked at Austin. They hadn't exactly told their friends that they were essentially living in slavery, being controlled by Imperator. She looked away quickly, hoping that Abria wouldn't ask any further questions. And, it seemed that her blonde friend was too bewildered by Fallon's ramblings to continue because she suddenly seemed distracted by a group of women and children dancing a funny jig, although she watched them with a confused expression.

Soon, Elena was given a plate, and she walked around with Austin to several different booths of people passing out food. She ate chicken that had been fried in a vat of oil and a roasted ear of corn. She tasted spaghetti and meatballs, beef empanadas, shrimp fried rice, and chicken stir-fry.

As Elena watched men drink beer from tall steins and throw dice, she couldn't help but feel amazed by the New Yorkers' distinct customs, diverse culture, exceptional food, lively music, and unique clothing. The underground of Manhattan was proof that life existed outside the domes and that people and customs were thriving. Hopper was right; there were civilizations surviving in secret.

As the festivities lasted well into the evening, the Firebirds gathered around a small campfire and roasted marshmallows. Fallon sat with them, smoking his hand carved pipe.

"So, Elena, how is your dad?"

Elena looked around at the other Firebirds and then bowed her head.

"What's happened?" Fallon asked.

"Truman and Hannah Ransom were killed in an accident," Austin explained.

Fallon's sharp intake of breath caused Elena to look at him; he searched her eyes deeply. "Imperator has killed them."

Elena nodded. "I think so."

Fallon was quiet for a moment, looking away into some far off place. "How about you kids tell me what you are doing in New York." Smoke rings were now coming from his nose.

Elena shifted her gaze to Austin who shook his head a fraction of an inch.

"We were just doing a bit of sight-seeing," Elena said. Her marshmallow caught fire and she blew it out quickly, blushing red with embarrassment.

Fallon looked at Elena with an amused expression on his face. "You were sight-seeing in the Bowen's old apartment?"

"You know, we just wanted to see where we grew up," Declan said nonchalantly.

Fallon looked around at all the Firebirds and smiled genially. "I know why you're really here. You're searching for the Island Station."

Elena wasn't entirely sure what he meant, but she knew that it's what Austin was waiting to hear because he immediately said, "Yes, we are. Did Hopper explain how important it is that we see the Station?"

"He mentioned it, yes." Fallon took a long drag off his pipe. "Long ago, I was the Communications Officer of the Island Station. Hundreds of us were able to hide there safely as Imperator was ravaging the city eleven years ago."

"Imperator was *here!*" Austin said. "How do you know that?"

"I saw him with my own eyes," Fallon said bitterly. "After the city was abandoned, we built all this underground so we'd be safe from Imperator knowing where we are."

Fallon was silent for a moment, staring off into space like he was thinking about something that caused him sorrow. Then, he stood rather abruptly. "I will take you to the Station tomorrow. But for now, get some rest."

As Elena watched Fallon walk away she couldn't decide if he knew about the mission to find the Amulet or not. But, she felt suddenly tired and overwhelmed. She made an excuse about needing sleep and slipped away to find the old subway car that had been prepared with seven camp beds for the Firebirds to sleep on.

Elena dropped into the nearest camp bed and crawled under a woolen blanket. She pulled the Kairos from around her neck and thought about the photograph she'd found in the Bowen apartment.

Were they able to trust Fallon? Apparently, her dad and Hopper did, but they didn't even know him. Would this man lead them to the Amulet? He'd only mentioned the Island Station; perhaps Hopper didn't tell him about the Amulet. Another secret? And if Fallon hadn't been told, how in the world would the Firebirds be able to find it?

Elena fell into an uneasy sleep and felt she'd barely rested when Austin was shaking her awake.

"Time to get up, Sunshine," Austin said. He was sitting on the edge of her camp bed, smiling. "Fallon said he'd take us to the Island Station after breakfast."

Elena sat down with Austin, Pigg, Fergie, Declan, and Abria around a square table and stared into a bowl of gray colored gruel.

"Has anyone seen Wheeler?" Austin asked. "He took off last night and never came to bed."

"Maybe he got carried off by the bogey man." Elena yawned. "We can only hope."

"That would be awful," Declan said. "He's the only one who knows how to operate the Independence."

"Nah, Fergie and Pigg have got the hang of it now, right?" Elena asked them.

"Not quite," Fergie said seriously. "At least, I would not wish to be responsible for the entire hovercraft until I have logged more flight training hours."

"And you know me," Pigg said between bites off his spoon. "I should not be in charge of anything where the probability of my clumsiness causing certain death is high."

After they ate, Fallon led the Firebirds back through the maze of makeshift houses and businesses to a flight of stairs that led up to the New York City streets. He took them through and around several buildings for a few blocks until they finally reached Abria and Declan's resident building.

The Touchdot flew from Fergie's Broadcaster and the door to the Independence opened out of thin air. At this same moment, Kidd appeared through a door of an adjacent building. He looked as though he'd slept well and was ready to go.

"I'm glad to see you," Austin said to Kidd. "I thought you'd abandoned us."

"I would have," Kidd said dolefully, "except Fergie has the key."

Once on board, Kidd took the command chair and Fallon sat in the navigator chair. He directed Kidd down a series of streets that eventually led out to the perimeter of the bay. Kidd slowed the hovercraft and it came to rest at the edge of Battery Park.

The Firebirds sat in silence for several moments, staring at dark waves that lapped against a sandy beach, which stretched along the opposite side of Ellis Island. The buildings on Ellis looked dilapidated beyond the point of repair. And Liberty Island stood somberly against an orange, red horizon while Lady Liberty lay crushed on her side.

"This bay was once covered with water," Fallon said. "But the sun has been evaporating the earth's water supply for nearly a hundred years."

As Kidd eased the Independence out over the dry basin toward Liberty Island, Elena couldn't help but feel sad as she saw the damage Statue. Corroded to the core and choked by grass that was running wild up her sides, the goddess was broken and forgotten. Her shining torch of independence was covered over by earth.

"The Statue that stood as a symbol of freedom to generations of immigrants was pulled down long ago by Imperator," Fallon informed them. "The seven spikes on her crown represented the seven seas and seven continents. Her torch once signified enlightenment, and the tablet on her arm represented knowledge. But notice, her right foot is still raised, moving forward. Her left foot still tramples broken shackles. So, you see, the destruction of our nation did not diminish her purpose in my opinion."

Fallon directed Kidd to land the hovercraft on an empty stretch of ground, and Elena was the first one on the ground after the door had been opened. The Firebirds hurried over to the base of the statue, to the main entrance doors that had all been shattered. Elena stepped through a battered doorframe and entered the remains of the Liberty Island museum.

The place had been ransacked, but Elena noticed a plaque set in the wall and read aloud, "Give me your tired, your poor, your huddled masses yearning to breathe free, The wretched refuse of your teeming shore. Send these, the homeless, tempest-tossed to me, I lift my lamp beside the golden door."

As Elena explored, she noticed that much of the museum's photographs, prints, and artifacts had been plundered. The full-scale replica of the Statue's face and foot were graffitied, and the original torch had been shattered throughout the lobby.

However, an eight-foot replica of the statue was still standing in one of the hallways. Fallon pulled a small, metallic square from a tooth in his mouth. He held it in the palm of his hand. Elena watched as it unfolded into a shiny orb. Then, the replica statue slid sideways, revealing a hole and the top of a ladder.

"I'm not going down the creepy tunnel first, right?" Pigg whispered to Elena.

Elena watched Fallon descend into the hole, and she quickly followed. The tunnel was extremely narrow; it would have been impossible for someone to climb up if another person was coming down. After a few dozen rungs, Elena's feet finally touched the ground.

"It looks like the Firebird Station," Elena told Austin and the others who were coming down the ladder.

The room was similar in size and shape to the Firebird Station and included a stainless steel kitchenette, an island cooking station, metal bunk beds, and a cluster of cushiony chairs that surrounded an Optivision pupil station in a circular fashion.

However, this room was filled from floor to ceiling with American memorabilia: small models of the Statue of Liberty flanked the bookcases like columns; flags of red, white, and blue adorned the walls. There were stamp collections, coin collections, and collections of antique toys. Music recordings of every single American song were alphabetized on shelves, along with every motion picture that had ever been made. A wall of sports memorabilia featured historic baseball bats, balls and gloves, footballs, and basketball uniforms.

Fergie and Pigg immediately went to work. Fergie inserted her Touchdot into a niche on one side of the station, and Pigg inserted his PocketUnit on the other. A holographic screen came to life as the two friends accessed every file they could find.

"Where's Wheeler?" Elena asked in general.

"Oh, he said something about how he's not, like, paid to do this kinda stuff." Abria flipped her blonde hair away from her face. "You know, he just gets nicer and nicer the longer we're on this trip."

Declan made a face at her. "Yeah, his ability to make friends is awe-inspiring."

Elena smiled and then stood beside Fergie and Austin at the Optivision station. She waited patiently as dozen of records flashed across the blue holographic screen.

At length, Pigg shouted, "I got something!"

A shiny, multi-layered object appeared on the screen. A golden ring formed the base and a triangular medallion was set on top. Fancy script was etched into the sides and, in the center of the triangle, was an emerald stone.

Quite suddenly, Elena felt the ground below her shudder.

"Fallon, what was that?"

"I'm not sure," Fallon confessed. "But we should return top side."

Elena and Pigg crashed into one another as they headed toward the ladder, but she let him go up first after she saw the distressed look on his face. As she climbed, Elena felt another quake vibrate up the ladder, causing her hands to shake. After she finally made it up the ladder and out through the museum door, she looked around and noticed something very strange. The island of Manhattan appeared to be moving.

"Um...why is New York City, like, sinking?" Abria asked in a panicked voice.

"New York isn't sinking," Fallon said, looking stunned. "We are."

# ¤ 24 ¤

## Kairos

Elena watched Austin's face fill with earnest determination. "Back on the Independence, NOW!"

She took off in a full sprint, covering the ground to the Independence in a minute. They all filed through the door and raced down the hall, skidding onto the bridge where Kidd was sitting in bewildered silence.

"Wheeler, take off!" Austin ordered.

The sound of Austin's command roused Kidd into immediate action as Fergie took the navigator's seat next to him.

"Wheeler, take off!" Austin ordered again as Liberty Island was sinking ever faster into the ground.

"I can't!" Kidd said, and it was the first time Elena had heard him genuinely distraught. "The hovercraft won't move, no matter what I do."

Fallon walked to the front window, gazing out at the top of the ground that was easing ever closer and whispered, "It's secondary protocol."

Austin hollered, "What's secondary protocol?"

Fallon turned to look at them. "Whatever you did triggered a series of actions that were invented to keep intruders from discovering the secrets inside the Station. We're caught in a force field that's pulling us under the ground. There is no way to escape!"

Elena gasped as, a moment later, they were covered on every side with sand. She scarcely dared to breathe as the Independence began to groan under the pressure. She could feel a strange sensation creeping up and down her arms and legs as the hovercraft creaked and moaned in a slow, sinking death.

"I have activated the additional oxygen reserves," Fergie informed them. "Therefore, we need to attempt not to panic."

"*Attempt not to panic*," Kidd mocked her. Then, he pointed at Fallon and said, "This genius conveniently forgot to tell us about the brilliant little trap, and we've just been sucked underneath the earth. So, I'm gonna go ahead a feel little panicky, okay? Anyone else want to join me?"

Pigg raised his hand.

"Just wait," Austin said, silencing the others.

Then, Elena noticed that the hovercraft was no longer sinking.

"I think we've landed," said Austin. "Now, if we could just be quiet for a few minutes, I'm sure we can think of something."

Fergie began accessing files from her Touchdot Optivision as Pigg held his PocketUnit out. Elena sat and closed her eyes. She tried to think about everything her parents had taught over the course of her life. She recalled all the Simulabs that she'd done and thought about the classes she'd had in school. Try as she might, nothing came to mind that would help in a situation where someone is buried alive in sand.

Then, Elena felt an unnatural shaking and noticed that the sand started to slide down the window.

"What did you do?" Kidd screamed at Fergie in an accusatory way.

"I did nothing that instigated this," Fergie said, pointing at the window as the sand kept sliding.

Eventually, the sand slid away from all the windows and Elena saw that they were in an underground chamber, more immense than she could have imagined. The entire Liberty Island fit inside it with ease.

Now that it seemed they weren't in mortal danger, Elena could only think of one thing. "I'm going outside."

"Whoa, wait just a minute!" said Pigg. "We were just dragged underground. There could be any number of things out there, and we have no way of knowing where we are or how safe it is to move around."

Elena looked at Pigg with a mildly amused expression on her face and then said, "Ok, so I'm going outside now. But, I think some people...Pigg...should stay here."

"Oh, I'm staying," Pigg said. "That's a great idea. You can just let me know how it goes when you get back."

"Actually, I think it would be best if everyone stays here while Lena and I scout around outside," Austin said. "Fergie will you work with Pigg to see if we can somehow turn off the force field so we can get outta here?"

Fergie went straight to work on the Optivision screen hovering above the command console.

"Lena," Austin whispered. "Grab your carrier bag and bring the Dossier."

Elena walked off, as Austin said, "Abria, may I have the Cryptext?"

In moments, Elena reached her cabin. She grabbed the Ransom Dossier from under her pillow, stuffed it into her carrier bag, and ran toward the main entrance where she found Austin and Fallon waiting for her.

"Fallon has offered to come with us," Austin told her.

Elena could tell by Austin's fake smile that he didn't want Fallon with them in case they found the Amulet, but she knew that he didn't want to arouse suspicion either, so she smiled politely and followed Austin out the door.

Elena stepped off the Independence and into a pile of dirt that had been left from sinking under the ground.

"Fallon, maybe you could go that way." Austin pointed off to the left. "See if you can find anything to help us get outta here."

"Sure," Fallon agreed as Elena and Austin headed off to the right and began walking toward the edge of Liberty Island.

"Sinking under the ground was too weird," Elena said.

"It was a great trap," Austin said. "Anyone standing outside would surely have died. But, now I'm more certain than ever that the Amulet is down here somewhere."

As they kept walking, Elena felt excitement rush through her body. They were going to find the Amulet, she just knew it, and then all their questions would be answered. But then, she stepped headlong into what felt like a wall and fell to the ground heavily. Her vision was momentarily blurry, but she could see that Austin had fallen beside her.

"What is this?"

As Elena's eyes came into focus, all she could see was an open space stretched out in front of them for miles. She and Austin helped one another stand and reached their hands forward, feeling the air. Then, she felt it. A wall. She felt as high and low as she could, and then she ran along the wall a few steps feeling her way to nothing.

"There's some kind of barrier here. Maybe we're trapped."

"Maybe not," Austin said as he reached for the hololight in his vest. He stepped back, far away from the invisible wall and shined the light into it.

Elena watched the light spread out and then felt confused as Austin brought it around in a strange, flashing pattern.

"What are you trying to do?"

"Remember when we were in the Vault," Austin started to say. "I mean, the simulation before the Vault? Well, the light in the room was moving in a strange way and that's when I saw the weakness in the simulation. What if this wall is also a simulation of some kind? Maybe we can find a flaw in the coding and get through the wall."

Elena folded her arms over her chest. "That's a bit optimistic of you, Austin. I mean, how would we even..."

"Listen," Austin said seriously as he pulled back his sleeve to reveal his Broadcaster. "Fergie said that when she first checked the Touchdot that it already had cryptology programming on it. If I can just read from the program, I might be able to see if there is a wall of simulation here."

Elena watched the Touchdot fly from Austin's Broadcaster and scan the area. Several Optivision screens appeared. He seemed to study the scans, though to her it looked like a jumbled mess of symbols and letters. Then, quite suddenly, he began to move his fingers through the air in a non-distinct way along the vacant space directly in front of him. A moment later, she watched as the apparent wall of the simulation began to break down and melt away.

"Okay, now that was just *unnatural*," Elena said. "And a little too easy. It can't really be that easy, can it?"

"Well, in all fairness, Liberty Island did sink into oblivion almost killing us," Austin reminded her.

"But, what if it's a trap?"

Austin smiled at her in a goofy way and said, "I guess there's only one way to find out. Unless, you'd prefer to go back to the hovercraft."

"There's no way I would leave you out here alone to have all the fun by yourself," Elena said.

And together, they stepped into a marble walled library that stretched farther than they could see and rose into the air at least seven levels tall.

"Do you think this is real or a simulation?" Elena asked in disbelief.

Austin reached forward and pulled a book off the closest shelf. "Definitely not a simulation."

"I bet this place has every book ever written," Elena said as her eyes scanned the floors above them.

"Do you think there's a book in here that will tell us where to find the Amulet?" Austin asked.

"I hope so, because I'm getting tired of…"

"You're glowing!" Austin exclaimed.

"Well, thank you," Elena said awkwardly, "but this is hardly the time to comment on how I look."

"No, I mean your Kairos is *glowing!*"

Elena looked down and noticed that her necklace was beginning to emit several outlandish rays of light. She pulled it off her neck and held it in her hand.

"What do you think it means?" Elena asked, but then the Kairos rose from her palm into the air.

The sharp angles of the star necklace were moving and sliding automatically, until it finally unfolded to reveal a clock-like face. The dial had two hands: one with a globe at the tip and the other with the shape of a sun at the tip and, like a clock, it had numbers. But it also had multiple round faces of all different sizes and each with a unique set of symbols.

Everything on the clock began to spin wildly, counterclockwise and clockwise, at the same time. The hands revolved and the elevated circles rotated around the face of the clock while the various symbols lit up at different intervals.

"Lena, get the dossier and turn to page thirteen," Austin ordered.

She opened her carrier bag and pulled out the Ransom Dossier. Page thirteen had strange letters and symbols that were scrawled along the binding, corners, and edges of the page. Austin took the Cryptext and manipulated the symbols on the cylinder to match the cipher from the diary.

Then, the mayhem continued as the Cryptext hovered out of Austin's hand into midair and flew with the Kairos down the main hallway between the rows of books. Elena and Austin ran to catch up until both pieces stopped moving. She watched, wide eyed, as the Kairos and Cryptext contorted until, at length, another object appeared floating in midair; it was a shiny, multi-layered object with a golden ring at the base and a triangular medallion set on top. Fancy script was etched into its sides and an emerald stone sat in the center of the triangle.

"It's the Amulet," Elena whispered, in awe. "It's actually here. We actually found it."

Austin reached forward and pulled the Amulet from its space. He examined it closely for a moment and then said, "Let's hope Fergie will be able to tell us what it does."

With the Amulet tucked safely inside Elena's carrier bag, she and Austin ran back through all the marbled chambers and back through the door to Liberty Island. Apparently, Fergie had disengaged the Masquerade because the Independence was gleaming in the distance. As quickly as they could, Elena and Austin boarded the hovercraft and noticed that Fallon was waiting for them.

"I didn't find an exit that way. Did you find anything?"

"No," Elena lied. "We didn't find a thing."

"Austin! Elena!" Abria said eagerly after appearing from the hallway. "They think they've figured it out."

Elena and Austin hurried to the command bridge with Abria and Fallon. Fergie was just finishing up with a multitude of holographic display screens, and Pigg was using his fingers to unlock some of the security protocols.

"That should do it," said Pigg.

From the front window, Elena watched a skylight hatch open far above them. The opening grew wider and wider until it was large enough to extricate Liberty Island.

"Wheeler, do you think you can fly us out of here?" Austin asked.

"This is a *hovercraft!*" Kidd said impatiently. "It can only propel us forward over a fixed surface. It can't *fly up.*"

"Precisely right," Fergie said. "But this island does have the ability to change locations using some type of platform. We simply need to find the correct sequence to stimulate the mechanism that controls it."

Elena watched Fergie access a grouping of files, and then she felt the ground moving below her feet. They were rising up on the ruins of Liberty Island, back where they came from.

As they rose, Fallon shook Austin's hand. "Sorry you didn't find what you were looking for. But you kids have a lot of gumption. You're welcome to come stay with us as long as you'd like."

"Thanks, Fallon. We'd be grateful to stay one more night, but tomorrow we've got to get back to school."

Later that evening, as the Firebirds sat around a camp fire under the city of New York, Austin handed the Amulet to Fergie who looked it over in silence while he and Elena took turns telling their friends the story of how they found the artifact.

When they finished recounting their adventure, Fergie handed the Amulet to Pigg. "Can you see anything?"

Pigg pawed the Amulet for a few moments and then exclaimed, "This is not really an emerald stone. It's a container full of green fluid."

Fergie nodded. "I believe that part of this riddle has officially been solved."

"Do you mean, this whole thing was never about, like, finding the Amulet?" Abria said, as Declan added, "We were supposed to find whatever is *inside* the thing?"

Then, Kidd spoke, his voice dripping with cynicism, "Yo, Big Ears, what are we supposed to do with it?"

"I don't know," Pigg responded in a defensive tone. "This Amulet was left here eleven years ago." Then, a little bravely, he added, "So perhaps *you* would like to have a try figuring it out."

Kidd didn't say another word as Elena dug into her pocket and withdrew the photograph she'd found at the Bowen's house.

"Bowen, I found this photograph in your dad's office," she said, handing it over to Declan.

Declan took the photo, and Abria looked at it from over his shoulder. They smiled at one another. "Dad and Mom said these people were like their family."

"These are my parents," Elena said, pointing down at the picture. "And these are Pigg's parents."

"And that's my father," Austin added.

Declan looked confused as Abria said, "And these are Fergie's parents."

"Did your parents work for the United Republic?" Elena asked.

"No," Declan replied. "They were scientists."

"My parents are engineers," Fergie said. "They work mostly with Humanoids."

Elena looked thoughtful and then held the picture up to Kidd.

"Wheeler, are your parents in the photograph?"

Kidd barely even looked at the picture, and then he stood up rigidly.

"No," he said simply, and then he stomped off into the busy tunnel.

Elena felt a little sad to see him go. After everything they'd been through together, he still didn't want to try to be friends. She found herself wondering if he was ever going to change.

Declan handed the photograph back to Elena, and she stared at all the smiling faces in the photo.

"My parents lost their lives fighting for freedom from Imperator," she said shortly, moving her fingers over her parent's faces. "I'm determined to carry on with my parents' work."

"Their work?" Pigg screeched. "You must be joking! Your parents were involved in, we don't even know what. We don't have any clues, we don't have any directions, and we certainly don't have enough supplies."

"I'm not suggesting that we start right this moment," Elena said impatiently. "I'm just saying that I plan to carry on with their work, no matter how long it takes me."

"Why do you want to do this?" Pigg groaned.

"Imperator has enslaved all of humanity," Elena said. "He puts us in those domes to keep track of everything we do. And, he's made it impossible for people like Fallon to live a normal life. Don't you feel like we should help?"

"Help what, Elena?" Pigg asked. "I like my life, and it seems like these people down here are making it just fine."

"But the life we're living isn't real," Elena said. "It's like a simulation. It makes us feel free when we're not. Imperator uses his power to control people. And anyone he can't control he gets rid of. He murdered my parents. What's to stop him from taking your parents as well?"

"Are you seriously suggesting that you can somehow stop him?" Pigg said. "You're just a girl, a thirteen-year-old girl!"

"Wow, Pigg, you're totally being, like, confrontational," Abria said. "Does anyone else feel weirded out by that?"

Elena remembered how she'd once told her dad that she was just a girl, but he'd reminded her that there had been plenty of extraordinary women in history and she would be no different.

She smiled sheepishly and said, "Actually, I'm fourteen today." She sighed deeply. "Some people are born slaves, and other people make themselves slaves, but both have a right to freedom."

No one spoke after she said this, but she looked around at her friends hopefully.

"I was hoping that you would help me finish the work our parents started," Elena said. "I mean, we've made it this far, haven't we?"

Fergie reached forward silently and took the photograph from Elena's hands.

"Many years ago, my parents began to explain their work to me. They do not merely create Humanoids," Fergie said in a tone of formality. "As members of the Renegades, my parents explained that I would one day be required to finish their work in ending Imperator's tyrannical reign."

Elena felt so stunned that she couldn't even speak.

"If you already knew, why didn't you say anything when we first started planning the trip here?" Austin asked.

"Firstly, I was bound to secrecy. Additionally, I was not aware that my parents' efforts were part of a grander scheme. I never imagined that it would require additional participants until I began to read the Alpha Manuscript. However, the photograph Elena took from the Bowen's home is proof of the Renegade alliance, as I believe it features all the original members. Therefore, I must conclude that we will need each other to finish the work our parents started."

"Can your parents tell us where we need to go from here or what we need to look for?" Austin asked.

"My parents work in the Galilee Province, and they certainly could tell us," Fergie said. "However, I already know the artifact that I need to find, and it is not in our home. The artifact is called the Catalan Atlas. It resides at the White House in Washington D.C. inside the Eagle's Nest Station."

Pigg moaned in disapproval.

"What's the Atlas for?" Declan asked.

"Unfortunately, my parents did not disclose that information to me. I was only told that one day I would need to retrieve it," Fergie said. "I could never have imagined that it would be this early in my life."

Elena buried her face in her hands. Fergie had known the entire time that she was on a quest to finish her parents' work, but she'd been sworn to secrecy. She felt confused by all the lies that had been unraveled in her life recently, but she was too exhausted to worry about it at that moment. She was only certain that there were other artifacts to be found and Fergie's artifact was in Washington D.C.

"Suddenly, I'm feeling so tired," Elena said, as she stood, not meeting anyone's eyes. "I'm going to bed. See you in the morning."

But, an hour later, Elena was still awake on her camp bed in the subway car. When the other Firebirds had come to bed, Elena pretended that she was asleep, but in truth, her mind was still racing. Several confusing incidents had taken place since her parents' murder, and she was having a hard time trying to piece together what it all meant.

Shortly after her parents died, Elena wanted revenge for their murder. But then, after talking with Hopper, she discovered that the matter of their death was a systemic problem dating back to when Imperator came into power. She had also learned that her parents weren't the only conspirators involved in trying to overthrow the dictator that had forced them into slavery. Therefore, Elena was filled with a renewed sense of purpose, one that came, not from revenge, but from an obligation to defend mankind.

Feeling that sleep was not going to happen anytime soon, Elena decided to take a walk. As she stood from her camp bed, she noticed Austin's eyes on her. She signaled him to follow. Together they walked in silence through the congested tunnels, passed dwelling tents and subway cars that had been converted into homes. Eventually, they found an adjacent tunnel that seemed deserted and settled down in a corner.

Elena rubbed her tired eyes and sighed heavily. "So much has happened in the past few weeks. I can barely wrap my mind around it."

"Me, too," admitted Austin.

"So, what was all that earlier today?" Elena asked.

"What do you mean?" Austin said.

"How did you know how to use your hololight to see the door through the simulation?"

"I'm not exactly sure," Austin said. "It's like I said about the simulation when we were trying to get to the Vault. I could just *see* the way out of the room. And earlier today, it was almost as if I could distinguish the boundaries of the simulation."

"But, how did you know how to use the Cryptext?" Elena asked. "I mean, you've only read through the dossier a few times."

"I don't know," Austin said. "When Abria first found the Cryptext the symbols looked familiar to me, but I wasn't sure why. Then, while we were down in that library I realized that I'd seen the symbols in the Ransom Dossier. It just all came together. I really can't explain it."

"I still think that's weird and we should have your brain tested, or something."

Austin opened an Optivision screen from his Broadcaster.

"After we met with Hopper, I started drawing a timeline of events so I could keep things straight. As we've learned more, I added extra lines."

Elena looked at the timeline and read the dates and descriptions out loud: "Around 2280 A.D. there was a world wide famine. Soon after was the election of the Oligarki. Then, the story about the Great Drought started circulating about a year later and genocide followed a year after that."

"Then, Imperator had people Trademarked and sent to live in one of three cities that were built to confine humans in the domes. At some point way back here" — Austin indicated an area on the timeline with his finger — "your dad started his work with the Renegades. And right here," He pointed to another section of the timeline, "Declan's parents left the Cryptext in the apartment. Here is the Amulet we found today."

"What is that red mark?" Elena asked, pointing to an area that had no writing.

"That's where," Austin said, his voice quivering slightly, "my father disappeared...or Imperator murdered him."

Elena squeezed his hand.

"The communication stations that Hopper mentioned are all around the world," Austin continued. "We don't know where all the Stations are, but I've written down the three we know about: the Firebird Station at Grimsby, the Island Station in New York, and the Eagle's Nest in Washington D.C."

Elena removed the photograph of the Renegades from her pocket and looked down at their faces.

"I've thought about this picture a lot. If all the people here are the original Renegades then..." she swallowed hard. "What if each couple has a kid in the Firebird Unit?"

"That's certainly possible," said Austin. "Remember, Hopper said that our Unit wasn't chosen randomly."

"What if each of these people has a Dossier or an artifact that has to be found? That would be twelve diaries or artifacts." Elena began to chew a fingernail. "You know, I didn't understand why Wheeler was in our Unit until today. He was put in our Unit because his parents were Renegades."

"But he said his parents aren't in the photograph," Austin reminder her.

"Well, he lied," Elena said.

"How do you know?"

Elena lifted her shoulders into a shrug. "I don't know. It's just the way he said it and the look on his face as he saw the picture."

She looked thoughtful for a moment. "Something awful must have happened to them. Why else would he be so nasty to everyone?"

"You have a temper, too," Austin said. "And you were like that before your parents died." He smiled at her in a friendly way. "You're not feeling empathy for Wheeler, are you?"

"No!" Elena said sharply, although in the quiet of her heart, she knew there was a reason Kidd was so horrible to everyone. And it was the same with her. She hated to admit it, but she was starting to understand him better. But this idea made her sick to her stomach, so she changed the subject. "At least we accomplished what we set out to do. We have the Amulet, even if we don't know what it's for. But, it's strange the Fergie knows so much already, right? Why would her parents tell her about the artifact they were supposed to keep secret? She's just a kid."

"I don't know," Austin admitted. "But I think we should go to Washington D.C. to get the Catalan Atlas before we go back to school."

"Me, too."

"But trying to convince the others to go might be difficult."

"Then, we'll tell them the whole truth about my dad's dossier and everything that Hopper told us," Elena said solemnly.

"That's a good start," said Austin.

"After everything that's happened, I've realized my goal shouldn't be revenge. I don't want people enslaved by Imperator. Our parents were trying to do what's right. They were trying to free people by removing him from power."

A profound silence overwhelmed Elena. She felt encouraged and dispirited; hopeful and desperate; brave and frightened. The task before them would be long and complicated. They hadn't deciphered all of the Alpha Manuscript or Ransom Dossier, they hadn't decoded the Amulet, they didn't even know what the Cryptext was for, and they hadn't even retrieved the Catalan Atlas.

But Elena knew that her parents had fought for freedom, that it had cost Truman and Hannah Ransom their lives. She was determined that their lives wouldn't be lost in vain. She was determined to remove Imperator from a place of ultimate control. She set her head back against the wall, longing for the day that they would all be free.

# THE ADVENTURE HAS JUST BEGUN

What will happen next to Elena, Austin, and their friends?

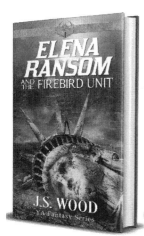  

Follow Elena's story @

## www.jswood.me

Made in the USA
Columbia, SC
28 November 2018